Tribulations

Tony Heck

Literary Haven Press, LLC

Published by Literary Haven Press, LLC
450 Lexington Avenue, Fl 2 #122
New York, New York 10017

"Kindness is the sunshine in which virtue grows."
Robert Green Ingersoll

Contents

Part I: Father   9

Part II: Mother   73

Part III: Brother   121

Part IV: Friend   177

Part V: Guardian   245

Epilogue   295

Chapter 1

Today

Small beams of sunlight sprayed through the cracks of the deteriorated barn's roof, as Clare Chestwick sat at the edge of the loft, gently rocking underneath the middle of five looped ropes. Several feet below rested a padded dirt floor and a few rusted tools no one in the family bothered to use or repair. Standing, Clare gripped tight to the noose, leaning back and taking account of the four people gagged and bound on wooden chairs. Ropes coaxed their necks, only to be tightened if they made a fuss. Throughout the barn, the smell of mangy wood and feces from invading wildlife mixed with the cool mist of morning, permeating the pores of the sodden prey as Clare reflected on her adolescent memories.

To bring together this modest congregation, Clare had drugged each participant with a tranquilizer obtained from a city vendor. She had asked what might happen if she pierced herself—inadvertent curiosity. The elderly gentleman, a slip of chew pushed against his lower lip, laughed at the scenario. Bits of his addiction slipped onto his chin without concern, telling her that such a predicament would be unfortunate, and would cause her to sleep for a few hours.

"Make sure you have someone with you, pretty lady, while you chase whatever you fancy. Just don't hurt any of those boys." He laughed until a coughing fit caused him to gag his wad into a neighboring can. Solemn, she did not partake in his jest, merely nodding and pocketing the needles.

Clare could not wait anymore, planning that night to stab, duck, and wait for the effects of the shots to take place. She tried the concoction on herself as a test, wincing at the self-administered injection, waking three hours later in a daze. Satisfied, she chose her father, Kelvin, as the first.

A rail of a man these days, despite hitting the tip of six feet, he had begun to relax now that he was in his mid-thirties, allowing the roving patches of wispy brown hair to reign wherever they lay, often fretting over the beginnings of a receding hairline. He wore only boxers this night, so once the tranquilizer took effect, Clare placed his ratty red sweatpants and generic black shirt on his body before proceeding to her mother.

Rhonda lay curled in a ball in the neighboring bedroom, wearing clothes that rarely changed. Her wavy brown locks were splayed over her pillow, unkempt by indifference. Clare's mother did not shy away from vocalizing her desire to maintain distance from Clare's father. At one time, her mother may have allowed her father's prick near the inner sanctum, pushing and driving its point until feeling his completion, saturating her God-given womanhood. Now, a divorce imminent, her mother enjoyed rest without sexual irritation. Clare placed her mother into deeper unconsciousness, aching to punch and wail the peaceful look off her face.

Though its inhabitant was gone, she walked up the stairs to look upon the haunting room of Tristen, a sixteen-year-old whiff of a boy, like his adoptive father, though smaller in frame and mind. He basked in mediocrity, trying to find the best way to make life passable; to make himself invisible enough to move through each day without strife; to make his way home in the luxury of isolation, telling her of his ecstasy in his masturbation escapades by trying to outlast or beat a record of staving off the final spurt. Clare missed the time when he was younger—innocent.

Walking into his room, she quivered in disgust of this pervert—no, rapist. She crept in, worried he may still be lingering in some hidden corner. She imagined his loose black curls, feeling his jagged bones pointing in furious directions. The ever-present smell of his relentless habits pierced her nose as she neared his bed. Sickened, she left without renewal.

Clare contemplated acquiring the other two for her plan, dragging all four bodies to the barn in quick succession, but she worried how long the tranquilizers would last given the hour that had already passed. She hoped the barn's distance would be enough so that the others would not be disturbed by any noises. She had thought far enough ahead to disconnect the security lights. Her grandmother, Edna, sleeping next door, rarely checked on night nuisances.

She hauled each with precision, careful to keep their heads from bouncing as she transferred them into the simplicity of her old childhood wagon. Upon wheeling one then the other to the barn, she began the arduous task of dragging them up the gently sloped stairs. After much deliberation, she had resorted to the use of a plywood board placed over a majority of the stairs to utilize the wagon. She also crafted a makeshift pulley system partially wrapped around a beam then around her waist in an attempt to keep the wagon from drifting, tugging them up to the loft.

Once they were situated upon their respective chairs, she bound nooses around their necks, the ropes then thrown over a horizontal roof beam and secured on a vertical support at the other side of the barn. She tied their hands to the armrests and ankles to the legs of the wooden chairs, wrapping neckerchiefs over their mouths. She wanted them to witness and listen, to know what they had done to her without giving incessant excuses.

After situating her parents, she continued on the light dirt path her family used to reach the backyard trailer where her ex-lover, Nick, resided. A rustic pissant of a man who had pined after her for years, his recent attempt at maturity had drawn her in until he'd reverted to his old bullish and careless attitude. After setting the creaking wagon next to the front door, she squeezed the syringe in one hand, ready to bring him into the fold.

Her limbs sore from dragging her parents up the stairs to the loft, she contemplated how she would place Nick upon the wagon, knowing this to be one of the worst parts of her plan to act alone. She had wanted to tell her friend Ryan of the plan. Though he may have respected the premise, Ryan would have kept her from going through with this task, never understanding the internal demons that tracked Clare.

Thankfully, Clare, at nineteen, 140 pounds, five and a half feet tall, with some lingering strength, fueled herself through willpower and adrenaline. She waited the obligatory time for the tranquilizer to work through Nick's system after pricking him in the thigh and hiding near the bed. She tied both ends of a rope around his legs, wrapped the rope around her waist, and heaved on the rope, dragging Nick through the living room and down the wooden steps, then an exhausting toss into the wagon.

Her ex-boyfriend now sat in the fourth chair, dirt and grime covering his back, a few bruises developing on his limbs. She doubled the amount of rope she used to tie his hands and legs. Despite his modest muscle tone, if any of them were able to attempt to escape in a fit of rage, he was the one. She inched Nick's chair away from the hayloft edge, having almost tossed him over as the chair scooted away with his heaved body. She pulled it back to the two feet of distance from the edge she had determined to be safe.

Clare took a break, breathing heavy against the back wall of the hayloft, her limbs blazing from this last endeavor. If she didn't hold tight to her conviction, she would probably stop and sleep. She inched herself back up, looking at her phone. Almost five in the morning. She would need to hurry before her grandmother woke, if she was not already disturbed by the noises.

Clare hastened to the abutting house, her grandmother's means of separation from the floundering marriage of her parents. She turned the doorknob, blessed that her grandmother had not woken and locked the front door from unknown fear. She walked up the familiar stairs, stepping over the sixth with a small creak.

"Kelvin, is that you?" Clare heard from her grandmother's room, though no light emitted under the door. Clare remained quiet, not wanting to stick the needle in her grandma while she was awake. "Whoever is out there, please identify yourself."

Clare wavered near the stairs on the second floor, waiting in silence for her grandmother to return to bed. With the click of the door, Clare knew she would have to improvise. "I'm sorry, Grandma. I didn't mean to wake you."

Unlocking and opening her door, Clare's grandmother, Edna, eyed her granddaughter. "Why are you up at five in the morning, Clare? You feeling okay?" Her grandmother smoothed her nightie, the light-blue frock swaying with the touch.

"Yes," Clare said, squeezing the syringe tightly in her hand, contemplating the recourse of stabbing her grandmother right here and now. This woman was the kindest and the cruelest, a tool of selfish idiosyncrasies, refusing to take honest responsibility for the neglect, the rape, Clare's loss. Her grandmother desired peace and ensured everyone knew. Every time a problem arose, Edna would make immediate efforts to smooth over the matter in secrecy. Clare knew her grandmother wondered why her granddaughter brought about such trials on the family.

"Well, what did you want then? I want to go back to bed, but I would feel better knowing you were tucked away first."

Clare breathed in quickly, then lurched the needle toward her grandmother. Edna fell back, stumbling to run to the other side of the bed. Edna prided herself on her youthful, firm physique in her fifties. Though she spurned most advances by men and kept an internal vigil for her long dead husband, Clare knew her grandmother still enjoyed the idea of being courted. Clare tried to ease the shot into her grandmother's rump, an area Clare thought would be safe to jab.

Edna cried out, falling forward, landing on both her wrists. "What is wrong with you, child?" The drug was working too slowly. "Why would you do this, Clare?"

Clare held the nose and mouth of her grandmother until she passed out. Clare fell to her side, exhausted by the lasting struggle, yet knowing she needed to finish this remaining task before the others woke. She embraced the body, taking a break at the bottom of the stairs, then managed to get her the rest of the way to the final chair. She tied and gagged her grandmother, then set herself back at the crowning epicenter of the empty middle noose.

Elated at her feats, Clare held the noose with affection, swaying in comfort, slipping at the loft edge, her right foot hovering. At the cusp of death, her body acted without pause, holding tight until she fell backwards onto the safety of the loft. She let the rope drift off, rocking back and forth over her head. She remained there, studying the cracks in the roof, considering how this decaying barn still stood over the years, conscious of her grandmother's concern that someone's ill touch would destroy its charm.

She was exhausted, unwilling to leave her design, drifting to sleep in satisfaction. She awoke to the sun glittering in patches on her shut eyes, exuding a soft red glow. She heard groans from beside her, along with intense moaning and shuffling.

After stretching and easing herself up, she said, "I assume all of you are awake at this point." Nick continued to fight in his chair. "I'll wait until you are done with your fit, Nick." A few more tugs, then he stopped. "As you can tell, you are able to hear me, but none of you can speak or move. A noose is wrapped around your necks, and you are in a chair hovering at the edge of the hayloft. You'll be safe as long as you listen and refrain from struggling. I'll allow each of you a turn to tell me your apologies and the reasons that you have murdered my soul but left my body to rot. You are to bear witness and understand the consequences of your destructive behaviors."

Clare felt tears on her face. She hit her thigh to increase her resolve, to feel the sharp pain of bruises patterned in that spot, dark black splotches of focus on her body. "I shot you all with a tranquilizer. If you cause any issues or try to escape, I will use another. Each episode will result in everyone waiting a few more hours until you regain consciousness. You will only be the source of suffering for the others, as I will not feed or provide any of you water until this is over. We could finish within the hour, or we can elongate this into a week. Eventually, you will relinquish and allow my final resolution—simply an apology for how you wronged me."

Her mother let out a muffled cry, but Clare knew the tears stemmed from discomfort, not from the pain she had caused her daughter. Her grandmother was quiet. Clare would not have known whether she had recovered if not for the occasional twitch of her neck or itch of her finger.

"Dad, you're first." She walked to him, undoing the bandana twisted into his mouth.

"What the fuck do you think you are doing, Clare? Get us the fuck out. Once I get out of this chair, you'll be sorry. How dare you!" He looked over at the others. "You've tied up your grandmother. What is wrong with you? This is how people go to jail. What do you hope to accomplish in kidnapping us? Do you think this will make me change my mind? Are you even my daughter anymore?"

With gritted focus, her father tried to burrow his hands out of the ropes. He pulled up, as if to break the arms of the chair, though his efforts did little but chafe his forearms and wrists. Clare was furious that he did not consider her base accusations, adamant that he knew of his role in her shattered life.

Relaxing, he said, "Clare, come on. This is not like you. Please let us out, and we'll pretend this never happened. I'm sorry for whatever you think I did."

"No, Dad. There are reasons you are here, and you very well know that."

Part I: Father

"Fathers, do not provoke your children to anger, but bring them up in the discipline and instruction of the Lord." Ephesians 6:4

Chapter 2

Clare has not been born

Kelvin's eyes glazed over the dark graveyard. He sat in his truck near the local church, just up the hill from his house. There was only one light, near the back entrance of the parking lot; he and Rhonda would not be seen outright. Kelvin tended to drink and get stoned here with his buddies. Even brought a few girls in his better attempts. He had yet to be bothered by any police officers, the closest house being a quarter of a mile around a twisting bend. This had been one of his favorite places, where he finally lost his virginity to Rhonda in a rapid action of his hips. Kelvin thought the condom would stifle the sensation, but he had been unable to help himself within minutes. Now, Rhonda's admission sullied that memory.

"How did this happen, Rhonda? We've been careful. We have to get you an abortion right now."

Kelvin hit the steering wheel three, four, five times, his hand pulsing with pain. He could not have a kid while still in high school, readying for college. Sure, no college had picked him for a soccer scholarship, but he could still try to attend, despite his failure to submit applications. Now he really saw no way out. Rhonda and his seed would root him to this damn town for the rest of his life.

"You know we've not used condoms sometimes. This is not my fault." She kept her eyes down, fingers locked in her lap.

Kelvin welled in guilt over his reaction. Four months of dating, and now he was to have a child with her. "I thought you were on the pill. That's why I felt safe."

She looked at him, her right nostril flaring. "Oh, come off it, Kel. You came in me. Begged each time." She looked down, twisting her fingers, lacing them back and forth. The pattern made Kelvin angrier. She needed to control every situation, even her emotions, with these ridiculous tics. "I guess the pill is just not fully effective. This is not my fault, so quit acting like an ass and let's deal with the situation."

"I can probably get a few hundred from Mom," he said. "Not sure how I'll explain why I need the money. Don't suppose you can get any from your folks?"

"Not without telling them what I need the money for. Kel . . . I'm not getting rid of the baby."

He swung the door open, scrambling out of the truck, and slamming the door shut. He would never lay a hand on Rhonda. He did not have the heart to be physically cruel. However, he had a harder time keeping his words at bay. Rhonda stayed in the truck, looking to him for sympathy.

He yelled through the closed window, "Why would you want to have my kid at seventeen? Rhonda, we can't keep this thing. I love you, but you must be realistic." He saw her mouth moving but could not hear the soft undertone of her voice. He threw open the truck door. "What did you say?"

She snorted, indignant. "Unless you are saying you will forcibly murder this child, then I will be having this baby."

"So, I get no say? You get knocked up, and I deal with the consequences. How selfish are you, Rhonda? How can we possibly become parents in high school and expect a bearable future?"

She stared through the windshield, refusing to look him in the eye. "Baby won't be born until after graduation, Kelvin. You don't have to take any responsibility. I'm merely telling you the situation."

Kelvin gazed at the graveyard, the chipped headstones, most more than fifty years old. The congregation for the church had slowly died off, a few stalwart families keeping it afloat with their weekly pittance. Once Reverend Shephard died, none of the parishioners knew who would take over the church. In this sparse area, few remained that felt obligated to praise God with minimal means. Kelvin's mom had gone to the church in her youth but drifted off after the death of Kelvin's father. As she told it, she did not feel supported by the church, some speaking ill of her predicament of living in her country house all by herself with an infant. Kelvin's mom persevered but refused to acknowledge the church's existence, ensuring her son knew exactly the hardships she endured and enemies she would never forget.

Oh, Kelvin's mom knew he came here for out-of-sight activities, but she minded her business if he did not cause trouble. Now with this growth inside Rhonda, the graveyard became his mom's business. He despised bringing his mother into his personal life, as she never found a solution that included his say.

How would he possibly keep this from his mother without her encouraging something preposterous? Would she see the matter his way? Encourage Rhonda without alarm? Her son knocking up some seventeen-year-old girl would not reflect well on how she raised him. She would need to help him somehow and keep the problem quiet. A mother's reasoning could sway Rhonda.

Once he soothed his thoughts, hoping his mother would fix his problems, he reminded himself that he loved Rhonda. She had been supportive when he failed to nab any soccer scholarships, saying they would manage and suggested they attend the same college. She wanted to study journalism, not caring where she went. She would allow Kelvin to decide the destination as long as she decided her journey. He loved the passive way she controlled situations. Until now. Now, she held both their futures in the forming hands of a mistake.

The wind whipped against the truck, rocking them on the side of the hill. He stepped inside the cab, away from the cold breeze. Kelvin did not fear tipping, but Rhonda held to the door, stabilizing herself. The quiet lingered as Kelvin had nothing more to say. She knew what he wanted.

"It's not that I want to have a child at this point in my life, Kel. And I'm not against a woman's right to choose an abortion."

Kelvin did not speak, hoping she would convince herself. Any words from him might spoil this beautiful one-sided conversation. True, he did not particularly care for the idea of an abortion, but he knew the chains of a baby would ground him to this spot. His ideals immediately expanded once the situation concerned him, but he dismissed the thought.

"I never saw myself needing an abortion. I've been so careful. Patrick and I never had a pregnancy scare for the year we had sex, so maybe I thought myself invincible." She started crying. "I don't know how I could have let this happen. What are we going to do?"

Kelvin adored this woman and became ill at her pain, watching her rare soft tears flow down her face. He wanted her to be happy, find fulfillment with him, but could that possibly include a child? She must realize the choice to be obvious. He scooted over to place his arm over her, unable to stop himself from consoling. He gritted his teeth as she shoved her face into his chest, sobs shivering over his plaid shirt, snot and salty tears seeping through.

"Do you think your mom would help us?" she sputtered, her head drifting closer to his crotch. His dick quivered as she drew near, but he fought the urge to pat her head down. Damn thing never quit, even when he supported its best interest. "My parents will throw me out if they know. I have no doubt. I'm torn too, Kelvin. Some part of me will always have regrets, no matter what we do."

Kelvin rubbed her back, shifting his lap so he did not bump her. He worried she would turn on him if she knew of his untimely desires. Maybe, just maybe, his mom could bring a better sense to the situation. His mom's indifference to Rhonda had not gone unnoticed, but that had been her best reaction to a girl so far. His mom had said that his prior girlfriend, Sheryl, was wearing "whore's clothing" the first and only time they met. Sheryl did not take offense, her skirt three fingers shy of the prize, but his mom still had no right. His mother took a different approach with Rhonda, barely acknowledging her existence, as if Rhonda was a minor annoyance that would drift off if ignored. He suspected Rhonda cared little for her either, though Rhonda never spoke an ill word of his mother. Rhonda was passive and kind until cornered, at which time she became strong-willed and stubborn. That's why he needed her to fight this battle within herself. If he pushed too far, she would sit there, arms crossed, fingers twiddling, until she had the baby on the floor of his truck.

"Let's go see her," he said. He did not expect this encounter to go well for anyone, but his mind floundered for a better plan. He pulled his arm from behind Rhonda to get his keys out of his pocket. She remained limp without helping, muttering incoherently, followed by pitiful whimpers. She drifted her face, still a swamp of distress, against the dashboard.

"Jesus, Rhonda." He grabbed the tissues from the center console, handing them to her. "You can't see Mom looking like that. She'll know something's wrong before we even utter a sentence and be on high alert. We must be careful in how we approach her. She's quick to judge."

Rhonda turned on the light over the rear-view mirror, wiping her face, then the dashboard. "I thought your mom liked me. She seems like a levelheaded woman. Raised you on her own, didn't she?"

"She raised me on her own because she had to. I was already born when Dad died. What are you talking about? You just said your own parents would never accept this. I have no idea what she's going to say."

"Stop it, Kel. You're being cruel. Let's talk to her and get this done with."

"Fine." The truck roared as he reversed out of the lot, swerving recklessly down the hill. He took a left turn too sharply, tossing them both as the truck rolled into a ditch and then back onto the road.

"Damn it, Kelvin! I'm pregnant!"

"Sorry, I honestly didn't mean to," he said in a dismissive tone.

They left North County Road, returning to paved roadway as they ventured deeper into the country; Illinois appearing barren and colder than normal. He turned right three miles later onto a gravel-pitched path named Granite Peak Road. The county talked about paving this area as more people moved into the farmlands from the city. The town committee was tired of people complaining of rocks beating up their misplaced vehicles. Kelvin hoped they never changed the road. Driving these few miles on the rustling and shaky gravel made him feel welcome, ready to be home.

Neither spoke the remainder of the ride. He made a final left, then maneuvered down the quarter mile driveway to his house. He weaved around the larger potholes out of habit. He filled them up every year, but more always seemed to develop near or at the same place. A two-story house with a large patio came into view. The security light went off, and Kelvin could hear his Labrador mix, Shelbie, barking around the truck.

He parked next to his mom's pale red Subaru, careful of Shelbie, who would not stay more than five feet away. He opened his door so he could grab Shelbie and keep her from Rhonda. The dog would never hurt anyone, but Shelbie never understood her size, barreling over everyone in excitement. Rhonda hurried into the house while Kelvin rubbed Shelbie's belly.

"Good girl. How's momma feeling today? I hope you have plenty of love left because she's going to be pissed. Yes, she will."

Shelbie's tongue lagged to the side as her feet shifted in excitement. Kelvin heard a familiar whistle, and Shelbie ran to the backyard to Kelvin's grandfather. He let out a long sigh and dawdled toward the house.

"Kelvin, you better have a good excuse for missing dinner. The pot roast is simmering in the cooker if you are hungry. I told Rhonda to set herself up with a plate."

He held on to the door handle, considered leaving. His mom would never scream at Rhonda, but she sure as hell would still scream at him in front of her.

"What are you doing standing in the doorway? It's cold. Come sit down with your girlfriend. She says you've something that you want to talk to me about."

Kelvin slowly closed the door, sulking past his mom. She gave him a pat on the back, grabbed a plate, and started loading it with slops of food. He sat at his normal place next to the head of the table. His mom never liked the idea of them sitting across from each other, so they always sat next to one another. She thought they could have better conversations with less distance between them.

Rhonda looked at him, her face scrunched. She was confused why he sat on the exact opposite side of the table from her. Kelvin motioned his head to the seat across from him.

"Oh, she's fine where's she's at, Kelvin. I'd like to hear what's so important before you two try to put something over me. You just keep eating your food, dear."

Kelvin looked at Rhonda, her fork swirling through mashed potatoes, clearly hurt at being excluded, as if already accused of some wrongdoing. Kelvin said nothing in her defense. That would only hurt his chances of his mom handling the situation to his satisfaction. His mom came around with her own plate. Kelvin stood and pulled out her chair, then pushed it in gently.

"I'm so glad for this surprise visit, Rhonda. Kelvin rarely lets his girlfriends meet me more than once. He thinks I'm overbearing and judgmental. Told me as much in a few of his adolescent fits." She laughed while Kelvin braced a smile, attempting to enjoy the pot roast. Rhonda returned a pained smile, her right eye twitching, but Kelvin believed his mother didn't notice.

"I like that you've had the bravery of dealing with me twice. Shows how much you must care about my Kelvin."

"I love him very much, Ms. Chestwick."

"Mrs. Chestwick, dear. I did not divorce Kelvin's father. He died tragically, and I still carry that man's name."

Rhonda froze beneath the glare from Kelvin's mother. Kelvin wanted to correct the faux pas but could not fathom words that would ease this slight. He had not prepared Rhonda at all for this second encounter, a damnable meal with his mom in force.

"I'm sorry, Mrs. Chestwick," fumbled Rhonda after a pained silence.

"No harm, though it took you long enough to say." His mom took another bite, in clear delight of her wit. Kelvin hated her like this and wondered how many glasses of wine she had drunk this evening. He should have checked, though Rhonda had sprung the whole baby situation on him only hours before.

"Mom, we should just tell you what we need to talk about. No use dragging this out."

"Oh, Lord, what are you about to tell me? You better not have gotten into an accident. Did you hit and run? Dammit, Kelvin! I've told you to watch these city drivers out here, driving in the middle of the road on those hills you can't see over."

"Mom! No one is hurt. My truck is fine. Calm down." He reached out and placed his hand over hers. "Can you just let Rhonda tell you?"

His mom drew back her hand, clasping it with the other. Kelvin hoped she would not be defensive, but his mom never took new information well; she considered herself fully informed of all facets of his life.

Rhonda's gaze dropped to the floor as the room filled with silence, then a jumbled utterance fell from her mouth. Kelvin wiped the sweat off his palms.

"Speak up, dear. I can't hear you."

"I said that I'm pregnant," she said in an outcry, then blushed.

Kelvin's mom studied Rhonda. *As if wishing Rhonda dead*, Kelvin thought. At least his mother appeared to support his side of the problem.

His mom cleared her throat. "How do we know the baby is Kelvin's? From what I remember, you tramped around with that Patrick Holdsteader for the past few years. Are you telling me you have not recently slept together?"

Kelvin was also curious about the answer. He did not doubt the baby was his, but he was amused by the vile accusation his mother presented. A good tactic, though Rhonda's anguished face quickly smoothed over.

"I've only been with Kel since September of this school year, so the baby is his. I have no doubts. I'll take a paternity test if you need me to," Rhonda said, as if she had expected to be called a tramp, unable to identify the father. Rhonda would certainly chastise him later for failing to rise to her defense, as if he had accused her of being a cheater. He felt her glare, though he focused on his mother, waiting for her rebuttal.

"Okay. First off, his name is Kelvin. Not Kel. I did not name and raise him for seventeen years for anyone to call him anything but his birth name." She took a bite of her food. Kelvin felt ill. "Now, assuming the baby to be Kelvin's. And I believe you, dear. I needed to be sure. I have no doubt my Kelvin would be stupid enough to thrust his seed inside you, despite my obligatory discussions with him about safe sex. Men can be so insistent, can't they?"

She patted Kelvin's hand. He pulled away, disgusted at his mom's depiction of the relationship he had with Rhonda. Did she not see the difficulty Rhonda had in revealing their situation?

"What do you intend to do about the pregnancy? I assume you've told me for a reason."

Rhonda waited until Kelvin's mom nodded her head, permitting her to speak.

"I want to keep the baby."

"Well, then," Kelvin's mom said. She stood, stacking all three of their plates, though Rhonda only ate half her food. She scraped Rhonda's leftovers into the trashcan and washed the plates.

Kelvin did not know what his mother planned to do next. Rhonda tried to whisper something to him, but he shook his head with quick inflection, a warning. His mom opened the wine cabinet, embracing a new bottle. She unscrewed the cap and poured herself a glass to the brim.

She considered the two of them. "Either of you want a glass? Appears you both want to play adult, so let's get to it."

"Rhonda can't drink, and I'm okay," Kelvin said, trying to find even ground.

"Suit yourself." She placed the top on the bottle, returning it to the cabinet. She glided to her seat, studying Kelvin.

"So, you want this baby, too? Don't look puzzled at me. You just told me not to offer your little lady a drink. Seems like you care, don't you?"

"No, ma'am," Kelvin said in a low whisper, hoping Rhonda would not hear.

"So, you don't want this baby?" Kelvin's mom yelled out, standing without spilling, slapping the table. "We have a predicament, now. Don't you think my boy should get a say about this pregnancy, Rhonda?"

Rhonda let loose, crying with her hands held tightly in her lap. Kelvin was mortified. The woman he had ached over for years, culminating in these past few wondrous months, now wanted to have his baby. Maybe this had been the Lord's way of leading them down their rightful path. He wanted and should have prayed for an easier test.

"Mom, I want to be with Rhonda," he said. "I just think that we are too young to be having a baby. I don't know the answer. I hoped you could help us find it."

"Well, you surely can't expect this young lady to want to stay with you if you demand she abort your child. Have either of you considered adoption?"

"No, ma'am. If I have the baby, I will find a way to raise her."

Kelvin's mom took a sip, a tic of her lip, then a smile arose. "Oh, Kelvin. I guess you are giving me a grandchild before I turn forty."

Kelvin leered at his mother, watching the hateful red wine tinting her lips. He knew she loved him dearly, but she could rip the worst of situations to the roots. She would ultimately defend him but always made sure he understood who kept him standing.

Rhonda stood. "Mrs. Chestwick, I can leave if you want. Kelvin told me we should talk to you. I'm sorry if this news upsets you. I know my parents will take this even worse, and I expect I will need to find a friend to stay with. I should plan accordingly."

Kelvin's mother walked to Rhonda and placed a soft hand on her shoulder, a light rub of encouragement. "Please sit down, dear. Though you may find this hard to believe, I am fully on your side. You see my son defended you quite admirably, did he not?"

Kelvin saw Rhonda coaxed down, guided like a feather to the fall. Kelvin's mom took a sip as Kelvin waited for the play to end. She had decided his fate at first utterance. "Do you like the ring on my finger, Rhonda?"

Rhonda looked at his mother, then over to Kelvin, appearing unsure of the proper response. "The ring is beautiful, Mrs. Chestwick."

"Oh yes, dear. A family heirloom of the Chestwicks, the ring Mr. Chestwick proposed with. A gaudy thing with its flower pattern of diamonds, weighing me down from the moment I said yes. Never thought I would take it off."

She marched to the other side of the dining room table, twisted off the ring, and slammed the band down, taking out a small chip in the wood. She patted Kelvin on the back and sipped her wine. Kelvin looked at her, then back at the ring.

"What do you want from me?" he said, studying the twisted confines of the band.

"Son, I am not going to have a bastard of a grandchild be raised in this house, nor will I allow this community to think I allowed my son to knock up any girl he wants and pay to have his business tended to. You say you care for this woman and want to be with her. Prove it."

He took the ring, holding it between his thumb and index finger. There never had been a choice. His mother was always the one who decided. He loved Rhonda well enough. He rose, shuffled around the table, and got to one knee.

"Rhonda. I know this is not what you imagined, but will you marry me?"

He extended the ring, expecting her to slip her finger through. She kept her hands clasped, gazing at the ring. Fury rose in Kelvin. He felt foolish kneeling to someone so unappreciative. His mother began laughing, spitting out a little wine.

"Well, are you going to answer him, girl?"

"Will I be allowed to stay here?" Rhonda said.

"Of course. What else would you expect?"

Rhonda's breathing quickened, and Kelvin's knee began to ache. He wanted to throw the damn ring on the ground, ask them to figure the whole mess out and tell him if he was to be married or not, but he kept in position. Rhonda splayed out her left hand, and he slipped the ring on the designated finger only to discover the ring to be too big. He pulled the ring back, unsure how to proceed. Rhonda grabbed the ring and jammed it on her thumb, resulting in a slight cut to her knuckle, causing blood to trickle around the band now firmly in place.

Chapter 3

Clare turns two

Kelvin was furious—at himself, his friends, and his teacher, Professor Trenton, who had claimed he understood the difficulties of being a young father. Now, he was forced to retake the final or face failing the class, delaying his associate degree to his mother's chagrin. He could not recall why he had thought it brilliant to write notes on his arm, covered with long sleeves in the midst of summer. He pushed off his shame, eager to celebrate his little girl's birthday.

Kelvin revved the truck, spitting gravel to the sides before turning into the driveway, parking in his spot. He heard a squeal of delight from the porch. His mom had Clare in her hands, brown paste covering his daughter's mouth.

"What the hell do you have all over her mouth?" Kelvin asked, grabbing his bag from the passenger seat.

"Hey, language," his mom said. "I let her lick one of the beaters of the brownie mix. You know how Grandpa loves brownies, and I think he deserves a treat after watching Clare today."

Kelvin kissed his mother's cheek and Clare's head, then rushed inside. He threw his bag on one of the dining room chairs and flopped into the neighboring seat.

"What do you mean Grandpa watched her?" he yelled out as his mother entered the house. "He can barely move around; what would he do if an accident happened?"

Kelvin's mother placed Clare on the kitchen counter, cleaning up the utensils around the sink, but keeping herself in front of Clare just in case.

"I hate when you do that. She could fall so easily. Maybe I ought to stop going to class so someone can take care of her correctly."

She spun around, soap flying from the spatula in her hand. "Kelvin Michael! You are so close to getting your associate degree. You are finishing that school."

Kelvin saw Clare wiping soap from her face, trying to understand what happened. When Clare noticed both of them looking at her, she began wailing, patting at her eyes.

"Now see what you did!" He took Clare and jostled her up and onto his shoulder, which only caused her to cry louder.

"Oh, Lord. You need to be more careful, Kelvin. Give her here. I'll wash her eyes out. You can finish the dishes."

Kelvin handed her off. Clare's hands waved wildly back for her daddy. "Mom, I need to get some sleep if I'm going to work this shift tonight."

Screams emitted from the sink as water cascaded over Clare's eyes. "I can't do everything! Go to bed, but you better be ready to help me with the party tomorrow. I have friends coming to see Clare, and I will not have both her parents absent."

Kelvin could still hear his poor baby's cries as he stomped up the stairs to his bedroom. No one cared that he did the work of three men. Rhonda lay there in her pink pajamas, the third day in a row. She had a pile of books on her dresser. Self-help books that his mother kept encouraging her to read. After Clare's birth, Rhonda's general interests dwindled, leading to her crying all the time. Kelvin eventually stopped trying to comfort Rhonda, as she only took offense, accusing him of not understanding her. He ignored her most days, biding time until she returned, still loving her.

"Clare's birthday is tomorrow. You coming down for it? Mom plans on having some of her church friends celebrate with us."

"I can't, Kelvin. How could I even know how I'll feel tomorrow? I . . . I can't see anyone I don't know. Tell your mom I'm sorry."

"Fucking hell, Rhonda. You tell her." He flopped on the bed, bumping her as she placed a pillow over her face—Rhonda's way of stopping a conversation.

"Rhonda, we can't keep having you live this way. Do you want to try seeing a doctor again?"

She turned over, giving him a kiss on the cheek, brushing his hair. "I'm getting better, Kel. I swear. Grandpa has been talking with me, and I'm reading the self-help books, I promise. I'm learning to accept that my reaction to Clare was not my fault. It just takes time."

Kelvin closed his eyes, having heard the same pattern of words coming from her mouth every few months for the last year. Her lack of empathy for her daughter turned to guilt upon seeing her, wondering why motherhood had not welcomed her. The cycle was exhausting.

"I understand, honey," he said, hoping he would find the passion for his wife another day. "Please just make sure you show your face. I know Clare would love to see her mommy at the party. I bought a few presents, including a doll and coloring book."

"I'll try. I really will. Please be patient. Get some sleep."

Kelvin drifted to sleep at her behest. He dreamed of easier times, which mostly centered on less responsibility amongst his high school buddies. Waking with a start, he wondered why he never heard from them anymore. He looked at the clock, which was blinking twelve. He grunted, never losing the daze of working third shift. He searched for his phone, unsure whether he had set his alarm on it. Not on the nightstand.

"Rhonda. Rhonda! What time is it?"

"Shhh, Kel," Rhonda said. "You'll wake Clare and your mom."

"Where's my phone?" he seethed. "My alarm didn't go off."

Rhonda reached around, smacking her hand on her books. Kelvin turned on the light, figuring his phone must have dropped on the floor. Rhonda groaned, attempting to block the light with the covers. Kelvin searched all over, but his phone was gone.

"What did you do with it, Rhonda? Did you snoop through my phone again? I haven't been talking to anyone. Now give me my phone."

"Shut up, Kelvin. I don't have your phone. Turn off the light."

Kelvin ignored her, shoving objects all over the place in desperation. He began banging his fist on the dresser, exhausted and frustrated by

Rhonda's indifference. When the hell would she start pulling her weight? The sound reverberated through the house, and a wail could be heard from below. Kelvin growled as he barreled downstairs, where his mom already held his little girl. Clare's fists rubbed her eyes, then struck his mom's shoulder.

"We don't hit, Clare bear. No matter how much Daddy scares you."

"Have you seen my phone?"

"It's on the counter, where you left it last night when you decided to help with your daughter for a moment."

He saw the phone on the counter next to his bookbag. He took the phone. 1:21. A text from his boss asking where he was. He opened the alarms, seeing that he had set two for 11:00 last night.

"What happened to my phone? I set my alarm. Did it not go off?"

Kelvin's mom weaved her hand through the baby's stringy auburn hair, blowing little bits around, then kissing her cheek. Clare did not smile but was visibly soothed by the affection. Kelvin waited with crossed arms, then slammed his phone on the kitchen counter with impatience.

His mother turned toward Kelvin, causing Clare to shift and cry again. "What's wrong with you? I turned your phone on silent. I thought you were getting calls at night when I heard the vibrating. Sorry."

"Well, I'm probably fired because of you."

"Kelvin, you didn't even know where your phone was. You need to take responsibility."

Kelvin fought against obscenities, incredulous at her demands that he maintain a job, then failing to help him keep it. He called his boss, who informed Kelvin that he no longer needed to return due to his prior tardiness and this unexplained absence. Kelvin tried to come up with some excuse about caring for Clare, but he remained fired. Kelvin sighed, noticing his mom observing, as Clare's head rested on her shoulder.

"That did not sound like it went well," his mom whispered.

"I'm fired, Mother."

"Oh, well, we'll figure something out. You'll find something better after you graduate."

"What about you demanding I keep a job if I want to stay in this house?"

Kelvin's mother placed Clare on her toddler bed decorated with Elmo sheets. A present from Grandpa, who thought the world of the high-pitched red vulgarity for children. Clare reached her hands out, muttering something that sounded close enough to "dada."

He sat on the floor next to her bed, stroking her cheek. "Sorry for waking you, Clare bear. Daddy missed work, but he'll make it up to you at your birthday party." He tickled her belly until she giggled in fits.

"Kelvin, you need to calm her down, not rile her up. Now it'll take me an hour to get her back to bed."

Kelvin's mom went to the sink, opened the second cabinet from the right, and poured herself a glass of red wine. Kelvin watched as she sipped, then let out a guttural sound of satisfaction. He looked to see Clare studying his mother in the same manner.

"Mom, I'll stay with her until she goes to bed. I'll read her a story or something. I'm usually up at this hour anyways."

His mother continued to sip her wine in exaggerated breaths, looking out the kitchen window. Clare was now on her knees, waiting for something new to happen. Kelvin searched for one of her books scattered nearby, spotting one on top of the television stand. It was about some little bear that got lost.

"Maybe it's for the best. This way you won't be tired for the party tomorrow. Did Rhonda say she'll join us? She doesn't need to make a big production. I would just like her there for the cake cutting and opening of presents."

"She said she'll try, Mom."

"Did you set up the backyard for the bonfire? I think it'll be nice to make s'mores and hot dogs. I know Grandpa is excited to sit by the fire like old times."

Clare began whining, pulling, and then patting at the book.

"I forgot, Mom. I'll set it up first thing."

"I wonder if people think we are trash for having that trailer in our backyard. Too bad Grandpa says he doesn't feel comfortable moving up and down these stairs, but then finds a way to make it up to entertain that wife of yours."

"Mom, why don't you take a bath and go to bed? Like I said, I'll take care of Clare."

"Yes, that's good. I hope your wife feels better, Kelvin. My prayer group keeps her in their thoughts every week."

His mom walked to her bedroom, taking the bottle and glass, and closing the door behind her. Kelvin craved to tell Rhonda that his mom gossiped about her daughter-in-law at church, praying over her condition, but he knew there would be no use.

Kelvin read and reread the book to Clare, using less animation and pretend bear growling each reading to calm her. Amid the third time, Clare drifted to sleep. Kelvin kissed her on the forehead, pulling her blanket up to her shoulders. He went upstairs, slinking into bed, unsure and indifferent about what he may need to do about work.

Kelvin woke to a loud bang and crying from downstairs. He turned to see Rhonda still asleep in bed. He threw on a pair of gray sweatpants, the drawstring pulled entirely to the right so he had to loop the string around and tie the one end to keep them up, and a shirt with large block lettering advertising Stanford that must have come from a yard sale. He strolled down the stairs to the dining room to see his daughter covered in brown batter mix. His mom was also splattered with mix all over her pants, as well as large areas of the floor and surrounding cabinets. He stared at them for a few seconds before laughing.

"It's not funny, Kelvin! Now I don't have any cake mix for the birthday party. All I wanted to do was give her a taste of the cake batter, and then she grabbed the bowl, and it all poured right on her head."

Kelvin laughed even harder. His mom tried to keep her pout but soon laughed along. Clare giggled after no one seemed to be afraid anymore.

"I'll clean her up in the bathtub upstairs," he said. "Why don't you take a shower, and we'll wipe up the kitchen afterwards."

"I'll still need more cake mix, or someone will have to pick up a cake."

"I'll pick up a cake from the supermarket. I can get a tube of that cake decorating stuff or the edible letters. Do we need anything else?"

"We have plenty of drinks, hotdogs, buns, plates . . . Oh, could you pick up ice cream?"

Kelvin nodded and grabbed a towel from his mother's bathroom to wrap up his daughter as he lifted her from the floor, hurrying to the upstairs tub. She had run her hands through her hair and face, licking both her arms. "We have to take a bath really quickly, darling, then

Daddy will prepare for your party. Are you excited?" He tickled her belly as he pulled off her shirt, causing her to giggle and bat his hand away. They played with a duck and boat in the bathtub, followed by fervent whining as Kelvin scrubbed out her hair.

Once she was clean and dressed, Kelvin left Clare with his mom, not feeling the need to press on Rhonda about today's festivities. He wanted to go to Walmart, but given his recent firing, he went to Loc-Stop, the smaller grocery store just up town, worrying they might not even have cakes. Luckily, the store had three options: chocolate cake with either a pink, blue, or green border on white icing. He asked one of the clerks if they had a vanilla version, unable to see the harm in buying both types of cakes, but he was told that was it. The only lettering he could find were those small, chalky, crisp letters. He wanted to ask about squeezable icing but could not take the awful monotone voice of the clerk again. He grabbed the pink-outlined cake, a package of lettering, and a bucket of Neapolitan ice cream and waited in the long line, sighing at the slow pace.

"I can get you over here, Kel."

Kelvin looked over, unable to recall knowing anyone that worked here, and saw his ex-girlfriend, Sheryl Bishop. He hurried over before one of the people in front of him complained.

"I had no idea you worked here, Sheryl. How have you been?" He put down the cake and ice cream, giving her an awkward hug over the counter, swooning over her thin navy buttoned shirt, her left nipple lightly visible.

"Oh, I'm the assistant store manager, but I saw the line and figured I could help. I came back from college a little while back—not the place for me." She scanned his items through in the lull as two people lined up behind him, ruining any extended conversation.

"I can understand that. I'm at Stillwell Community College, taking classes for finance." He pulled out a twenty as she bagged his groceries.

Quick exchange of cash, she said, "What's the cake and ice cream for?"

"I'm having a birthday party for my little girl. She's already two." He laughed, not knowing what else to say to break the tension. Sheryl followed his laugh with a kind smile. "Why don't you come to the party? Everyone should be there around six. Some of my college friends are coming by. It'll be fun." The woman behind him started pushing her food along the conveyor belt.

"Um, sure. I don't get off until six, but I'll try to make my way over after that. Same address?"

"Same address." He grabbed his two bags. "Nice seeing you again, Sheryl."

He did not think she heard him at first, as she furiously scanned the woman's ten cans of tuna. As he neared the exit, he heard, "You too, Kel!"

Kelvin felt a slight increase in his mood, now considering his unemployment with little concern. He hoped to graduate soon and move on to better opportunities. He walked into the house yelling out, "Daddy saved the day." Clare sat with his mom, bundled up on the couch watching cartoons. He set the bags on the kitchen counter as his mother scooted behind him.

"Oh, let's see what you found." His mom took out the bucket of Neapolitan ice cream, frowning. "Is this the best they had at that wretched store?"

"I thought you wouldn't care."

"Well, I thought you would try a little."

"Before you start, they had limited options for the cake. I asked." His mom shook her head, taking out the small lettering. He went to the cabinet to grab a packet of powder donuts. Clare clapped her hands when she saw, so he tried to sneak her one.

"You know I hate her having so much sugar. She'll be eating fistfuls of cake later."

He tried to shove a donut into his mom's mouth, but she pursed her lips, shying away. He wiped a little of the powder on her cheek before eating the donut whole. She wiped her face off, picking up Clare, who had licked rather than eaten the now soggy donut.

"Can you set the wood for the bonfire?"

"Sure." He walked out the back door, hoping to see Grandpa on the isolated porch swing. His grandfather liked to sit and look out amongst the fields and wooded area, smoking a cigar without judgment from his mother. Kelvin rarely joined him, understanding Grandpa needed these times to think about Grandma.

Kelvin moved some of the scattered rocks surrounding the fire pit into a makeshift circle. He then placed the wood Grandpa had delivered into a teepee. He thought he should tell his mom about Sheryl but could not anticipate her reaction of either disgust or delight. He figured Sheryl wouldn't show anyways.

After an hour, his wood pile was only a bit slanted, though braced enough from all sides. He worried one side might cause the whole thing to tip over once the fire began, but he checked that the logs would still fall within the extended confines of the pit. If his mother made sure her drunk friends respected the rock barriers, it would be okay.

"Looks good, Kelvin," he heard as he placed more brush in the center to start the fire. "Your mom taught you well."

"Thanks, Grandpa." His grandfather walked around the pile, performing his authoritative review—his right hip shuffling with exaggerated movements to keep the weight off.

"Seems a bit slanted over here, but I think you'll be fine. I bet you already knew." He laughed, sitting on one of the benches placed near the pit. "I can't believe your little girl is turning two. Seems like yesterday you brought home this little pink rough patch, wailing like a banshee." Kelvin kept his eyes on his unlit project. "Your mom does right by that girl. Takes care of us all, really. I hope you repay her in kind, Kelvin."

"You don't need to watch Rhonda the way you do, Grandpa. I don't think you should be taking those stairs anymore." Kelvin sat on the neighboring bench, both still looking at the fire pit.

"You need to care for her, Kelvin. She needs patience. Having a child can take quite a toll on a woman, even if they don't mean for it. Your grandma went through something similar with your Uncle Roger. Kids are tough. Thankfully, Clare is sweeter than some. Your wife had a major bout of postpartum depression that no one will discuss. Now she carries this hanging guilt because she feels so detached. Depressed from being depressed, if that makes sense. She needs to know that you don't hate or look down on her. She's getting there, but she needs you more than me."

"She should go on medication like Mom said. I can't convince Rhonda of anything."

His grandfather stood, boosting himself off the bench. "I hope you think over my words and can figure out why your response is shit, boy. You need to be a husband, so start acting like it."

Kelvin could not find an appropriate response, so he ventured off topic. "Where's Shelbie at? I haven't seen her slobbering face for a few days."

"Good lord, Kelvin. Shelbie hurt her foot a few days ago, came around hobbling. She's holed up in the trailer with a cone on until she can put more weight on that leg." He patted Kelvin on the back. "You really are oblivious about what happens around here. I'll see you tonight. Good job on the bonfire. Keep in mind what I said about Rhonda." Kelvin observed his grandfather limping toward the trailer, ensuring he took the steps okay.

Once his grandfather was inside his trailer, Kelvin needed an escape. He moved through the neighboring rows of corn, stalks taller them him, ripe for harvest in a few weeks. He longed for Shelbie to come bounding with him, a companion for any mood, and simmered in guilt that he had not known the poor thing was suffering. After twenty minutes, he found himself at the edge of a patch of woods, an isolated quarter mile circle surrounded by the sweeping farmland. When he was younger, Kelvin had hoped he would find his own Terabithia, but he never discovered the bridge.

He stepped under the shade of a large sycamore tree, in a better state of mind, knowing he did not want to leave Rhonda. Though he despised her when she lay crooked in their bed for days without end, he had pined so long for her in high school, promised to love her indefinitely, and he wanted Clare to have a two-parent household. Yet he had carnal needs that Rhonda failed to acknowledge, let alone satisfy. Had he invited Sheryl to fuck her or did he want to get a rise out of Rhonda, an emotion, proof that he meant more to her than a safe place to sleep? He would not allow guilt about his extramarital activities. He had kept them from encroaching upon the glass frame of a home life. Could Rhonda blame him for an escape if he kept happy otherwise?

Kelvin looked through the canopy, light streaming around him, hoping to find some woodland creature to occupy his mind. He fretted over the lack of wildlife, wondering whether the isolated woods had relinquished its fauna to the surrounding countryside. He sat and leaned against a neighboring oak, enjoying the seclusion. He closed his eyes, listening to the melody of birds, an orchestra of shrill sounds that complemented each other in their final note. He let himself drift into the ease.

He woke with a start. A squirrel chattered nearby, falling at Kelvin's jarring movement. The squirrel jumped to a smaller tree, staring at him. Kelvin smiled at the squirrel, pleased to find a furry friend after all.

He heaved up, ignoring the squirrel's agitation, looking at his phone to find thirteen missed calls from his mother and texts ranging from "Are you okay?" to "You better get your ass to your daughter's birthday party, Kelvin. I am so disappointed in you." He deleted the voicemails without listening, figuring they contained the same overall message. Needless alarm. The party started at six, and it was only fifteen after.

As he headed toward his house, he felt greater conviction that he would sleep with Sheryl if the opportunity presented itself. He passed through the corn once again, planning to sneak a bottle of wine from his mother. He needed something to loosen his charm.

He saw the flames of the bonfire and reflections of five moving figures enlarged by the light. Some were closer to the firepit than he would have liked, but his mother's friends would fall where they may. He heard a rush of screams as he grew visible to the party, an eclectic group of women adorned in necklaces, wristbands, and dresses. Of course, his mother would not be outdone, planning an outfit of a red dress, cream cardigan, and pearls.

"How have you been, Kelvin? I heard work gave you some trouble last night," said Evelyn, the pride of his mother's friend group, though primarily thanks to his mother's sentiment of keeping one's enemies closer.

"Oh, Evelyn," said another woman in an orange pantsuit that had no place at a bonfire. "Edna told us that in confidence. The boy wants to focus on his studies, which I find admirable." The woman began rubbing his arm. Kelvin guessed they were already into their second bottle of wine.

"Hands off, Chelsea. The boy is married," laughed Evelyn. The others followed with feigned laughter, even Chelsea.

"Where's Mom?"

"Oh, she's in the house taking care of your lady friend. I haven't seen Rhonda. Will she be joining us?" asked a woman with flowing red curly hair, wearing a simple black dress and emerald earrings.

Evelyn interjected as Kelvin twisted in place. "We love the dress your mom put on your darling baby girl. Ladies, remind me to ask where she found it. I would love to buy one for my granddaughter."

"Well, I need to go find Clare and Mom. Hope you enjoy the bonfire." Kelvin scurried away before he could get a response, bounding up the steps into the house. "Mom! I'm back!"

"Hi, Kelvin," Sheryl said, sitting on the couch with Clare on her lap. Clare was adorned with black strappy shoes, a pink tutu, and a matching shirt with the words "Two Cool." Kelvin realized Evelyn's comment had not been a kind one.

Clare reached for Kelvin. He picked her up, giving her kisses on the cheek until she giggled. He sat down on the other side of the couch, a respectable distance from Sheryl.

"When did you get here?"

"Maybe thirty minutes ago. Your mom told me to wait here until you arrived, though I'm not sure where she went."

"Well, thanks for waiting. Want a drink?"

"Yes! I didn't feel comfortable asking your mom for a glass of her wine. After all these years, she still has that polite sneer toward me."

"Oh, she's like that with most people. You only met her the once. You get used to her demeanor."

"I'm glad to see you joined us, Kelvin," came a voice from his mother's bedroom. She held a bottle of Sauvignon Blanc, chilled in the wine fridge she pretended not to have in her room. Kelvin and Sheryl were both looking at the bottle in her hand. "Oh, the ladies have decided we should be bad and switch to white wine." She strayed toward the door as they watched. She twirled, stumbling a small step, but keeping the effect. "Sheryl, dear. Stern manners do not make me a bitch. Please remember, as I pray for your children." She pushed open the door with a wide swing and glided down the wooden steps. "Bring out Clare!"

They paused, waiting for an encore. "Did you know she was in there?" Kelvin finally said. Clare remained mesmerized by her book, not recognizing the adult games occurring around her.

"Not at all," whispered Sheryl. "She must have come in while I read to Clare. Maybe I should go."

"Please don't. Let me take Clare out, and I'll meet you upstairs. We can hide in the guest bedroom and try to catch up without Mom around," he said with nervous laughter.

"Are you sure that will be okay with Rhonda?"

"We'll leave the door open. We aren't planning anything, are we?"

Sheryl shrugged. Kelvin swallowed hard, picking up his daughter, who immediately cried out, reaching for the book depicting pictures of bears in funny costumes. "Come on, sweetheart. Grandma has to primp and prod you around the church group." Clare started screaming. Sheryl swooped up the book and placed it in Clare's hands. Kelvin mouthed "thank you" before rushing out the door, feeling Clare's tantrum growing.

Kelvin returned to his grandfather sitting in one of his outdoor chairs, prodding at the fire, keeping a watchful eye on the ladies now spinning around, two bottles being passed between them. He handed Clare off to his grandfather, telling him to be careful. He gave a knowing nod and began bouncing Clare on his knee, book still in hand, flopping all around.

Kelvin snuck back into his mother's room and grabbed a bottle of champagne that he would pay for tomorrow. Two glasses from the cabinet in the other hand, he nodded his head toward the stairs, signaling Sheryl to follow. She giggled as they tiptoed up. Kelvin collapsed on the floor at the edge of the empty bed. Sheryl sat next to him, brushing his hand to grab one of the glasses. He glanced at her to see if there had been any meaning, but her attention was now on the simple room.

"Not very welcoming, is it?"

"It's the guest room. Mom doesn't see the need to add personal effects. She thinks it makes guests feel more welcome when they can make the space theirs. Can't remember the last time we had a guest in here, though."

He poured champagne into both glasses, a rush of bubbles forcing them to sip quickly.

"So, what's new with Sheryl?"

She laughed, swallowing the first glass, sticking it out for a refill. "I already told you I came back home and became the assistant manager of the store."

"Well yeah, but why leave college?"

"Who likes college if you can't get drunk and fuck around? I liked being studious but could not escape the pull of the party life."

"That doesn't sound like a reason to leave," he said, refilling their glasses, then clinking them together. "I'm jealous you got to have that time away. I was tied down with a baby."

"Oh, you know you love that little girl. She's precious as hell."

"I would never trade Clare for anything, but I miss what I never got to experience. Just getting a year of drunken debauchery sounds exhilarating. A bit of freedom."

"Freedom from what, Kel? We all end up in a token family; you just got there faster." She stood, catching herself on the bed. "I left because of my boyfriend. We were together for a year, but I got drunk and slept with someone else. I told him right after in a tearful plea. He seemed to understand and forgive me, never even asking who the guy was. Two months later, he tells me he is in love with some woman in his physics class and wants to break up. He promised up and down that he did not cheat. He just felt something for this woman that he wanted to explore." She sat on the bed, breathing out continuous sighs. Kelvin stood, refilling both their glasses. "It's not fair for me to blame him. I just could not accept the breakup, stopped going to class, and failed my spring semester. My parents told me that I had to take a year off to get my head straight. Now I'm back in the hometown I had sworn off."

Sheryl swayed, taking a sip of champagne, pacing around the room, opening the closet, then relaxing on the bed. Kelvin watched her from the floor, unsure what he could say to comfort her.

"Rhonda never leaves her room anymore. After she had Clare, she couldn't face being a mother and became despondent. She's better now but still rarely leaves the house."

"Poor Rhonda," Sheryl said, then put her glass down. "Maybe we should get more."

"Hell, why not. Mom's going to be pissed either way." He rushed down the stairs, grabbed the first white wine he could find, tried to quickly take the cork out, and pinched the corner of his finger on the bottle opener. He yelled, then slunk down, looking around to make sure no one noticed, then finished opening the bottle. He hurried off, taking the stairs two at a time. Sheryl lay on the bed, glass balancing in the air on her palm.

"Pour me up!"

"At this rate, you'll have to stay in the guest room."

"Seems I've already made myself comfortable, so why not." Sheryl patted the bed. He sat down but refused to scoot closer. He had never strayed from his marriage in the sanctity of his home. It seemed blatantly cruel to Rhonda. Was infidelity in such close proximity to his wife an unrealized boundary for him?

"Kelvin . . ."

"Yes," he said, turning his body toward her, knee bent on the bed as a buffer.

"Kelvin, Kelvin, Kelvin."

"What do you want to say, Sheryl?"

"Why did you choose Rhonda over me?"

He swallowed the last of his glass, then took a swig out of the bottle. "Is this why you came over?"

"No. I came over to meet and celebrate your little girl's birthday. Seemed like the best time to ask her daddy why he left this fine ass. I don't even think you properly broke up with me. Just stopped talking to me, and the next thing I hear, you were fucking Rhonda."

"Everyone knew I wanted Rhonda since freshman year. I never thought the opportunity would come that she would even want me."

Sheryl grabbed the bottle from him and guzzled a quarter before falling back onto the bed and spilling a little on her blouse. He grabbed the bottle from her hand before the whole thing tipped onto her. She laughed, wiping her mouth on her sleeve.

"I cannot think of a single complaint I had about you. I just wanted Rhonda so bad and for so long that I could not stop myself. Now you see me years later, and she's locked in her room barely giving me the time of day. I'm lucky if I can get her to touch me anymore." He slapped his hand over his mouth. "Shit, I shouldn't be telling you that stuff."

"No, it's fine. I just wish you would have stayed my friend."

Kelvin relaxed next to her. He still kept an honest space between them, namely the bottle of wine. "I'm sorry, Sheryl. You did deserve better. Sometimes I wonder what life would be like without Rhonda, but I don't let myself get far. I still love my little girl, even if her mom is cold."

They both jumped at the thunderous slam of a door, looked at each other, and then began laughing. They filled their glasses until the bottle was empty.

"Do you think that was Rhonda?"

"Probably. I'll deal with her. She's supposed to be downstairs celebrating our daughter's birthday. Guess I should drag her down."

"Kelvin, be nice. Being a young mother and wife can be hard."

"Don't you think she should be celebrating her daughter's birthday?"

"You're right. I don't know. Do what you need. I should go downstairs, anyways. I'll see you outside." She leaned her head against Kelvin's shoulder, lingering there as if she might fall asleep, then pushed off, taking a few steps to catch her balance. "I'm all right," she said, laughing and holding the doorknob. "I hope the ladies are just as drunk."

Sheryl weaved down the stairs. He listened for any signs of falling, but the stumbles did not result in any thud. He stewed over Rhonda's brisk action in slamming the door without even a greeting. What the hell could be her problem now? He had not done anything he regretted. How dare she act so childish in front of guests.

He went to their bedroom door. Locked. He twisted and turned the knob to make sure he had tried to open the door correctly. No movement. He banged and beat on the door in frustration that his wife would lock him out of his own bedroom.

"Open the damn door, Rhonda. You need to come downstairs and celebrate your daughter's birthday. We are waiting for you."

He heard a muffle. He banged on the door harder, pain coursing through his hand. "What are you saying? Unlock this door!"

"I said leave me alone. Go play with your whore in the other room!" The voice was close, so at least she was out of bed.

"We were just talking. Quit being a bitch and come downstairs with me."

"No! You've embarrassed me."

"You better open this door and celebrate Clare's birthday like a fucking sane person, or I'm dragging you down." He pounded on the door with both hands, then punched the door, causing two of his knuckles to bleed.

"You're being a drunk asshole, Kel. Go to bed and leave me alone!"

"I warned you, Rhonda." He backed away, trying to get a running start in the hallway, though he did not have much space. He slammed his right shoulder into the door. Pain shot through his body, but he swore he heard a crack. "I'm getting this door open!" He switched sides, slamming his left shoulder against the door. A little more movement, but still no breaking.

"Will you calm down before you break the door! I'll open it if you promise not to hurt me."

Kelvin clung back to the wall. He never thought of hurting her. He just wanted her to get over these issues and enjoy life a little. "I would never," he said.

The door opened, and he saw her scurry under the sheets on the bed, turning her back to him. "I'm not going. I don't want to be around all you drunk fools. I can celebrate with Clare tomorrow."

"Today is her birthday, Rhonda. Today. Not tomorrow. When are you going to start being there for her?" He grabbed one of her books stacked on the nightstand. "What is the point?" He slammed the book down. "There is no point. For over a year you claim you are getting better, hiding in this room, reading these nonsensical books. I'm done with this shit, Rhonda. I'm burning every one of these unless you come downstairs and stop me."

She kept her back to him. "You won't, Kelvin. You're better than that."

"Nothing works for you! I need you back. We all need you back. Sheryl is not my wife and never will be. You are!"

"Endearing words, Kel. I promise to try. Tomorrow."

Kelvin began stacking the books. Two fell off the shelf, but he piled as many as he could into a two-foot tower. "I'm done, Rhonda. I'm burning these. No fucking point."

She did not respond, further driving his fury. He carried the stack of books, kicking the door twice to get her attention. He charged down the steps, slipping down the last two, dropping the books and falling into the edge of the last step. He felt intense pain in his lower back, but he intended to see books burn. He was collecting them when Sheryl sauntered inside.

"There you are. I thought you planned on coming out right after me. Here, let me help you." Sheryl grabbed the three remaining books. "What are these for? *Strong Mother*? Why do you have these books?"

"They're Rhonda's. Can you stack those on top of mine and open the door?"

Sheryl gave him a puzzled look, though she placed the books as asked. She held the door as Kelvin marched out, looking at his bedroom window. He swore he saw a stirring behind the curtains.

"I'm burning these fucking books!" he screamed at the window. He saw Rhonda move the curtain, catching Kelvin's eyes. She quickly placed the curtain back, but he could see her shadow lingering.

He looked around and was met with stares. No one spoke or moved. He marched forward and threw all the books on the fire, their pages catching and flickering up.

His mom finally broke the mesmerized silence. "What the hell are you doing, Kelvin?"

Kelvin spun to face his mother. She stood next to the table of food and gifts, all opened. "You opened the presents without me?" He noticed Clare still on his grandfather's lap, playing with the doll he claimed came from Rhonda. "Did you tell Clare that Rhonda gave her that doll?"

"Well, Kelvin. We didn't know where you were, and it was getting late." Flutters of burning paper blew around, though everyone pretended nothing had happened, swatting them away. "If the present had her name, then I'm sure we told Clare that it came from Rhonda." She tugged on his arm, pulling his ear down to her. "You need to stop this right now. You are embarrassing me."

Kelvin jerked away from her. He seethed as Clare continued to play with the doll she thought Rhonda had given her. Clare should know her mother for what she was, not this feigned barrier of pretend. He marched to Clare, grabbing the doll from her hands. She began bawling, reaching out for the doll.

His grandfather snarled at him. "You need to stop this now, Kelvin."

"No, Grandpa," he whispered. Kelvin bent down on one knee to face his crying child. "Clare, your mom did not buy this doll for you. Your mom has done nothing for you, and I fear she never will."

"Stop this, Kelvin!" his mom screamed from the other side of the fire.

With Clare's eyes still on the doll, Kelvin threw it in the fire. Clare reached toward the melting face, crying louder.

"Your mom does nothing, Clare. This is her real present," he said, gazing upon the destruction, the sound of his daughter's wails ringing behind him.

Chapter 4

Clare is six

Kelvin's eyes glazed over the packages to his right, lost in thought about his little girl starting kindergarten. He hated missing her first day, but no one would change shifts with him. His mom would get the precious moments, once again.

"Kelvin, you need to get a move on the cold products. We don't want ice cream melting."

Kelvin blinked, looking at the woman bearing down on him: brown framed glasses on the base of her nose, black hair in a neat ponytail, clipboard in hand for some unnecessary check. "Sorry, Tina." He opened the back of the fridge and started stacking the ice cream.

"It's fine. Just keep on task."

She left through the side door, out to the CVS patrons. Tina had been assistant manager for less than a month and bothered Kelvin at every assignment, refusing to give him this day off, even though she could stock these shelves just as well herself. He caught himself staring at her from behind, disappointed again that her ass seemed to divot and swell in the wrong areas, as if a permanent indentation had pressed the poor thing. Three months since Rhonda had even flicked at his penis, and he felt the itch to stray. However, the chlamydia incident had resulted in the current lurch with Rhonda, and he hadn't been able to advance beyond awkward gawking without guilt.

Four hours of stocking followed by four more with self-checkout morons. People had an inordinate amount of ineptitude in scanning a bunch of black lines, only a few able to make the process quicker than going to a cashier. Then you had the ones disputing prices with you, as if the longer they bothered you, the higher the discount they'd get. Knowing he hated this purgatory, Tina basked in his misery. At the end of his shift, he changed his clothes and hurried to the exit to prevent delay.

"Thanks for your help today, Kelvin. Sorry you had to miss your daughter's first day of school. I promise I'm hiring more people."

He stood before the exit, trying not to turn around. "Thanks, Tina. I usually don't mind all the hours, but today was for my little girl."

"I get it. Hopefully, we can be more accommodating in the future. Have a good evening."

"You too," he said, bursting through the door. He felt a little better with the acknowledgment of his sacrifice. Maybe Tina would eventually be a welcome addition to his work life.

He drove the twenty-seven minutes home casually, not caring to speed back. He only really wanted to see his daughter and hear about her day; he did not look forward to encountering the rest of the household. Two more blowouts after Clare's second birthday had caused his mom to demand the fighting cease. Grandpa suggested Rhonda move into the trailer, as neither Rhonda nor Kelvin wanted the divorce, largely due to his mother's umbrella of money and support that kept them comfortable.

Rhonda returned to their shared bed without explanation last year. He theorized it was because Rhonda was growing closer to Clare, as she realized her daughter did not judge her for any misgivings, and she had not completely damaged their relationship.

He liked having her back. He had never gone to the trailer for release, not liking the idea of having sex in his grandparents' trailer. Then he tripped up with some dried stalk of a woman, leaving him with a cold wife, though she thankfully remained in the same bed.

He brought Clare's favorite treat, Zebra Cakes, which he stole from the store. He felt no remorse in thieving from the abstract entity. He never received a bonus for his hard work these past two years, so he awarded himself small incentives. They wanted him to stock shelves until his mind was numb, so a few items might find their way to his house.

He pulled into the driveway, puzzled that his mom's car was absent. Immediately, he felt a pit of nausea that something had happened to Clare. No one had texted him with updates, so she must not be at the hospital.

Shelbie bounded over, at a slower pace as age had started to grip her. She seemed to be purposely keeping stride with Grandpa's decline. Kelvin stepped out of the truck and bent down, giving Shelbie a proper belly rub, her tongue lolling to the side. He had hoped Clare would rush out, too. He grabbed the snack cakes and walked into the house, hollering out and wondering why everyone would be out so late. He threw the box on the counter, looking in his mother's and Clare's bedrooms. He walked upstairs to find Rhonda missing, too.

He fought the urge to call them, expecting they must have gone to dinner, but he deserved to see his daughter on her first day of school. He worked a twelve-hour shift and got screwed from seeing his daughter the whole damn day. Kelvin kicked off his shoes, leaving them in the middle of the kitchen. That should annoy his mother well and good. He flopped on the couch, searching for an escape.

After twenty minutes of channel flipping in annoyance, he called his mother, who answered on the second ring. Loud screams came from the background. "Sorry," she yelled, then the sound of a screen door slamming.

"Where the hell are you? I wanted to hear about Clare's first day, but I find myself home alone."

"Oh, Kelvin. What time were you supposed to get home? I thought you said later. Rhonda and I are at a church function with Clare. We are wrapping up now. The kids are putting on a skit for church, and our first practice was tonight. Clare is playing one of the adorable angels. Rhonda promises to finish up her costume after I show her how to sew properly."

"Did anyone think to tell me what my daughter would be doing? When was this play nonsense decided?"

"It's not nonsense, Kelvin. Quit being this way. I'll be right in, Denise. Sorry, Denise is trying to put everything away with the kids running around. Thankfully, Rhonda is here to help."

"Whatever, I got to go." He hung up, satisfied that he had gotten the last word.

After throwing a mild tantrum of boredom on the couch, he stepped out to his grandpa's trailer, hearing the blaring sound of some reality television show. His grandpa had a guilty pleasure for *The Real World*, a pull to a youth he could never return to, Kelvin guessed.

"Hold on a second," Kelvin heard, standing silent at the door after knocking. The door opened to his grandfather in pajama bottoms and a black tank top, loose on his declining frame. "Kelvin. Your mom told me you wouldn't be home until late, so I didn't do anything about dinner. Come on in." His grandpa shuffled against the door, giving Kelvin just enough space to slip by and sit on the gray couch neighboring his grandfather's brown reclining chair.

"Don't worry, Grandpa. I already ate. I just came to see how you were doing. Rhonda, Clare, and Mom are all at church."

His grandpa raised the recliner up until his forehead was tilted to the sky but still low enough to see the television. "That's right. Little Clare bear will be in a play, I hear. An angel, of course," he said, chuckling.

"No one told me," Kelvin said. "I wanted to see Clare before bed. Hear all about her first day of kindergarten. Now I'm missing out on the whole day, you know?"

His grandpa changed the channel to some historical program, as if to hide what he had been doing. "Oh, I'm sure she'll tell you. That girl will rattle on about everything she can remember. Don't you worry."

"I just don't understand why I work so much when Mom has enough money to keep us all happy. I could have seen Clare off to school today," he grumbled.

"Stop right there, Kelvin. What your mother chooses to do with her money is her business. You be grateful for what she provides you. We all have a good thing going here, but you still have to earn your basic keep."

"Rhonda gets to laze her ass around; meanwhile, Mom demands I keep a job. Makes no sense. I'm her son."

"Rhonda has that online business she's been putting together. Been doing quite well, from what I hear. Sold four boxes of lotion last week."

Kelvin rolled his eyes, sinking himself further into the couch. "Is that what Rhonda is telling you all? She sets herself up in some pyramid scheme and is now an entrepreneur? She'll be lucky to make a thousand dollars in a year."

"Dammit, Kelvin," his grandpa spat. "You need to be more supportive of your wife. She is still sticking by you, and she's good to Clare."

"Oh, thank God, she's *finally* taking responsibility for her child." Kelvin waited for some other defense of Rhonda, but his grandfather kept his eyes on the television projecting some program regarding ancient Egyptians. Kelvin toiled over his grandpa's defense of everyone but him.

"Maybe Rhonda and I should have another kid, now that she's decided to own up to motherhood. I've always wanted a boy."

"What the hell are you talking about, Kelvin? You don't want another kid."

"Sure I do. Rhonda might as well have another baby if she's planning on staying home for the rest of her life."

"I don't imagine that's the case, especially after what happened last year, and you giving her that God-awful disease earlier this year. Don't look at me like that. Of course she came crying to me. I'll be damned if I let you rag on her to me. If you are going to cheat on your wife, at least put on a fucking condom, Kelvin."

"Thanks for the advice, Grandpa. Mind telling me what happened last year?"

With a puzzled expression, his grandpa looked at him, then the television, then over to the fridge. "Can you grab me a Coke? I hate getting up and down off this thing. Liable to break it."

Kelvin eyed his grandpa, who remained fixated on the program. He grabbed two Cokes, placing one on the collapsible shelf next to his grandfather's lazy chair. Kelvin knew when his grandpa was withholding.

"Did Rhonda cheat on me? No . . . that wouldn't affect us having kids," he reasoned. "Has she made some sort of pledge? Is she adamant to remain on the pill?"

"Oh, stop. You're the one that doesn't respect your marriage, not her. I told her to discuss the matter with you. I never asked after that. Figured you knew. Not my place, son."

"If Rhonda hasn't told me already, she has no intention of ever doing so. I feel you are hiding something I deserve to know. As your grandson, can you be upfront with me?"

His grandpa slammed the Coke down on a shelf, causing it to wobble before he quickly stabilized it. "I've told you time and again to respect that poor creature. Be kind to her, try to understand, but you never do. You get sweet on her every now and then, but you don't really try. I'm not surprised she didn't tell you. You would default to acting against her wishes."

"What the hell did she do, Grandpa?" Kelvin said, his voice calm despite the heat in his chest.

"Oh, you aren't going to leave this alone, are you? She swore me to secrecy, Kelvin. If I find out you told her that I told you, I won't ever let you in my house again. You are a grown man, and that is my ultimatum."

Kelvin was taken aback by his grandfather's threat. Generally an even-keeled man amidst chaos, Kelvin wondered if he still wanted to know his grandfather's secret.

"Agreed."

"Can you get me another Coke first?" Kelvin rushed to the fridge, pulled out another can, and dropped it on the stand before sitting down. "You can be a little kinder, Kelvin."

"Come on, Grandpa."

"Fine, fine. Well, you know Rhonda had all those problems with the baby, even before our precious Clare was born?"

"Yeah, of course. She was on bedrest the last two months. The doctors worried Clare would be premature."

"You have no idea, do you, Kelvin?" His grandpa shook his head. "Well, you know Rhonda also had a long, difficult childbirth, and she did not take to Clare right away."

"Yes, but why are we revisiting that awful time?"

"Well, Rhonda got pregnant last year. She still lived with me at the time. She came to me crying when she found out, not knowing what to do. She was worried she wouldn't be able to go through the experience again. With all the trouble between you two, she felt lost."

"What did she do?" Kelvin asked, looking to the ground. He felt tension throughout his body but stifled the impulse to lash out at his grandfather, loving the old man. It seemed unfathomable that his grandfather would keep secrets from him about his wife, yet here he sat, letting the silence linger, compelling Kelvin to ask once again, gruffer, "What did she do, Grandpa?"

"The only thing she could think to do. I told her that I was sure we could come up with something else, but when she put me to task, I had no alternative to offer. I did not want her to get rid of that baby but did not want to lose her either. So, I gave her my car keys to do what she saw fit."

"You mean she got an abortion. If you are going to help her get one, you should probably say the word."

"Kelvin, I did what I thought best. I beg you not to harass your wife over this. Please don't cause more trouble. What's done is done. There's no good bringing that kind of past back."

Kelvin considered his hands, shaking with quiet intensity, not knowing what to do with themselves. How could a man's wife find it okay to make this decision without telling her husband? Was he so terrible that Rhonda could not express these concerns? A doctor could have confirmed her worst fears or helped set them aside. Instead, she chose to rid herself. He would not yell at her given his unwillingness to betray his grandfather in tandem with Rhonda's expected denial of the act, but he would never relinquish this feeling of pulsating disgust.

"Kelvin, please say something. It's tearing me up what you two do to each other, but there must be peace. Please let it go."

"Sure. I'll make sure Rhonda never needs to make this decision ever again. At least not because of me."

"What do you mean, boy? You aren't planning to hurt that poor girl, are you?"

"I've never hit her all my life, Grandpa, and you damn well know I never would."

His grandfather looked shamed by his suggestion. "You're right. I just don't like the way you are talking, is all."

"I won't tell her. You've just given me a lot to think about."

"Well, that I can understand," his grandpa said, nodding his head vigorously, as if he had won a hefty battle. A pleasant look of relief spread over his grandpa's face, which made Kelvin feel a little better about his half-hearted honesty. "Why don't you stay here and watch some television with me? Better than you waiting on the women to finally make their way home. Your mom takes on too much, I tell you. Has to be in charge of anything that remotely sparks her interest."

"I'll watch television with you. I don't mind." Kelvin looked around, seeing how lonesome his grandfather must be now that Rhonda had moved out. Empty bottles and roughed-up self-help books sat on the table next to the couch, as if enticing Rhonda to come talk with him more. Kelvin's concern wore thin, his mind jumping to Rhonda's failure to honor the sanctity of their marriage, but not necessarily by the act itself; the real betrayal was not involving him and merely hoping he would never discover it. He simmered with these thoughts until he heard the car pull into the driveway.

"Do you want to say hi to them, Grandpa?"

"Oh, my legs are feeling a little rough. If you don't mind, you can bring Clare over before she goes to bed."

"Sure. If she's still awake."

"Thanks, Kelvin. And please don't bring anything we discussed to Rhonda. I don't want to be in the middle of any spat that you two have. I love you both and hate taking sides."

Kelvin looked at his grandpa, incredulous that he would not take his grandson's side. *He must be sweet on her*, Kelvin thought. Kelvin had always suspected this, given the way his grandfather doted and let her stay with him. He would never act on it. His grandfather was a better man than he; impulse drove Kelvin to promiscuity.

Over the next few weeks, Kelvin continued the façade. He got a vasectomy scheduled and performed within the month. He did not want children with any other woman and would never trust Rhonda about this. Plus, he did not want to put forth an ultimatum to his mom about who must leave in the event of a separation, fearful that he might end up with the short end of the stick because of Clare. He underwent the vasectomy with a clear conscience.

Once he rid himself of one possibility, he mulled over the recompense Rhonda should have to undergo to make amends. Kelvin expected a confrontation would only lead Rhonda to reason that the child had been lost due to her body and hormones, not her choices. He deduced the answer lay with adoption, but he worried that Rhonda would wile her way out of the lengthy process. He formulated a plan based upon finances, tied to a benevolent act that would appease his mom.

Foster care beamed as a solution that he could present to his mom as a healthy means for Rhonda to put effort toward a charitable cause. Moreover, the state paid benefits to households who cared for these pour souls. The more he researched and put together his case, the better he felt over his lost child. He considered what Clare might have to experience with changing strangers in the house, but he convinced himself that having other children around would be more fun for her than her current isolation.

Two weeks after his vasectomy, Kelvin took his mother out to lunch, as a purported treat. She enjoyed the small box of an Italian restaurant with six tables that exuded the intimacy of a family-run business. Leonardo, the owner, always flirted shamelessly with her, usually offering some of the shelf wine free of charge for his "prettiest patron." Kelvin relied on this ceaseless flirtation, despite his misgivings and poorly disguised disgust, so his mother would be more agreeable. Amid his spaghetti Bolognese and her angel hair with shrimp and garlic sauce, he opened the discussion about his concerns for Rhonda.

"I know you worry about her wellbeing too. Now that Clare is starting school, maybe she needs more to care for around the house."

"What are you getting at?" his mother said, pouring another half glass of the white wine, too impatient for the server. "Rhonda seems to care for basic tasks around the house."

"I think she does the minimum required," Kelvin said, taking a mouthful of his spaghetti. A trickle went down his chin, but before he could wipe, his mom reached over and took care of the issue. "I hate when you do that."

"Of course you do, but you will always need me, Kelvin. Now, please get to the point. She does our laundry and cleans our dishes. As far as I'm concerned, that helps me out enough."

"Okay, okay," he said. "Fair enough. I just think there's more that she can do that could benefit Clare."

"She helps me out with the church when I ask her to. She doesn't volunteer outright, but she never says no when asked. Tell me what you want, Kelvin."

"I found out that Rhonda and I can't have any more children."

His mother dropped her fork and grabbed her glass. He could not tell if she looked shocked because she actually felt this way or just thought she should appear upset. He figured it was best to not assume and push forward.

"I know. I felt a little shock, too, but the doctor told me I had little chance of conceiving again."

"I didn't even know you two were trying. With all the trouble happening between you, bringing another child into the mix almost seems a sin. I care for Clare as it is."

Kelvin remained calm, though he wanted to dump the remainder of his spaghetti on his mother's head. "I think Rhonda has stepped up as much as she can handle, Mom."

"As much as she can handle is right, Kelvin. Now, what the hell are you driving at?"

"I still want more kids, but I'm not sure adoption would be right for us. After what happened with Rhonda when Clare was born, I'm unsure what a baby would do to her."

"Then why even bother with this conversation? Seems you have your answer right there."

Kelvin squeezed his fist under the table. He knew better than to try to manipulate his mother. He would have done better by just placing the foster parent documents on the table. Now he found himself pushed back into reasoning that held no truth.

"Fine, Mom. Do you want the truth?"

"That would be nice. You know better than to lie to me."

"I found out Rhonda had an abortion last year. She told Grandpa about the pregnancy, and he helped her out. She never told me about any of it. He accidentally revealed it to me when I talked about having another baby, trying to convince me that it may not be the best idea. He feels awful about it, Mom, but I don't want this to be about Grandpa."

If his mom had been surprised by the admission, she kept a face of absolute precision, focused on the glass.

"Do you think we should get another bottle? No. I think I have some at home. Much cheaper that way. I know you are working now, but let's not kid ourselves." She raised her hand, then asked for the check from the waiter.

"I told you this was my treat."

"We both knew I'd pay. Now, why did you feel the need to tell me this?"

"I thought we could find a way to satisfy your desire for more grand-children. Also, Rhonda can remain home with a clear conscience."

"Oh, good God, Kelvin. Did you memorize this?"

"Not necessarily. I think we should become a foster home. For all the reasons I said before, plus the state pays to take in foster kids. Isn't that a great idea?"

"And you have come up with this idea entirely to support the house-hold, not as some shallow reprimand against your wife?"

Kelvin felt brief pause upon being discovered, but his resolve quickly recovered. "Hardly, Mom. I thought you would jump at the idea."

His mom rifled through her purse, pulling out her wallet, dropping her credit card at the edge of the table. Kelvin felt slight embarrassment at his mom paying for his meal, though he made no effort to persuade her otherwise. He began speaking, but his mom raised her hand for silence as she looked through her phone.

"I have been considering adding to the house—building a separate connecting home for myself. I've wanted my own space and have been looking into various developers. Perhaps this is the motivation I need to move forward. I'll go along with your ploy. And maybe you're right. Rhonda could use a focus, and this would make our little family look better within the town and church. The foster care would be your re-sponsibility, Kelvin. I won't be dragged into caring for more children. I will, however, make the presentation to the state for whatever boxes they need to check for the financial wellbeing of the home."

She let out a long sigh, waving to the waiter and pointing to the credit card. At times like these, Kelvin speculated how much money his mother possessed that allowed her to make flippant considerations about things such as this building upon their home. He had not asked since he was fourteen, when he had wondered aloud what money he would be entitled to from his father's death. One of his friends had read something about an infant winning a lawsuit because of the wrongful death of her parents. His mother did not scream or cry at his question. She smoothly told him that she cared for him and the household and asked if he had something missing in his life. At the time, he had no immediate desires, unsure what he would do with a thousand dollars other than buy video games. He shook his head and left the question unanswered, though as an adult, he considered his lost earnings frequently, feeling the thumb of his mom press down on his life. However, if he found himself to be in the wrong, what would he have left but a faltering family in a drab neighborhood? He knew better than to force the subject.

"I appreciate this, Mom. Are you sure you want to build onto the house? Wouldn't you want to build a separate house?"

"I don't see why, Kelvin. I can share utilities, pay upkeep, and still be close to the family. I've contemplated this for a number of years but wanted to be there for Clare. If you truly want to expand your family in this way, without vindication," she said, rolling her eyes, "now would be the time for me to get my own space. You two can move into the bigger bedroom, and the kids can take the upstairs bedrooms. It's perfect, Kelvin."

Kelvin's mom looked around, agitated at the waiter's absence, abhorring inept service. He regarded his mother, dressed in a far superior outfit, including a repertoire of necklaces that accessorized her elongated neck. Kelvin wondered why she did not date more. He could remember a few male friends she had around the house when he was growing up, but the same could have been said for female friends of hers. She seemed to keep everyone at a platonic level, enjoying her solace, never mentioning any feelings of loneliness. Now, she had found a way to distance herself a little more from their lives, and Kelvin felt a pang of emptiness at his mom moving out.

"Finally," his mom muttered as the waiter picked up the card.

"Do you care if we present the idea to Rhonda together? If she knows you already agree, then I think she will be more reluctant to argue against the idea."

"I don't think she would have much to support an argument in the alternative, Kelvin, but I suppose having myself in the conversation would be helpful. I can discuss my plans to turn the house into a duplex, as well. I'll ask your grandfather to be there. Family meeting this Saturday, then."

Kelvin observed his mom begin to write the numbers for a 20 percent tip, then scribble them down to less than 15. Few people made his mom wait.

That Saturday, they all sat around the dining room table, aside from Clare, who had a playdate with some girl from church. Kelvin sat on his mom's right, Grandpa to her left, and Rhonda at the other end of the table. Grandpa eyed Kelvin from across the table, attempting to wordlessly inquire what this family meeting was about. Kelvin had not spoken with his grandfather regarding his plans, as if the whole business had truly been forgotten, as requested. He loved his grandfather, but penance must be made.

"We might as well get this moving forward," his mom said, looking across to Rhonda. "I've decided I want to build an addition to the house and make it into a duplex. I've felt for some time I should give Rhonda and Kelvin space, and this way I get to build a new home for my pleasure and remain close by."

"But there's four bedrooms here," Rhonda said. "There's plenty of room. We still have a guest bedroom."

"Quite right, dear, though I'm not moving out because of you or Kelvin. If that were the case, I would have started building years ago. I've been encouraged to finally begin, and I'm hoping it won't interfere too much with your lives. I don't think the process will take more than a year, according to my builder."

"You already have the plans?" Kelvin's grandfather asked, though he sounded as if he cared little for the answer.

"Of course, Dad. I had plans drawn up a few years ago but didn't care to move forward with Clare in the house. Her now being in school, along with Kelvin's announcement, made this the perfect time to move forward."

"What's Kelvin's announcement?" his grandfather said, maintaining the same weighty eye upon him.

Rather than proceed with some inverted soliloquy, Kelvin said, "We are going to start raising foster children at the house. Won't that be great?"

No one responded. Rhonda kept her head down. Grandpa's glare deepened at Kelvin. Kelvin's mom smirked.

"I think it'll be great for the family. Rhonda and I have been wanting more kids, and this is a terrific way to utilize the additional space. Rhonda will be able to care for them, since she works from home, and the state will give us subsidies for providing for these children. Think of what a difference we will be able to make," Kelvin said, his hands laid out as if presenting this unbelievable gift.

"What about Clare?" Rhonda said.

"What about Clare?" Kelvin retorted. "She'll finally have kids to play with. We won't accept anyone with dangerous propensities. These children just need a loving home for their situation. I thought you would be the first supporter."

Rhonda sucked in deep and looked at the empty chair to her right.

His grandpa glanced at Rhonda, then back at Kelvin. "Did you discuss with Rhonda whether she would be willing to care for foster children? Seems presumptuous, Kelvin."

Kelvin opened his mouth to respond, but his mom chimed in first. "Well, Rhonda has plenty of spare time since Clare is in school now. She's done quite well as a homemaker, and this is the sort of compassion that makes a person feel good in their daily lives. Don't you agree, dear?"

Rhonda kept her gaze on the chair, seeming to weigh her next words. Instead, she simply nodded.

"Well, that takes care of that. I've told Kelvin that I'll help him with the paperwork however he needs. You two can take the downstairs master bedroom once I move out. If you have concerns for Clare's wellbeing, you can always have her remain in her bedroom down here. That way you can have your foster children upstairs, though I must admonish this separation a little. You'll just have to see how everything goes."

"Doesn't this all seem like big changes, Edna? I think we've been doing great so far," his grandfather said.

Kelvin's mom patted her father's hand. "I've been wanting to do this for a while, and I think it is admirable what Rhonda and Kelvin will be doing for the community."

Rhonda stood, bowed her head to the table, and walked upstairs to their bedroom.

"She'll come around," Kelvin said. "It's the least she could do."

"I'm not saying what you are suggesting is wrong, Kelvin, if it is for the right reasons. If you are using these poor children to get back at that woman up there, you are only inviting heartache. I know she has her problems, but so do you. You should take some time and reflect over that."

His grandfather stood, placed his hand on his daughter's shoulder, then slowly made his way towards the trailer, eased by the cane. Kelvin and his mom watched him go without a word. The addition to the house would be built. The caring of desolate children would follow.

Chapter 5

Clare is seventeen

Kelvin looked across his desk at the young man, straining to understand how someone who had missed work twice without calling did not expect to be fired. Even more, he had tried to convince Kelvin that these no-shows had not even been his fault. He did not know the schedule, or forgot to look, or wrote the dates and times down wrong.

"I'm sorry, Shawn. We have a corporate policy at CVS, and I don't get to make the decision. Everything comes from above. I'll be sending your last paycheck to the address we have on file."

"Whatever. This is bullshit. I told you it wasn't my fault, but here you are blaming me. I'll sue this place. I swear."

"Shawn, I've warned you that everything in this meeting is being recorded. Please leave in a cordial manner."

Kelvin opened his office door, as Shawn stomped out. The kid, as Kelvin kept thinking of him, was only a few years younger. Kelvin gave many chances to younger team members, knowing he had his own attitude, but he despised lying. Own up to your failures and move on. He would have had more respect for Shawn if he just told him he hated this job and didn't care anymore.

Kelvin had thought moving up the ranks within the store would bring him fulfillment, but the higher he rose, the fewer peers and more isolation he discovered. No one wanted to be friends with the disciplinarian.

He leaned back in his chair, bumping his head against the wall, almost falling. He swore, then realized he'd forgotten to turn the recorder off. He began the paperwork that the store required in order to protect their interests in the minimal chance of a lawsuit, even from the most ludicrous of sources.

Another day gone by, Kelvin powered down the gravel road in his sturdy pickup truck. That jumble still gave him the ease of knowing he was almost home. He was eager to get there, as a new foster kid had arrived—a fifteen-year-old boy, Tristen, with a turbulent history. Rhonda had been hesitant to allow this one at the house, given Clare was only seventeen. The social services representative, Brenda, had all but given up on finding the boy a placement, as older kids were difficult to situate, especially with past sexual trauma. Brenda preferred finding placements with kids of the same sex at this age, given the possibilities, but she had come to an impasse. Kelvin agonized over this, knowing he could properly care for the poor kid.

Brenda disclosed that the past sexual abuse concerned the activities of the mother, a prostitute of necessity due to drug use. "The mother kept the boy in the same room while these activities took place," she had said during a meeting. "The mother lived in a box of a studio and would hide him in the closet. One of her customers called the police when he discovered the little boy, and Tristen was taken away by social services. The mother kidnapped him from the foster parents, and they were hiding ever since. A recent tip came in about the situation. The mother was arrested and transported back to Maryland, and Tristen came into our care."

Brenda did not know if anything further happened to the poor child, since he refused to speak about his home life or his mom. Tristen demanded to be returned to his mother, to protect her, to make sure she stayed safe, but social services could not permit this.

Kelvin talked with Clare, despite Rhonda's hesitation, and Clare was oddly amenable. In the past decade, Clare had been around an eclectic group of children, which Kelvin hoped would give her a greater social disposition and awareness. Kelvin had long ago pushed aside his initial reasons for taking on the program, believing he truly meant to help the less fortunate children. He now hoped his own child would venture off to the Peace Corps or some other endeavor he never had the opportunity to undertake.

Kelvin parked in the front driveway, waving to his mom. She was gardening in the mulched area before the front porch, wearing her large straw-brimmed hat. She had built the duplex in such a way that the only separation between the two homes was the five feet the family had to cross to get to her door. His mom refused to put an adjoining door inside the original portion of the house, though the builder advised it would have been little trouble. Instead, his mom had an additional adjoining wooden porch built in the front. Her place was simple—an open space containing the kitchen, dining room, and living room, not too different from the original house except for the color scheme that delved into brick reds, forest greens, and meadow blues. A guest bathroom was placed in the far back of the first floor as if to ensure that everyone's necessities stayed as private as possible. The spiral staircase had been the prize she truly sought—a monstrosity that swirled up near the kitchen to the two upstairs bedrooms. His mom wanted a spacious master bedroom, over seventeen feet long, not including the flowering bathroom with a jacuzzi tub. A small bedroom abutted her room for any guests, though the room had rarely been used. His mom still found reasons to visit her neighbors and make herself noticed, including the new gardening fascination that took up the front yard with a variety of unknown flowers and bushes.

"Hi, Mom. These plants sure do seem to need a lot of tending. We could probably hire a professional if you want."

"I think I'm doing a good job." She stabbed a little deeper underneath one of the empty areas. "I met the new boy. Seems like a nice fellow, though a little sullen. He may be a runner, Kelvin."

"I can't keep them from running away if they don't want to stay, Mom. I don't manage a jail. If they can't appreciate our home, then maybe they are better off."

His mom took off her hat, squinting at him. "I don't believe you mean that. You know how awful you felt when that eleven-year-old girl, Jenny, or Julia—"

"Josie," he interrupted.

"Yes, well you searched for days when she left," she said, returning to mulching the dirt.

"Of course I'm going to worry, but I've learned that I can't control them."

"You seem to be doing a fair job for Clare, though. Are you really going to make her try out for girls' soccer again? You know she hates it."

"She's so good, Mom. And it'll look good on her college applications next year. She needs something on her resume besides playing the flute."

"But that's what she loves, Kelvin, and soccer interferes with band practice. You should respect that."

"Yes, Mom. I get what you are saying. I just don't think there's anything pushing her to improve in other areas."

"The girl is seventeen, Kelvin. Best let her steer her own life because anything you direct her toward will get a giant KEEP AWAY sign. She needs independence. Let her figure out her mistakes through years of regret like the rest of us."

"I know, Mom. You okay? Need any help?"

"Oh, yeah," she said, flinging off her gloves, putting out her hand for Kelvin to lift her up. "I'm just jabbering about nothing."

"Well, I need to go and check in on Rhonda and the new kid."

"Oh, you go," she said, grunting as she picked up her tools. Kelvin watched her agonize in front of him, shook his head, and walked inside the house.

"Anyone home?"

"Quiet down, Kelvin," whispered Rhonda from their bedroom.

"Why am I whispering in my own house?" Kelvin said without regard.

Rhonda grabbed his arm, pulling him into their bedroom and slamming the door.

"Well, I'm sure that helped keep the place quiet," he retorted, sitting on the bed, unbuttoning his shirt. "What's going on?"

"That kid creeps me out, Kelvin. He just stares. The only word he's said since he arrived at the house is 'Hi.'" She began pacing around the room. "I gave him the tour, showed him the clean room where he'll be staying, and told him dinner would be at seven. I asked if he needed anything or had any questions. He sat on the bed with his luggage, back turned away from me, staring at the closet door. I coughed a few times, but he refused to engage."

"Rhonda, come here." He reached out for her and pulled her onto his lap. "You know each of these children has something in their history. We've never taken anyone this old, so you're just used to the talkative kids—the ones that called you bitch, cunt, or whatever nasty words they heard in their past. Why does this kid's solitude creep you out so much?"

"I don't know. Maybe you're right." She pushed off him, bracing her back against the headboard. "These kids used to make me cry," she said, laughing lightly to herself, shaking her head. "This poor thing, Kelvin. To be in the system at fifteen without relatives. I hope his mom's case goes well, but the sexual perversity he must have seen . . ." She hit the board of the bed with her palms a few times. "I know. I already raised my concerns, and Brenda convinced us that we were the right family. I just have this feeling, Kelvin."

Kelvin looked upon his wife. Over the years, he had felt a stronger connection to her, though more out of forced vicinity than a conscious yearning. He failed to recognize the stark changes in her through the minutia of moments that had passed these seventeen years, knowing that he had no desire to leave his wife anymore. Still, he despised the excuses she came up with for anything that required effort beyond her pattern displays of housework.

However, Kelvin still drew most of his excitement from the attention he received from women. He tried to limit his outside exposure after one woman began a *Fatal Attraction* approach of finding his home phone number and calling it. Thankfully, he disconnected the landline before his wife ever heard from the woman, claiming the line to be a waste of money, since they all had cell phones. Rhonda knew his habits. She just kept herself within these walls so she did not need to face them.

"Let him get situated, Rhonda. He'll adjust. If you are so worried, Clare can sleep in our room."

"Can you talk to him? To make sure you don't feel anything wrong? I can't shake it, Kelvin."

Kelvin sneered. "Are you worried he'll hurt you?"

"No," she stammered.

"I just don't get why you are being so judgmental with this one."

Rhonda looked upon her fidgeting hands.

"I'll knock on his door, but he may just need time. You don't even know him apart from his situation, Rhonda."

He took off his tie, unbuttoned his shirt, and threw on a large gray sweater over his black undershirt. He did not want to appear as some formal presence the first time meeting the boy. He left Rhonda to her thoughts and walked up the stairs, wondering if Tristen had any interest in sports. After Grandpa died five years ago, Kelvin had little masculine interaction aside from when he was at work. He thought another male presence might help Tristen, offer him the support his grandfather had provided him, but then he considered Tristen's upbringing—a single female presence without a dominating male figure.

Though he believed Rhonda to be acting out, he felt a wave of discontent while walking up the stairs. He knocked on the door, softly at first, then firm knuckles on the third try.

He heard a slight click at the door, a twist of the knob, and the door opened a few inches. He waited a few moments before pushing the door open. He knocked on the door once again to signify his entry. Rhonda and Kelvin kept strict rules that all the kids should have a sense of privacy. He did not want their home to feel like a penal system with inspections at inopportune times. Rarely did Kelvin find his trust betrayed, so he felt the system held merit.

"How are you doing, buddy? Looks like my wife got you set up in your room."

Tristen sat on the edge of the bed, peering out the window next to the closet to a view of the clandestine surroundings of gravel roadway that leered out into neighboring pastures and woods. Kelvin sat on the other side of the bed near the door, giving Tristen his space. Rhonda had a point when it came to Tristen's age. They had never had a boy older than ten stay with them. Kelvin had few interactions with teenage boys other than passing conversations with customers at work or Clare's friends, which were awkward conversations for everyone. Tristen gave a slight nod, indicating he did not want to be entirely rude, though he failed to turn around.

"I'm Kelvin. You are free to call me Kelvin or Dad—if you want. We are here to help you as much as we can during this time. We know a little about why you are here, but if you ever want to talk to Rhonda or me about anything, please do."

The quiet swayed over the room, giving Kelvin a dreamy feeling rather than discomfort. He knew Tristen wished him away, given the rigidity of the boy's body enclosed upon itself, and focused out the window. Kelvin stood, unsure what else he could say that would make Tristen feel more welcome.

"Did you need anything else, Mr. Chestwick?" Tristen said, turning his head just enough to catch Kelvin's eye. The kid had black hair that wisped in wavy formations, drifting down just above his eyes and over his ears. Kelvin thought he might style it purposely this way but could not be entirely sure. He had two earrings in his right ear—one on his lobe, another in the upper ear, both silver studs—and tan skin with a few pimples marring his complexion.

"No, Tristen," Kelvin said. "Clare should be home soon, then we'll have dinner. If you are feeling unwell, you can have your food up here in your room, but we would much rather you eat with us. I think you'll like Clare. She's a fantastic flute player and gets along well with her peers."

"Thank you, Mr. Chestwick," Tristen said, watching Kelvin until he turned toward the door.

Kelvin trudged down the stairs with a feeling akin to what Rhonda described, but he would not give in to the unsettled feeling. The boy had had his entire life tossed about and was now in a stranger's home. Kelvin returned to their bedroom to discover Rhonda asleep, a pillow clasped between her arms. Not wanting to bother anyone before dinner, he walked out the back door toward the empty trailer.

The family had discussed what they wanted to do with the trailer after Grandpa died. Everyone knew the contraption to be an eyesore, thankfully not visible to passersby. However, no one could stomach being the person to suggest destroying the last remnants of Kelvin's grandparents.

Kelvin walked into the trailer and sat on the couch. At these times, the desire to get a dog—a large, furry, nuzzling thing that would place a slobbering jaw on his leg—overcame him. He missed Shelbie. He thought a dog would be good for Clare and would give her a greater reason to visit once she moved away for college. A dog would also help these foster kids, comfort them during these transitions. Despite the positives, his mother and Rhonda had vetoed him, worried that a foster kid might be allergic or, worse, agitate the dog to the point the poor thing might harm the child. Kelvin thought that would reflect worse on the kid, but he let the matter be.

He settled himself into his grandfather's chair, leaned back with the leg rests up, and turned on the television to the History Channel. A moment of calm reflection as Kelvin fought to stay awake through the rise of Napoleon. Soft light rolled over his closed eyes until he drifted off to sleep.

He woke with a jolt to Rhonda's cries at the doorway. He tried to swing down but was kept in place by the stubborn chair, causing a pinched feeling in his stomach. Rolling off, he approached his wife, who was emitting pitches of noises without words.

"What the hell is wrong? Is Clare okay?"

"That boy was spying on your daughter," she screeched. "I told you he was no good. She arrived an hour ago, and he already can't help himself. An hour, Kelvin!"

Kelvin blinked, trying to wake fully to his wife's ravings. "What do you mean he spied on Clare? What did he do? Go into her room?"

"No, Kelvin," she said, her voice dropping to a whisper. "Clare took a shower after her marching band practice. As I'm walking up the stairs to see how that boy is doing, I see him peering in the bathroom through the open door. He didn't say anything. He just stood there, gawking at me."

"Do you think he accidentally walked in on her?"

"No, Kelvin! You can hear the damn shower running from the outside. He purposely walked in and spied on your daughter. Why is this not making you mad? That is your daughter!"

"Will you sit down?" he said, motioning to the couch.

"No, I won't. You need to handle this now. I told you I did not want him in this house and see what happened. I'm holding you responsible."

"Fine, fine," he said. "Is Clare okay?"

"I think so. She didn't know what happened until after I screamed. Then she saw Tristen standing there and yelled for him to get out. He ran past me, nearly making me fall down the stairs. The kid has no control."

"Where's Clare now?"

"She's with your mom. She's a little shaken but seems to be handling the matter well. Your mom also thinks this was a misunderstanding. What is there to misunderstand, Kelvin?" She writhed. "I caught the boy in the bathroom spying on our daughter. I wonder what would have happened if I had not walked up the stairs when I did."

She began crying into her hands. Kelvin rolled his eyes but rubbed her back for some attempt at comfort. She grasped his hand, keeping her head down.

Only able to keep appearances for so long, he said, "I'll go talk to him. Why don't you stay here and watch television until I sort everything out?"

"Thank you."

She remained fetal as he hurried out the door. Kelvin initially thought Rhonda was overreacting, but anger welled within him once the thought of Tristen walking in on his naked daughter settled. Kelvin prayed the boy had a good excuse but wasn't holding his breath.

He walked in the back door and yelled, "Tristen! Are you here? I'm not mad. I just think we should discuss what happened."

No sound. Kelvin walked around upstairs, through the rooms, but no sign of the boy. Kelvin noted Tristen's luggage still remained by the closet. Kelvin considered his next steps and walked to his mom's place.

"Mom! Clare! Are you here?"

"Upstairs, Dad!"

He entered his mother's bedroom to see Clare with a maroon robe draped over her shoulders, sitting on the bed. His mother sat next to Clare, massaging her hand.

"Did I interrupt?"

"I don't think so," his mom sighed. "Clare was more shaken up by Rhonda's screaming, to be honest. Did you find the boy?"

"Not yet. His stuff is still in the house, so I doubt he went far. Did either of you see him run down the road?"

They both shook their heads. Clare sighed, her hair soaking the top of the robe. He bent down to Clare to study her reactions. "Clare, can you tell me what happened? I have your mom's ravings, but I want your side."

Clare shook her head. "I honestly don't know. I heard a knock at the door and yelled, 'Who is it?' I thought I heard a muffle, so I said I couldn't hear what they were saying. There was silence for a minute, so I went back to washing my hair. Next thing I know, this boy is standing at the entranceway of the bathroom, and Mom is screaming at him to get out, calling him a pervert and all sorts of names."

"Do you think he meant to walk in on you?"

"I don't know, Dad. He must have knocked, so maybe he needed something. I just don't understand why he would walk into the bathroom when he knew I was taking a shower."

"The whole thing is very suspicious, Kelvin, but I think you better hear from the boy before making any rash decisions on calling social services," his mother said.

"I mean, he seemed terribly shy but nice when I greeted him," Clare said. "He asked how my day went, and we had a short chat before I showered. I didn't feel threatened at all."

"Well, we need to find him. Mom, do you want to take your car and see if he's down the road?"

"What if I find him?" she whispered. "Do you expect me to pick him up?"

"I'll go with you, Grandma. I'll bring the mace Mom bought me a few years ago. We'll be fine."

"I'll keep looking around here," Kelvin said. "He may just be scared and hiding."

"This ordeal is making me ill," his mom said.

Kelvin shook his head and led them to his house. Clare changed and went off with his mom to check the roadways. Once he made sure both had left, he searched the house again, calling out for Tristen. Kelvin had a feeling the boy was still here, though he did not understand his endgame. Would he run off in the middle of the night? Kelvin questioned whether Tristen had a phone. Maybe he'd had someone pick him up.

Rhonda appeared at the back door, asking if Tristen had been found. When Kelvin shook his head, Rhonda scurried back to the trailer, saying, "I will not feel safe until we find that kid." Kelvin figured he would not tell her even if he did find Tristen. Kelvin found the situation regrettable and disappointing, but to treat the child as a predator was unnecessary.

After he searched every room to no avail, Kelvin began opening supply and closet doors. Kelvin felt uneasy about snooping this far if the boy did not want to be found, but he had a responsibility to Clare. He would try his best, for everyone's sake. When he opened the closet doors to the downstairs guest room, he found Tristen huddled, asleep on the floor. Kelvin felt bad for waking him as he gently poked the hunched boy's shoulder. Tristen woke with a start, pushing further back into the closet.

"I didn't mean to startle you, Tristen. We didn't know where you went; we've been worried sick."

"Please don't tell Brenda what happened. I didn't mean to. Honestly, Mr. Chestwick. I'm very sorry. Please believe me." He started crying, wiping his face on a neighboring dress.

Kelvin struggled as to what he should do next. He texted Clare that he'd found Tristen but told her to wait a bit before returning home. He studied the poor, scared teenager in his closet, covered by Rhonda's extra Sunday dresses. He did not feel comfortable pulling the kid out. Kelvin grunted and maneuvered his way into the closet, sitting next to Tristen, then squeezing his arm around him. Tristen recoiled from the touch, shaking his head and looking at Kelvin in surprise, then leaned forward and began crying into Kelvin's shoulder. After a few minutes of Kelvin patting him on the back, Tristen eased into a soft whimper, then silence.

"I'm not going to tell Brenda, but you need to tell me what happened. My wife can get easily spooked, so I'm sorry if she scared you, but you did walk in on my daughter showering."

Kelvin watched as Tristen blinked a few times, then took a few deep breaths. "This week has been awful, Mr. Chestwick. I lived with my mom, and now I'm here feeling lost."

"Tristen, tell me what happened today. I promise we will discuss everything else, but first I need your story."

"I . . . I'm sorry. I really am. I was cold to you and Mrs. Chestwick. I'm so uncomfortable with all this. Your daughter was so nice, and we spoke for a few minutes. I never meant to see her naked or bother her at all. I didn't even really see her. I had to pee so bad," he said, fumbling over his words.

"What happened, Tristen? You knocked on the door, right?"

"I knocked twice, Mr. Chestwick. I tried to ask Clare if she could wrap herself in a towel, so I could go to the bathroom, but I don't think she heard me. I opened the door with my eyes closed, to ask her again. I did not want to see her, Mr. Chestwick. I just wanted to keep myself from going in my pants."

"So, you knocked, then tried to ask Clare if she could step out of the bathroom so you could use it?"

Tristen nodded, his breathing beginning to slow.

"Why didn't you just ask if you could use our bathroom?"

"Mrs. Chestwick said I was to never enter Clare's or your bedroom under any circumstances. I didn't know what else to do. I only opened my eyes when I heard the screaming behind me. I looked to see Mrs. Chestwick, then back at Clare, then back at Mrs. Chestwick. I was frightened. I ran down the stairs and hurried into this empty room. I hide in closets when I get overwhelmed."

"It's okay, Tristen. Again, please call me Kelvin or Dad, whenever you feel comfortable. I'll explain everything to the family. I don't think you did anything wrong, at least purposefully."

"Really?" Tristen said, relief on his face.

"Yes. I think Mrs. Chestwick . . . Rhonda may be a little high strung about all this. Do you want to come with me or wait until I tell you the coast is clear?"

"Do you mind if I wait in here until you explain? I don't want anyone to be mad at me. I swear I'm not a pervert, Mr. Chestwick."

"I believe you, Tristen."

Chapter 6

Today

C lare studied the sad, aging man. The father, who only had a kind word to say if the compliment did not interfere with his daily living. A man who had no room or accommodation for his family, other than handling them. She heard him rattle about letting them go, twisting in his chair. This encouraged Nick to begin a tirade of grunting, his veins pulsating as he pulled on the twisted ropes holding his wrists in place. Clare no longer heard her father, her eyes now focusing upon Nick.

"Nick, you need to calm down," said her dad, eyeing his daughter.

Clare took a few deep breaths, then snatched a tranquilizer from the bag she had placed nearby for such matters. She smacked Nick in the face, whispering, "You have to listen to me, now." She then placed the needle in his arm, the effects drifting within, as she watched his pained face slowly relax into sleep.

Kelvin did not protest, as if concerned that speaking out of turn would result in the same treatment. Clare waited a few minutes before focusing back on her father.

"What happened to you?" he said. "We can get through this, Clare. If you let us go, we'll forget the whole thing. Are . . . are you going to kill us?"

"No," she said without inflection. "But you wanted to kill me." She moved to the edge of the loft under the empty noose, letting her legs kick gaily in the air. "We'll just have to wait until he wakes. I told you all to calm yourselves."

Her father began making these awful yelps and cries for help, though he must have known that no one outside could hear him. He quickly changed to calling her deplorable, a liar, ungrateful, a bitch, a spoiled brat. She did not entertain him.

Her father's voice grew hoarse with curses, so he began a different approach, saying he never meant to hurt anyone, to at least spare her grandmother, a frail woman who did not deserve this torture. She acknowledged the begging for her grandmother and began laughing. She stood to face him.

"That woman has never been frail in her life. Perhaps if you treated Mom with a sliver of the respect you have for Grandma, you would not be in this predicament. Any slight, any insinuation that you were not the head of the household, you found ways to force us back into the fold, under the thumb of Grandma, you as her noble steed. You rarely paid attention to me unless you needed me to speak against Mom. Anytime Mom tried to express herself, you would belittle her."

"I never abused any of you," Kelvin cried out. "I did the best I could, taking care of you and your mother. I love you both."

"You really believe you did your best? Or do you want to call something 'your best' to feel like you actually accomplished something in your life besides a middling existence built on the back of Grandma's generosity?"

Kelvin began to retort, but she screamed out, "No! I will not entertain this conversation anymore, Dad. We will wait for Nick to wake up. I told you the rules. Now, we wait, unless you want the same treatment." She grabbed the bandana and another needle, shaking them in front of him until she felt sure he would remain stifled.

Clare was unsure how to fill the time, curling against the wall. She drifted to sleep once again. Now that the scene had been set, her fervent dread had relaxed. In passing, she heard a soft murmur of her name being repeated until she awoke with a start.

Her dad smiled. "I think Nick is awake if you want to continue yelling at me."

Clare studied Nick, his arms flexing, but his head still tilted to the side. She thought making them each wait for the others would be a fine punishment. For them to know of their collective terror toward her, converging into this pinnacle. She began to weary of the waiting, already nearing into the afternoon, deciding the idea to be pointless. Why would any of them care about the others' transgressions? Selfish creatures only wanting to know the reasons they specifically were trapped. She would administer the medication only in the event one tried to free themselves. She waited for her father to meet her gaze.

"Dad, your actions had consequences that always fell on everyone else. I just need you to admit you hurt me. Admit you hurt us with your lies, cheating, ultimatums that we all had to follow."

"I never hurt you, Clare. I never struck you once."

"I'm not saying you beat me, Dad. You knew so much and did nothing. Nothing! Unless something affected you. The only person that could reach you was Grandma. You hurt me with your absence, your insensible selfish attitude that never helped me unless it helped you. I'm me despite you, not because of you."

"I'm sorry if you feel this way, Clare, but that is no reason to trap your whole family in this charade. Let us go so we can discuss like a family."

Clare set her face within inches of his, twiddling one of the tranquilizers still in her pocket. She smirked as she studied his face.

"That's good, honey. We'll forget this whole thing. Just let me go."

All she wanted from her dad was an honest apology, an understanding, an admission that he had not bettered her life, a sense of continuous falling as his shadow came and went. He was a failed support system in which the patient, barely alive, was considered a success exclusively by that one breath that keeps coming, though a pittance of effort would have brought meaningful life.

"What do you think we are here for? You turned your back on me, failed to listen, and left me to rot."

She jabbed him in the leg, harder than necessary from the adrenaline tingling throughout her body. He cried out and began another tirade of screaming. Once the drug took its final effects, she gagged him, then took a few steps over to face her mother.

Part II: Mother

"Can a mother forget her nursing child? Can she feel no love for the child she has borne?" Isaiah 49:15

Chapter 7

Clare has not been born

R honda sat on the bathroom floor, considering the consequences of the second positive pregnancy test. She skipped school that day, unable to stop the constant fretting over the delay of her period until she no longer could stand the unknown. She wanted to buy a third test, praying another would give her the result she needed, but she refused to purchase more false hope. She was simply pregnant with Kelvin's baby.

Her parents would not understand; they'd always been devout advocates of abstinence. She went alone to obtain birth control from Planned Parenthood last year so she could safely have sex with her prior boyfriend, Patrick, though her parents knew none of that.

The one blessing was not being pregnant with Patrick's child. Despite Kelvin's faults, she did not expect he would stop speaking to her after he found out the news, unlike Patrick. Patrick never concerned himself with consequences, and when they came along, he ignored those as well as he could. She hadn't planned on dating Patrick after he went off to college, but he had begged her. She stayed until she learned of his escapades—he used her for sex when home, then returned to whoring at college. She did not feel disappointed or disgusted. Patrick behaved exactly as expected.

Having been lauded as a bright student, Rhonda thought of her vague future of success. However, she could never pinpoint what field she wanted to enter. She liked the idea of being a doctor or scientist, though her parents had spent most of their savings on sending her older brother off to college. She knew her parents did not want her seeking higher education, preferring that she find something more practical nearby. Despite her parents' rigid devoutness and ignorance, she loved them as best she could and didn't want to disappoint them.

Both tests in hand, she began crying. She did not want a baby nor an abortion, as evident by her preventive care. Her future was being defined by the double lines before her.

As she dropped both sticks, she sank to the ground next to the toilet seat, unable to avoid the jostled declarations altering her life. The smell of light urine wafted from the toilet. The soft red rug, normally nestled around the bottom of the toilet, had been pushed off as she slumped to the floor. It had been tangled amongst her lower extremities in the twisted fall. She was disgusted by the touch of the rug and could not recall the last time it had been washed. Maybe "bathmat" was the correct term, she wondered, though the absorbent square had more of a shaggy texture, akin to a towel. "Fancy bathmat" sounded preposterous, but it would align with her mother's taste in décor. No matter that the mat or rug had absorbed countless drops of water and Lord knows what else. Rhonda did not observe any mold but figured mold and bacteria relished the wet environment. At this thought, she violently tossed the mat from underneath her toward the door of the bathroom, as she now rested on the cold tile with no inclination in how to proceed with life.

A baby would need a protector—a mother who would love unconditionally through all bouts of screaming, shitting, and general mayhem. Rhonda abhorred disorder and did not know how to prepare. Patrick had been obnoxious but only with his buddies, as she refused to tolerate any playful belittling or bullying. She never bothered anyone, nor did she inspire anyone's ire. Even in sex, she found satisfaction in reciprocation. She did not feel shamed about sex despite her parents' design, and she had enjoyed sex with Patrick by restricting him from her body until he respected her own pleasurable desires and needs.

She grabbed and threw one of the pregnancy tests at the door, causing it to bounce, then rattle on the floor. Did Kelvin have some version of bionic sperm to get her pregnant within three months of dating? And more importantly, did she truly intend to term and form a genetic binding between Kelvin and herself? She had known of Kelvin's crush for years but played aloof. She liked his offbeat attention and did not want Patrick to thrust around his ego at Kelvin. She had no doubt that Kelvin would scrap with someone if threatened, but she could not foresee an outcome in his favor. That kindness gave her hope in his ability to be a father, though she questioned whether they truly understood each other. She knew that a child would be beautiful, but they had no monetary safety net. They would be mere children having children with no familial support, at least not from her parents.

Maybe her parents would surprise her. A grandchild might be a warm, unanticipated gift that her parents could try to appreciate, premarital sex aside. She would not tell them of any considerations of abortion, instead pointing them to the celebration of a new life they could guide. However, she had to talk to Kelvin first. He had a right to be a part of the conversation, though she would make the decision that she thought best in the end, his support or not. Maybe, he would be so swept up by the events and propose on the spot, envisioning a young married couple in love scraping to get by.

The growing discontent pinching the insides of her chest knew these fantastical hopes had no threshold in reality. Her parents would have nothing to do with her and her pregnancy. If she wanted to forge a continued relationship with them, she would need an abortion without their knowledge.

Rhonda slumped further until she lay fully on the ground. The smell of the recently cleaned bleached floor flooded her as her hair scraped the side of the bathtub, her face a mere foot from the toilet bowl. Rhonda noticed the cleanliness of the toilet, a habit developed from her father, who could not find happiness in silence. Movement with purpose tended to result in cleaning, if he had no other projects he could grasp in his hands. She often found herself the first mate to his captain, bleaching the tiled surfaces of the house, as her father thought her brother had more productive ways to spend his time. She took offense but rarely complained. She saw the desire in removing deficiencies, dirt, defects, disgust, a meditation in removing abnormalities in a clean household—aside from the rug.

The cold tiles encouraged reprieve from thinking about the future. But immediate decisions needed to be made. She had taken both the SAT and ACT exams with sufficient scores to apply to better-than-middling colleges. If she chose to have this child, could she still attend college? A single mother continuing her studies would not be an impossibility, but certainly a difficult trial. She did not know if she had the stamina or means to try to be both a mother and student. If Kelvin stayed with her, perhaps they could attend the same college. She felt ill again. Her thoughts returning to Kelvin's receptiveness of the baby, she became annoyed by the limitations she felt Kelvin would not be forced to experience. She fought the resentment, knowing that she had chosen to participate in their sexual engagements leading to this burden—a double-edged sword that would leave her wounded, no matter the decision.

She admitted in a soft, soothing tone in the back of her mind that an abortion was the obvious choice—no limitations, no decisions and retribution from her parents, and no forced connection with Kelvin. The forefront of her mind, however, despised that her doubts stemmed from others' assumed control over her body, that either decision would be tantamount to an admission that she did not control her own life. Maybe a baby would be a sign that she could be strong enough to stand on her own and not only control her life but care for one, too.

Rhonda thought she could be loving and supportive of a baby if she did not lapse into self-doubt and loathing, a part of herself that was shoved, throttled, and chained down to its recesses—a result of the discrimination she received from her parents. She shuddered, wondering if such malicious thoughts would plague her children. She had overcome much to be a bright student who participated in extracurriculars, attended weekly church service with independent thought, and made healthy sexual choices with monogamous parties.

She had friends that would support her. Would Brooke understand if she chose to have Kelvin's child? Brooke took a staunch view on abortion at this age, seeing the option as the only choice. Chelsie Becker had her baby last year with some creepy twenty-year-old that tried to attend prom. Brooke spoke vehemently against Chelsie's personal choice to bring a child into obvious poverty, viewing the option of ridding herself of the infecting cells to be the easiest test Chelsie could have taken all year, yet still failing. "The prison of men infecting our bodies," she often said to Rhonda. Rhonda wondered if such hatred developed from the sexual frustration of desiring women or not getting men.

A noise from the front of the house, a creak of brakes, caused her mind to return to the bathroom. She planted her feet on the door, worried the lock would also fail her. She did not want to encounter her family. With the touch of her fingers to the markings of her tears, she felt the worry plastered upon her face. Her mother may not realize, but her father and brother would inquire until she revealed her secrets.

A knock on the door. "Who's there?" she said, barely audible.

"Is someone home?" Her brother's voice. Had he planned to come home today? Close to the holiday, but Christmas still a few weeks away. She did not want to expose her sexual proclivities to her older brother, whom she got along with on the surface out of camaraderie against her parents, never admitting the pedestal placed under him.

She spoke louder. "It's me, Ben. I'm not feeling well. Can you use Mom and Dad's bathroom?"

"Uh, sure. Do you need anything? Ginger ale?"

"No, I'm fine. I'll be out in a few minutes."

"Okay. Excited to see you, Rho. Yell if you need anything."

Rhonda closed her eyes, praying that she could find the will to remain silent until she could talk to Kelvin. Her brother would tell her to keep the child, not vehement against all abortion, but still disappointed. He might even try to bribe her with periodic payments to keep her afloat, knowing their parents would want nothing to do with her. Maybe his opinion would open her mind from the hazy anticipation. He tended toward the positive more than the rest of the family.

Rhonda pushed herself against the tub, grabbing the two pregnancy tests. Despite slight disgust, she placed both in her bra, having no pockets in her dress. She pushed against the sides of the sink to study herself in the mirror. The pregnancy tests were clearly visible in her bra, pointing in odd directions, like misshapen nipples. Her breasts could not hide these results, but she could not fathom placing the tests in her underwear. She moved them toward her armpits, so the points neared where her nipples were, hoping they stayed in place.

Once she was satisfied with the hidden tests, she only then noticed her sunken brown eyes and hair tossed in a cascade of directions from bobbing around on the floor. She could not conjure a smile at the sight. When she lifted the outer cusps of her lips, the rise of her cheeks emphasized her misting eyes. She eased out a complacent breath to ploy a smile for her brother. She wiped her face, the light runs of mascara taken care of, then opened the door.

Rhonda walked toward the living room, uneasy, holding one hand to the wall. She searched for her brother, surprisingly absent from the couch. She considered that the ivory plush cushions might be able to hide the tests until she could find a private time to remove them. She shook her head. Her father would probably choose that day to clean the living room, which entailed removing and vacuuming the cushions.

"What's in your bra?"

She swung around, her brother appearing from the dining room. She covered her chest in exaggeration, hoping to play in jest.

"Why are you looking at my chest?"

"Jesus, Rhonda. I'm not. You look like you have two spikes sticking out the side."

She looked down—one test pointed downward to the right, the other to the upper left, a shish kebab display of her breast. She tried to think of an excuse. A reason she could have two pens, markers, or some other device in her bra, but all these examples felt exhausting. Ben gazed at her with tender confusion. She began crying. He immediately held her, and she embraced him in turn.

"I'm pregnant, Ben. I just found out."

He squeezed her a little tighter. Slight sobs still erupted from her, but she pushed him away gently, letting the pregnancy tests fall to the floor.

"How could this happen? Mom and Dad are never going to accept this."

"I know. I was on the pill. Do you think I should get an abortion?"

"Oh, Rhonda," Ben said, shaking his head and sitting on the couch. "I came home to de-stress. Now you are asking me about an abortion?"

"I don't know what to do or who to talk to. I just found out five minutes ago."

"Have you told the father?" He waved his hands in front of his face. "Never mind. You haven't told anyone. You should talk to the father. If Mom and Dad ever find out, though . . ."

"I know! I know exactly what they will do. I'm frightened. One part of me wants to get the damn abortion without telling anyone." She motioned one arm toward him. "Except you. What harm could the ignorance possibly do to our family? As long as you don't tell."

"I think you need to tell the father, Rho. That's not a choice you should make for the both of you. Also, if Mom and Dad ask, I'm not going to lie to them."

"Why would they ask?"

"You know how intuitive Mom can be about unplanned situations. She saw some look on my face after I came home from my first touch of a girl's breast. Made Dad give me a thirty-minute sex talk, which generally consisted of the words 'Don't do it' and 'Wait for marriage.'"

Rhonda sighed, sitting down on the other side of the couch. "Don't you think I should have some idea what I want first?"

"I've never knocked anyone up. How the hell would I know?"

"Very helpful, Ben." She slumped further into the couch, holding the edges of her dress as they began riding up.

"Guessing that's how it happened."

She jerked up, punching him in the arm. "You suck."

"Rhonda, do you want my opinion?"

"Yes, please. Some type of guidance. Anything better than wallowing in a lonesome hole."

"I don't believe in abortion, Rho, but I think you know that. I get why you are open to it as a choice. I would not hate you for choosing to rid yourself of the baby, but I think it would take me some time to face you again. You will never be able to undo having an abortion. If you have the baby, there's plenty of options for you: marry the father and raise the child together or even raise the child on your own. I know you have a good head on your shoulders. You would be a good mother. I would even offer to help you out, as much as I could. Or you could give the baby up for adoption, Rhonda; provide another family an option. Later in life, when you feel ready for a family, you could even try to open your heart to the child you gave away. I would never judge you for trying to give a baby a better chance, Rho."

"You think I should have this baby?"

"Yes, Rhonda. These events happen for a reason. Let your blessing grow. I think you'll be happy with your choice."

"Thanks, Ben." Rhonda felt no better but surrendered to the decision. She would have this child, aware of the divide it would cause her family.

Chapter 8

Clare is five

Rhonda reached for one of her books, seeking a highlighted passage about looking for the hopes of tomorrow, rather than the sorrows of yesterday. She felt supported in these words—the notion that tomorrow may hold a brighter future, a gleam of sunshine in the torrent cloud that basked in her mind.

A light knock on the door of her trailer bedroom. "Rhonda, do you want anything for lunch?"

She smirked at the inviting face, deep lines on his small forehead and along his wide eyes, a testament to his profound thoughts. A man of immense vision and purest heart, the only person that had tried to understand her mental storms that were followed by the emptiest of calms which left her feeble in the bed. Kelvin had long given up trying to understand the wanes of her depression. He would never understand the immensity of her drawn-out, painful labor, the days of hospitalization, the fear she felt for her own health, and the numbness that followed Clare's birth.

"I could use a snack. Maybe some apples with peanut butter. Do you think you could share with me?"

"Of course, dear. That sounds great."

"Thanks, Teddy," she said, urging out a fuller smile.

Teddy turned, resting his hand on the doorknob, then looked back at Rhonda. "Clare is doing great today. Edna is focusing her on math this week. She said if you want to help, you are welcome anytime."

Rhonda's smile waned, clawing to preserve its kindness. She nodded. Once he left, she burrowed under the sheets, exhausted from the interaction. She could not stand to see Clare's face today. A haunting look of innocence would hurl Rhonda into the lonesome cave she had discovered after Clare's birth. She accepted that the guilt she felt about not being a mother with instantaneous gratitude came from internal judgment, and she needed to welcome forgiveness. Yet facing that little beauty brought about deeper reflections.

Early on, Rhonda oft found herself lectured on the profound benefits of medication for the mind by Kelvin's mother. Edna would feign compassion about Rhonda's wellbeing, provide updates on Clare, then segue into medications that would "do wonders" for her depression. Rhonda did not want to die, though she sometimes wished she had not been born, dreaming of burrowing into a minefield of blissful decay on her bed, forgetting all trials and disappointments.

She acknowledged her diagnosis of postpartum, clinical, and other words to describe depression. She dumped the medications, steadfast to familial ideas of keeping the natural mind from being altered; the medication made her feel like she was sinking. Edna rarely brought up the issue anymore, accepting that either her daughter-in-law was grown or not worth the effort.

Rhonda believed her problems existed outside of herself in the banalities of the world. Dreary Rhonda existed in others' expectations and judgment: her parents, Kelvin, Edna, Teddy, and even Clare. Despite her brother's careful support through her pregnancy, she had not heard from him since her parents threatened to withdraw their financial aid for his schooling if he continued to funnel her money or speak to her. Rhonda did not fight their decision, mandating that Ben follow their directives for they should both not have to suffer. Somehow, she felt his kept promise, praying for her in the only contact that remained.

Teddy walked through the door, placing the sliced apples and glob of peanut butter on her nightstand, along with a glass of water. He patted the bed, indicating she should scoot over to allow him to sit. She closed her eyes, then twisted her body over until she gave him just enough room.

"How are we feeling today, darling? Want to go on a walk with me and Clare to the woods later? A nice day out for some fresh air."

He dipped an apple slice into the peanut butter and handed her the piece. She gently took the treat out of his hand, munching tiny bites. She felt childish but liked the care from Teddy. She teetered on an attraction to the man, only in his early sixties, purely on this type of affection. Part of her attraction to Teddy came from his love for family, but his friendliness was truly the little she needed to ease each day. Kelvin did not have time for such trivialities or the tolerance to be patient with anyone, especially her. Instead, she compressed these feelings around him.

"I don't know, Teddy. That sounds nice, but I have something more pressing I need to talk to you about."

He nodded, waiting for her to continue. Another reason she loved his company. A man who waited for her words instead of guessing what he thought she would say.

"I've been worried about a certain problem. I should have mentioned this to you before, but it's such a personal issue. I don't want you to feel uncomfortable."

He softly touched her shoulder. "Please just tell me. We don't need to be keeping secrets now, do we?"

She gritted her teeth, desperate to dull this confrontation. She had wished, prayed, even contemplated possible medications or injuries that she could ingest or experience in order to rid herself of this conversation. She had been unsuccessful with any half-hearted plan, though she had searched online for daunting means of self-mutilation for this task. She felt for those poor women without any escape.

"We need to keep this secret, Teddy." She pushed herself up to the headboard, then found and squeezed his hand. She searched his face until their eyes locked. "I need you to promise me you will tell no one what I'm about to say. I mean it, Teddy. I don't know what I'll do if I can't trust you anymore."

"Oh, okay," he said with a murmur. His eyes drifted, but Rhonda kept the stare until he faced her words.

"I think I'm pregnant, and I need an abortion."

Teddy jolted, studying her face. His eyes squinted, as if judging her honesty. She waited for his complete reaction. She had no other option, and she would threaten more drastic measures if he refused to help. He would not let her harm herself; that would result in a heavy eye and daily monitoring. Rhonda believed she gave him purpose since his wife died—a reciprocal relationship that kept them both alive.

"Why would you want to do that, Rhonda? That doesn't sound like you. Are you sure?"

"I haven't taken a pregnancy test, if that's what you are asking, but I'm sure. I haven't had my period in a few months, though I've been praying for the blood."

"Should I get you a test first?"

"If that's what you need me to do, but I know I'm pregnant. Now, I just need your help in getting an abortion."

"Why are you saying it like this, Rhonda? I know you better than that. You aren't taking this as lightly as you sound. This must be eating you up." He sat at her side. "We can get through this together, dear. I'll help you along."

"Teddy. I don't say this lightly. If I do not get an abortion, I will kill myself."

He smacked her, but Rhonda did not feel hurt. He needed to express his shame at her revelation. He put his hand over his mouth, tears forming.

"I'm sorry. I just can't hear you talk this way. You can't get rid of a baby just like that, Rhonda. Think of Clare, how grateful you are to have such a beautiful daughter."

"Teddy, stop." She closed her eyes in reprieve from his gaze. "You know what I went through with Clare. The labor, the hospital stay, all the complications, the unending guilt. I love my child, but I cannot stand to go through another one."

She opened her eyes. His back was turned to her, looking out the door to the dark hallway. She knew he would relinquish his hesitations and help. Ultimately, he loved her more than any conviction. She did not know how long he would toil within himself before he would admit her result to be the best decision. She waited in silence for more than five minutes. He held the power for the moment.

"I need to think this over. I can't talk about this right now." He pushed himself up with an inadvertent grunt and ambled out the door.

She leered at the open door, hating that he left her exposed. She sighed, scurried to close the door, then slunk into the bed, emerging solely for the apple slices. She briefly fretted over Teddy's reaction, before turning on the twenty-inch television mounted to the wall, hoping to find an impactful drama on Lifetime. She loved the fight of these women, blustered against trying forces. She felt hope watching them, as if she related to trials against maniac murderers or rapists. She had demons that tormented her, but they did not depict those well enough on television. Even if they tried, she would be presented with either boring, oversimplified, and trifling representations, or repeated screams for mercy to the masses. Her pain was too personal and severe to be gathered in an hour-long depiction.

Over the next couple days, she spent time playing with Clare, pleased at her effort. She pretended to not understand the source of this inspiration, as she surveyed with anxious patience Teddy's mood and demeanor. He acted ordinary, being cordial, helpful, and supportive without a hint of their conversation. She waited him out, as past record suggested discomfort resulted in Teddy's eventual willingness to agree. On the fourth day, she lost the patience, frightened by the passing time, albeit far shorter than a looming first trimester. She made him a sandwich, calling him into the house kitchen. Rhonda held the plate out, unwilling to release as Teddy pulled.

"I need to talk about our discussion a few days ago," she said, pointing to her stomach.

"At the trailer, your room, bring the sandwiches," he said. She looked around the empty room but followed instruction, hurrying to the trailer with sandwich in hand.

Rhonda placed the plate of food on her nightstand and sat at the edge of her bed. Teddy slunk into her room and closed the door.

"I can't do it, Rhonda. I always want to help you, dear, but this doesn't feel right. I think you should tell Kelvin."

"No. Can you let me borrow your car at least? I'll figure the rest out."

"I don't like this." He sat next to her, taking her hand. "Think of the child."

"I am, Teddy. I'm thinking of everyone. I know what is best for me and my family."

He stood, nodding his head. "You know where I keep my keys. Just don't tell me when you go or when you come back. Lie to me. I'll figure out well enough in a couple months."

"Thanks, Teddy."

"Please don't thank me. I don't want any part, Rhonda. Just know I love you."

She watched him leave, then called the closest Planned Parenthood—near forty miles away. The lady who answered, Trisha, warm and receptive to Rhonda's questions, advised that Rhonda may be able to drive the same day depending on how far along she was in the pregnancy. When Rhonda told her she didn't know, she told her not to worry, they would do an ultrasound before proceeding. They would discuss her options after the ultrasound, but they expected to be able to conduct a procedure the same day. If they thought she would have to be sedated, they could help her with alternative arrangements including having volunteers bring her to a local hotel to stay nearby overnight. Rhonda scheduled an appointment at 9 a.m. that Friday. Trisha warned her that there might be protestors at the clinic, but they were not allowed to impede or physically prevent her from entering the facility. However, they might yell and say disgusting things to her. If she encountered any issues, she should run back to her car and call the facility on her cell phone. Rhonda knew the woman could feel her hesitation—being confronted seemed too much for her to handle—but Trisha told her that their facility had very few violent protestors, so she would be safe.

Rhonda ended the call with far less relief than she had sought, as unease clawed deeper into her chest. She was making the right choice. However, the choice was not settling as easily as she had hoped.

As she waited for the day, she remained distant and solemn in bed, taking a few extra moments to interact with Clare. She considered that this ongoing attention might appear out of character, raise questions, but she admitted in personal affirmations that such thoughts were egocentric and untrue. She longed for support from Teddy but respected him enough to remain silent.

She left at eight that Friday morning, wanting to arrive when the facility opened, hoping to be awake, ready, and inside before any protesters could appear. She did not understand the power and incentive of such hatred, yet a group of six stood in the front, blocking the entrance to the facility. She inched closer with the car, not feeling confident about her ability to ease through them, given her limited driving over the years. She would not allow them to stop her, as signs about going to hell, and abortion equating to murdering babies slammed against the windows of her car. Rhonda was scared—not by the signs but by their bloodlust.

She parked in the back of the lot, then realized the distance required a lengthy walk to the building and possible confrontation with the protesters. Thankfully, they had not followed her, though she questioned whether they genuinely respected a false line that kept them from encroaching on private property. She breathed deep, closing her eyes, struggling to picture a rolling cloud, a meadow, anything that could be considered a happy place; she only found blank notions that scared her. She looked at her phone. No texts or calls, thankfully. She opened the car door, hurrying to the back entrance.

A woman jogged up next to her, resting a hand on Rhonda's back before stepping in front of her. Rhonda wiggled in discomfort, but the woman's hand kept her in place. Rhonda was trapped and curled her shoulders forward in protection. The woman stepped away from Rhonda, waving her hands in a display of purported innocence.

"Apologies. I'm Tanya. I didn't mean to scare you. I just wanted to make sure I got your attention before you stepped inside. Can I have a few minutes of your time?"

Rhonda looked around, hoping someone would come to her rescue. She saw another woman walking in the back entrance, giving Rhonda a nervous look. Tanya maneuvered to lock eyes with her, open and ready to reveal some missive.

"I just want to get inside. Sorry." Rhonda pointed toward her intended direction, hoping to bypass this confrontation.

"Oh, please just listen. My boss will be all over me if I don't at least tell you what I need to say." The woman put her hands in a pleading display. Rhonda thought this woman must be edging her forties, embarrassed by her need to beg to keep from being chastised by some boss. Rhonda assumed the woman could be lying but also wanted to believe Tanya was telling the truth. She craved honesty. Rhonda nodded her head.

"Oh, thank you. What's your name?"

"Rhonda."

"Bless you, Rhonda," she said with an exaggerated smile. "Why do you want to walk in that facility? You know what they do there, right?"

"Yes," Rhonda said, faltering in her speech for a moment.

"Are you pregnant, Rhonda? What did you hope would happen today? Because I can tell you the Lord has better plans for you."

"I don't know," Rhonda said.

Tanya laughed, placing her hand on her hip and wagging her finger at Rhonda. "Now, why would you go to such a terrible place not knowing why, silly? Do you have questions that you need answered? Because I'm quite knowledgeable about matters of the heart. Are you seeking birth control? Because I can teach you better methods. The Lord teaches us that the sanctity of marriage allows the fulfillment of marital bliss without the fear of such consequences. Abstinence outside of marriage is an absolute method that is church-approved. Isn't that great?" she said with a smile and clapping of her hands.

"I don't know. I think I'm okay. I'm married." Rhonda felt at a loss about how to make this woman go away. She thought of running toward the building but worried the damn woman would follow her or the medical staff would chastise her for causing a distraction.

"Oh, you're married," Tanya rang out with glee. "Congratulations. You look so young. Your husband must be one lucky man."

"I suppose."

"Oh, I know he is, Rhonda," she laughed, patting Rhonda's arm. Rhonda looked disgusted at the touch of affection, but Tanya did not appear to register. "Does your husband know you are walking into a Planned Parenthood? Why did he not come with you?"

Rhonda felt a fury well within her, as if Tanya had any right to delve into her marriage. "I'm okay, Tanya. Thank you for your time."

Rhonda moved to the left, causing a soft squeak from her white tennis shoes. Tanya stepped in front of her, arms out as if ready for an awkward embrace. "Please listen to me, Rhonda. I know the Lord can help you through this. You just need to think through the consequences. Protect the souls of you and your child. We can help you."

Tanya stepped closer, so Rhonda took a step back. Rhonda grew frightened. Would this woman chase her if she ran? She searched for someone to scream at for help. Tanya had not been violent, but her actions suggested increasing hostility. Rhonda felt for the keys in her pocket. Tanya moved another step closer, her eyes unblinking as if to hypnotize Rhonda into absolution. Rhonda took another step back, pivoted, and sprinted to her car. She thought she heard clopping sounds coming behind her. She clicked the open-door button, swung the door out, then slid into the driver's seat, slammed the door, and locked it. She looked to see Tanya's head tilted to the side, right where Rhonda left her.

Rhonda scrolled through her past calls, finding the phone number for the facility. She called—five rings before someone answered the phone. A husky sound grunted hello.

"I'm sorry to be calling. I have an appointment today. Rhonda Chestwick. I'm parked in the back of your facility, and I can't get this woman to leave me alone. She keeps blocking me from walking in."

A knock on the door caused her to drop her phone onto the passenger seat. Rhonda looked to see Tanya waving at her, motioning for her to roll down the window. Rhonda put one finger up, then grabbed her phone. "She's knocking on my car. Can someone please come out here and help me inside? I'm scared."

"Of course. Someone will be out there in a moment."

Though disconnected, Rhonda kept the phone to her ear, pretending to continue the conversation. She wanted to keep the woman waiting, maybe even bore her into bothering someone else. Another knock on the door. Rhonda turned to see Tanya, still there, raising a finger to request another moment. Rhonda then saw a tall woman in pink scrubs marching to the car, and she breathed out in relief.

The woman pointed to Rhonda, screaming for Tanya to leave their patients alone. Tanya raised both her hands, yelling an apology. Rhonda then noticed her wallet in Tanya's left hand. Could she have really dropped her wallet when grabbing her keys? How could she be so stupid? She banged on the steering wheel, causing the horn to blare out a terrible shriek. Both Tanya and the woman in pink jumped. The woman took the offered wallet from Tanya, then pointed her away.

The woman knocked on the window, pointing to her nametag. Rhonda unlocked the car, gently opening the door as the nurse stepped back.

"Sorry about that. I haven't seen Tanya around here in a while. She's usually pretty good about being respectful when people don't want to talk. Please come with me, and we'll take care of you."

"Thank you," Rhonda said with a slight nod and followed the nurse into the center, desperately trying to control her feelings.

Chapter 9

Clare turns nine

R honda sat at the kitchen table, watching as Clare pressed her face against the living room window, rain pelting at her in turn. She had warned Edna that having the birthday party that weekend was a mistake given the gloomy weather forecast. No parent of sound mind would drag their child through the dark and meandering country roads for cake and ice cream in this storm. Edna reasoned that invitations had been given out before the end of the school year, and she had no intention of disinviting everyone through an exhausting telephone list, expecting some would show.

"Clare, please don't press your face against the window. You never know when a stick or rock will smack the window. Remember the branch that cracked it last year?" Rhonda said. "How about we watch the *Muppets Christmas Carol* while we wait?"

"No," she said, her lips now pressed against the glass, causing forced smudges.

Rhonda sighed, refusing to punish the poor child on her birthday, dismayed that Clare's favorite movie could not cheer her up. Where was Edna with these promises of a birthday party of fanfare and children's laughter? The woman could not even be bothered to deal with the elements for the few feet to the neighboring house. The clown with a pony had cancelled earlier that week, followed by a few classmates' parents phoning apologies for their inability to attend, two being Clare's closest friends. At least Edna had bothered to place the roving rainbow of streamers and "Happy Birthday" banner in the living room.

"Listen to your mother, Clare," Kelvin said, connecting with Rhonda's gaze in shared dismay as he moved closer to the window, pressing his own face against it in some defiant display.

"I think that's enough for tonight," Teddy said, excusing their newest foster child, Jeremy, from the table. Teddy had been a model grandfather figure for the children, taking on the role of tutor.

"Don't run up the stairs," Rhonda snapped, as Jeremy climbed the steps on all fours.

"I think we just call that crawling fast," Teddy said, smiling at Rhonda.

"We can't have another child fall down the stairs like Becky, spraining her wrist. I thought the state was going to press charges of neglect the way they interviewed everyone, as if one of us had pushed her down the steps."

"That's why we don't hop down the stairs, right Clare?" Kelvin said, tickling the side of Clare's tummy. Clare struggled to maintain her grumpiness but eventually relented to the flurry of fingers, giggling as she begged her father to stop.

Edna burst through the door, slamming it shut in exasperation, her silver blouse and tan slacks speckled with rain drops. "I can't believe how hard it is coming down out there. I know you said severe weather was reported, Rhonda, but this feels like a hurricane."

Rhonda felt mild pleasure at Edna's edging toward an admission of the insane notion this party would be a success—that is until Clare flopped to the ground, crossing her arms, minutes from a tantrum that would ruin any chance of celebration, even amongst family. Rhonda looked to Teddy and then Kelvin, attempting to come to a silent decision of how to handle Clare's disappointment. Thankfully, Teddy grasped the clues, easing himself up on his cane.

"Why don't we open some presents, Clare bear?" Teddy said. "Grandpa got you something you can play with right away. Won't that be nice." Teddy tried to ease himself down to Clare, but Edna shooed him back into his seat before he fell, causing a poor ambulance driver to be the only one to make the trek out here for Clare's birthday. Teddy tried to wave off Edna, but Kelvin picked Clare up, bouncing her around until she faced Teddy with a smile.

"Okay, Grandpa," she said.

"Thank goodness," Teddy said. "As I got a gift for a big girl. Thought we lost her. How old are we turning? Must be a hundred, right?"

"No," Clare said, shoving her face into Kelvin's neck, laughing.

"I'm sure your cake can help us?" Edna said, looking around then at Rhonda in puzzlement.

"Of course," Rhonda said, taking the cake out of the fridge, though not before rolling her eyes in the safety behind the door, turning around to show nine candles in bright yellow—Clare's favorite color for this month. Edna began piling presents on the table from the spare bedroom, as Clare beamed brighter with each new box, patting Kelvin's head to be let down.

"Which one is from you, Grandpa?"

"Oh, you know I'm a sucker for Snoopy," he said, gently pushing a box covered with images of Snoopy sleeping on his doghouse. Clare grasped at the present with youthful greed, beginning to rip the paper before Rhonda suddenly told her to stop. Both Edna and Teddy looked at Rhonda in puzzlement.

"Shouldn't we get Jeremy? I know the child has only been here for a month but doesn't seem right."

"Of course," Teddy said, looking abashed. "I completely forgot about the child up there. He sure is quiet."

"Suspicious," Kelvin said, heading up the stairs two at a time in a blatant display of how Clare was taught not to take the stairs. "Jeremy? Oh, where could Jeremy be?" They could hear giggling as Kelvin made a roaring noise, appearing with Jeremy slung over his shoulder. "He was hiding in his closet, though he couldn't quite shut the door." Kelvin placed Jeremy down between Rhonda and himself as Rhonda patted the young boy's head. She hated growing fond too fast, just when the kids would move on to a more permanent placement or return to their parents.

"Clare, open your present," Jeremy said, clapping his hands. The family joined in his enthusiasm as Clare ripped off the wrapping, squealing at the pristine paint set with book. Clare held up the present so everyone could see, and Edna took a picture on cue.

"What do we say?" Rhonda reminded her.

"Thank you, Grandpa," Clare said, hugging tight onto Teddy.

"Where's mine?" Jeremy said, placing his hands on the table, looking around.

"Where's your what?" Kelvin said, bending to one knee.

"Don't I get presents? Mommy always gave gifts to all of us," he said, eyes welling in growing despair.

"Why?" Edna said.

"Edna," Teddy said, putting his hand up for her to stop. "Jeremy, why did your Mommy give you all gifts?"

"We had our birthdays on the same day," Jeremy said, beginning to cry in confusion. "I wasn't bad, was I?"

"When is your birthday?" Kelvin said.

"Today," Jeremy whined, beginning a rippling effect as Clare began to whine in return.

"Is his birthday really today?" Kelvin said, looking to Rhonda.

"No," Rhonda mouthed, rushing to the drawer with the paperwork saved for each foster child. She flipped to see his birthday had been in November. She shrugged her shoulders, shaking her head. Rhonda tried to urge Kelvin to call out the blatant lie with her eyes, but he shook his head in turn.

"Mom, didn't we save that present for Jeremy in the other room?"

"Oh, yes. I think we kept a special gift for good boys. You don't care, do you, Clare?" Edna said, brushing the hair of the poor girl who appeared distraught, indicating she minded very much. Kelvin pulled Edna into the guest bedroom, closing the door.

This forced Rhonda to ease poor Jeremy against her leg as he twisted his face onto her flower dress, streaks of snot in tow. She gagged but kept patting the back of his head in comfort, though annoyed and knowing this display would only cause her problems later, as Jeremy related this lying and crying with getting his way. She and Teddy needed to always be the foundations of patience and kindness. This mother-son combination discovered new ways to strike against each lesson, innocuous or not. Teddy eased Clare onto his lap, going through the princess pictures, emphasizing the decadent colors that would bring them to life. In turn, he softly pushed one of the other presents towards Rhonda. In unspoken understanding, she grabbed the present and bent down to Jeremy.

"Look, Jeremy. We found your present. Can you open it for me?" At first, Jeremy batted at the present, so Rhonda sat down, feigning motions of ripping off the wrapping. "Guess this present is for me, then."

"No," he said stomping, reaching for the present.

"Now, now," Rhonda said. "That is not how we open gifts, do we? Why don't you sit down next to me, then we can show everyone what you received?"

He paused, appearing confused by the instruction, then flopped to the ground after grasping the present. Rhonda sighed, figuring this was as close as it would come to genteel behavior for the boy. He squealed at the cover with a shining knight, sword presented, before a castle riddled with towers. He sprawled over the kitchen floor, opening the book to a fire-breathing dragon, dumping the box of crayons onto the floor.

Serenity be my restraint, she thought as she took a purple crayon. "Should we color the dragon purple?"

"No," he said, immediately rubbing in crass red lines all over the dragon. Rhonda stood, having enough of the fit, inadvertently touching the snot, rushing her hand to the sink with floods of soap and furious scrubbing. Only then did Rhonda notice Edna and Kelvin speaking with Teddy in whispers as Clare opened a third present in mid cheer. Hurt by her exclusion, Rhonda understood her part in keeping Jeremy preoccupied, but she still felt left out.

Lights then flooded the front window, and they all turned in surprise. Edna hurried the presents into the spare bedroom as Kelvin attempted to quell another outburst from Clare. Rhonda observed Jeremy still marking furiously with the red crayon, as a tree, fairy, and princess suffered the streaking wrath. A rushed knock followed. Kelvin opened the door without consideration of what insanity was on the porch.

Four people stood at the front door—an older boy near Clare's age and a younger girl were both shielded by their mother and father, who looked earnest to escape the rain that now seemed to travel sideways into the house. Kelvin motioned for them to enter, pointing to an area to the side for their coats and shoes, as he fought and eventually succeeded in closing the door against the wind.

"We are so sorry for being late. My name is Rex Teruptil," he said, shaking Kelvin's hand and nodding to the rest of the family before removing his coat.

"I'm Loretta," the petite woman said, mussing up her son's hair a bit in his apparent shyness. "This is our boy, Nick, and my daughter, Isla. We moved here—oh, some weeks ago now, and I know that we are all taking a bit of time getting transitioned." She glanced at Nick, though Rhonda could not tell if this had been a purposeful sign or inadvertent slight. "So, I'm not sure how much Clare and Nick have gotten to know each other since Nick only attended those last few weeks of school, but this seemed like a great opportunity for the whole family to meet more of the community, despite that horrendous downpour."

"We are all in a bit of shock you made it," Edna said, graciously shaking Loretta's and then Rex's hand. "We are of course honored that you came all this way. How was the drive?"

"My wife can drive through anything," Rex said, rubbing his wife's back. "I would never trust anyone else to get our family through a snowstorm, tornado, or worse, God forbid. I still say she missed an opportunity to be a storm chaser."

"Please," Loretta said. "We again apologize for being late. Did everyone already leave?"

"No one else made the trek, so you really must be quite the driver," Kelvin laughed. "Please step in and make yourself comfortable. We haven't even blown out the candles on the birthday cake."

Clare looked awkwardly at Nick in puzzlement. Jeremy took no notice of the new guests, still fiercely mutilating any semblance of the intended colorful characters. Then again, his present should be used how he wanted, Rhonda figured, only really dismayed that he would grow tired of the coloring book far sooner than hoped despite the many pages with barely a few scribbles.

"Oh no," Loretta said, clapping her hands together. "I forgot your present outside. I'm sorry, Clare."

"I'll get it," Nick said, boots and coat on before his parents could voice concern.

"Brave boy," Edna said, motioning to two chairs at the dining room table for Loretta and Rex to sit.

"When he wants to be," Rex said, grinning. "Well, who is this on the floor?"

"That's our foster child, Jeremy," Rhonda said, unsure whether to pull him up, instead making a broad motion to the floor. "He's currently coloring his birthday present. Isla, would you like to color with him or would you prefer to see the presents Clare received?"

"Do you want to see my room?" Jeremy said, jumping to his feet, fingers caked with red crayon. "I have Hot Wheels and Legos. Oh, and we can play the Wii. Do you like *Mario Party*?"

Isla looked to her mother, who nodded her head. "As long as the door stays open, mind you."

Isla quickly followed Jeremy up the stairs. Rhonda witnessed crayon markings streaking parts of the banister. She considered walking up to force him to wash his hands but did not have the heart to play disciplinarian in front of company. Thankfully, the Wii was downstairs, so he could do minimal damage.

Nick barreled into the house with a sopping box, appearing to fall into the door rather than properly entering, as he struggled to stand after squashing the box into his chest on the foyer floor. Instead of standing, he overcorrected, falling backwards, yelping, then looking abashed at the outburst.

"Oh, son," Rex said, easing his son up, then grabbing the mashed box. "Thankfully, the present isn't easily breakable, or we would have really made a bad first impression. You can go ahead and open it now if you want." He passed the present to Kelvin, who then gave it to Clare.

"We weren't sure what to get you," Loretta said. "I hope you like it, though it may be a bit impersonal."

"I'm sure it is perfect," Edna said, helping Clare open the soggy wrapping and box, revealing a mint-green wallet. Clare blinked a few times at the gift, then looked to Edna for some signal.

"Open the wallet," Nick said. "There's more." Clare followed instruction to a gift card for the jewelry store, Claire's, then smiling in realization.

"We know she doesn't spell her name that way," Loretta said. "But Nick thought of the idea, and we had to admit that it was quite cute."

"Now you can get yourself more jewelry like you've been begging," Rhonda said, feeling a bit left out of the celebration. "Should we go ahead and serve cake and ice cream?" As if hearing her, squeals came from above.

"Children," Kelvin yelled. "Come down. We are blowing out candles and having cake."

Jeremy rushed out, nearly falling down the last three steps onto his face. Thankfully, Isla had the patience to hold the banister, taking one step at a time. "We've talked about this, Jeremy. Please be careful, okay?" said Rhonda, who had been ready to brace the mindless child.

"Sorry," he said, rushing around her to the table, hopping from one foot to the other while staring at the cake as Isla squeezed next to him. Once Nick had recovered to the kitchen table, sitting next to Clare at Kelvin's invitation, Rhonda lit the candles and pushed the cake before her. She began to sing "Happy Birthday," the others quickly joining. Clare blushed while blowing the candles as they clapped. Rhonda began serving the cake and ice cream, mostly to appease Jeremy's dancing next to her. Before she could say no, he rushed up the stairs with his dessert, Isla following in giggles. Rhonda sighed, figuring there was no harm this time.

"I'm sorry more people couldn't show," Edna said, kissing Clare on the cheek. "I'm just thankful that you have such a wonderful new friend to celebrate with and hope for a lasting friendship. Rex, Loretta, have you picked out a church yet? You should come with me one of these upcoming Sundays. I'd be happy to introduce you and your family around."

"That sounds fantastic," Rex said, swirling a bit of cake with his ice cream before eating. "Loretta was just saying we needed to find ourselves a new place of worship."

"No requirements or expectation that you have to keep going," Edna said, smiling. "But I'm very hopeful."

Rhonda was barely listening. She saw Clare and Nick whispering to each other with hands over ears, neither having touched their dessert, and was curious as to what secrets were being exchanged. Teddy must have followed her gaze, as he chuckled. "Look at the two of them. Bit of romance budding." The room laughed as the kids blushed, though Rhonda questioned whether the jest was all that funny as she forced a soft chuckle.

Chapter 10

Clare is seventeen

Rhonda burrowed herself into the couch, furious that Kelvin did not find the situation serious, that he would diminish what she had seen with her own eyes, as if there could be another way to interpret a boy walking in on a girl in the shower. Tristen had the look of shock at being caught in the act; she recognized the eyes of a boy who wanted more. She had a daughter to protect, especially now that Edna had given Clare condoms, taking any chance she could find to undermine Rhonda's parenting.

Rhonda had adored many of the kids the minute she met them. Tiny forlorn faces, scared, helpless, wanting a kind word to make their day. Others, mostly boys, put on a posture of hostility, requiring Kelvin to talk with them about the welcoming environment and driving off fear by lashing out. No one was punished unless they threatened the family or themselves. Some took to Kelvin's open candor, as he had a knack for speaking to rather than down at them, yet Kelvin also spent little time at the house, busy traipsing at work or Lord knows what else.

Maybe Kelvin's even reaction resulted from the debauchery of men. A camaraderie of the destitute, for when one's acts of perversion were pinpointed, then came the collective fear of being branded.

She listened for a sign of a struggle. The boy was unaware of the trailer, but that would not prevent him from venturing idly into her haven.

Rhonda ran to the door, locked it, and scrutinized her surroundings, as if the boy could have made his way inside the trailer without her hearing. Could he squeeze himself through one of the windows? Perhaps the bathroom and spare bedroom, she considered, hurrying to each and ensuring the lock was in place. She then went into Teddy's old bedroom, forgetting the sorrow it held.

Over the years, the family had all found their way into the trailer for one reason or another. Kelvin for solitude, Clare to study away from family, and Edna to periodically "tidy up the place." Rhonda thought Edna really came to reminisce about her father and mother. Rhonda tended to find Edna with a drink when she caught her inside the trailer, though for Edna a drink in hand was a staple.

The thickening layers of dust in the room verified that Edna could not have stepped into Teddy's bedroom. Rhonda confirmed both windows were locked, then sat on the bed. She understood Edna's difficulty in this room, the last year of Teddy's life having been spent bound to the bed, primarily cared for by Rhonda. She had refused to allow Edna to hire a home caregiver. All those years Teddy kept to Rhonda's side, helping her through trying times. Rhonda sickened at the idea that she would not give Teddy the same honor in return.

She rested on the bed, fretting over Kelvin's search, worried the boy would conceal himself in the house crevices until they went to bed and then strike. She rolled her eyes, letting out a deep sigh, knowing Teddy would lecture her on such arrogant thoughts. Teddy always found the best in the kids, coaxing them into expressing their feelings and discovering where their anger originated.

She had ignored the therapy treatment that Teddy pushed her toward. However, he'd eventually convinced her to seek help from her primary care physician about her running thoughts and panic, always followed by wallowing. She was permitted a rolling prescription for Xanax meant to tamp her thoughts down under her control. She did not take it often, hating the numb feeling that coursed through her the remainder of the day, so she stocked bottles of Xanax in cupboards around the house for bouts of hysteria. Rhonda realized that she should have taken one before this teenage boy arrived at the house. The children were what stressed her out, and Clare had been less helpful as she got older, finding little interest in the younger children as she grew into her teenage years.

Rhonda's mind turned to the years she'd spent burrowed inside the house with only brief escapes with Edna to church or with Kelvin on sporadic romantic outings. She smiled at the thought of Kelvin being romantic: her big, strong protector. A cynical curl drew over Rhonda's mouth as she wondered how Kelvin's spine could possibly support a relationship without his mother around to keep him propped up.

She looked at the pictures Teddy left on the nightstand: Clare as a baby, his wife and him on their wedding day, and a family picture of Kelvin, Rhonda, and Clare, just before Clare started kindergarten. She wondered if Edna took offense to the absence of her picture in the bedroom, though other pictures of her were plastered in the living and guest room.

"Teddy deserved better," she muttered, reflecting on the chestnut casket, small funeral, vague ineffectual eulogies that had not properly idolized the man who had given to everyone and asked for nothing in return. She had wanted to give a eulogy that would make the heavens praise the welcoming of his spirit, but she could not find the will, still devastated from discovering him that dreary Tuesday morning. He had appeared to be doing well the night before—no weakness of breath, only a slight wheezing that gave no alarm. She often reflected over that Monday night, and how she had missed some clear sign that the Lord meant to take him.

Rhonda found sleep overcoming her, enjoying the sweet embrace of being away from it all. She had slept little the night before, worried about this exact predicament, or something like it. The soothing calm washed over her, and she fell asleep wishing Teddy would take care of the situation like only he knew how.

She woke, eyes agape, startled by the moonlight as her only guide. Rhonda chastised herself for falling asleep when her daughter needed her. She scuttled to turn on the bedroom light, then the light in each room until the entire trailer looked ready and alive. "No sign of that boy," she said with relief. Should she go back to the house to help in case they had not found him? For all she knew, Kelvin had given up after ten minutes and gone to bed.

Rhonda placed her hand on the front doorknob, breathing in quick rasps for the bravery to unlock and pull. In two quick motions, the door opened and she stepped back. She waited to the count of five—no movement. She looked outside, expecting Edna's motion detector to turn on the light. Rhonda jumped two times in quick succession for the flood of light all around. She found no one in the backyard. She studied the barn, far removed in the back, the dark mouth of the building agape—no visibility without a flashlight. If the boy stayed there, that was his decision, she reasoned.

She scampered to the back door of the house, then opened, slammed, and locked the door. She turned around to find Kelvin and Edna at the dining room table with Clare.

"Well, there she is," laughed Edna with a grand gesture toward Rhonda.

"Kelvin knew I was in the trailer," Rhonda said.

"Well, when we saw all the lights off, we figured you planned on staying the night there," Kelvin said with a shrug.

Rhonda ignored him, sitting next to Clare, touching her shoulder. "Are you okay, sweetheart? This whole situation has gotten out of control." She looked at Kelvin. "What did you do? Did you find the boy? I hope he's not here anymore!"

Clare gently took Rhonda's hand. "Mom, I think you overreacted. Tristen did not mean anything; he explained to Dad what happened."

Rhonda felt her face scrunch, furious that they would take the side of this boy over what she had witnessed. "What could he have possibly said that explained why he walked into the bathroom while you were taking a shower? There is no reasonable excuse." Rhonda stood, her voice rising to a furious pitch. "I want him out of this house, Kelvin. I will not permit him here for another second."

"Keep your voice down, Rhonda. Maybe you should take a Xanax," said Edna with ease. Rhonda wanted to slap her but did not have the courage. Rhonda marched to the cabinet over the sink, took out one pill, and swallowed it dry.

"Happy?" she said, hands shaking.

"Very," Edna said.

Clare motioned for Rhonda to settle back next to her. "Mom, please. I know what happened frightened you, but Dad talked to Tristen. Then he came to Grandma and me to apologize. Everything was a misunderstanding. I promise you."

Clare patted the chair, continuing to coax her. Rhonda felt trapped, accused, as if her hysteria was the real cause of this debacle.

"This is not my fault," she said. She grabbed a glass, pushed it into the refrigerator button for water, drank two sips, and sat next to Clare.

"No one said it's your fault," Kelvin said. "The poor boy did something stupid, but he didn't mean to invade anyone's privacy."

"Then why walk into an occupied bathroom?!" she said.

"Will you just listen? That poor boy up there can probably hear you," Kelvin said, slamming his hand on the table. Edna took his hand, patting it for reassurance. Rhonda eyed the touch, knowing she would be in the wrong for whatever occurred next.

"The kid felt lost and lonely. He was sitting in the room trying to figure out what the hell happened to his life. He missed his mom, and he just went from living in town to our country house. I can see how that can be alienating. You told him that he could not go into our bathroom, so he tried to hold his bladder all that he could."

"I did—" Rhonda started.

"Shut up, Mom," Clare whispered. Rhonda looked at her daughter, wounded that the one person she had fought to protect was now telling her to stop. Though no tears formed, Rhonda motioned to her eyes, as if to wipe away her shock. She sipped her water, then returned her attention to Kelvin.

"Okay," he said. "He knocked on the bathroom door to say something to Clare, ask if she could leave the bathroom quickly. Evidently, neither Clare nor Tristen could hear each other, so Tristen opened the door to ask again, not wanting to see Clare naked. You just happened to walk upon the situation of him opening the door, when you scared him, causing him to fall into the room. I could see how you may have thought he meant to spy on our daughter given the situation you encountered."

She could feel the soft wash of relief beginning to formulate from the medication, but this respite could not yet soothe her anger. "You're blaming me for finding that boy peeking at our daughter? Do you want me to apologize to him while I'm at it? Are you looking to whore your daughter off, Kelvin?"

"Oh, Mom," Clare said, shaking her head. Edna sneered. Rhonda thought she would get another reaction from Kelvin, but he looked bored.

"Why do you hate this kid so much?" Kelvin asked earnestly.

She looked at him, then down, trying to articulate the feeling the boy gave her. She could say she was worried that he would harm Clare in some way, but she had to admit that some of the children had been more actively dangerous than the reserved, scrawny child upstairs. Had his story of a prostitute mother that kidnapped him bothered her? No, she reasoned, shaking her head. Rhonda knew the underlying rationale that Kelvin would not accept. The boys in this house had been actual boys, none older than ten. She knew they would move on, find homes. This fifteen-year-old boy would be sexually charged, looking for inspiration in conquests such as Rhonda. Kelvin would carve his design into the boy, turn him into another version of himself, preying on women. Rhonda did not need another testosterone-engorged male presence in this house, spoiling proper men for her daughter.

Rhonda wondered whether she really thought the boy had committed an atrocious act or if she merely saw the chance to be rid of him without guilt of her misplaced blame. She sought to speak a truth, without taking back the events she witnessed. The Xanax poured over her ridges as she strained to warn of her fear that Kelvin's influence would poison the boy, turning him into another disgusting, oversexualized rendering —Kelvin's greatest prodigy.

Before she could form the words, Edna decreed her ruling. "This is madness, and the boy stays. He has done nothing wrong, and I do believe it best you go to his room and apologize. I have little doubt that he is still awake, upset by these awful events."

Rhonda let the final touches of the drug soothe her. A figurative kind hand descended on her, easing her down before she screamed at her mother-in-law and her condescending tone. Rhonda breathed into the sweet touch, then placed her own on Clare's shoulder.

"I'm sorry if I scared you, honey. I only meant to protect you."

Clare gently nodded her head. "I know, Mom. It's okay." Clare pulled away from Rhonda's hand and stood. "I'm going to bed now. I'm tired."

"Okay, darling," Edna said. Kelvin followed with a whispered, "Goodnight."

They waited until she slumped up the stairs and they heard the door shut.

"I will not apologize, Edna. I witnessed and stopped that boy. If he has an excuse, then I expect you and Kelvin will be keeping a close eye on him. I will not force him out, but I do not think I am wrong for being suspicious of a fifteen-year-old boy whose mother happened to be a prostitute and likely drug user."

"Are you concerned because of the morals of his mother?" Kelvin said. "He did not do these things. He's just a lost boy who needs a home."

"Oh please, Kelvin. A mother has great influence over her child. You aren't worried about the thoughts that go through this kid's head?" Rhonda heard the words tumble from her mouth, unsure of their foundation. She had never been so ruthless to these foster kids, but something inarticulate lingered.

"Goodness, Rhonda," Edna murmured. "You may want to consider this train of thought more before we continue."

"What do you mean?" Rhonda snapped, forgetting the ease of tension she just felt.

"Well, if that were the case, Clare would be tied down to her bed, reading books to inspire her, yet finding no fix. She may even find herself pregnant in the next year, don't you think?" Edna swirled her hand in the air. "I mean, if we are to believe she'll turn into her mother."

Rhonda pulsed with fury, thankful she could stifle the desired words from her mouth. "Are you going to allow her to say these things to me, Kelvin?!"

Kelvin briefly looked at Rhonda, then the table.

Rhonda stood, her chair falling back, and she slammed her right hand on the table. "Fine! I will be moving into the guest room tomorrow. You will raise this boy on your own, Kelvin. Don't shake your head at me. You will do it! Tonight, I'll be staying in our bedroom alone."

Rhonda marched around them, slamming their bedroom door, locking it behind her. She began sobbing, hurt by the jagged truth and raw falsehoods alleged at her. She stripped, crawled into bed, crying over her isolation. She curled under the bed sheets, wondering why she continued to stay in this horrid house, wishing Teddy would visit and comfort her to a deeper sleep.

Chapter 11

Clare is eighteen

"I t's not that I haven't thought about leaving, Ben. Ben? Ben?" Rhonda checked her phone signal, surprised, as she generally had consistent reception at the far corner of her bedroom near the closet. It was no longer the guest room, now that her books were piled onto the nightstand and most of her clothes were placed in the closet. She hit the speaker button, tossing the phone on the bed.

"Oh, sorry," Ben said. "I had to put you on mute. Kathy asked me about one of the kids' basketball practices this weekend. Looks like I'll be doing the rounds. She's off to Tulsa or Tampa for a week. I can't keep track. Anyways, yeah, I understand. I've told you, if you need a place to stay until you get situated, we have a spare bedroom. I know you're waiting until Clare leaves the house, but it's her senior year. She'll be off to college soon, and you'll be relieved of any obligations."

"What would Mom say if she discovered me at your house? She would probably stop talking to you."

"Oh, she's not that bad anymore. You should reach out. I know she would love to hear from you, as long as you don't expect her to admit any wrong. You'll have to be the one to break ground between the two of you."

"Not a chance in hell," Rhonda said, flopping on the bed, causing her phone to jump into the air. With unexpected dexterity, Rhonda caught the phone before it crashed to the floor.

"Rhonda, I'm glad we're talking more, but you need to try with Mom. She's at my house quite often. I think meeting for a casual dinner at my place would be a nice transition to developing your relationship."

"I don't know. I'll think about it. I can't forget being thrown out and ignored, Ben."

"I know. Please take care of yourself. Everything will get better if you try. I need to go cook dinner for the kids. I'll talk to you later."

"Bye, Ben."

Rhonda threw her phone against the neighboring pillow, then sprawled over the covers of the bed. She glanced up, ensuring she had locked the door. She wanted time to read through some smut book she had taken from Edna's house. Rhonda had to look twice at the book on the small shelf in Edna's guest bathroom. Rhonda studied the cover featuring a woman's gaping face of ecstasy and a man groping her breast over a string bikini, kissing her on the neck. Rhonda did not find the picture overly interesting or new but needed to know the contents of an explicit book that her mother-in-law would buy. Twenty-two pages into the book, the lead discovered she needed to escape the mundaneness of her desk job by managing a bar at the beach. Rhonda fell asleep, wondering how a twenty-six-year-old could possibly understand the tedium of daily life.

Once Rhonda woke, she grabbed her phone, groaning at the hour—just after 1 a.m. She rolled her tongue around her mouth, encountering the rank taste of failing to brush her teeth. She peeked out the door, ensuring Kelvin had not fallen asleep on the couch. She preferred less interaction, appreciative of having her own space in the guest room yet despising that she needed back-up toiletries in the upstairs bathroom when she could not sneak access to the bathroom in their old, shared bedroom.

She had not reached forty, yet she hobbled up the stairs, hating every step, trying to remember when stairs became the bane of her day. She lugged from the final step, wanting to be quiet, but unable to calm her heavy foot. She paused to catch her breath, not winded, just disoriented from waking up so late.

She flipped on the bathroom light, then stopped in position. Had she heard whispering? Both kids knew better than to be up this late. She kept the bathroom light on for guidance, then softly tried to open Clare's door. Rhonda would normally knock, but she took the risk of getting brutalized later about privacy. Rhonda peered at the bed, trying to find Clare in the pile of blankets, not seeing any light indicating phone usage. Rhonda closed the door, walked to the bathroom, and began brushing her teeth. She would normally close this door to reduce the noise from the electric brush, but she still felt disturbed.

Teeth brushed, she crept toward Tristen's room. The now sixteen-year-old boy performed moderately well in school, despite his inherent social awkwardness, going through a dark clothing phase that Kelvin mocked at any chance. Despite the passing year and adoption, Rhonda never found the strength to interact with the boy longer than necessary. She felt pleasant but weary during their exchanges. Even after Tristen's fulfilled request for his adoption after his mother had been sentenced to three years in jail, he did not seem happy.

She gently opened the door to Tristen's room, terrified she would find the teenage boy masturbating. She saw mild shuffling under the sheets, quickly realizing the body design did not make sense. Tristen remained a scrawny creature, despite his inhalation of food.

"Tristen, are you okay? I thought I heard something."

She hoped the boy would not respond—that the whispers had been the eeriness of the night—but the sheets rustled once more. Why was he tossing and turning so much? She stared at the pile in the bed, now perceiving the outline of two bodies. Had Tristen brought someone into his room? He knew no guest would be permitted on a school night, especially in his bed. Had he discussed this with Kelvin? She felt disrespected that Tristen and Kelvin would break these modest rules without her input. She grasped the top of the blanket, sliding it down just enough to confirm her worst fears, revealing the wide eyes of both Tristen and Clare. More from horrific instinct than curiosity, she ripped the blanket down to reveal their naked bodies entangled within each other.

Rhonda could not feel anything beyond shock. She had been prepared for some possible promiscuity, but she tore through the thought of killing the boy now. She considered screaming, the force etched in her throat, yet she could not produce a sound. The devastation of finding her daughter with her brother, by blood or not, had brought a level of disgust that could not be processed.

Clare pulled the sheet up to cover her breasts, grimacing as if daring her mother to comment on the sight before her. This was the fruit of Rhonda's life—her daughter punishing her with a conundrum that no parent deserves. Rhonda could not bring herself to chastise the boy, the scars from the admonishment last year still running deep, yet here the boy lay with her daughter, proving Rhonda a prophet of the boy's nature. Rhonda heard soft utterances from the boy. Low apologies repeated in terror, looking at no one—an open-eyed disbelief, perhaps ridding his mind of what he had been caught doing.

The guttural scream initially came out as a moan, the pitch rising. Clare dove over Tristen, kneeing him in the stomach, causing him to heave. Rhonda saw her coming, but the sound would not halt. Clare gripped her mother's head, forcing her mouth closed, her front teeth piercing her tongue. A cry of a different sort now muffled forth. Clare pushed her mother over, then closed the door, locking it behind.

"Put your clothes on, Tristen. Mom, if you stop the dramatics and keep quiet while we dress, I'll explain."

"Explain what?" she cried out, a splash of blood dripping from her bottom lip. "Did he rape you? Please tell me you did not agree to this. Oh God, Clare, do you not care about me, this family? What will everyone think?"

"No one will think anything if you shut the fuck up. Now quit talking so loud," Clare said.

Rhonda twisted her focus away, mostly out of embarrassment for Tristen's erect penis wiggling around as he rushed for his pants. How could he possibly be excited after this?

"Mom, can you turn around?"

"I don't want to. Please just tell me this will stop, and I'll pretend I never saw anything."

"No, you won't. You'll try to swallow this until you scream it out at some inopportune moment at the dinner table."

"Is that what you think of me?" Rhonda asked, whirling around. "Clare, you slept with your brother."

"Oh, Mom. I've known him for a year, and he's not even related to me."

Rhonda pressed against the wall, grasping for something to hold. Instead, she eased herself to the floor, coming to terms with what took place in this household. How could she be so ignorant, so blind to the daily musings of her daughter, unaware that Clare could be having such shameless sex under this roof?

Rhonda pounded the floor, dismayed at being convinced that staying in this house had been for Clare's benefit. No one needed her. Kelvin's daughter sat on that bed, barely dressed, looking at her with disdain, annoyed that her mother had caught her.

Tristen! The boy was sixteen and had fault in this affair, too. "How could you do this, Tristen? Look at me! How could you defile my daughter? You *are* just a little pervert," Rhonda said, then spat on the carpet.

Tristen was silent, focused on the floor. Rhonda kept her gaze upon him, waiting for him to defend himself, help her understand how screwing her daughter could be anything but a betrayal. "Wait until Kelvin hears about this, Tristen. Oh, I fear what he may do to you."

He looked at her, aghast, tears welling in his eyes. He began mouthing, "I'm sorry," the words barely audible.

"You will be. Oh, I promise that we will not stand for this."

"Oh, shut up, Mom. I mean it. Shut up. You will do nothing of the sort. If you mention any of this to Dad, I'll tell him you made it up. I'll also tell him you've been talking to your brother about leaving him. He'll kick you out on your ass, Mom, so don't pretend that you have some power in this situation. If anything happens to Tristen, I'll run away. I'll walk out of this godforsaken house for good, leaving you and Dad to actually talk to each other."

Rhonda numbed at her creation. The revulsion, the anger, the cold, blunt threats, dissipated in the same air that shared her daughter's words. She could not understand what sins she had committed in her life to warrant this disgrace. She had always been and would always be the victim in this house. A creature swept into the corners, hoping these vile people would not paw and dismantle her fractured psyche. Rhonda kept silent; in a deep, forgotten world of misery, she relished in undiluted torture.

Clare turned to Tristen, gently stroking his hand. "Do you mind leaving for a moment? Maybe take a shower or just hang out in my room."

Tristen nodded, glancing at Rhonda for apparent permission. Rhonda motioned her hand for him to leave, as if she had any control.

Rhonda studied the faded gray carpet on the floor. She could not recall any explicit words or touches that would have revealed some underlying sexual tension between the two. Clare had been gentle and guiding with Tristen, similar to all the other foster kids that had come through the house. Clare would show them the way to school, help them with their homework, and teach them how to cook for themselves if Rhonda found herself unable to that day. Rhonda had seen no longing looks or pining from Tristen upon Clare, but she had not been especially scrutinizing. She had worried the boy would become a pervert, possibly a rapist, but never a voluntary lover.

"Mom. Mom, will you look at me?"

Rhonda considered her daughter, trying to understand how she could suffer so from her own flesh. She would not dig herself out of this pitiless state, tired and determined to go to bed. She decided to pretend that nothing of this sort had happened, keeping her false strength downstairs—safe there.

"I'm sorry I said those nasty things, but I hate when you get so hysterical. I know this is shocking. Please don't blame Tristen. I'm the one that started it. He's never forced, asked, begged, threatened, or required that I have sex with him. He's a good person, Mom, and I love his kindness."

"In our house, Clare."

"Where else, Mom? We both live here. Would you rather us go to Grandpa's trailer?"

"No," she sighed. "No, I'd rather this all had not happened. I'd rather not have found out and left well enough alone. He's sixteen, Clare. You're an adult, despite what you may think. Is that even legal?"

"Yes, Mom. I believe sixteen is the age of consent."

"Oh, God. Why, Clare? You could have asked me if you had questions."

"Mom, I love you, but I would not want to talk to you about any of this. Also, I didn't have questions. Are you even listening to what I'm saying? I wanted to have sex, not understand how condoms and birth control work."

Rhonda's hand swung to her mouth. "Please tell me you've been using condoms. We can put you on birth control, too."

"Grandma already took me for birth control, remember? And yes, we usually use condoms. I'm not dumb. I don't want to be pregnant at eighteen."

"Why would you say it like that?"

"I didn't mean that as an offense to you. I'm saying that for myself. Stop making this all about you. *Everything* affects you. I just need you to understand that this is not some ploy or excuse to get back at you. Tristen is kind but vulnerable, and he's been there for me this past year. We are not a couple. He is just a source of comfort with occasional bouts of sex. I never meant for anyone to find out. I wish you hadn't barged into Tristen's room tonight."

"Me too, honey. Oh, me too."

Clare slumped from the bed, dropping against the wall next to Rhonda. Rhonda felt an arm push behind, then clasp tightly over her shoulder, yet didn't find the gesture comforting. Rhonda perceived the act as an aggression of Clare's control of the situation, wondering if her inability to handle the worst of her own problems had caused Clare to gain this ardent strength, akin to her grandmother. Rhonda could not recall the last time Clare had asked for her insight. She finally grasped the extent to which she had become a stranger in this home. The feelings she had in Clare's youth, that sense of unqualified motherhood that caused abandon, coursed through her mind.

"Mom, I don't think you are a bad person. I just don't get your hostility to Tristen."

"I don't hate Tristen."

"Oh, come on, Mom. This whole house knows. You barely acknowledge his presence. He's not stupid. He can feel the disgust coming off you when he passes. He avoids you, not for his sake, but to make you feel better.”

“Clare, I was worried he would take advantage of you. Maybe what you say is true, and you instigated this promiscuity, but he had to agree. This would never have happened if he did not live here.”

“I would be having sex with someone else, Mom. I’m eighteen. You should be happy I had a safe place and the foresight in pregnancy prevention, instead of a quick fuck in the back of a truck.”

“I’m done, Clare. I won’t tell your father or grandmother, but please stop this. If you’re found out, that’s judgment that I don’t think the family will survive.”

“Fine. We can pretend that I’m not a sexually active woman, and that you are not holed up in the guest bedroom. I love playing pretend.”

Rhonda nodded her head, knowing that Clare was mocking her, but losing interest in fighting. She did not want to be hated by Clare, so maybe ignoring this predicament would be better for everyone. Clare was right; no blood relationship connected Clare and Tristen.

Rhonda accepted that she had been correct in her foresight, but perhaps Clare had been the one to turn into Kelvin. Clare had shown such determination, spite, and a blasé attitude toward her sexual relationship. Rhonda was curious why Clare would be hesitant to tell Kelvin. She could not fathom Kelvin threatening Tristen or Clare. He would likely just buy more condoms and force them to promise that he would never catch them. But Rhonda acknowledged this Kelvin was an invention of her mind based upon the teenage boy she once knew.

Clare stood, still staring, waiting for some sign of Rhonda’s intentions. Rhonda tried to push herself up, but her legs were too numb. Clare rushed and helped her mother, holding on until Rhonda patted Clare on the arm. “I’m going to bed. I won’t say anything.”

Rhonda shambled down the stairs, exhausted and silent.

Chapter 12

Today

"Clare, please let us out. I'm sorry for whatever you are feeling, but we are all hurting. We can talk about this."

"Mom, it's too late! You don't get to pretend to be a mother now! Not a day of my life has gone by when I have not seen this imprisoned gaze in your eyes. You relish being the victim. You don't know what else to be."

"I tried," Rhonda cried out. "I tried to be a mother. No one taught me. My own family abandoned me. After I had you, I felt so much shame. I did not want to touch you or hold you, afraid I may just drop you on the floor. Your great-grandfather helped me, but that guilt never left, Clare. I can't look at you without seeing my failings."

"You think telling me how I am your personal failure is the way to talk to your daughter?" Clare laughed, a desperate act to keep from crying. "You two are a broken foundation, and why I'm standing here today. I never relied on you. How could I? I had to take care of you."

"I certainly do not think you can place the blame entirely on me. Your father went out whoring with all those women. Plus, Tristen and Nick are the real reason you're unhappy. You did that, Clare. I tried to stop you. Remember? But you threatened me."

"You're my mother! Of course I threatened to run away or tell Dad some awful story about you. I was acting out. I went to Tristen because he listened, Mom. He cared for me at a time when I did not seem to have anyone's attention. He held me while I cried about school or a fight that you and Dad had once again. You two made the house so toxic, and I found a person that could relate to what I had gone through for years."

"Tristen raped you! Nick hurt you! I'm not the one that caused you to spiral into this mess. This is not my fault," Rhonda cried out.

"It is. I hope you understand you are just as much at fault as everyone next to you. I don't think you have an honest apology to give me, do you?"

Clare saw her mom open her mouth multiple times then scream for help. Clare knew that this discussion had been a waste. Her mother would never accept her part in any wrongdoing. Clare loomed upon her mother, needle in hand.

"Do I need to drug you, or will you quiet down so I can gag you?"

Rhonda tugged at her bindings, begging to be let go. Clare stabbed her in the thigh with the syringe. The screaming slowed until her mom no longer fought the inevitable. Clare placed the gag on her, finding relief that she would no longer hear those screams.

Clare rested against the barn wall, studying her grandmother. She had barely moved these past couple hours. Clare worried that she may be on the verge of dying, and she could not let that happen until she was done. She would need to monitor her. Ignoring these concerns, she considered the empty noose and its lost occupant.

Part III: Brother

"For the Lord detests the perverse but takes the upright into his confidence." Proverbs 3:32

Chapter 13

Clare is eleven

Tristen rested on the floor of the closet, looking through his math problems—a series of fractions that he needed to reduce to their lowest denominator. His mom had placed a light in there long ago, for when she needed to work, along with the required earbuds. Tristen hated the feeling of the earbuds at first but soon found them to be a comfort, bringing thoughts of away, though he occasionally heard the sounds from the outside: the grunting and moaning of men in his mom's bed.

Tristen needed to ask his mom for help with his homework, though. He thought he understood Mr. Retvan's lessons, but the lines daunted him. Why should two numbers that work turn into two lower numbers that worked? He knew multiplication and division, but this new focus on fractions in the third grade had turned his love of math to loathing.

He had to keep trying, knowing his mom would scream and cry if interrupted. Only twice had he ever pushed himself out of the closet, both so he did not go to the bathroom in his pants, but his mom had frightened him so much the second time that he peed in the closet the next time. Soon discovered, a frosted man bellowed about being tricked, disgusted by Tristen's appearance and smell, running out the door before paying. His mom now demanded he pee before she began work and placed a large bottle in the closet for him to use if he could not hold it.

Tristen hated the bottle, always making a mess and causing the closet to keep that lingering smell of urine.

The second-hand lamp flickered over his work as the wires became faulty with movement. Tristen went to his knees, reached up, and slowly moved the lamp to find that right spot for steady light. Pain pulsed through his ring finger. Tristen jerked back; a small spider scurried to one of the dark recesses of the closet. He tried to steady himself, but the jerking motion caused him to lose balance on his wobbly knees, numb from the cramped space. He fell into the closet door. He held his breath, thankful that the force had not caused the door to open.

Then Tristen heard yelling—his mom screaming. The closet door opened, Tristen's face suddenly inches from the man's thing. Tristen fell back, hitting his head on the closet wall, one of his earbuds falling out.

"What is this? What the fuck is this? You have a kid in the same room. This is sick. I'm out of here." The man scrambled around, pulling up his worn gray underwear and grabbing pieces of a frayed suit.

"Not without paying me first," his mom screamed, pulling at the pants in his hand. "You owe me a hundred dollars."

"I don't owe you shit. Get the hell off me, you whore. I ought to call social services."

He pushed her back, causing her head to hit the metal bedframe. His mom slowed as she patted the back of her head, then looked at the spots of blood on her hand. Tristen hollered at the man, aiming to punch him in his private region. His mom had taught Tristen that if anyone tried to hurt or touch him in a way that made him feel bad, he should strike that area to cause the bad man to go away. Finally, Tristen jabbed a small fist into the man's scrotum. The man roared, shoving Tristen into the nightstand. Tristen cried as his right shoulder throbbed.

The man left with his clothes draped around him, calling Tristen's mother more names. Tristen cried over the searing pain throughout his arm, longing for his mother. He knew she was disappointed at him for ruining her night—that they needed the money and could be kicked out for failing to pay rent for another month.

"Get in the closet, Tristen."

He cried, "Mom, I'm sorry. A bug bit me, and I got frightened."

"I don't care," she said. "Get in the closet. I need to figure out how we are going to stay in this shithole." She pushed herself off the floor, her face grimacing with pain. Tristen did not move, hoping she would change her mind. "Do you want to be homeless, Tristen? Do you want to live on the streets? You need to be a good boy and stay quiet. Now, please get in the closet."

She pointed at the door. He passed by her, flinching at the blood. He whimpered, upset that he had done all he could to be a good boy and still found himself in the closet. Tristen turned off the light, curled himself up in a ball, and tried to forget that bugs bite in dark hovels.

He woke in the morning to his mom frantically pulling him out of the closet, begging him to be on his best behavior. He started crying, picking himself up, hating the disruption of his sleep. He had neared forgetting about the events of last night.

His mom held him by the shoulders and whispered with fear, "Tristen, I need you to be good. There's a woman from social services at the door, who asked to look at the place. I bet that man from yesterday called. Unless you want to be taken away from Mommy, I need you to keep quiet. If she asks you questions, you should tell the truth but don't mention the closet or that man. That'll get us both in trouble. Okay?"

She wiped his face with her shirt, ridding him of the startled tears. She perked up a smile and hugged him. "Everything will be fine."

Another knock on the door. "Miss Etivil. Is everything okay? I know it's early, but I need to have a look through the premises."

His mom squeezed her eyes shut a few times, and Tristen wondered if the pain in her head remained. She then opened the door with an emphatic greeting to the homely older woman who walked right through the door. Tristen stood in place, afraid to make any wrong movement and upset his mother. He did not want to leave her.

The woman looked at the tiny boy in his plain orange shirt with jagged hems, blue jeans, and no socks. Tristen then saw her focus on his hair. He patted to find tufts of it sticking up on the right side, where he had lain.

"He just woke up," his mom said. "No time to fix his hair."

"Oh, that's all right. I'm sorry to have disturbed you so early, but we got an urgent call." The woman walked over to Tristen and bent down to his level. "I'm Deborah Lonert. What's your name?"

"Tristen," he said, being truthful without revealing too much, remembering his mom's words.

"Tristen, can you tell me where you sleep?"

His mom interjected, "Oh, he sleeps on the pull-out mattress from the couch over there near the bathroom. I know it's not the best setup, but I've tried to make do with our budget."

The woman opened the door of the closet and looked inside. Tristen could see her observing the blanket, pillow, lamp, and scattered homework. She sneered at his mom, then looked back in the closet.

"Can you please explain why it looks like a child sleeps in this closet? I don't see any blankets or pillows on the couch."

"Oh, Tristen just likes to play inside the closet sometimes. You know. Gives him a bit of his own space and all."

The woman turned to face him once again. "Tristen, do you like to play in the closet? I don't see any toys."

"Sometimes," Tristen said, not sure of the right answer.

"I wish you would direct your questions to me, ma'am," his mom said, eyeing the woman.

"Miss Etivil, I have been called with serious accusations, and I need to be able to conduct my job. I appreciate your patience."

"Call me Lilin," his mom said.

The woman looked down at her papers. "Ah, yes. Tristen, these next questions are going to be a little personal. Has your mom ever done anything naked with someone else while you were in this room?"

"How dare you?" his mom screeched, getting between the two of them. "What are you trying to insinuate?"

The woman sidestepped and looked down at Tristen. "Please answer the question, sweetheart."

Tristen did not want to lie, but he did not want his mom to get in trouble either. "I've . . . I'm not sure what you mean."

"See?" his mom said, waving her hand in front of the lady. "Can you please leave now?"

"Ma'am, you need to sit down, or I'll be required to take him with me right now and figure this out later."

His mom sat, arms crossed, glaring at Tristen. Tristen began to cry, not sure what he had done to make his mom so mad. He had not told on her, yet she still seemed frustrated with him. He looked at the lady, taking in shorts gasps of air.

"It's okay, honey. You're not in trouble. Were you ever told to get in this closet while your mom did stuff with a man on the bed?"

Tristen's crying had fogged his mind. He just wanted the woman to go away. He nodded his head, hoping that would end the conversation.

"Thank you, Tristen. I think you'll need to come with me until we can sort this all out." The woman placed her hand on his back, leading him out the door. "I'll be in contact."

"Why are you taking my boy?" his mom shouted. "I've never done anything perverted around my kid."

"Lilin, even if that may be so, having sex while a child is forced to sleep in a cramped closet is not appropriate. We will need to place him into foster care until such time you can provide him with a proper room without being privy to your private matters."

"How dare you judge me? I've raised my son to be a fine boy. Get your hands off him." His mom pulled Tristen back, shoving the woman away.

"Ma'am, if you touch me one more time, I will call the cops."

"Call the cops. You're trying to kidnap my son!"

The woman beckoned Tristen to follow her. His mom placed a hand on his shoulder. He did not know what he'd done wrong and just wanted to sleep. He pouted, waiting for someone to tell him what he was supposed to do. Deciding for him, his mom pushed the woman out the door, then slammed and locked it. They both listened for a response, but no noise came from the outside.

His mom spun to Tristen. "How could you tell that woman I've had sex while you were in the room? How could you do that, Tristen?" She got down to her knees, level with the frightened boy. "They are going to take you away, honey. Don't you understand? I'm going to lose you."

"Mommy, I didn't mean to do anything wrong," he wailed. "I'm sorry. Please don't let them take me away!"

His mom pulled out a suitcase from under the bed and began packing clothes.

"Mommy, are we moving?"

"We need to leave, Tristen. Start grabbing anything you want and throw it into the suitcase. We can't take everything, so choose your five favorite toys."

A loud knock on the door. "Police, open up!"

"Shit," his mom said. Tristen almost told her she said a bad word, but the look on her face made him keep quiet.

"Ma'am, we need you to open this door, right now."

Tristen headed to the door. He did not want his mom to be in trouble with the police. They would help him.

"Tristen. Don't touch that door. You need to stay by mommy."

"But Mommy, it's the police. Shouldn't we let them in?" A slam on the door caused him to fall backwards to the floor.

"Oh, dear God," his mom said, rushing and opening the door. "Sorry, I was in the bathroom. Can I help you?"

"Ma'am, I'll be arresting you for assault on Deborah Lonert. Your child needs to go with her for now."

His mom began crying, causing Tristen to sob on the floor. The officer that spoke handcuffed his mom while a second officer helped Tristen up. The officers led his mom out the door, saying things about "rights" and "silent." Deborah appeared after the officers departed, reaching out her hand for Tristen to grasp. Tristen kept his hands to his side, not wanting anything to do with the woman who had just stolen him from his mom.

"Tristen, you have to come with me. I'll be setting you up in a nice home, just until your mom gets herself situated. We don't want you to feel upset or bad, okay?"

He still would not look at her as he began to numb at the events, similar to the internal place he found in the closet when his mother worked—a zone that kept him from understanding the worst of the situation, remaining patient until he could return to the reality he preferred.

Through the disillusion, which Tristen felt must have lasted days, he found himself strapped in the back of the woman's car, a suitcase of his clothes and other toys next to him. She continued to talk about the wonderful home, that he would still get to go to the same school, and he would even get his own room.

Tristen perked up at the end, wondering what his room would be like. His own room sounded nice, but the closet had not been as cramped or confining as this woman claimed; he had the space to move and do his homework. Sure, he wanted to watch cartoons and go to the bathroom when needed, but these seemed like small sacrifices for his mother.

Tristen rolled his head back and forth, refusing to speak to the woman despite her questions about his friends and school. Given his insolence, she turned up the radio. He did not recognize the song but found the fun beats to be more uplifting than the drone of the woman. The constant twists and turns through the city left him unable to keep track of where he was being taken.

The clock indicated only ten minutes had passed when the car jerked a few times as the woman tried to parallel park, failing twice, horns honking at her. Once she had settled the vehicle at an odd angle but out of traffic, he turned his attention to the front of a brownstone building. He had never lived in a building with fancy iron rails. He wondered if these people owned the whole building. Would he get to live with someone rich? He began to forget his loneliness, thinking about all the wonderful toys and games these people might have. Maybe they would even let him take some back when his mom came to pick him up.

"When will my mom be getting me?" he said, unbuckling his seatbelt.

"I'm not sure, Tristen, but we hope soon. I'll be here to check in on you, to make sure everything goes well, okay? The Biltors are a wonderful family. They have one son, who's thirteen, and a dog named Theo. I'm sure you'd love to meet Theo, right?"

Despite his disappointment in not getting an answer about his mom, Tristen found the idea of a dog exciting. His mother would never let him have an animal. They simply did not have the room, his mom claimed, though he knew he would dutifully care for any creature.

Tristen got out of the car, trying to lug his suitcase with him. The woman ran around to help him pick it up, but he kept a hand on it, not wanting anything else to be taken from him today. He counted nine steps up to the door, each one closer to a new world. Instead of walking into a house, they walked into a hallway similar to his apartment. The brown boxes to the left, marked for mail, along with the mahogany wood floors and vibrant white walls contrasted with his old hallway with markings all over the wallpaper and matted carpet. He wondered if he was being forced to live in a church, the only place he could fathom being this clean. Even school did not make him feel so foreign.

They walked further down the hallway, bypassing the stairwell to the right. He tried to peek up, curious as to what lingered above, but hurried along, not wanting to lose sight of his suitcase. The social worker knocked on the first door to the left. Without pause, the door opened to a considerable woman wearing a flowery dress, ready to welcome them.

"Oh my gosh. Hi, Deborah." The women hugged each other while Tristen stood outside the door, unsure if he was welcome. He had learned well enough to wait until invited.

"Oh, this must be Tristen. He's so big and strong. You described him perfectly," the woman said, tapping the social worker on the arm. The boisterous woman walked over to him and gave him a hug without warning; his arms squeezed to his sides. The woman crouched down to Tristen's face. "I hope you'll feel welcome here, Tristen. You will be just as much a part of the family as anyone else. I'm Donna, but if you prefer, you can call me mom. I'm happy with whatever you are comfortable with."

Tristen would not be calling this woman 'mom' anytime soon, but she seemed nice enough, so he spoke out a soft, "Thanks, Donna."

"Oh, what a gentleman," Donna said, scooting him inside. The apartment seemed both large and small to Tristen. Large because he had only ever slept on either the pull-out bed, Mom's bed, or occasionally the closet, all in the same room. However, he did not see any bedrooms, only the wide kitchen with a center aisle, a dining room table with an ornamental chandelier, and the living room to the left with an area rug of crisscrossed designs, a matching black couch and love seat, and a massive television attached to the wall.

"Would you like any cookies, Tristen? I made a whole batch of them to celebrate your arrival." Donna presented the tray. He looked at them, unsure if this meant he should grab one now. How many was he allowed to take? He reached out when Donna pulled back the tray. "Oh, dear. Do you have any allergies? These have nuts in them. I didn't even think to ask beforehand. Jonathan—that's my son," she said with a beam. "Oh, his school is just adamant about being aware of other students' allergies, and look at me possibly poisoning the poor child."

Tristen had not been aware of any allergies that would keep him from eating the cookies ripped away from him. One time, his face had swelled up when he fell into a patch of poison ivy at the park. His mom had been distraught over the doctor's bill, so he learned to tread carefully on the trail of any park they visited thereafter.

"I don't see any allergies listed in his paperwork," Deborah murmured.

"I'd rather not risk it until you are sure. Let's show you your room, Tristen. You can get settled in while I talk to Deborah here."

Donna led him down a small hallway in the back with a banner stating, "Welcome, Tristen!" Tristen saw the hallway ended at a large bathroom with a circular tub and two sinks. Another door stood across from his with a clear warning: "Keep Out."

Donna must have seen Tristen's confusion. "Oh, that's just Jonathan's little joke on the family. We had an argument a few weeks ago when I went to clean out his room. I must remember to respect his privacy." She laughed, blushing slightly.

Tristen did not know what to do with this bit of information, so he turned the knob of the room that was now his. He had never seen so much Pokémon memorabilia in his life. Sheets and pillows covering a queen-sized bed with a "Gotta Catch 'Em All" logo and various Pokémon that Tristen recognized but could not name. Three posters with legendary Pokémon, including his favorite, Articuno. A giant dresser with a mirror placed in the back-left corner of the room, a shaggy royal-red area rug, and a desk with paper and pencils. A closet with no door rested next to the desk with more clothes in it than Tristen had ever owned.

"I hope you don't mind the Pokémon. If you want us to get you something else, we can certainly go to the store and have you pick. Everything here is from one of Jonathan's phases when he was your age. I also found a bunch of his old clothes that may be too big for you." Tristen walked to the enormous bed, placing his hand over the soft sheets. "We just want to make you feel welcome. Please let us know if there is anything that you want or need."

"Thank you," Tristen said, embracing Donna, needing someone to understand the unfathomable loneliness he felt in that moment. He could tell Donna was a good person, despite his unrelenting desire to be with his mother.

When Tristen finally relinquished his hold, he looked upon Donna's face, tears resting on her cheeks. "If you want to take a bath or shower, there are towels in the bathroom, though I set one aside on the dresser. The right sink is yours with a new toothbrush and toothpaste just for you. I'll give you some time to settle in, but if you need anything, please come out to the kitchen, and I'll be happy to help."

She placed her hands on her hips, a smile splashed on her face. Tristen did not respond, looking down, unsure what he could possibly say to reciprocate the kindness. He knew he could not bring up wanting to see his mom. Donna gave a nod, then walked out and shut the door behind her. Tristen ran to the bed, threw his face into the pillows, and cried. His body convulsed with shudders of sobs as he tried to stifle the sounds to keep from bothering Donna.

He knew that he alone could not solve this despair. He did not want to like Donna—a feeling of betrayal toward his mother. What if he began to like this place more than his own home? His mother needed his protection. He would not come to care for these people but would bide his time until he and his mom could be safely together. He fell asleep, wondering if his mother was concerned about him, desperate to know where he slept too.

Tristen woke to a knock at the door. He shook his head, a patch of drool slinking from his mouth. He wiped his face on his sleeve and went to the door.

"I'm sorry for waking you, dear. I wanted to make sure you weren't hungry. It's almost 2 p.m., and I can't imagine leaving you hungry."

"Yes, please," Tristen said, then Donna led him to the kitchen. A cascade of Chinese food had been placed on the dining room table with more than five different types of dishes. His mother rarely left him hungry for long, but he had never seen so much food at one time.

His eyes must have revealed his thoughts, for Donna followed, "Oh, we don't expect you to eat all this, dear. Paul and Jonathan will be here sometime this afternoon. Paul just landed from a meeting at some place I forgot to write down," she laughed. "Thank goodness he never quizzes me. Jonathan should be home from school sometime around three." She brought Tristen over a plate and guided him to the line of rice and other dishes. "Don't be shy, now. We are a family that loves a good appetite. Oh, and don't you fret about school. You don't have to go this week while you settle in. Next Monday, you'll be going back like nothing ever happened. You don't have to tell anyone about your mother if you choose. We don't expect you to think badly of her. Bless me. If we all thought something ill about a mother who made mistakes, it would be a wonder why we ever stayed after exiting the womb." She laughed again, though Tristen did not quite understand, aside from knowing he did not need to feel shameful about his mother being taken by the police. Alas, meaningful words that did not change anything. He sat on the other side of the dining room table, unsure what was expected of him.

"You can sit in the living room and watch television if you want. I'm sure you can find something fun. Just try to keep the food on the table. Otherwise, Theo will be getting himself quite a meal." She dropped her plate down, causing some of the food to scatter onto the table. "Oh my God, I forgot about Theo! I didn't want him to jump on you first thing."

She rushed to a small central nook at the back of the apartment, between the dining room and living room, and opened the left door. "Wait, are you scared of dogs?" Donna said, as a little brown and white Cocker Spaniel barreled out, sniffing all around, then placed his paws up on Tristen's leg. Tristen smiled so big that his mouth began to hurt. He petted Theo behind the ear, to which Theo responded with a lick on the hand. "Oh, he loves you. I knew he would. I'm so happy you get along. Theo's been with us almost six years. He's been my buddy while Paul travels. Oh no, you won't be able to eat on the couch. Theo will jump all over you."

"I don't mind eating at the table," Tristen said. "I like him being out here." He glanced at the dog, sitting in patience, tail wagging furiously for some fallen food from Tristen. Tristen dropped two small pieces of chicken, giggling when Theo lapped up the food in two swift gulps.

"Don't feed him too much. He'll be going to the bathroom all over the place with too much Chinese food."

Tristen blushed. "Sorry."

"No need to be sorry," Donna said, sitting down with her mound of food. "I just hate the poor thing getting sick, and you don't know his bowels . . . yet," she laughed.

Tristen hurried with the remainder of his food, then asked to be excused. Despite their one-room life, his mom always demanded that he ask to be excused before running to some corner to read or play games. Donna nodded her head. He hurried to his room, checking to see if anything had changed. He really did have a room full of posters, toys, and Pokémon memorabilia along with a closet of clothes. He went to the bathroom, realizing just how dirty he felt in the pristine house. He stripped off his clothes, turned on the shower, and let the water rush over him for more than fifteen minutes.

When Tristen heard a door shut outside, he worried someone else might need the bathroom. He looked around for a towel, only then realizing Donna had left the towel in his room. He saw the small hand towel but did not think it polite to use that for anything but drying hands. He stood in the tub, letting himself drip for more than five minutes, the cold air making him shudder. When he felt dry enough, he opened the door to no one, then scurried to his room.

"Why are you running around naked?" came a voice from the room across from his. He slammed his door shut, then quickly put on the first pair of underwear, pants, and shirt that he could find. A knock on the door almost caused him to stick his head through the arm hole.

"Just a minute," he mumbled, then opened the door once fully dressed.

"Are you okay?" said a boy half a foot taller than Tristen with short black hair and a pudgy face. Tristen visualized this kid being quite the bully, but he had a pleasing smile that disarmed Tristen's instincts.

"Yeah. I forgot my towel."

"Oh, that's fine. I just wanted to make sure you knew where to find clothes. Why do you look so surprised to see me? Wait, did Mom forget to tell you she had a son? She is something else. I'm Jonathan," he said, putting his hand out. Tristen looked down at the extended hand. "Dad taught me a handshake eases any situation."

Tristen took the hand in hesitation. Jonathan squirmed around Tristen, looking at the room. "Wow. I hope you like Pokémon. I really can't believe she put all this out. Did you tell them you were obsessed or something?"

"No."

"Well, I hope you like staying with us. If you need me, just make sure you knock. Mom thinks barging into my room is okay and won't let me put a lock on the door. Anyways, nice meeting you." Jonathan raised his hand, walked past Tristen, and shut his door.

The following six days felt like a welcoming whirlwind, more of an onslaught to ensure his happiness than a warm environment in which he could ask for anything. He felt bombarded by pleasantries, having gotten used to him and his mother being in the same room with large bouts of ignoring each other in pretend privacy.

Tristen met Paul once, later that first night. A stocky, short man with a crew cut, he had a similar demeanor to his wife with a gruff layer added. Tristen saw the salesman in Paul, feeling he could not trust the constantly shuffling man, yet he wanted to trust him and have Paul like him. Paul left for another trip the following day, and Tristen did not see him again.

Tristen asked Donna about his mother a few times. Though Donna was never rude about his question, she would direct the conversation to the first random thought on her mind after a quick comment that his mother was doing her best. Tristen did not think Donna knew what his mom's best could be. That Sunday, Tristen asked if his mom was good, whether they could all live in this house together. Tristen loved living with Donna, but he yearned to have his mom back. Donna laughed, claiming that his mom would probably need more space, but they all wanted him to see her soon. Donna had spoken to the social worker, and his mom would be calling sometime that week to talk to Tristen. Tristen did not feel better about this, but at least he could find out how his mother had been doing.

That Monday, Donna escorted Tristen to the train to school. She asked if he wanted her to go with him, as she knew he was capable but still would love to make sure he was okay. Tristen nodded that he would be fine, telling her that he had been on trains alone many times. Donna did not look eased but handed him his backpack and a brown bag with a sandwich, apple, cookie, and drink.

Tristen's classmates pestered him as to where he had been before he could even place his bag on his set hook. He told them he got the flu, an excuse his mother had used at one of her past jobs that did not seem to get her into trouble. They quickly lost interest, having hoped that his absence held a story beyond the mundane. Tristen enjoyed being back in class, especially since his teacher pulled him aside at lunch to tell him he would not need to make up all the work from the prior week.

Though he missed his mother, he was beginning to enjoy the new foundations of his life. As he walked to the train station after school, thinking of the possibilities of food Donna could be making for dinner, he felt a hand on his shoulder. He jerked, ready to sprint away.

"Tristen, it's me."

He spun around to hug his mother. He began to cry, so happy to finally see her.

"Mommy, I missed you."

"I missed you, too," she said, squeezing him tight as people scurried around them to the train. She gently pushed him off, then squatted down to look him in the eye. "I've come to take you. The bad guys are saying you can't come home until I've made impossible changes that could take me months, if not a year. I can't be away from you that long, baby. You understand?"

Tristen did not understand, but he did not want to disappoint his mother, so he nodded his head.

"Good. I'm parked close to the school. I tried to find you earlier, and I'm glad I finally spotted you. We're going on a trip! Won't that be great?"

"Don't I need to get my stuff? Should I tell Donna and her family?"

"No, honey. We need to leave now. We'll move far away in the country, where we can get a big house for cheap. You'll make all kinds of new friends."

Tristen began to cry at all the changes. What had he done?

"I don't want to, Mommy."

His mom looked around at the people taking notice of the crying child. She tried to soothe Tristen, hugging him again, but he felt so alone. His mom grabbed him by both shoulders and looked him in the eye once more.

"Do you ever want to see Mommy again? You need to stop crying. We have to leave now. If we don't, you will lose Mommy."

Tristen tried to fight the crying, pulling back into sniffles, shaking his head no. He allowed his mom to pull him along, his arm starting to ache as she dragged him through the crowds. He soon found himself in their dilapidated brown Cadillac, sitting in the backseat with piles of their stuff from the apartment.

Once he saw the last of the city, he knew he had done something bad but did not know what. "Where are we going?"

"West, baby. We are going to drive as far west as we can go and then a few miles further. You'll get to choose the town! Won't that be fun? We'll pick a country lane on the map, and you can let me know if the town is okay."

Tristen wanted to call Donna. He had her number in his backpack, but he understood well enough that this would betray his mother. She needed him more than he needed that other family, so he accepted he would venture west with her. Perhaps they would find a nice town. They could have a two-bedroom apartment, a dog, eat mounds of Chinese food, and watch cartoons together, just like he'd always wanted.

Chapter 14

Clare is seventeen

Tristen sat in the solemn room, maintaining the same position at the edge of the bed facing the closet. Kelvin had been nice enough, but he already despised Rhonda. She hated him before he even spoke two words, her face unable to mask some preexisting assumption. He did not want to be here, deep in the country, stuck with these people that were no better than strangers, forced to take him for state money.

How could his mom have been so stupid? They had lived a better life once they drifted from the city, even if his mother continued her love of booze at the local bars. She told that shadow of a man, Roderick Oaper, about her escape with Tristen six years ago, while drunk at the bar. His mom reasoned that she had been dating him for close to a year, so what was the use of secrets?

She was right, at first—he kept their secret. That was, until Tristen caught the man in their living room getting a blowjob from some strange woman. Tristen did not believe Roderick spotted him, as he left and hurried off to tell his mother at the liquor store. She had been taking some backstock out to the front when he yelled for her to come out. He had been warned by the owner that his mother would be fired if he ever caught Tristen walking into the store.

His mom rushed out, telling him to calm down, questioning why he was back early.

"I found Roderick at home getting a blowjob from some skank."

"Don't say skank, Tristen. What are you talking about? Are you sure?"

"Mom, I saw him with his pants down, and she was licking his penis. I know what a blowjob is."

"Oh God," she said, dropping the carton of beer to the ground. "What am I going to do?"

"Kick him out, Mom."

"I suppose you're right, but I thought things were going so well."

"On our couch, Mom. Our couch!"

"Wait, why were you home so early? Weren't you going to the water park with Philippe's family?" she said.

Tristen looked away, feeling guilty. "I felt sick. I told them you were at work, so they dropped me off at home."

"I guess you do look a little pale. I wish they would have called."

"Mom! That's beside the point! What about Roderick?"

"I don't know. I'll think about it. Just go home and get some rest."

Tristen stepped back, disgusted at the idea of catching that man in the act once again.

She sighed. "I'm sure he's not there anymore."

Unfortunately, Roderick was there, though the woman had left. Tristen got into a yelling match with him, telling him his mom would be better off if he was gone. Before any physical altercation could begin, Tristen ran to his room and locked the door. He put in his headphones and drew up the volume to drown out the banging. He could see the door shaking with each pulse, but he focused on the music.

Tristen woke to the music still blaring from the headphones, though they now lay to his side. He thought he heard whimpering. He creaked open the door and looked out. No sign of Roderick. He walked into the living room, where his mom was crying into her hands holding a note that said, "I left like you wanted. I'm going to tell them what you did, bitch."

That was when Tristen discovered his mom had told Roderick their secret. Tristen proposed they run again, but his mom refused. She believed Roderick would not follow through and did not want to uproot their lives after so long.

One week after the incident with Roderick, his mom was arrested and taken across state lines, and he once again found himself in the foster care system. Only this time, he was left with a mediocre family with a middling income that lived in a country house connected to a gravel road. He also had no means of meeting or communicating with his mom.

The social worker was intent on keeping him in the same school district, but being tossed into the wilderness still felt like a punishment. So, he plastered himself into that position at the far corner of the room, looking at his phone every few minutes, wondering if his mom had memorized his number to call. Tristen could not think of a close friend that he could reveal his situation to. How do you explain you had been kidnapped from foster care by your own mother? He wished he could go back and make her follow the proper channels. The more he investigated the foster care process, the greater his belief that his mom would have gotten him back in less than three months. Now, she could end up in jail for years. A tear trickled across the bridge of his nose at the uncertainty.

That social worker made his mom out to be some pervert, but he believed his mom had done her best in the worst of situations. He did not agree with placing a child in a closet to have sex in the same room, but his mom had not been fornicating for fun—it was for survival. She did not deserve to be judged for keeping him alive and fed.

Tristen knew this family must think the worst of him. Why else would the mother take him through the house in such a rude fashion, telling him what he should not do, rather than any joys of living in the house? He kept silent throughout her instructions, offering only an initial smile and greeting. The more house he saw, the greater the longing for his home, his stomach wrenching at his plain room in this cold, lifeless house. He felt like a rolling cog for the family, a cylindrical continuance of lost children with no intention of making this space welcoming.

Tristen was in a haze, stuck in a meditative grasp of wishing himself out of the situation. He sat like this for more than an hour, fearful that if he moved, the intensity of his desire would falter, and his wish might not come true. Only until a soft knock, followed by more knocking, then another bout of knocking, did he release his tension and open the door. He smiled at the beautiful girl standing before him, taller than her mother but recognizable in features: flowing brown hair and a plentiful bosom that he tried not to be too obvious in observing.

"Hi, I'm Clare." She stuck her hand out, poking him in the stomach. She stepped back and laughed. "Sorry."

Tristen fought blushing. "That's okay. Nice to meet you. I'm Tristen."

He stepped back, sitting on his bed. Clare looked around the room, then at him. "I hope Mom wasn't too much to handle. She can be snappish when a new kid arrives. She takes to the younger ones more. You're the oldest boy we've had, so I can't imagine what she put you through."

"It's fine. I think I'm just overwhelmed by the sudden change."

Clare gave a smile, nodding her head. "Well, if you need anyone to talk to, I always try to be a helpful ear. Also, I know the room is lacking personality. You're welcome to look through some of the stuff we have in the closet if you want to put anything on the walls. Mom thinks leaving the space blank allows the kids to make the room their own, but it always makes me feel a little alienated and cold."

"I suppose I can try to find something to make the room mine."

He kept his gaze to his lap, discomforted by her compassion. He felt the pressure shift in the bed, the feeling of her body next to his. Tristen could not believe this lovely person had come from that woman, and suddenly he felt an arm embrace him. His head fell into the nape of her neck as he sobbed. He was embarrassed, but the agony poured out nonetheless. He prayed that Clare would be his friend.

He opened his eyes, a light glistening of snot evident on her shirt. "I'm so sorry," he said, jerking his head back, causing her to fall backwards onto the bed, her shoulder yanked with his embarrassment. "Oh my god. I'm sorry. Are you okay?"

Clare laughed, sitting up and looking at the mess on her shirt. "I'm fine, quit worrying. I planned on taking a shower anyways. Everyone cries when they get here. You've been torn from everything you know."

Clare patted him on the back, then closed the door behind her. Tristen groaned over the messy encounter. She had enchanted him with her kindness. Few women gave him attention—not that he looked ugly or disgusting, but he possessed a curt shyness that left him appearing aloof, indifferent, or insolent.

He had kissed three girls during his tenure at school, but only one led to a relationship involving a boring symphony of weekly phone discussions, hand holding, and a few moments of awkward discovery of the bottom portion of their bodies, leaving them feeling raw. She had moved on to someone else, who he expected discovered far more of her. He did not mind, wanting to keep his promiscuity to an elevated standard of lust, rather than a desire to not be left behind in teenage sexual awakening. His three friends claimed sexual completion, though Harold never identified the woman, insisting it was some friend of a cousin he met. None believed him, but Tristen supported his friends' endeavors, even the ones they dreamt.

Tristen lay back, studying the smooth white ceiling, save for a slight crack near the bottom right corner of the fan base. He should not be thinking of Clare in these crass ways. He must focus on her as a friend, ignoring the bubbling hunger.

Tristen double checked he had locked the door, even testing to see if the lock might be faulty, then pulled down his pants. He jerked off, trying to focus on an image of a naked woman from his phone. He wanted to play a video, but he could not get the data to work. He did not dare to ask Rhonda the Wi-Fi code, worried if she asked why, he would blush. Five minutes later, tissues in the trash, he lay on the bed, guilty that he had masturbated to thoughts of Clare. Now that the impulse had passed, he thought Clare deserved better than his imagination.

Suddenly the urge to pee struck. Had he needed to go to the bathroom all this time and forgot? He knew masturbating forced the urge. He listened for and heard the shower. Rhonda had mentioned another bathroom, but that was in her room, a space he was not permitted to roam. Rhonda's attitude would only get worse if he begged to use this prohibited bathroom within mere hours of introduction. He looked around for a bottle but could find no quick fix. He also worried that any attempt could cause spillage on the floor, possibly staining the carpet. He could not fathom explaining a urine stain.

Maybe he could pee outside. Within the darkness, he could sneak out the back door and urinate in the grass. But what if the grandmother or Rhonda caught him? He would be shipped off to another home; a home that might not have someone like Clare. A woman who let you bawl your deepest, most heartfelt sorrows into her shirt.

The most obvious solution startled him, but the reality stopped him, considering how absurd to have impure thoughts about a person, then to knock and ask her to exit the shower. Oh, but he had to use the bathroom so badly. He could not pee himself, oh lord, he could *not* pee himself the first night. Tristen tried punching himself in the crotch, hoping the pain would alleviate his need for some time. No relief came from the torture of his throbbing balls, and his need to urinate persisted. He was left with no choice. He must beg her to leave the bathroom.

Tristen crept to his bedroom door, unlocked it, then peeked out. He did not want to converse with Rhonda unless necessary. No sign. He tiptoed to the bathroom door, gave a soft knock, and said, "Clare, I need to use the restroom. Can you come out for a moment?"

Silence. No response that allowed him permission to enter the bathroom. He needed to pee, desperately at this point, furious at his position, upset that he had no logical choice at the end of this predicament. A small trickle of urine caused him to twitch. *Oh, help me,* he prayed. Tristen banged on the door. He waited, believing he heard the opening of the shower curtain but could not tell. Should he open the door?

"Oh, I'm going to pee myself," he whispered.

He opened the door a fraction. He waited for a scream. Hearing none, he opened the door further, eyes caught in the mirror, noticing Clare's back, the gentle glide to her butt. He thought he yelled out for her attention but did not know, lost in admiration.

"What the hell do you think you're doing?"

He fell into the door, causing Clare to scream at the sudden slam.

"Get out of there! You get out!"

Tristen pushed himself up, slipping on the bathroom floor, smacking his face. He crawled backwards and turned around to see Rhonda with a snarl, glaring through him into portions that he hoped would remain a mystery. He maneuvered up, trying to run by her down the stairs, falling into her. She cried out, but he could not check on her. He must get away. Away from Rhonda and her screaming, away from this cold house, and away from Clare, her lustful reflection still pounding through his head.

He ran out the door to the backyard patio, urinating through one of the spaces in the slats—a small relief until he recalled his predicament. He looked at the trailer in the dark. He did not know who or what resided in the dilapidated metal structure. He snuck back into the house, wishing only to grab his bags and make his way to the road. He would walk until he died. He could not live here. Lord knows the words Rhonda had said to Clare about him.

Then he heard screaming upstairs. Rhonda erratic, calling him a pervert, a monster, followed by Clare's soft voice of reason. He would not enter Rhonda's room. She would call the police with accusations that he waited to rape her, the horrid woman. The names that streamed from her mouth left him heartbroken. Had he been a pervert? He hadn't meant to catch a glimpse of Clare's beautiful body, and he would not have assaulted Clare within any stretch of his fantasies.

He went into the spare bedroom, softly opened the door, then closed it. He feared turning on the light. He sat on the floor, trying not to be seen through the window facing the front yard and driveway. He wanted to close the blinds but knew that any change would be recognizable to Rhonda's heavy eye. He fought crying. He did not want to make noise and feared that if it started it would not end. He longed to call his mom in prison.

He breathed deep, once, twice. He looked around for a plan. He could hide until everyone went to sleep. A clean escape in the safety of night. Two options, he reasoned: under the bed or in the closet. Tristen chose the closet, finding a certain safety in the confined space. No walk-in closet, but enough room to prop himself in the corner with bent leg room.

Lights beamed into the window, then stopped. He scrambled into the closet, closing the door. He practiced his breathing exercises, fighting the panic. His mom usually helped him, but this time he was alone. Tristen tossed his head, trying to maneuver out of the dangling clothes, deducing from their design they must be the grandmother's. Rhonda had mentioned the woman lived next door. He yearned for a kind, lovely older woman who would forgive him. He fell asleep as time ticked by, fighting the temptation to scramble into the countryside, accepting the inevitable.

Chapter 15

Clare is eighteen

Tristen passed Clare the opened Coke. "You know, I can drive some of the way." Clare smiled, keeping her eyes on the steep highway roads. "I know I just got my license, but come on, I'm a good driver. Your grandma even said so."

Clare took a sip of the Coke. Tristen eyed a dribble falling from her mouth, swept onto her sleeve. Nothing awkward or unusual about her actions, yet in his unrelenting passion for her, he found her quirky temperament irresistible. He never expressed his feelings. The past year had been a gust of going to school, explaining his situation without judgment, which had failed, enduring Rhonda's bitter hatred, his mother's scheduled trial which thankfully did not move forward, and a plea deal resulting in three years in prison followed by probation. His mom told him that the jail time could have been more severe. Her attorney had told her that this was the best result she could hope for in front of this judge. Tristen felt deserted.

Clare convinced Tristen to visit his mother in person, despite the sixteen-hour drive. Rhonda refused to see the woman, Kelvin could not take the three to four days off work, and Edna had general obligations with the church that she did not feel comfortable missing. At first, Rhonda refused to allow Clare to take Tristen, but Kelvin talked Rhonda into the trip, explaining that Clare had proven herself to be a responsible driver. Tristen also deserved the opportunity to see his mother.

Rhonda agreed only if the two slept in separate rooms at each hotel. Kelvin was chagrined at the increased charges. Eventually, Edna offered to cover half the expenses. Three weeks later, Clare and Tristen drove the hundreds of miles to the jail. Kelvin called ahead at each hotel, requiring they stop halfway in each direction. No consideration was made for flights due to the comparably extravagant costs along with the difficulty of getting to the prison from the airport.

Tristen spoke little during the drive, letting the myriad of radio stations guide their way: country, to classic rock, to country, more country, then NPR.

Tristen debated inviting one of his friends but enjoyed the idea of just him and Clare together. Harold, Tom, and Philippe all chided him that this was his chance. They made up stories of Tristen watching some romantic television with Clare in her room, the distance weakening to cuddling, then more. He played along, of course. They had known of his crush from the very first week. So deep that he'd turned down Trina Noret for a date. He could not fathom going with anyone but Clare, but he could not ask her. He maintained a simple lack of interest to Kelvin and Rhonda, who never seemed to notice anything.

Clare would probably go to prom next year with her friend Nick, who held no qualms about showing his infatuation with Clare. Clare had privately told Tristen that she was worried she led Nick on, though she told Nick consistently how much she valued their friendship. Nick refused to listen. He appeared to hold on to the old theory that being a nuisance would wear a woman down. Tristen was firm that Clare could not be that woman. He told Clare that Nick pushed too hard; she needed to be careful around him. She laughed, claiming Nick to be nothing more than a harmless, gangly bear. In jealous rebuke, Tristen pointed out a bear is still a bear; their instinctual nature would reveal itself whether you wanted to believe it or not.

They neared the halfway stop around Columbus, Ohio. Tristen mentioned doing a little sightseeing, but neither found a point of interest. They arrived at the Best Western just after four in the afternoon. Tristen lugged both suitcases while Clare checked in, being the adult with a credit card on this trip. She led them to their rooms, next to each other, and they agreed to meet for dinner at seven. Clare claimed desperation for a nap and waved him goodbye.

Tristen stood in the hallway, his keycard in hand, wishing he had the pride to knock on Clare's door and kiss her. Instead, he slumped, inserted the card, threw his luggage on an isolated green chair, and flopped down on the queen-sized bed. He threw off his shoes, flipping through channels without purpose until Clare knocked on his door.

"You ready?" he heard behind the door.

He looked around, worried Clare would judge him for not changing clothes. Nothing he could do now, slipping out the door to greet her. Thankfully, she also wore the same clothes from the drive. She smirked, then hurried down the stairs toward the car. He followed in quick step, looking anywhere else but the fantastic outline of her jeans.

"Where do you want to eat? I hate to admit it, but I'm craving Olive Garden. All I can think about is unlimited breadsticks. Those snacks did not fill me up during lunch."

She slipped into the driver's seat, not waiting for his response. He rushed into the passenger seat and gave her a marked, "Sure."

"Great! There's a location about six minutes from here. I knew you would say yes, so I scoped one out."

Tristen smiled, unsure how to respond. Clare turned up the music as they coasted through the light traffic. The restaurant had a twenty-minute wait, and Clare wanted to call one of her friends about some project she wanted to work on during the trip. Tristen sat on the edge of one of the benches against the wall, surrounded by families squeezed together in corners. Tristen studied Clare through the clear doors, walking back and forth, laughing with exaggerated hand motions. Her hair twisted with the wind, slapping her in the face twice. Someone might have thought her messy, but he liked her carefree absurdity.

"Is that your girlfriend?" asked an older gentleman next to him.

Tristen kept silent for a moment, then shook his head no.

"Well, you better snatch her up. She's very pretty, and I see the way you look at her." He laughed with a soft wheeze. Tristen looked around, terrified of other patrons eavesdropping on this conversation and telling Clare, yet no one took interest.

"I like her, though," Tristen admitted.

"Attaboy. I thought I saw that look on your face. Young love is a beautiful thing. Does she know how you feel?"

"Phileke, are you bothering that poor boy?" said another man.

"I'm just trying to tell the boy he needs to tell her how he feels. It took me years of wasted time to tell you how I felt."

Tristen prayed for an out from this conversation, answered by the buzzer letting him know their table was ready. "Thank you for the advice," he mumbled. He tapped the window near Clare and hurried to the waitress.

They each got waters and the free unlimited soup, salad, and breadsticks, saving their money for a better dinner after the jail visit, noticing the waitress roll her eyes at their order. While they waited, children screamed and spread their food amok. Some parents looked regretful, others enamored by every gesture.

"Are you excited to see your mother? Only two more days. I thought about leaving early tomorrow so you could visit her twice, if you want."

"Wouldn't work. We would have to arrive by one in the afternoon, meaning we'd need to leave around four in the morning. I don't think I'll be in the mood." Tristen played with his straw wrapper, stealing quick glances at Clare. He hoped he had not hurt her feelings. She focused on her phone, paying no mind.

"Oh, sorry to hear. Are you happy to see her?"

"I miss my mom, if that's what you're asking. I'm not sure if I want to see her in a prison setting, though. I'm worried that I'll start crying. I hate the idea of her being trapped in that monstrous place just because she wanted to be with me."

Tristen clenched his fingers tight into his leg. He fought the panic, the pain, the need to cry. He wanted to show Clare that he could be a man during the worst of life, that she could look to him for comfort, not the other way around. He dreaded the idea of her coming to his side of the booth and consoling him. He suddenly craved solitude in the busy restaurant.

Clare glanced at him. He darted his eyes down to the breadsticks, grabbing and shoving one into his mouth. Divergence. Clare eyed the breadsticks and took her own as well.

"I'm sure your mother doesn't blame you for what happened. You were nine. We've talked about this. There is no way this is your fault. I know that doesn't help, but you must know."

Tristen quickly nodded his head, then began to choke on the breadstick. He grabbed water to help him swallow. He could not find his breath, and the water gurgled in his throat. He pushed against his diaphragm, needing release. He panicked, motioning to his throat, signifying his struggle. Clare yanked him out of the booth and began giving him the Heimlich. Pain wrenched into his ribs, though his fear of dying prevented him from shoving her off. The breadstick spewed into the booth, and he immediately gasped for air. Clare guided him down to sit, rubbing his back, asking him questions that he could not understand—just whooshes of sound spiraling around him. He hated the stares, feeling reduced to a boy who could not eat a damn breadstick.

"Please, can we leave?" he croaked out, his body aching.

Clare grabbed the glass of water and led him to the front, resting him on a bench outside while she paid. Tristen rocked a little, the near-death experience pulsating through his body.

Clare rushed out, an Olive Garden bag in hand. "Let's go," she said, leading him to the car. He shuffled inside, leaning his head on the window as soon as Clare shut the door. He tried to remember what had startled him so much that he almost lost his life. Tristen's mind kept circling to his mother's restrained predicament, along with his tumultuous feelings for Clare. Had God intended to punish him for one of these plights?

Tristen did not latch onto faith like Clare's grandmother. None of the family cared much for the sporadic forced church gatherings, other than Rhonda. Out of sheer boredom, Tristen figured.

Imagine dying by choking on a breadstick. His friends and classmates would have talked about his absurd loss of life until their final days. A warning to children to chew thoroughly before swallowing. In that capacity, Tristen could be a folk tale, a fun mechanism in saving lives. Tristen smiled at the thought of being a choking legend.

Back at the hotel, he made it to his room on his own, though he still ached. Clare gave him four Tylenol and asked if he wanted her to stay over. He wanted nothing more, but not in his current state of botched rigor mortis. He told her no. A look of sadness came over her face, or maybe worry, but Tristen thought he also saw hope that he would have said yes. She respected his answer and left. He fell asleep, wondering what his mother would say to him first.

Neither spoke the next morning other than short spurts of no substance. Tristen's throat felt scratchy, and he thought he sounded like a wheezing smoker, but Clare reassured him. He swallowed a chain of cough drops to lubricate and ease his throat. Neither talked about his mom, quickly arriving at the second hotel with little fanfare.

Clare brought a Subway sandwich to his room, knowing he preferred roast beef on rye. She did not ask to stay, and Tristen did not offer. He was still disgusted over the restaurant debacle, wanting to wade through his misery alone.

Clare could not even attend the prison visit—only one visitor allowed per inmate. Some exceptions could be made for children with an adult, but not in their context. He throbbed in silent fear of going into the prison alone, the iron gates shutting, trapped with a cascade of strangers visiting other detained women.

Tristen contemplated getting back at his mom's ex-boyfriend, the sniveling lunatic. He'd discussed with Clare possible retribution: extreme toilet papering, but the man did not have a house of his own; stink bomb, but he lived in an apartment complex that would cause harm to others; pooping in a bag and setting the bag alight, but the same problem regarding the co-tenants. Tristen rarely thought of Roderick Oaper anymore, not until this trip had been proposed. He wanted to punch him in the face, but Tristen knew that prison would destroy him.

Tristen questioned what he could tell his mother that would interest her. He did not want to tell her about going to an amusement park, relaxing with his friends and playing video games, or that he'd managed to pass all his classes this year. How would the ease of his life make her feel better? On the phone, his mother had grown stifled and tired, sounding uninterested in their conversations.

Tristen finished his sandwich, turning up the television to soothe himself, though he soon drifted into self-pleasure. Only moments later, a knock at the door startled his rhythm. Tristen strained to zip up his pants, careful not to harm himself. He hated having to stuff himself away, worried someone would look down at the bulge, "Pervert" screamed through the hallways. He then realized the knock was likely Clare. He turned red, hoping she would not notice, her likeness in full nudity now roaming in his mind. He looked through the peephole to Clare and opened the door.

"Hey, I wanted to make sure you were okay. You all set for tomorrow? You want to talk?"

"No, not really," he said, fidgeting behind the chained door. He had not offered to let her in, and she became visibly uncomfortable by the separation.

"I guess I could have texted. Sorry. After yesterday, and with tomorrow, well, you know. Just please come to my room if you need anything."

Tristen nodded, then closed the door. His erection would not dissipate, moving the flush of blood to his face. He knew how rude he had been, but for her to see him in that state would have been worse. The trade-off for now over eternity seemed clear to him. He grabbed his phone to send her a text.

"Sorry for being so out of it. I just woke from a nap. I am nervous but more for Mom than me. Thanks for being so supportive."

He threw his phone on the bed, not wanting to second guess his decision to hit send. A buzz came immediately. He rushed over, throwing himself on top of his phone.

"No worries, lol. Of course. I'm here for you."

Tristen folded the phone into his arms. He had fallen for a perfect, unattainable woman: a beacon of support, a furtherance of his every need, a caretaker and friend in one. He realized that she might never want to date someone with his characteristics. She would want a man, not a boy. He would need to relinquish some of his reliance on her, display his resilience. He went through his normal routine and fell asleep early that night.

Tristen awoke exhausted and nervous. He had failed to sleep a solid two hours without startling himself in sweats. He did not know the reason for his increased apprehension other than his abhorrence of prisons. He needed to visit his mother, to show his strength to Clare. He refused to show trepidation.

He met Clare in the lobby at 7:30 to be at the prison by 8 a.m. They arrived at the lot, which already seemed quite full, concerning Tristen over how many visitors the prison allowed in per day.

"I don't think you have to stay out here," Tristen said once Clare parked. "I expect they get nervous when people wait in their cars. I'm sure they have a lounge area that you can relax at."

"Honestly, I don't want to wait in the lounge area of a prison, Tristen. I can deal with any questions out here. Unless you want me to go with you?"

Bravery in mind, Tristen shook his head. "No. I just wanted to make sure you'd be okay."

He closed the door and lumbered toward the entrance, careful not to catch the eye of any other visitors. He could not fathom discussing his reasons for being here.

Luckily, no one spoke to him except the officers in harsh tones of judgment. A small, fit woman asked that Tristen place all his personal items in a small container. He tossed everything he had from his pockets, then she placed the container on a conveyor belt. Tristen kept his eyes on his property, not noticing another voice until he yelled, "Sir, do you want to walk through or not?" Tristen turned to see a stretch of a man, who clearly wanted to boom but only sparked. Despite the man's lack of intimidation, Tristen rushed through the metal detector. A loud beeping made him freeze. The man, now identified as Trip, led Tristen to the side. Another man asked if he had any metal on him, then patted him down thoroughly. Though uncomfortable, Tristen tried to make his mind escape these awful touches. Of course, he had no identifiable contraband. Tristen grabbed his personal effects, then moved to a visitor's room on the side of the long hallway.

Only a scattered few sat around the tables in the room, some standing in line near a desk. He worried he needed to check in. No one had told him what to do next. Everyone seemed to be a regular. Did they know he did not belong here? No one paid him any mind, so he sat at one of the empty benches off to the side. Thirty minutes passed, then Tristen saw people continue to step into the line at the desk. He knew he needed to report at this point but felt awkward that he had already sat for so long. He did not want to embarrass himself any further.

When the line dropped to two people, he shimmied toward the desk, trying to exhibit the attitude that he had meant to wait the whole time. His turn came quickly, and he had not prepared, so he said, "I'm sorry."

"Sorry? For what?" said the gentleman, eyes behind glasses studying Tristen's face. "Who you here to see?"

"Oh, Lilin. My mom."

"Who? I don't see her here."

"Lilin Etivil."

"Okay, okay. Let me look through my lists. I don't see her, but you just wait a minute there."

Tristen thought he might be in trouble, as if he had reported his mom to the police for some crime. He looked back at the crowd as eyes began to focus on him as entertainment, a steady cycle thrown off course. He tried not to engage, but the more he fought their gaze, the more his awkwardness increased with side glances and twitches.

"Hey kid. Your mom can't have visitors today. Sorry." Tristen did not find him apologetic at all, as the officer flipped through his paperwork.

"What do you mean? We drove a thousand miles to get here. What happened?"

The man stared, brow furrowed into his glasses, nose flickered in annoyance. "Sorry, sir. I can't tell you that."

"Do you know when I can see her?"

Exasperated sigh. "Let's just say I would not wait around for less than thirty days."

"What happened?" Tristen yelped. "Is she okay? Is she in the hospital?"

The officer stood. "You need to calm down, kid. She's fine. She got into some trouble and lost her visitor privileges. I honestly can't tell you more than that because I don't know more." The officer took two deep breaths, as tears welled in Tristen's eyes. "Look. I'm sorry, but I can't do anything. I think she may be allowed calls soon, so she'll probably call you. I would just head home. There's nothing more for you here."

Tristen nodded his head, more in observance of the officer's authority than in agreement. He refused to look at all the faces—masks of pity. He walked by the metal detector, out the prison door, and then knocked on the car window. Clare turned with wide eyes, then hit the unlock button.

He rushed inside the car and let out a flood of emotions. Tristen could not identify his greatest sorrow: his shame, his mother's situation, or his feelings of abandonment. He felt them all in a whirl. Clare rubbed his back, not asking what happened.

After five minutes, Tristen's chest still heaved in pain, but he managed to bawl out, "Can we just go home?"

"Sure," Clare said, turning on the car and exiting the parking lot. She turned up the music to some classical station. Tristen wondered if she felt embarrassed by his display. He had prepped himself to stifle these damn emotions, but another problem arose with each new resolution. He would never be the man Clare would want. She needed someone with greater resolve and an understanding of timing in these unpleasant displays. He tucked his head against the corner of the seat, falling asleep.

Tristen woke to the smell of fried chicken. He fought against his mood, focusing on his hunger. Clare smiled when he turned to her.

"I hope you're feeling better. You slept for over three hours. I stopped at a Popeyes. There's a meal in the backseat if you want." He nodded his head and ravaged the chicken in quick bites. "Did you want to tell me what happened? Did your mother say something?"

He swallowed the clump of fries in his mouth. "I didn't get to speak to her. They told me she wasn't allowed visitors. Honestly, Clare, I don't want to talk about it. What am I going to tell your parents? How is this going to look to them? We travel all this way, and my mom can't behave well enough to see her son."

"You don't know what happened, Tristen. Maybe she was defending herself. I'm sure she would have called if she could have."

Her words did not ease his wounds, and he was determined not to talk about this debacle of a trip. They made their way to the next hotel after four more hours on the road, heading straight to their rooms, each exhausted for their own reasons.

That evening they got dinner at a local Chinese restaurant and ate in Tristen's room. Tristen put on a Julia Roberts movie, *Runaway Bride*, knowing Clare adored Julia Roberts. Tristen ate at a corner table, and Clare at one of the nightstands.

"You know, I'll support whatever you want to tell Mom and Dad. If you want to say that everything went fine, then you should. How would I even know unless you told me?"

"I don't know. I don't want to lie, and my mom may call to tell them that she's sorry for missing the scheduled visit."

"You're right. Mom would hassle you for lying if she found out. They won't say much. It's not like you knew beforehand."

"I wanted to see her, Clare. I don't care about appearances. I just wanted to make sure she was okay." Tristen began crying once again. Furious at another display, he pounded his hand on the desk, causing the rest of his food to flip and fall on the floor. "Shit, I'm sorry."

"You don't have to be sorry to me," Clare said, pity all over her face. "We'll just leave a bigger tip for the hotel staff."

Tristen regarded her carefully, exhausted at the excuses she kept making for him.

"I'm sorry I'm such a mess, Clare. I had hoped this trip would bring us closer, but I feel I've been a sniveling baby the whole time."

"Oh, come off it, Tristen. Anyone in your situation would be crying nonstop. I think you are brave, given all you've gone through. You have to remember that I've met many foster kids, each with a reason for living with us." Clare patted the bed. "Come lie next to me and watch the movie."

Tristen eyed her, then the bed. He slumped over and lay on the far corner, though his excitement welled up. To his chagrin, Clare kept to her side of the bed, feet on the floor, eating off the nightstand, attempting to keep any food from dropping on the floor. He scooched a little further to the center, praying for Clare to take the hint, attempt to comfort him.

"You keep looking at me," Clare said, though she did not sound offended.

"Sorry. I'm just appreciating how nice you are. I don't think you know how much you mean to me, Clare."

Clare moved toward Tristen. Tristen sat up, not sure what she planned to do. She grabbed his arm and placed it over her shoulder.

"There you go. Now I feel appreciated," she said.

Tristen felt the heat rising from her touch. He fought himself, trying to think of any object that would sway his body. None. He tried to be sly, pushing his penis to the side to keep from rising too obviously. He appreciated just holding her this way and did not want to creep her out.

Tristen then felt a soft kiss on his lips. He did not move into the unexpected affection, jerking back. Clare looked at him, expectant. Tristen did not know what to say, so he kissed her back. Clare pulled away as soon as he went to caress the outside of her breast.

"Tristen. I know we aren't related, but I think my parents would still be upset if they found out. You have to promise that you won't act weird or do anything obvious. Mom would immediately try to get you sent to a new family. Physical clinginess would be apparent to Mom. We'll have to be sly. Can you promise to keep a secret?"

"Yes, of course," Tristen said, though he would have promised to give an organ, if it meant he could touch Clare again. He pulled her closer, kissing her neck, and thanking the gods that wishes do come true.

Chapter 16

Clare is eighteen

Tristen once more found himself lamenting—the worst breakup he'd ever experienced and now he was forced to live near Clare's friend, lover, whatever she called him that day. Nick had intruded on his life and made winning Clare back infinitely harder. Ever since Rhonda had discovered their sexual trysts, Clare had all but formally declared the relationship over. He had not seen her naked in six months, though she had wandered twice to his room in a drunken stupor, as if she sought some forlorn memory. He had tried to rekindle passion, but she could not be reasoned with.

He had told the boys in the vaguest terms about his sexual conquest, though he knew they did not believe him, since he refused to tell them who, where, or even when, in fear they could figure out Clare's identity with these details. He stopped bragging when he realized none of them listened, preferring concrete facts over his alleged exploration of the mystery woman. For them, the allusion was no better than a spirited tale of their youth when they had to use their imagination of a woman's secrets. Now old enough to easily search porn, these boys needed referenced physicality of the domain.

After Clare refused any further advances, Tristen thought of slamming her name to her friends, spreading rumors during the final moments of her senior year of high school. He did not know what he expected from the rumors but guessed it would somehow affect her. He made no such revelation, though. He reasoned that this profession would shatter any chance he had of winning her back. He just needed to bide his time, or so he thought.

Regrettably, Nick moved into that damn trailer. Tristen knew better than to hate Nick outright. Given the recent death of Nick's father and his choice to raise his sister, Isla, so she could continue at the same school, any slander would result in his own demoralization. Nick possessed the status of sainthood at the moment, even to Clare's parents.

Tristen could not fathom Clare having feelings for Nick. She had firmly stated that they were friends, despite Nick's advances. Nick never shied from showing his feelings for her, but she had expressly told Nick that his moving into the trailer would need to make these displays stop. This seemed to be Clare's one condition in offering the space of the trailer for free. Rhonda frowned on the idea, so naturally Edna supported it wholeheartedly, which granted Nick instant access to the trailer.

Three weeks into the invasion, Tristen felt even more like an outsider, as Clare spent inordinate amounts of time at the trailer. Now no affection drifted his way. He longed to have Clare for his own once more and could not understand what he had done wrong to end their love so quickly. Not that Clare had ever used that word exactly—love—but she smiled when he uttered it to her after another bout in his bed. He did love her. Undeniably, the best person he had ever cherished, so this increasing distance ripped at his emotional core.

As Tristen withdrew from his friends the last few months—rarely offering to hang out or play video games—Philippe had been the only one to ask how life was going. He engaged Tristen, invited him for pizza, encouraged him to tell him what was bothering him. Philippe guessed girl trouble, but Tristen adamantly denied it. He ultimately offered the reason of missing his mother, a reason none of them could fight or fix.

Not an outright lie. Tristen did miss his mother, though the calls had become less frequent over the last few months. Another flaw in his emotional wellbeing. His mom had been repeatedly apologetic for the debacle of missing his visitation, though she refused to expand on the reasons.

"Not safe," she said.

He wanted to express his troubles with Clare and obtain her advice, but his mother's situation made him feel constricted, expecting someone else in the house would eavesdrop on his childish predicament. He considered talking to Kelvin, in the vaguest of terms, but worried Kelvin would investigate. He got along with Kelvin well enough but figured the man would throw him out if he discovered the violation of his daughter under his roof. Thankfully, Clare's threats to her mother had kept Rhonda from telling the others, though her quiet hostility against Tristen was ever present.

Tristen heard a knock on the door. He grunted into his pillow, hating being disturbed in the deepest of his wallowing. Another knock forced him to roll out of bed and open the door. He smiled; Clare stood before him.

"Hey, Nick is having a few people over at the trailer tonight if you want to join. Probably just to play cards." She continued, whispering, "Someone is supposed to be bringing over a fifth of whiskey, maybe more, so once we're sure my parents are asleep, we'll be really ready to party."

Tristen hesitated before her, blank. He knew her offer to be friendly, but he could not extinguish the continuing lust in every glance at her. Her withdrawal made him yearn to touch her, just one more time.

"You okay? I think it'll be fun. You haven't really gotten to know Nick and his sister very well."

"Are you dating him?"

"What?" she said.

"Are you seeing Nick? Is that why you won't be with me anymore?"

Clare shoved him inside his room and shut the door. "What the hell do you think you are doing? What if my dad heard you?" She sat on the bed with a bullying glare. "And it's none of your business, Tristen. I'm not, but it's none of your business. We had our fun, and I'm sorry that everything got awkward, but I thought you understood this was over."

"But why?" he whimpered, dropping to his knees.

"What do you mean, why? People our age see other people. You're cute. Go meet a nice girl. Give her that sweet, sensual touch you're so good at."

She smiled, pushing back his hair. Tristen wanted to believe this affection to be more than just a pitiful display toward a child. He felt lectured at rather than supported.

"Does that mean we'll never have sex again?"

She laughed. "Oh, I don't know. Who knows what might happen in the future? But I need you to understand that you should go and explore, meet others."

Clare patted his head, then walked out of his room before he could respond. She gave him hope—a hope that they could find entangled happiness once again. Tristen knew the chances were small, but the spark of possibility still existed. He needed to go to this party. Maybe, if he buddied up with Nick, Clare would appreciate his efforts, finding him charming.

Tristen wondered if Nick's sister, Isla, would stay in her room or come enjoy the party, too. He had spoken to Isla only a few times—outgoing, though a little aloof, and a year younger than him. Maybe he could convince Isla to help him with Clare, especially if she also did not like the idea of Nick and Clare dating.

Tristen stood, looking at the dimming sky. A smile broadened on his face as he imagined another chance with Clare. He did not want to see other women. They bored him. Clare gave him excitement, a challenge. He looked through his closet, hoping to recall outfits that Clare had told him looked good.

A few hours later, Tristen walked out to the backyard, knocking on the trailer door that burst open to a tower of a man looking down at him. Nick seemed daunting due to his height, but once anyone got to know his mildness, pot usage, and lack of ambition in working out, his intimidation dissipated. Tristen still hated being forced to look up to talk to Nick, as if this quality alone made Nick superior.

"Hey, Tristen. Come in." Nick moved to the side, welcoming him. "I'm not sure when everyone else will be here, if they're even coming at all. Clare's in the bathroom. She stole a box of her grandma's wine. You want any?"

"Sure."

Tristen slid down onto the worn couch. Nick had not removed any of Clare's great-grandfather's furniture. He wondered if her great-grandfather's clothes remained in the closets. Nick seemed like someone that would wear anything if it fit. Tristen reminded himself that this man was putting off college to raise his sister for three more years. Competition for Clare, yes; asshole, probably not.

Tristen then noticed the paused screen for *Call of Duty*. The faint smell of weed lingered under the rolling scent of Febreze. Tristen despised shooting games, mostly due to the childish behavior in online play. He either played with friends or alone.

A red Solo cup was thrust under his nose with a sickening bland smell of white wine. "I'm sure you've had some before, but I'll warn you anyways, take three big gulps and let the alcohol simmer. Then the taste isn't so bad."

Tristen took the cup and followed Nick's advice, taking three big gulps that left a bitterness in his mouth. He had no desire to smoke pot, knowing he would reek when returning to the house. An unspoken understanding took place that proclivities stayed out here.

"Where's Isla?"

"Staying at some friend's house. Kayla Perterken."

"How's that going?" Tristen said, his mouth feeling a little looser, taking another sip.

"As well as can be expected, man. It's weird being the parent of a sibling, but she's so responsible. She'll take care of herself. I just wear the badge of protector."

"It's great you stayed."

"Yeah," Nick said, looking in his cup.

"Look who came," shouted Clare, coming out of the bathroom, her glossy red eyes punctuated by her swaying motion to the couch.

"I figured I should get to know our backyard neighbors," Tristen said, followed by another gulp.

They all laughed. Clare slapped Tristen on the back. Tristen stood, suddenly made uncomfortable by her touch.

"Where's the box of wine? I need another refill."

"You want a hit, Tristen? I know Clare smoked the hell out of the bong in the bathroom, but you can go in there, if you want." Tristen's face creased, puzzled. "We aren't gross," Nick laughed. "We hide it in the bathroom to keep the smell from getting into the furniture. Pretending to keep secrets from Clare's parents and all. Just spray the Febreze afterwards."

"I'm good. Maybe later. I'll stick with wine for now."

"I've got Fireball," Clare said, jumping up. "Let's do shots."

Nick shuffled in the chair. "Isn't it a little early, Clare? Let's wait for Joe and Yarto."

"Naw. You know they take forever."

Clare walked into the kitchen area of the open space, taking out three shot glasses. From another cupboard, she brought down a fifth of Fireball, poured the liquid into all three glasses, placed her mouth over one, then threw back her head, swallowing without pause. She looked at Nick and Tristen, then smiled. Silence hung in the air, as if she was waiting for applause.

"That's an impressive trick," Tristen said to appease her. "Where did you learn that?"

Clare swayed a bit, still smiling, though her eyes took on a thicker glaze. Tristen wondered how much pot she had smoked in the bathroom. She had been in there for over five minutes after he arrived, and he had no idea how long before.

Nick leaned back in the recliner, rolling his eyes. He grabbed the remote control from the neighboring table and unpaused his game. "She learned from Yarto's girlfriend. His girlfriend gets quite slutty when she drinks even the smallest amount, so she likes to find ways to impress other men. He usually stops her after a bit. She claims he's just jealous, but we know he doesn't really care. Yarto's just embarrassed for her."

"Are you saying I should be embarrassed for showing you boys that little trick?" Clare took another shot in her mouth, made sure Tristen caught her eye, then licked the outside rim of the shot glass before performing the same trick again.

Tristen almost choked with excitement. Did this mean she had changed her mind? Or was she trying to make Nick jealous? Why would Nick need to be jealous? He was the one that had been after Clare all these years. Had he heard wrong? No, but something in the dynamic had changed.

"So, seeing anyone?" Tristen said, trying to find the mark.

"You haven't heard about Julia?" Clare said, mocking the name with a pitched tone.

"Lay off, Clare." Nick rattled on the controller without turning his head. "I'm dating this girl who lives about an hour from here, so I don't get to see her all that much. You might have noticed her at the funeral." He slammed the controller down; his death displayed across the screen. He leaned back in the recliner, taking a sip of his drink, studying the ceiling. "I'm hoping once she's in college, she'll be able to stay here on the weekends. As of now, her parents would never allow it, even though she's eighteen. She's strapped to their purse strings until she gets through college. But they won't know she's here unless they surprise her with a college visit. There's issues, but I like her a lot."

Clare poured another shot, this time picking it up and throwing it back. "Oh, Julia. Oh, Julia. Oh, Julia," she said, laughing to herself, then wobbling over to Nick, falling on his lap. "Been dating for three months, and she's all you talk about."

"You may want to slow down, Clare," Nick said, though he cradled her in his arms, rather than push her off. Tristen wondered why Clare had invited him. To watch her nuzzle up on Nick?

"Are we going to play video games or what?" Tristen said. He looked around for more controllers, finding some piled in a box on the other side of the television. He grabbed two and tossed one in Clare's lap.

"You'll have to get up if we're going to play, Clare."

"You both are no fun," she whined, letting the controller fall to the ground.

"Hey! Watch it. Damn things cost sixty bucks."

She picked it up, petting it gingerly in Nick's face before sitting on the couch. She jumped up. "We forgot to do shots together!" She wobbled to the counter, refilled her glass, then brought over the three filled shots to Tristen and Nick, spilling a little on the carpet. Tristen saw him roll his eyes but no remark.

"To friends," she said, raising her shot glass in the air. "To good times and forgetting the worst of our past, looking only to the future." Nick and Tristen muttered a "Cheers," swallowing their shots as well.

Tristen gagged at the blast of cinnamon in his mouth, the liquor sinking into his stomach, a cement block billowing his insides. He did not care for liquor, the quick intoxication, the deadly line between fun and continuous vomiting. He preferred beer but rarely got the chance unless Tom's older brother bought them a case, charging them twice the amount he paid as a "service fee." But he didn't want to appear weak in front of Clare. Her careful words of hope still lingered, a *never say never* thought swaying in his mind.

Tristen played *Call of Duty* with Nick for an hour or so, neither commenting much on the other's technique, though Nick clearly had put hours into the game. Clare played for a few minutes, killing Tristen twice before switching to scrolling through her phone, laughing to herself. When no one asked her what was so funny, she slunk off to the bathroom, then Nick's bedroom, slamming the door. Tristen hoped she'd gone to lie down and take some time away from the booze and weed.

Nick's phone rang. "Yep," was all he said before hanging up. He turned to Tristen. "Yarto's at a house party over in Luck. I'm going to head there if you don't mind. I'd offer to take you, but I don't think you'll know anyone. Also, if you go, Clare will want to go, and Clare is in a state, as you can tell. I think it's best that I just head off. Feel free to stay and play if you want. Clare can sleep in my bed if she doesn't wake up. I'll sleep on the couch or Isla's bed. You can drink or eat whatever's around here." Nick grabbed his wallet and keys from the counter, then headed out. Tristen thought he heard him say, "Good luck" as he left.

Tristen looked at the closed door for a few moments, unclear as to what was expected of him next. Should he care for Clare in the next room? Sneak out? Or just hang out in the trailer in case she got sick? Tristen decided to play games for an hour or so longer, check on Clare to make sure she didn't choke on her own vomit, then escape this mess of a night. Despite Clare's clear annoyance at Nick having a girlfriend, Tristen still wanted her to notice him.

He looked in the direction of the bedroom, curious if he should snuggle up with her, yet feared she would scream and throw him out, ruining the small likelihood of them getting back together. Tristen flipped through the stack of games on Nick's PlayStation, choosing some Batman game. He had heard good things from either Tom or Philippe. He found himself enamored with the game, floating through the sky, zipping through the city, fighting off all sorts of bad guys he vaguely remembered. Though quite drunk, despite only two cups of wine and a shot, he kept a certain rhythm, forgetting why he had stayed in the trailer until he heard a loud groan from the bedroom.

Tristen paused the game, listening for further sounds. Another groan, though much softer—a word escaped her lips that Tristen could not understand. He slowly pushed open the door.

"Niiiiick," she said, looking toward him.

"No, it's me, Tristen. Nick had to head out, but I stayed around in case you felt sick. You okay?"

She shook her head, then mumbled "Nick" once more, before telling him, "Come here." She patted the bed a few times until Tristen walked over and lay on the bed.

"I missed you," she said, rolling on top of him.

"Clare," he grunted. "Are you okay?"

"Let's fuck. Come on. I want it. Please," she slurred in his ear, the wretched smell of weed and Fireball taking over his nose.

"Are you sure?" he said. Tristen quivered, his penis erect at the immediate prospect. He blessed the world that Nick had left, and that he'd had the chivalry to stay.

Clare mumbled something back, though he could not make out what she said. He began taking off her pants, kissing her neck, though she did not show sincere signs of reception. A slight groan escaped when he kissed her mouth. He hurried off with his own pants, so excited to be with her. All the months of yearning coming to this sweet moment, Clare begging him to be inside her again.

Tristen reached down, feeling the wet of her eagerness. He moved his hand around, unskillfully, but he generally remembered what Clare said felt good to her. Tristen looked at her face—eyes closed. He wondered for a moment if she had fallen asleep, but then how could she be so wet? Her body must want him. He rocked her until she mumbled some words that he accepted as a request to continue. He tilted so she lay splayed on her back and smoothly placed himself. She made a light grunt, and he stopped, worried he had hurt her. Should he continue? She seemed to be enjoying it.

"Clare. Hey, Clare. Do you want to keep going?"

Clare tossed her head around, then made soft pats on his chest. He did not know what this meant, but he had already started, feeling his balls begin to throb as he rested within. She had left them open to the possibility of a rekindling, and they had had drunken sex before. He began pumping in her, eyes closed, feeling the euphoria of making love to her once more. He felt a slap on the face, though not hard, and opened his eyes.

"Stop," he heard her mutter, head rested to the side.

He was close and needed to finish. Maybe thirty seconds to completion. He hurried his rhythm, streaming inside her. At that moment, he realized he'd forgotten to wear a condom, so excited for the opportunity that he hadn't even contemplated protection. He looked around the floor, then rushed to the bathroom to grab a towel, wiping both him and Clare off. He then lay next to her, nestling half-naked, thankful for this night.

Chapter 17

Clare is nineteen

Tristen opened the fake bottom of the closet floor. He'd made it a couple months back. He reached down, moving the black cloth to take out the bag full of white pills. He swallowed two with the glass of water next to him, then sat in the closet opening, praying for the pills to work faster. He needed relaxation, a quick fix.

He had stolen a few bottles of Xanax from Rhonda after Clare and he had the fight that awful morning. She'd claimed to know nothing of what had taken place when she'd woken up next to him, both semi-naked. She accused him of vile things, of taking advantage of her in that diminished state. He'd tried to argue back, claiming she had asked for him to come to the bed and seemed excited. She seethed that he was a rapist, and he took advantage of incoherent girls. He began crying, begging for her to forgive him. She claimed if he just let her alone, she would try to forget the whole thing.

For two months, he feared seeing Clare's face. Though he did not believe himself to have done anything wrong, how could he convince anyone else? He had thought through that night over and over—the groans, the soft pats on his chest, her excitement. He fought against the slap and that one word that came into his mind at the end. *Stop.* She could not remember saying that word, since she claimed to have been so far gone, but he could not forget. He hadn't meant to hurt her. Afterwards, he began taking a Xanax a day to calm his obvious nervousness, pointed out by the entire family. Rhonda had stacks of bottles in the cupboards, so she did not miss the few he stole.

And now this. Why had Clare told him, of all people? She could have handled the matter on her own without pressing, no, terrifying him. Pregnant. Of all the possibilities, he hadn't expected to hear those words from her, showing him the results of his sins.

"I'm not sure it's yours," she had whispered near the door. After that one night, she no longer allowed them to be alone together. He despised this ploy, believing she was doing this to belittle him, make him uncomfortable.

"What do you mean you're pregnant? Who do you think the father is?" he said, breath rising.

"None of your business, Tristen. I felt I should tell you and now I have. I don't know whether I plan on keeping the baby. I'll need to tell Ni—" She slapped a hand over her mouth.

"Nick. Nick! Are you fucking kidding me, Clare?" Tristen stood, fuming with jealousy.

Clare pushed him down. His right arm struck the bedframe as he hit the ground. "You don't get to judge anyone. I still have to explain why I don't know who the father is, so you just wait." She slammed the door shut behind her.

He felt exposed, raw, needing an escape, so he had turned to the pills. Five minutes had already passed, but he did not feel the relief he needed. The anxiety trembled his body. He reached for the bag, taking two more, not caring about the lethargy that would ensue. He needed his mind to stop. What if she did tell? Would they tell Kelvin? Tristen could not survive in jail. He heard they murdered accused rapists, proclaimed innocence be damned.

The act of taking the medication helped him for a few more breaths, as if downing them gave him hope of relief. Tristen started punching his leg, anything to discharge this pent-up energy. The budding ripples of pain in his leg helped give him a little focus—a point to charge his mind into a plan, as if he could escape this pregnancy unscathed.

Could she comprehend accusing a possible father of such heinous acts? Tristen had always thought he would be a good father. He would stay, be nurturing, become the father he had always prayed for yet never received . . . except, maybe Kelvin. What would Kelvin do?

Tristen began crying. He'd never meant to hurt anyone. He loved Clare so much that he wanted to be with her always. Why would such passion be a crime?

She needed to have an abortion. An obvious solution which would give him time to convince Clare of the error of her feelings. She had wanted him that night. She had begged for him to come to that bed and comfort her. Her body had desired him, and he'd obliged. How dare she accuse him of any wrongdoing, when she'd slit his heart out with her coldness all those months? She'd hurt him and now she wanted to punish him with accusations and teenage pregnancies.

What if that night had been hazy for them both? He had been drunk, too. If he tried, there seemed to be some gaps in his memory. How could he have done anything wrong if he barely remembered having sex with her as well? She had enticed him. That's right. He had been ready for a fun night of video games, and she'd forced him to drink, then asked him into bed. Also, he was a minor. How dare she, the adult, try to trick him into feeling awful about her personal mistakes: drinking to excess and swooning over children?

Yet he did remember that night. He remembered her grunts and pushes on his chest, slapping his face, the soft "stop," and his decision to continue the thrusts. Though Clare did not indicate she recalled any of these actions, Tristen could not push himself to be so unaware that these memories would cease when he thought of Clare. He'd committed an atrocious act, good intentions or not.

He reached for a pill but pulled his hand back. She could not have that baby. Nothing could make that baby's life fruitful given the circumstances. Tristen would never get a chance to be happy with Clare if she saw that baby every day, a physical recollection of past crimes that could otherwise be forgotten over time. He loved her so much that he would sacrifice everything just to remove some fragment of those torrents of isolation he saw within her, in some misunderstood penance.

But then Nick. Tristen punched his leg once more. Nick must have known of Tristen's feelings for Clare, the connection between them.

Oh, Isla. What would she think? He had come to respect Isla, viewing her as a common ally amongst enemies. They had recently grown closer as outsiders, discussing the trivialities of their lives: Kelvin's external absence, Rhonda's internal absence that made Isla uncomfortable, and Edna's queer eccentricities mixed with alcohol, though neither could identify the exact exploits that made them identify Edna this way. Tristen tried to support Isla, listening to her explain the death of her father, the wonders of her brother. Tristen tended to be merely a presence, a diary for her despair, but he did not mind. This allowed him to ease from his reflection of the one topic that would never leave. Now, Isla would never speak to him again . . . well, if she believed Clare.

Believed! What if they did not believe Clare? He could control the narrative if he could find a way to present their sexual exploits as predatory on Clare's part.

But how could he expect Clare to ever forgive him? What was one accusation versus another? One was clearly baseless, he reasoned, drifting his head against the wall. He prayed the damn pills would let him live without this turmoil. *Work faster*, he thought, tears welling in his eyes.

He circled back to the central necessity: convincing Clare to get an abortion. She would have no way of substantiating any accusations if there was no baby. The baby might not be his, though. Then let Nick take care of the problem. But Clare would never come to him again if she had a baby with Nick. She would force herself into the idolatry of married life in a trailer placed in the backyard of her parents' house. A horrid fate for someone he admired so dearly.

Tristen wanted to help her rise above her recent minimalist approach. She had been an athlete and musician until something removed her pleasure in these activities. Had she ever genuinely enjoyed anything, or had she just performed for the appearances of success? A smooth cloud drifted over his body, the desired relief. The mind boomed, yet the body did not subject itself. He needed to convince Clare the best course of action was an abortion.

Tristen looked at the small mirror on his wall opposite the closet, his eyes still red from misery with no way to calm them. He practiced his smiling, trying to find a perfect approach to persuasion. He lost himself in a reflection of overwhelming remorse.

He opened his bedroom door and walked down the stairs to the kitchen. Kelvin sat at the dining room table, leering over piles of paperwork. Tristen thought he should be nice and ask what Kelvin was working on but did not want to get caught in some discussion regarding the household expenses. He had a mission. Kelvin did not look up, so Tristen went to the back door, hoping to stop Clare before any declaration to Nick. The cooling feeling continued, though his stomach grew nauseous.

"Nerves," he said, keeping focus on the trailer door.

Screaming emanated from the trailer. He realized he had heard voices with increasing intensity, but his mind calmed their entrance. He stopped in place, ducking down from view of the kitchen window, halfway between the two residences, afraid of that scream's meaning. Nick's roaring voice, then another scream, this one different. Why would Isla and Clare both be screaming in the trailer?

Tristen needed to escape. Whatever events occurred in that trailer could not be productive, even if not about him. He was scurrying toward the house when he heard the trailer door slam.

"You disgusting bastard," Nick said. "You raping piece of trash." The second set of words moved closer.

Tristen darted to the back door. He heard, "I'm going to fucking kill . . ." before the door closed behind him. He scrambled up the stairs on hands and feet. He prayed to find sanctuary in his room, locking the door. He could prevent these people from hurting him.

Tristen huffed behind the locked door, the Xanax fighting to calm him down, but the floating feeling would not keep. He felt jagged, like a useless, rusty serrated blade. Kelvin had yelled as Tristen whizzed by him, knocking papers over. Kelvin must be asking the others about the commotion. Would they call the police or break the door down? More yelling. Tristen listened with his ear against the door.

"Don't go up there, Nick. You don't know what's going on," screamed Isla. She sounded distressed, upset by the uproar caused by her brother.

"Shut the fuck up. He's dead."

"Hold on, Nick," yelled Kelvin.

More screaming and yelling, but Tristen lurched away from the door when he heard stomping in the stairwell. He fell backwards, hitting his back on the nightstand. The pain did not help him escape. Sounds of frustration—so close. Then a scream, followed by a loud thud. Another scream.

Tristen thought to look out the door. In that moment, he hoped something horrible had happened: someone tripped and cracked a rib; Nick had assaulted Clare or Isla; Kelvin had tried to fight Nick off and broke his nose. Would Clare's accusations be sustainable in such an environment? He could only deny and hope.

Tristen could not fathom acts of bravery, for he knew that no matter what horrid events had just occurred, they all connected back to his original transgressions. There could be no escape. He could not hide behind anyone. He hurried to the closet and slammed the door shut—a dark space of comfort.

He thought he heard more stomping, maybe a knock on the door. He squeezed his eyes shut, placed his hands over his ears.

"Please, Mom. I need you," he whimpered.

He felt around, bumping into the loose hovel of the Xanax, searching for the bag. A glorious supply of pills that would make this whole predicament disappear. Clare had done this. She would know. He grabbed a few. Swallowed. Grabbed a few more. Swallowed. He felt a slight choking from his dry throat.

Maybe he should stop, confess, and let the Lord take charge. He swallowed more pills, wondering how long the effects would take. Would he throw up? Convulse and cause a scene? Or would he drift into sleep, sorry that he had ever hurt anyone? He swallowed five more pills, then rested against the corner of the closet. He softly cried into unconsciousness, as his wish came true, and he slowly disappeared from the house.

Chapter 18

Today

Clare considered the empty noose, waiting for something to escape her mouth.

"Coward," she eventually yelled, spitting at the noose, just as she had done at his body in the casket, still not finding any relief. "You all let him rape me, and then felt sorry for him. He violated my body. My. Body." She ran to Nick, her mouth to his ear. "I know some of you think I asked him that night, even though I could not recall anything that happened. Tristen admitted it," she screamed.

Nick jerked, mumbling into the gag.

"You'll get your turn, Nick. Now shut the fuck up."

She wondered if she could find common ground with a rapist, feel his presence, so she could discover how to compel him to understand the violation she felt every time she thought of him. She had felt for him, once. She twisted the rope in her hand, letting her body sway with its grip, as the words whispered from her lips.

"You thought I didn't see the obvious desire you had for me, though that bathroom debacle certainly provided clues." She tried to smile, but too much pain prevented her. "Your longing looks, jerking motions when I caught you, beads of sweat at your temples as you smiled, stuttering to say something that would convince me that you had not just been lusting for me. Your warmth in contrast to my family drew me towards your desire, and in the same way your kindness pleased me, I wanted to do the same for you. Mistakes and regrets amongst innocence. I wish I could keep only that memory of you."

She had thought this over many times, reasoning that just because someone saves a saint does not justify the subsequent murder of twelve babies, and neither should months of kindness justify Tristen's rape. We are taught as toddlers the meaning of "no." Attempting to reason that the hormones of adolescent boys are provided carte blanche with automatic forgiveness is ludicrous. "You stole from me, Tristen. Not only in violation and in respect of my body. You stole my grief, leaving me with doubt and forcing me to feel guilt for your response to my pain. Many here should be mortified, as I should never have had to justify my reaction to the rape. I did not kill you!" screamed Clare, throwing the rope off her hand, losing balancing and falling back. "You died because of your actions, not my reaction."

She cried in howls of both her pain and her loss of Tristen, a mash of confusion and sorrow, unashamed at the display before her family. Was this not the reason she had brought them here? She prayed in the infinite possibilities after this life that he understood his crimes, that he could fathom the betrayal, that some part of him felt sorrow. She hoped God had punished him for his transgressions, then allowed him the freedom to grow into the man she had wanted for him to become the first time she'd kissed him in the hotel.

Clare grasped her abdomen and began to cry once more—that baby with no hope. She should have done a damn paternity test before confronting Nick, never telling him the truth about there being two potential fathers. She had needed Nick to want the baby, to take her in his arms and propose marriage, a family.

Clare considered the dangling rope above, an escape away from this monstrosity of a life. However, she still could not feel the dark compulsion of the rope, despite her family's inability to express remorse.

Wiping her face on her sleeve, she stood and slapped her face into focus. She smacked at the noose in a final gesture of this debacle of a eulogy. "I never would have wished for his death, no matter what you all think."

She walked behind Nick, touching the back of his head. He flinched. "Before you scream, rant, or beg, Nick, you must know that I'll have to drug you, causing this charade to continue. Just listen and leave well enough alone. I'm not sure Grandma can wait much longer for her turn." His head did not ease into her hand. "I'm not going to hurt you."

Clare untied his gag, then circled around, waiting for a torrent of obscenities that would only hold her steadfast. He did not speak, nor lift his eyes to catch her gaze. He had fought so hard before. Why did he not care to break free now?

"Are you okay?"

"Just get on with it, Clare. If you want to die, then die. You don't need this whole performance. What do you expect from us? Beg for our lives, while you shackle us to chairs and take away our speech? You don't want to hear from us. You only want to judge. I told you I was sorry about the baby, but I'm not the one to blame. Tell me what you want, so I can move on with my life."

"Fine."

Part IV: Friend

"Above all, keep loving one another earnestly, since love covers a multitude of sins." 1 Peter 4:8

Chapter 19

Clare is eighteen

"Come on, Isla, or we're going to be late for school," Nick yelled down the hallway. He hated driving her in the morning. Her homeroom teacher never gave out tardy slips, so she paid no mind to the harshness of his consequences. Mr. Oliwmer had already handed him two detentions for being tardy. One more and he'd be stuck with a Saturday detention. "Isla, I'm going to leave without you. We have a minute window, or I'll be late."

"You are not going to leave her," Nick's father said, looking up from the newspaper. Nick knew his dad loved him, but his dad worshipped Isla. Isla, the track star, the honor roll student, the popular girl voted princess of some freshman dance earlier this year. She did not need anyone else to remind her that she was royalty in this household.

"Dad, I'm going to be stuck in Saturday detention if I'm late one more time. All these late slips are her fault, I hope you know."

"I know, but she has a lot to do in the mornings. After her run, she needs to shower and get ready. She follows a tight schedule for her achievements, so I think a few late days on your part is a worthy sacrifice."

Nick slumped on the couch. His father, a widower for seven years now, furrowed his black eyebrows and short auburn hair, same as Isla and his mother. Nick wondered where his sharper, pronounced features came from, though he looked similar enough to his grandmother, who often bragged that they stole the looks of the family.

"You still desperate for that Clare girl?"

"What?" Nick said, disgusted.

"Well, you keep staring at me with that annoyed face, so I figured I would ask something about your life."

"She's just a friend."

"That's not what you want, though."

"Well, no, but I'm happy being her friend."

His dad laughed. "No man is happy watching the girl he loves with other men. You're a good-looking boy. You should have tons of girls knocking at our door."

"Isla, are you ready yet?" Nick urged down the hallway. His dad laughed again, returning to the paper.

"Almost," she said, appearing from the room, brushing her hair. "Sorry. I got lost in thought during my run."

"It's fine," Nick said, knowing his father would not accept any other response.

"Just five more minutes," she said, smiling. "I can go to your teacher and tell them it's all my fault, if you want."

Nick rolled his eyes. Though Isla received special favors from school staff given her track star status, he did not enjoy her flaunting that in his face.

"Have you heard from any of the schools you've applied to?" his father asked. Isla intended on ruining his day with this waiting.

"Not yet. That's a good sign, I'm sure. Must mean they're combing through my file in detail," Nick said, cracking his neck, averting his father's scrutiny. Nick had been rejected from two schools already, but he'd hidden the letters. He had two more schools he prayed for acceptance to, but his hopes were not high, given his middling 3.1 GPA and scant extracurriculars, preferring to relax and enjoy the now rather than consider the rest of his life. One of the two rejections came from his safety school, so Nick figured he would wait for the final rejections and destroy his father in one go.

Nick wanted to study at one of the local vocational schools rather than a college, anyways. Learn a trade. He had not considered any particular field, figuring a student learned his specialty by not entering with a firm idea of his strengths. His father pestered, vocalizing that he had raised a pizza delivery driver, only partly in jest.

"Well, you let me know as soon as you hear any word from them. I want to make sure we have a solid plan for you, Nick. You have less than four months of school left, and you will be expected to pay rent if you don't have any intention of schooling."

"I'm trying, Dad."

"Mmhmm," his father said.

"I'm ready," Isla said, her arms waving in a grand entrance from the hallway.

"I swear they plan this time for Dad to harass me," Nick muttered to himself.

He left the house, holding the door open for Isla.

"What time do you plan to be home, Dad? Should we get food?"

"You should plan on fending for yourselves all week, dear. The plant is asking for cuts again, so the employees will be upset, leading most to complain to me. Everyone will give their sob story. I hate this job sometimes."

"We need to go," Nick said, motioning for Isla to come outside.

"You are a great manager, Dad," Isla said, kissing him on the cheek. "They must know you do everything you can for them."

"Thanks, Is."

She bounded out the house and into the passenger seat. Nick drove the fifteen minutes with the morning's top hits playing from the radio. As normal, Isla spent the drive on her phone, taking in as much social media as possible. She never took her phone out at school, though. His sister had a reputation of impeccably following the rules, or at least the rules that affected her.

"You going to prom?" she said, eyes on her phone.

"No. I went with Dianne Turner last year. Too expensive and boring."

"So, she wouldn't let you get anywhere?"

"Isla, what the hell?"

"I don't know," she laughed. "Isn't that half the point of prom?"

"Not to me," Nick muttered. "Why do you ask?"

"Chan Petro asked Trinity to the prom, and he needs to find a date for his friend, Trent."

"Your fourteen-year-old friend is going to prom with a senior?"

"Fifteen, and yes. I'm thinking of going with Trent, but I have no interest in him. I just think it would be fun to dress up and be driven around in a limo."

"Did you ask Dad?" Nick knew his father would fight against the idea of his baby girl going with strange men to a dance known for promiscuity.

"No," she said, putting her phone down, studying him. "I wanted to talk to you first. I thought if you went, you could go with us. That way Dad won't be so hostile to the idea."

"Nope. Not going."

"Come on, Nick. This is your senior year. Prom is all about the seniors. It's your year to shine."

He turned the steering wheel hard to the right, speeding into the school parking lot. He braked abruptly, causing Isla to jerk forward into her seatbelt. Fifteen minutes late.

"Ow, you asshole. Please, Nick. What if I find you an awesome date?"

"Still no."

"What if I promise you Clare?" She had her hands wrapped tight around her phone, praying for his agreement.

"Clare won't go with me, and you know it. Crosses some unseen boundary line of our friendship. That's why I went with Dianne last year."

"That's right. You had to sit at a table with Clare and Marcos. Oh, Marcos. What a gorgeous oddity."

Clare had pined after Marcos their junior year. One of the best musicians in the band, Marcos played alto saxophone with a smooth jazz feel. He'd transferred from some school in Connecticut, then went back after the end of last year. His parents had reconciled, Clare had discovered, and she still messaged him from time to time. Nick did not recall anything negative about Marcos other than his knack for isolation, always focusing on his music, even during lunch.

"Shut up."

"Does that mean if I can convince Clare, you'll go?"

Nick rolled his eyes, got out, and dashed toward the school building.

Isla ran next to him. "I'll take your silence as acceptance," she gleefully said. "I'll let you know, as soon as she says yes."

Less than ten minutes later, Nick walked to the principal's office, ready to accept a Saturday detention for Isla's selfishness. He knew Clare would not attend prom with him. She had told him flatly that she viewed him as a brother; anything further between the two would be weird. He respected Clare's boundaries with insincere apathy.

His thoughts wandered to the other two of his trio: Yarto and Joe. Nick felt he was drifting from Yarto, since Yarto's girlfriend, Tiffany, stole most of his time. Nick and Joe, meanwhile, agreed to wingman for each other when the opportunity arose. They had gone to a few parties, but Yarto always ran off with his girlfriend, leaving Joe and Nick to attempt flirtation and feel worse. Clare and her friend Ryan sometimes tagged along, finding more fun with the drunken crowd, both often discovering someone's mouth or more.

"Isla kept me," he said to the principal after handing over the tardy slip.

"I see. So why don't I have your sister here with me, as well?"

Nick would not take away Isla's privileges, at least for now. "I don't know."

"Well, this is the third time, so you'll be here for Saturday detention from 8 a.m. to 12 p.m., Mr. Teruptil."

"Yes, ma'am." Nick slunk out of the chair, thinking Isla owed him. He returned to civics class, ignoring the lesson. He thought about going to prom with Clare. He looked down at his notebook, considered making a pros and cons list. However, he knew the one giant con that would preclude any possible pros: Clare would go to prom only as his friend, and he found the image depressing, sitting pitifully next to Clare at a table with his sister and her freshman friend with two creepy seniors gawking at them. The idea of that debacle made him ill.

At lunch, Clare approached Nick, who was talking to Yarto and Joe about the reasons he wasn't going to bother with the party that weekend.

"You could have just asked me to prom yourself. You didn't have to send your sister," she said, shaking her head. "I couldn't believe when she asked me. Said you were too scared to ask me yourself, that you practically begged her. She wanted to keep the conversation a secret but what the hell, Nick?"

Yarto and Joe both inhaled in tandem, then excused themselves, unable to hold their laughter out of Nick's earshot. He rolled his eyes; he had not understood how desperate Isla must be for this damn prom.

"I don't want to go with you," he began. When she looked ready to pounce, he continued. "Wait! I don't want to go at all. Isla thought if you went with me, I'd want to go. I don't. She wants to go with Chan, Trent, and her friend, but she knows Dad won't let her without me there."

Clare sat next to him, placed her head on his shoulder. "That sounds more like what I expected. I haven't had you beg me for a date in a long time. Thought we were past all that."

"Yep," he said, looking around the gymnasium at all the better conversations he could be having.

"Sorry. I didn't know what to say to her, so I told her I would think about it. I came to yell at you for putting me in such an awkward spot. I should have known better."

"It's okay," he said, resting his head onto hers. "You know Isla. If she wants something, she'll work harder than anyone to achieve it."

"Remember when she wanted to go to that Adele concert but couldn't find anyone to take her, so she convinced me that we should go? She never mentioned that she didn't have a ride until you told me your dad was forcing you to escort us there." She laughed. "I love her."

"Yeah," he said. "She's manipulative, she's bossy—"

"Oh, come on," Clare said, slapping his leg. "Why don't you want to go to prom? It's your senior year. This is the one outing everyone is required to attend. You're attractive enough. Plenty of girls would accept your invite."

"Thanks, I guess," he said, annoyed at the day's spiraling events—Saturday detention and now a rejection that he never wanted in the first place. "Are you going with someone?"

"I think Ryan. I'm not sure I'm in the mood to take someone in a romantic way, and Ryan doesn't have a date that he wants to bring. He claims that unless he can find a Greek god to present to the class as representative of a gay couple, then he would rather stay home."

"That's nice of you," he said.

"I guess, though I'm not sure if Ryan even wants to go with me."

"So, why not go with me, as friends?"

Clare slid a few inches away. Nick felt shamed, though he did not see the harm. He looked at Clare, situating his head to catch her eye. She kept quiet, looking off at freshman girls practicing a cheer.

"Never mind. Forget I asked. You should still go. We don't even have to be at the same table. Sorry."

He zigzagged down so he did not have to brush by her. He would not touch her, even accidentally; she'd shown him yet again how much she detested him.

He felt the soft touch of Clare's hand before he could find Yarto and Joe. "Don't be like that, Nick. I'm sorry if I hurt your feelings. I hate sending you mixed messages. You are handsome, smart, and funny. You'll make a girl giddy with happiness one day. I just don't feel that way. My head is just swimming right now with graduation so soon."

"No worries," he said with a nod, though he would not look at her. "I'll let you know if I decide to go." He pulled his hand away. She let out a soft sigh, but he could not be around her anymore.

Nick found Yarto and Joe standing with a few other guys they played *Call of Duty* with online. Nick gave a nod and sat a few feet away. Yarto and Joe waved them off and circled around him.

"What the hell was that with Clare? Did you really ask your sister to do that?" Yarto said, putting his hand on Nick's shoulder. "You could have asked me or even Joe. I know you want her, but that's a low guilt trip."

Nick sat with no response. He waited for them to begin laughing, but they stayed in place, patient.

"No, I didn't. Isla wants to go to prom, and she thinks Dad will let her go if I'm there. I don't want to go, as you both already know. Isla decided to ask Clare anyways, thinking that if Clare went with me, I would change my mind. I still don't want anything to do with prom and now I need a girlfriend to show Clare that I'm not some needy, detestable monster."

"She's always kept you at arm's length," Joe said. "Sorry you had to hear it again. It's not fair."

"Damn right," Yarto said. "That's why you're both coming to the party tomorrow. Instead of you two hanging out in the corner jerking it, you can try to mingle with the rest of the crowd and find nice girls. You aren't going to find them talking to each other. How do you think I met Tiffany? I sure wasn't going to find her in this cesspool of a school."

Joe laughed, and Nick gave a meek smile. "Cheer up, Nick," Joe said, punching him in the arm. "We'll make a solid go at talking to women, support each other."

Nick softly laughed, not at Joe's upbeat humor, but his inability to wingman. Nick loved the man—acne prone, greasy brown hair, and an incessant need to be the buddy. All these qualities made him a great best friend, but he was inept at convincing a woman of anything but escaping.

"Sure, buddy. We'll definitely double up and find dates."

At the end of the day, Nick sat in his car, waiting for Isla to show and head home. He tapped at the steering wheel to the beat of an AC/DC song, the name of which he could not recall. If he paid enough attention to the lyrics, he could catch the chorus, but he did not know the point. He started banging his head, indifferent to the occasional gawks.

A surprise knock on the window caused him to smack the power button on the radio. He looked over at Clare signaling him, then motioning for him to roll down his window. He looked down at the button, unmoving. Clare pulled at the door handle, but Nick had the doors locked since he hated when Isla barged into the car, scaring him. He sighed, letting the window slowly drop.

Nick never identified the pull that kept him focused on Clare. She looked plain, with auburn hair, reasonable complexion, a stiff body, and dressed to cover with no intent to make herself glamorous for others. He had first talked to her the summer after second grade at her birthday party. For a period, through fourth grade or so, she seemed to want their friendship. She had then found a different crowd that had left Nick alienated and pining for her affections. That feeling never left. His feelings tumbled through the years, as he developed crushes on other girls, but whenever he found himself heartbroken and yearning, Clare came to mind. During junior high, their friendship rekindled as they worked on projects and hung out in big groups, but she made no indication of finding him anything better than an aloof friend.

Nick's now ex-friend, Beau, had then told the whole school about his pining crush, even showing the notebook where Nick had written Clare's name a few times without thought. They survived the mocking, but she maintained a distance. Once Marcos moved away, Nick thought she would turn to him for comfort. Nick had grown taller, more muscular, more attractive, if he could be objective. With still no reciprocation, he was exhausted.

"Hey, everything okay?" he asked.

"No," she said, hand on hip. "Joe let it slip to Ryan that you're going to a party tomorrow that you never told me about. You don't want to hang out because of this prom nonsense or what?" Clare stuck her head in the car. Nick pushed back into the limits of the seat. "What's your excuse, Nick? I want to go."

"Then go," he said. "Find someone else to drive you, though. I have Saturday detention, I doubt I'll even want to go afterwards."

"Oh, shut up. Pick Ryan and me up at Ryan's place tomorrow. I'll text you to make sure you go. Quit being such a downer," Clare said, walking off with a flip of her hand in dismissal.

A knock on the passenger door, and he unlocked the car. "Bout time." He drove out of the parking lot before Isla could reach her seatbelt. Every part of Nick abhorred the thought of going, but he did not want to disappoint Joe. Let Clare witness him meet other women and control her jealousy.

"So, I saw you talking to Clare. Does that mean you're going to prom with her? I'm so excited," Isla said, clapping her hands.

"No. She told me that I should find better ways to ask her out than use my sister. How the hell do you think that makes me feel, Is? Now she thinks I'm desperate again. Are you trying to ruin our friendship?" He banged on the steering wheel. "Oh, and now I have Saturday detention because of you. So, no, I'm not going to the fucking prom."

"Sorry, Nick. I know Clare can be obnoxious, but I thought she understood when I asked her. Also, if I could go to that Saturday detention for you, I would." He eyed her before focusing back on the road. "Seriously. I feel awful, and I'll make a better effort in the mornings."

He sighed, rolling down the window. He yelled out for a few seconds into the wind, then rolled the window back up.

"It's fine. Really. You know how I feel about Clare, and this brought the memory of all her nasty rejections back. I know you didn't mean it."

"I really didn't, Nick. I wish I could help."

When they got home, Nick spoke with his dad about his Saturday detention. His dad tutted and called Isla into the living room. A family meeting was initiated, with Isla made to understand that she could not continue with this tardiness. Otherwise, the school might question his ability as a father. Nick knew his father despised anyone condescending to him about his parenting style, with multiple acquaintances having referred to them as "those poor children" when they discovered his dad was a single parent. On the contrary, Nick thought his dad a bit of a hero and despised any insinuation otherwise. Isla apologized and moved on with her night, though Nick still had to be at school at eight in the morning on a Saturday. Nick knew Isla wanted to ask about prom, but this weekend would not be the right time.

Nick struggled through the Saturday detention, working through one of his English assignments, then trigonometry problems; the teacher would not permit sleeping. Nick monitored the clock, though the incessant peeking caused the four hours to creep.

At noon, he dashed out to his car, took a few hits of a joint he had hidden while driving home, and fell asleep upon reaching his bed. He woke refreshed, though he soon discovered that he had slept for nearly two hours. Nick groaned, feeling this detention had thrown off his whole weekend.

He looked through his texts, mostly repeats of Clare reminding him to pick her up. She never drove, always too drunk to drive after a party. Nick and his friends had tried to force a rotation with Clare and Ryan, but neither ever stuck to the plan.

Nick found leftover pasta in the refrigerator, taking huge bites from the container, figuring he would finish it. His dad yelled for him to have some manners, so he snuck the container to his room, playing video games until party time. Getting ready, Nick slapped the aftershave on his face, examining a few irritated bumps on his neck just below his chin. He grumbled, deciding he could not go to the party after all. What girl would possibly want to kiss him with this patch of razor burn? Nick pushed on his nose, knowing his flaw stood out on his face. When this kind of mood struck, he preferred to stay home, reluctant to subject himself to rejection on top of a dejected feeling, which would spiral into a sour Sunday.

Finally giving in, Nick told his dad he would be home late. His dad gave a light wave, eyes on some sports game. Nick drove to Joe's house, then picked up Ryan and Clare. Clare and Ryan had started festivities early, screaming when they saw Nick drive up, raising their fists, as each took a swig out of a flask before tumbling into the backseat.

"Either of you want a drink?" Ryan said, holding the flask between Joe and Nick.

Joe grabbed it and took a few gulps before making a retching noise. "What the hell do you have in here? It tastes like rubbing alcohol."

"It's vodka," Clare screamed, then giggled. "All I could get my hands on unless you wanted me to bring my grandma's backup boxed wine. I'm sure you old ladies would love a little Franzia."

Joe thrust the flask in Nick's face, but he pushed it off. "Put that down. Do you want me to get arrested?"

"Oh, is little Nicky scared?" Clare said, rubbing the side of his cheek.

"Do you want to go or not? I'm not taking you if you can't act normal in the car," he said, annoyed by Clare's nonexistent boundaries.

"Woof," Ryan said. "Someone is not feeling in the party mood."

"Damn, Nick. I'll leave you alone," Clare said.

Nick saw her arms crossed in the rear-view mirror, face against the window. They rode the rest of the way in silence, aside from the sloshing of the flask, as the music eased him the forty-five minutes to the party. Nick parked his car a few houses down the street in case the cops appeared. He figured he would have some plausible deniability if he kept some distance from the drunkenness. He brought out a joint and began smoking it while walking up to the party.

"Let me have a hit," Clare said, as Ryan urged her to pass it to him after.

"No. I'm only smoking because I'm not drinking so I can drive you. Go find something to mix that vodka with."

Clare rolled her eyes, then screamed her arrival upon entering the house. A few people cheered back but most sneered, then went about their conversations.

"What the hell is going on with her?" Joe said. "I mean, she's never one to stay sober, but she's being crazy. We may want to watch out for her."

"Fuck that," Nick said. "She can watch herself. Let's go meet girls and do what we came here for."

Nick and Joe found Yarto in a back room with Tiffany and two other girls playing beer pong. The two girls were ahead by four cups, making the second to last cup as the boys entered the room.

"Damn, Yarto. You suck at this game," Joe said.

"Shut up," he said, punching Joe's shoulder.

"Don't let him talk to you that way," said Tiffany, a stumpy woman with long black hair. "He does suck." The two girls laughed and nodded their heads.

"We want next," Joe said.

Nick elbowed him, shaking his head. "I'm terrible at this game," Nick whispered.

"We can hear you," one of the girls said. "You'll probably lose, but it'll be fun for us." They laughed again.

Nick watched them aim for the last cup. The short-haired redhead on the right, light freckles on her cheeks, threw the ping pong ball first. The ball swished into the cup, not hitting the rim. She high-fived her partner, then Nick and Joe. Nick laughed at her enthusiasm, feeling better by her energy.

The girl on the left, with long dyed blonde hair, roots starting to show, and a crisp complexion, threw next. The ball bounced off the rim, then went up. Everyone in the room roared when the ball landed in the same cup with a soft plunk.

"Ohhh," yelled the girls, everyone laughing. Nick gave them each another high five.

"Are you sure you want to go against them?" Yarto said. "They're only getting better."

"I think the tall one can handle himself," the redhead said, smiling at Nick.

"Nick," he said, putting his hand out.

She looked at his hand and gave a strong handshake. "Nice to meet you, Nick. I'm Julia, and this is Kimmy. This is her house with a few other girls. They go to college nearby. Golden Valley."

"Nice house," Joe said.

"It's my friend Lisa's house. Her family never visits, so they rent it out to college students," Kimmy said, smiling at Joe.

Yarto clapped Joe on the back. "Tiffany and I are going to the backyard. We've had enough losing for one day."

Joe began setting up the cups, pouring beer into each. The conversation trickled as Nick scrambled for a topic.

"So, what do you study, Kimmy?"

"I'm going for nursing right now. I like it okay. I'll be more excited when we get to actually practice what we're learning." She sighed and tossed her hand around. "But I know I need to learn the fundamentals first."

"Kimmy's smart. She should have gone to be a doctor, but she wants to be more hands-on with the patients. Supportive," Julia said, evening the cups into a triangle.

"What about you, Julia?" Nick said. "Do you go to college too?"

"Oh, no," she said. "I got into Golden Valley, but I'm still a senior. Kimmy is begging me to move in, since another housemate is graduating. I still have my heart on an Ivy League school, but I've been rejected by everyone except Brown. I'm still crossing my fingers, though I loathe the idea of living in Providence." She grabbed both ping pong balls. "Winners go first. How about you guys?"

"I'm still waiting to hear back from a few colleges," Nick said. "But I may just go to a vocational school. Still not sure what I want to study." He made a nervous chuckle when no one responded.

"I'm heading off to a small school in California to study computer technology. Hoping to find myself in Silicon Valley one day," Joe said, taking out the ping pong ball that Kimmy dunked and drinking the beer.

Nick roared internally, feeling overshadowed by Joe's incessant need to brag about his business dreams. Nick threw the ball first, making the corner cup. Julia smiled and drank it. Joe missed by almost a foot, hitting Kimmy in the chest. Julia laughed, while Joe turned bright red, mumbling an apology. They threw back and forth until Nick and Joe's team had two cups left and Kimmy and Julia's team had one cup left. Julia seemed carefree at their closing loss, but Kimmy stayed focused, visibly annoyed that the boys' team might win. Kimmy gritted her teeth and bounced the ball. Joe remained ready but missed the swipe, letting the ball enter the first cup. Julia threw quickly, the ball landing in the same cup. Nick looked down at the two balls, then up to Julia and began laughing.

"Well, that sucks," Joe mumbled.

"Oh, come on. You have to give it to them. That was amazing," Nick said. "Julia, do you want to get a proper drink?"

"Sure."

Joe looked at him, pleading without sound for him to stay. Nick shrugged his shoulders, shaking his head toward Kimmy.

"We going?" Julia said, standing by the doorway.

Nick nodded, then placed his elbow out to escort her. She took his arm with a "Thank you, monsieur." Though he had meant to lead, she directed them back through the living room, down a corridor, to a wide but small length kitchen. Julia dropped his arm as they squeezed past three people at the doorway to reach the kitchen table with the mixers.

"What's everyone drinking?" she said. One of the guys yelled, "Booze." She stared at him with disgust, and he smiled sheepishly.

"Bourbon, gin, or vodka?" she said to Nick.

"Make me whatever you're having," he said, praying he didn't sound as passive as he felt.

A gin and Sprite in hand, Julia led Nick to the backyard. A few people sat around the porch, and others could be heard making honest efforts at each other in the dark near the bushes. Julia led him to a porch swing hung next to an enormous oak tree branching out into the neighbor's fenced yard. They talked about school—Julia's favorite subject was biology; family—Julia had two younger brothers and she was closer to her father than her mother; religion—Julia did not find much benefit to organized religion but liked yoga; and dating—Julia's recent year-long relationship had been ended mutually seven months ago. They rocked on the swing, no one bothering them, when Nick stooped over and gave Julia a light kiss on the lips. She moved into the kiss, so Nick pushed harder until their tongues caressed. Nick had forgotten the sweet taste of a woman, enjoying the gentleness.

Julia pulled back and giggled. "You're fun, Nick. Though you taste like weed."

"Oh, God," he said. "I'm so sorry."

"It's fine," she said, patting him on the chest. "If I hated the taste, I would have stopped."

"Julia, can I ask you something?"

"Why not? Though I think we should go on a date before you suggest sex." Nick could feel heat rising in his cheeks, embarrassed to ask after her blatant suggestion that he just wanted sex, though he would partake on the very grass below their feet if she desired.

"You're blushing, aren't you?" she said, touching his face. "You are so cute."

"Thanks," he murmured. "I know we just met, and I would love to go on a date."

"Yes, Nick. I'll go on a date."

"No," he said. "I mean yes, please, but that wasn't my question." He looked around, unable to relax his hands. "Would you have any interest in going to my prom?"

"Oh," she said, scooting far enough away for Nick to notice.

"I'm sorry. I shouldn't have asked. I'm so stupid. You're just the first person I've even thought of asking to prom this year. Wasn't even sure I wanted to go."

"Well then, yes," she said, patting his leg. "You're still cute, even when you blabber."

Nick reached for her hand and leaned into the wooden swing. They sat in silence, watching the night sky. Nick wondered if Julia could identify any of the constellations but kept himself from asking. He could not identify one connection in the streaming lights in the sky and would only show himself to be foolish if she asked in return. Though he knew her only in this moment, he felt comfortable.

"Nick. Nick, you out here?"

"I'm here, Joe," Nick yelled out toward the porch.

Joe appeared before Nick, looked at Julia for a moment as if hesitant to speak, then focused on Nick. "Clare threw up in someone's bedroom.

Ryan cleaned it, but people are still upset. Yarto is trying to smooth everything over, but he suggested we leave."

Nick let out a drawn-out sigh, squeezing Julia's hand.

"Trust me. I don't want to leave either," Joe said. "Julia, I like your friend Kimmy. She's very knowledgeable about climate change. We had a great discussion. Alright, we should go, Nick."

"I'll be there in a second. Make sure you grab a bag for her to throw up in. Also, get rid of any clothes she vomited on. I don't need my car stinking of puke."

"Yep," Joe said, marching back to the house.

"I'm so sorry about this. Clare can be sloppy sometimes. I think she must be going through something."

"Not your fault," Julia said. "I'm glad you're taking care of your friend." She held her phone out. "Put in your number. We'll make plans next weekend, if not sooner."

Nick dialed in his number, gave her a kiss, and strode toward the house to save Clare from herself.

Chapter 20

Clare is eighteen

Nick loosened his tie after rustling into the driver's seat. Isla ventured into the passenger seat. Joe, Clare, and Julia squished into the backseat, trying to keep any noise of discomfort from escaping their mouths. Nick knew life could always get worse and dreaded the future might provide just that: more disparaging news.

"It was a lovely service," murmured Clare.

"Yes," Nick said.

Nick felt the touch of Julia's hand on his shoulder, but he did not have the energy to return the gesture, letting her hand slink back. The quiet in the car felt overwhelming, the tired engine keeping them company. Nick could not fathom music, and no one asked. Nick drove the car from the funeral to their home, no longer sure what he expected.

He could still recall the principal's practiced face of concern as Nick had walked into the office. An officer stood next to her. Nick instinctively patted his pockets, as if he had forgotten some remnant of marijuana on his person.

"Take a seat, Nick. We're just waiting for your sister."

"My sister?" he asked incredulously, unwilling to relax. "What does this have to do with my sister?"

"Please sit down, Nick. I'll explain as soon as Isla is here."

Nick eyed the principal, unsure if he should accept the offer, worried that the decision could never be taken back. Neither of them said a word more, as he shuffled his eyes between them. He sat and waited. Nick heard Isla walk into the principal's office, the carefree gait of someone who never received any chastisement.

"Nick, why are *you* here?"

"I don't know," he muttered.

"Isla, please sit down."

"Why is the officer here? Did something happen? Did you do something, Nick?"

"You two are clearly related, aren't you?" said the officer without any lightness to her tone.

"Isla, just sit down so we can find out what the hell is going on," Nick said, annoyed at this ongoing delay.

"I'm not sure the best way to tell you this. I'm sorry, but your father has been involved in a terrible accident at the plant. He was conducting an inspection, and the mechanism holding the car fell on top of him. I've been told by Officer Traynor that he did not suffer."

"What do you mean he did not suffer?" Nick yelled. "Is he dead?"

Isla started crying. Nick wrapped his arm over her shoulder as she turned into his chest.

"I'm sorry," said the officer. "He . . . he did die. I've been in touch with your aunt, but she won't be able to arrive until tomorrow. Nick, I'm told you are eighteen. Will you be able to stay with your sister for the night until your aunt arrives? Is there any other relative you'd prefer to stay with?"

Nick nodded, then shook his head, annoyed by the officer's mixed questions. He pinched his nose, fighting off his own feelings. Isla needed this moment for herself.

"I'll watch over Isla."

"Please know that the school is here for you," the principal said. "We will do everything in our power to make sure that you get all the support we are able to provide. You will be excused from school for at least a week and any further time that you may need. If you would like to head home now, I can excuse you."

"Yes, please," Isla squeaked.

Nick preferred Isla's sobbing over her stifled pain. He helped his sister up from the chair, nodded to the officer and principal with a soft thank you, and led Isla to her locker. The fog in his mind increased—a hazy, deterred, squished reality, as if moving through gelatin with no clear direction of escape. He found the world continuing to harden as he parked in their driveway, absent his dad's vehicle. His stomach panged at the thought that he needed to figure out a way to get it back to the house.

Isla made no movement to exit the car, no external sound; her body writhed with shock. Nick coaxed Isla out of the car, leading her to the couch.

"We can sleep out here tonight if you want. I'd rather not be alone anyways," Nick said.

"Me neither," she said, grabbing a pillow, squeezing it between her arms. "Can you put something on TV? I think I'll just rest on the couch. I don't know what we're going to do, Nick," she sobbed, her calm tone faltering at the end. "Where am I going to go?"

"What do you mean, where are you going to go? You'll stay right here with me." He stood, arms circling around the room, as if the question were ridiculous given his presence.

"Maybe, Nick. Don't you think Aunt Jeannie will demand I go with her? You're only eighteen."

"That woman has barely dealt with us but once a year. I doubt she wants to drag you back to her house. She already has three kids to handle."

"You're probably right," she said, nodding. "Everything is going to be worse."

"Yes," Nick said. "But we'll get through it. I promise, Isla."

Nick had tried to keep his promise, helping Isla and his aunt through the grieving process, guided by the faint remembrance of his mother's death. His aunt clearly did not know what to do with the two of them.

His aunt also fretted over money, as Nick's father did not have a life insurance policy; only being in his mid-forties, he still cherished the idea of invincibility. His aunt had told Nick, when Isla was off on a run, that there was still a significant mortgage on the house, though his dad had saved a fair amount for emergencies. Nick strove to convince her that he could take care of the payments. He would quit school and get a job, yet when she told him the monthly amount, he gagged. She had then told him that she thought the mortgage would have to go under his name, and no bank would give him that amount of money without a credit history. The bank would likely sell their home and give them any proceeds above the auction price unless they tried to sell it themselves. Nick had given his aunt permission to begin selling the house if she thought it necessary. He would find somewhere else for Isla and him to live.

Nick saw the "For Sale" sign stuck in the front yard as he parked the car on the roadside. Aunt Jeannie had invited some people over to help her with some of his dad's things: clothes, books, and other generalities. Aunt Jeannie had already spoken with family services about Isla's situation, and they had told her that as long as Isla was comfortable and Nick could show the ability to care for her, she could continue to stay in the area. Aunt Jeannie had reported this back to him without judgment or expectation.

Once parked, Nick opened the door for Julia, while everyone else slowly exited the car and headed up to the house. Silence hurt in the moment, but an improper sentiment could echo damage for a lifetime. Gestures filled the void, as Julia held his hand, and the others walked into the house with him. Yarto and Tiffany arrived soon after. Tiffany commented on the beautiful service and the lovely sentiments of the preacher, who knew Nick's dad more through social calls in town than his fervent churchgoing. She praised Nick for his words in remembrance of his father—something he had found online about the effect that one man's strength could have on a community, ready to fight for the betterment of tomorrow. Nick was pleased that his spun-out declarations held some meaning, even to those who had not known his father.

"I'm not sure what I'm supposed to do now," Nick said. "How can I afford an apartment? Dad had so little money saved."

"Maybe you'll get something from workers' compensation like my grandma," Clare said. Nick looked upon her with confusion. "My grandpa died in a construction accident, and Grandma got a settlement. I'm not saying you want to profit off your dad's death, but I think you would be entitled to some money, since your dad died at work."

"I think she's right," Joe said. "You should hire a lawyer that can help you."

"Can't we talk about anything else?" Isla said, running off to her room. Everyone glanced at each other, trying to figure out if they should follow or stay.

"I think we should give her some time," Nick said. "I'll check on her in a few minutes." Bodies relaxed though forlorn looks remained on the floor. "I understand what you're saying, Clare. And I agree, but I need a place to stay now. Without somewhere for Isla to call home and with family services visiting, she'll have to go to Texas, leave her friends, the track team that she adores. I want her to have stability."

"I wish I had a place for you, buddy," Yarto said. Tiffany rubbed his arm as the others nodded along.

"You could stay at our farm," Clare said. "No one has lived at Great-Grandpa's place since he died. It's a small two-bedroom trailer, but that should be great for you two. I can't imagine Grandma would mind. The place just rusts there."

"Clare, do you really think that we could stay with you?" a soft voice said from the hallway. "Please, Nick. Please let us stay with Clare. I can't imagine leaving my friends. We can take more of Daddy's stuff to Clare's so Aunt Jeannie doesn't have to sell it all."

"I suppose we could try. I'm not sure how all this works, though."

"Don't worry about that," Clare said. "Remember, my family takes in foster kids. I'm sure we can take care of all the paperwork and figure it out. Dad and Grandma handle all of that. As long as you don't mind Tristen being around," she said, a gray swoon overcoming her face.

"I don't know why we would," Nick said, "though I barely know the kid."

Aunt Jeannie walked in with Nick's Uncle Jerry and three cousins, Trina, Betsy, and Liam. The kids scattered to Nick's room, knowing he had a gaming system they never got to play with at home. Aunt Jeannie pressed upon her enormous bosom, startled by her kids rushing past, as she trudged up the few steps. Uncle Jerry stood behind her, hands ready for his wife's misstep, though he had to make the same effort with identical breathlessness. Though Nick saw them maybe once a year, he had fond memories of their banter and lighthearted demeanor.

"You should at least say hi to your cousins," Uncle Jerry yelled. "I'm sorry, everyone. I hope they straighten up when they become teenagers like these two." He patted Nick on the back. "I hope you're both holding up as well as can be expected. I told your aunt that we'll take care of the mortgage until this place sells, though I'm not sure if you should stay here. It would be very tense, never knowing when you may have to leave. Have you decided whether you'll be coming to Texas with us?"

"There's plenty of room," Aunt Jeannie said through gritted teeth. Uncle Jerry smiled at her with a nod, as if she had been trained to utter the words without balking thereafter.

Nick could understand why his aunt would be hesitant. Her three kids screamed and ran around enough that she could not handle more bodies, pleasant or not. Betsy had whined about wanting to leave throughout the service, until Uncle Jerry had to take her outside.

"Clare just offered a trailer her family has on their property," Isla said, standing and smoothing her dress—the floral pattern of yellows and pinks being one of Dad's favorite dresses on Isla, though she had long outgrown such decorations. "I think that will be a great place for us to transition, as long as Nick doesn't mind."

"The boy can take a few classes at the local community school or even take some courses online," Uncle Jerry said. "But we can get that all settled later. A few more people are coming over, including your family, Clare, so maybe we can discuss then. I'm in need of a beverage."

"Did all the catering come to the house? I forgot to ask before the funeral," Aunt Jeannie said.

"The food is in the refrigerator," Nick said. "I'm not sure what we have in terms of beverages, Uncle Jerry, unless you mean a soda."

"Oh," Uncle Jerry said. "I suppose that will suffice for now." Nick could hear him rifling through the refrigerator.

"Don't mess everything up, Jerry. Oh, goodness. Why don't you all go outside or into another room while I set some chairs up and heat up the food?" Nick's aunt looked around in dismay, though Nick knew his house to be spotless compared to the constant mess left by his cousins.

"Do you want us to help?" Julia said. Yarto stood by her and nodded.

"Oh, no. You kids have enough to deal with. Go take a walk. Get some fresh air."

"Text me if you need anything," Nick said, gently pushing Isla along, walking out the door. He was disappointed that his aunt seemed to be making this ordeal into a party. "Because she treats this as a social engagement rather than a memorial," he mumbled.

"What?" Julia said, her hand caressing his elbow.

"Nothing. Just a lot to think about."

"I know, honey. I'll help however you need me to."

"Thanks," he said, followed by a soft kiss.

Nick looked over his shoulder at Yarto, Joe, and Tiffany in a three-person conversation while Isla and Clare huddled in a discussion that Nick assumed concerned the trailer. He knew Isla despised the idea of leaving this town. He needed to do this for her. He could sacrifice a few years. A penance for failing to tell his father about not getting accepted to any colleges.

"Where are we going?" Julia said. He saw her eyes drifting along the cinder roadway, houses sparse along their path.

"I figured we could go to the gas station and grab drinks and snacks. Aunt Jeannie didn't buy all that much food, despite her calling in catering. I think the walk will do us good, anyways."

"I wish you would have told me before," she said, looking worried about offending him.

"Why, what's wrong?"

"I still have heels on. I don't think I'll be able to walk that far. I'm sorry."

"Don't be sorry. This walk is stupid. Come on. We'll just wait at the house." He turned around, guiding her with his hand. "Hey, everyone," he yelled. "Julia and Clare still have heels on, so I don't think a walk will be feasible. Let's just wait at the house. We'll hang in Isla's room, out of Aunt Jeannie's way."

No one responded, but all turned and trudged back the few hundred feet to the house. As they neared it, two cars appeared and honked. Isla and Clare hurried out of the driveway, as Clare's dad and grandma parked their vehicles. A few cars followed behind, though everyone looked confused about where to park. Nick released Julia's hand and directed them to park on the obvious roadside in front of the house. *Church folks*, he thought, rolling his eyes.

"Isla, go tell Aunt Jeannie everyone is arriving."

All matched in their suits, dresses, and Sunday best, approaching Nick outside the house to give further condolences. Nick waved his friends inside, but Julia waited diligently beside him, while Clare stood near her family with soft greetings. Gail and her husband, Steve, friends of Dad's from work, told Nick how awfully this tragedy had affected them; Cherit and Lou, friends of Dad's from some club that neither Isla nor Nick had visited, told him that his dad was one of the best men they ever knew; and finally, Kelvin, Rhonda, Edna, and Tristen were all lined up behind them, patient despite arriving before the others. Even with Nick's torturous relationship with Clare, he did not feel uncomfortable, having known her family since he was young. Edna and his dad had gone to the same church when his mom was alive, both prior members of the church board.

"Your dad was a great man, Nick—a godly man who would help anyone in need, even when he drifted away. I'm sorry for your loss," Edna said, giving him a tight hug, then squeezing him on the arm. "If you are ever in need, don't hesitate to ask us for help."

"That's right," Kelvin said, patting Nick on the back. "Losing a dad is never easy, kiddo. If you need to talk to someone, we're always here for you."

"I told Nick he can stay at our trailer," Clare said. "They have to sell the house, and Isla wants to stay here for school. They can for free, right? No one's lived there in years."

"I don't know if now is the time to discuss this," Rhonda muttered.

"Now is exactly the time," Clare said, crossing her arms. "What's the use in waiting? Nick will need to take guardianship of Isla, and a place to stay is the hardest thing to figure out. He should finish his last few months of his senior year here. I say we help him out."

"Okay," Edna said.

"Okay?" Kelvin responded, looking at his mother. "Are you sure, Mom?"

"Of course. Nick's father would have done the same for Clare without thought. We will help you however you need, Nick. Don't worry about money or moving expenses. Our family is your family."

Nick breathed heavy, unable to calm himself from crying in front of everyone. Edna stepped to him, enveloping him in her arms. Nick's body convulsed upon the eruption of loss contrasted with divine kindness. Edna reached out for Julia, pulling her into the embrace. Nick felt uncomfortable at all the eyes staring, but the emotions poured. He hoped that his dad would still guide him, wherever he may be.

Chapter 21

Clare is eighteen

Nick sat on the couch, Julia in his lap, when a loud banging on the door caused him to flail, almost dumping Julia to the floor. Julia's nails clung into the back of Nick's neck.

"You're worse than a cat," he said, moving her hand off his neck. "Am I bleeding?"

"Oh, stop. You almost threw me off the couch."

"Can you see who's at the door?"

Julia groaned, then walked to the door, still wearing shorts and a shirt Nick had given her. Nick watched her, the large shorts drooping, showing the beginnings of the beauty underneath. He wanted her again, resulting in the need to fix himself and his growing excitement.

"Hi, Julia. Is Nick awake?"

Clare, he realized, rolling his eyes. What the hell did she need at ten in the morning on a Saturday?

"Yeah, but we just woke up. If you come back a little later, then . . ." Julia said, before Clare shoved past her into the living room.

"Are you planning on getting a job? Grandma wanted to know if you've been looking now that graduation and school are done. She doesn't want to rush you, but I think she'll get annoyed, unless you show you've been applying. I thought I should let you know. If you need help, I'll be around."

"Sure," he said, feeling annoyed at the accusation that he had been lazy. No one had told him about some hidden requirement when he'd moved in. Clare's grandma had promised to take care of Nick and Isla, but Nick had not considered what her expectations might be. Isla was going to some running camp soon, so Nick wanted to relax, hang out with Julia, and smoke pot. Most kids took the summer off after graduation, Nick reasoned.

"Is this because your grandma smelled weed in the trailer?"

"No, Nick," Clare said, shaking her head and sitting on the lounge chair. "She genuinely wants you to start making a living for yourself. I think she's just concerned that you'll get depressed without a purpose."

Julia stood, one hand keeping up her shorts and the other hand out, appearing confused at Clare's abrupt entry into the trailer. Nick motioned for her to sit next to him on the couch, worried that another issue would arise between the two. He considered embracing Julia, but she looked ready to argue. He knew there was no way back from her frustration.

"Clare, don't you think when I say that Nick just got out of bed, you can respect our privacy? I know your family owns this trailer, but Nick has the right to a private space."

"Sorry," Clare said, snickering. "Nick, are you mad I came inside? I just thought you should know what Grandma said. If you'd like, I can report back to her that Julia wouldn't let us talk."

"No, it's fine."

"Well, it's not fine to me. What if Nick had been naked? I don't know what has gotten into you, Clare, but this candid flirting and ordering Nick around is inappropriate. I know your family did a nice thing, but you should still be respectful."

"Piss off, Julia. I've known Nick longer than your relationship can even be imagined. My grandmother is not a patient woman—generous, but not patient."

Nick watched the two of them. Clare pushed into her chair, smiling at Julia, while Julia twisted the large shorts into a ball, her fingers rigid in the fabric.

"This is not about your grandma, and you know it. Nick told me about all the flirting you've been doing when I'm not around, barging into the trailer without knocking, sitting on his lap, ruffling up his hair, even trying to kiss him. Grow the fuck up. You are not his girlfriend."

"And neither will you be if Nick realizes how controlling and pretentious you are."

"Oh, come on. I've helped Nick with school, with taking care of Isla, with everything. He's never complained. He sure as hell complains about you and your drinking, though. Face it. You're becoming a sloppy, red-necked bitch."

Nick stared at Julia, shocked by the outburst of frustration. "Julia, you need to apologize," he said, though he hated having to say it. Everything Julia said had some merit, but he knew to keep quiet; Clare and her family had opened her home to Isla and him at their dire time of need. He had told Julia all these issues in confidence, not realizing how much Clare's blatant disregard for their monogamous relationship tore at her. Nick knew Julia understood his predicament, so why utter this riot of words?

"I will not. You should be asking her to apologize to us, Nick."

Nick looked at Clare. A prick of hurt glittered in Clare's vacant stare toward the television.

"I can't, Julia." He swooped himself up and over to Julia, ready to console her. She remained apathetic despite his efforts.

"I can't anymore, Nick," she said, pushing him off. He shifted away, hands propped behind him. "I'm tired of worrying about this situation. College was going to put too much distance between us anyways. I'm sorry I'm doing this in front of her, but you've clearly made your choice."

"Choice? *Choice*?" Clare yelled, throwing herself from the chair. "You think it's fair to make him choose between his girlfriend and one of his closest friends? You can say whatever hurtful things you want, Julia, but I've never given him a ridiculous ultimatum."

Tears finally trickled down Julia's face as she looked to Nick for support. Instead, Nick turned his focus to the Saturday morning cartoon, *Teenage Mutant Ninja Turtles*, one of his favorite shows as a kid. Though the turtles may have had their own crime-fighting problems, they did not have crying women bothering them on a Saturday morning. He wished the two of them would leave and solve their problems amongst themselves. The idea of him choosing between these two self-involved women made him want to choose isolation, sex be damned. Well, at least for the moment, he figured, chuckling to himself.

"What the hell is so funny?" Julia sobbed. "I'm out of here. Please don't bother me while I pack." She tramped to the bedroom and slammed the door.

"Oh, dammit," Nick said. Clare leaned back in the chair, a smug look of triumph on her face. "What is wrong with you? Are you trying to ruin my life?"

"Ruin your life!" she said, her nose flared. "You are in this trailer with your sister because of me. I've always supported you, Nick. Even by keeping you distant, I've helped you! Don't pretend that creature in your bedroom isn't toxic because she bounced on your dick." Clare grabbed the closest thing to her, a glass of orange juice on the end table, and threw it against the wall before leaving. "When you grow the fuck up, then you can come apologize."

Julia opened the door, looking at the mess of glass and juice all over the wall and floor, some splattered on the back of the television. "You get what you deserve, Nick." She slammed the bedroom door once more.

Nick looked upon the shattered fragments of glass. He considered stepping on a few, cutting his foot. Maybe that would get them both to calm down and help him. He chose to believe that he was not the root cause of what was happening. He reached into the bottom right-hand drawer of the cabinets next to his sink and pulled out his pipe and baggie. He packed the pipe and began smoking next to the kitchen window over the sink, waiting for the tension in the room to dissipate with each inhale.

"Are you kidding me, Nick? We're breaking up, so you decide to smoke weed. You're useless." She dragged her bag through the hall, gave a small huff, and left the trailer door open as her bag bounced on the steps.

Nick felt only relief with everyone gone. He continued to smoke, letting the wind blow the door around. Julia never let him indulge unless she did too. She had taken avid concern and decisive control over his future, worried that he would never "find himself" without going to college.

He'd never informed Julia that he'd received money from Dad's accident, afraid she would dictate its use. Edna had warned him about letting too much information slip, as people suddenly found a multitude of reasons for needing to borrow money when discovering a person with some. If people were rude enough to ask, he told them he had gotten just enough to raise Isla until she turned eighteen. Thankfully, the extra he did not mention should allow both of them to go to college without the burden of loans. Even in death, he'd experienced his dad's helping hand.

"Why is the door open?" Isla said, returning from her run and waving away the smoke. "Come on, Nick, it's before noon."

"On a Saturday, Is. I'm allowed to enjoy my weekends."

Isla considered him until Nick's gaze turned away, then she sat on the couch, tossing her running shoes off. She flopped down to the floor and began stretching her legs, head curved to her knee. Nick felt slightly disgusted, witnessing his sister staying in good shape while he reclined in the chair with no active plans.

"So, Julia and I just broke up."

"Oh, yeah?" Isla mumbled. She tossed her head up. "I thought she was here last night. Took you long enough."

Nick flashed his sister an incredulous look.

"Oh, come off it. You bickered all the time. Why do you think I stopped hanging out in the living room with you two around?"

"Fair," he said. "She never left me alone. Always needed to make life plans. I'm raising you. Isn't that enough?"

"No," she said, standing up and leaning against the wall. She lifted each leg, stretching out her quadriceps. "I mean, yes, but you can't use me as an excuse to do nothing. I thought you planned to take community college classes."

Nick scoffed. "What is it about today? Between you, Julia, Clare, and her grandmother, I'm not good enough for anyone."

She stomped her foot down and eyed him. "What about Clare and her grandmother? Did you do something to make them angry?" Nick did not respond, inhaling deep and holding his breath. "Nick, what happened? Tell me now."

He let out the smoke and coughed a few times before smiling. "Edna is demanding I get a job. She doesn't like that I'm not doing anything with my summer. I think she just hates that I'm relaxing in the trailer and my marijuana use."

"We don't have to pay rent, Nick. Go get a job if that's what she requires. I'll be off at camp for a few weeks. It'll do you some good to get out, instead of moping here."

"I don't mope."

"I'm sad, too. I miss him every day," she said, ruffling Nick's hair. "But he would want us to do something, Nick. He would want to see us trying to be happy."

Nick waved her away, fighting off the conversation. Everyone demanded he talk about his father's death. The man had died and caused Nick to suffer through the limitations of his life in the betterment of his sister's. Nick would never admit any such selfish reflections, especially to his sister. She deserved the wellbeing he provided, thus resolving to tuck away the hostility he felt for his situation whenever placed on the spot. This torrent of abandonment, despite vocalized support, kept him seeking relief through increased bouts of the numbing substance he smoked. If he found a job displaying himself to the public, the continuous appraisal of his wellbeing and bombardment of phony well wishes would drive him into madness. Julia pushed, almost daily, on his feelings when he merely desired to sulk. Clare never asked, and he appreciated that, a caring touch in her self-involved persona.

"I can't face people out there, Is. Where would I get a local job without feeling like I'd failed?"

"Maybe you can work with Kelvin. He doesn't work in town. He might be able to get you an easy job of taking in deliveries without seeing anyone." Nick pursed his lips, despising the idea, annoyed most by its reasonable thoughtfulness. "Well, think about it," she said, heading to her room.

Instead, Nick relaxed and fell asleep on the chair, waking in the mid-afternoon to a *Judge Judy* rerun. He turned off the television, looking around to remember what he had meant to do today. Right. Julia broke up with him, followed by Edna, Clare, and Isla's demands that he get a job and move on with his life. He yawned, then yelled out while stretching in the chair. The chair rocked back, causing him to whoop. A knock on the door. He groaned and yelled for them to come in.

Clare walked into the trailer with a tray full of brownies. "Sorry about this morning. I hate Julia's greater-than-thou attitude. I hope you can work everything out. If you want to, that is."

"I don't know, Clare. I'm stuck figuring out my life, and I don't see Julia in that future. What you did wasn't right," he said, sitting up and taking the plate of brownies. He placed them on the counter next to the microwave. "But you helped in your way. Do you want any ice cream with your brownie?"

"Thanks," she said. Nick saw her eyeing the glass still on the ground, stains of orange juice on the wall. "I'm sorry about the glass." She walked to the small side closet next to the bathroom and picked up the broom and dustpan, sweeping the fragments of glass.

Soft sighs escaped Clare's lips as Nick watched her clean, waiting for the microwave to heat up their brownies. He scooped ice cream on top, placing the plates on the small kitchen table by the back window, as Clare grabbed a wet paper towel and wiped the wall and floor. Nick enjoyed the treat, not offering to help. He accepted her penance for this morning's debacle, though he worried about her personal wellbeing. Clare seemed to move in extremes these past few weeks, from bouts of utter silence and looks of longing fright to screams of euphoria and blistering anger.

Her grandmother's request for him to find a job seemed out of place, given that Clare had removed herself from attending college this upcoming year without any alternate plans. Clare provided no substantive reason, giving a vague allusion to finding herself, unsure of what she wanted to study.

Clare dumped the jagged pieces, washed her hands, and then sat on the chair next to him. She took nibbles of the brownie as melted ice cream oozed through the creases. Nick glanced at her, then shot his gaze back down to his own half-eaten brownie. He did not feel awkward in the silence, still a little buzzed from earlier, but felt that Clare needed some words to escape his mouth to fill a void he did not understand.

Instead, she said, "I don't think Grandma means for you to find a job tomorrow. She wants to make sure that you don't sit around the house for the next year, moping over your father. 'He needs some escapism and might as well make some money for his own future,' she said. She wants me to do the same, you know. I didn't have the chance to tell you after Julia screamed at me."

"Do you think your dad needs help at CVS? I wouldn't mind working for him, and we could carpool."

"I think he would like that," she said, a fleck of brownie drifting from her mouth to the table. "He's been encouraging me to possibly work there, so that would help me push him off. I have no interest. He's afraid I'll become despondent and sulk like Mom."

"I'm surprised he didn't ask Tristen to help him out. You can work at sixteen, right?"

Clare dropped her spoon, then quickly grabbed it. "I haven't seen Tristen in a while. He's been holed up in his room as far as I know."

Nick noticed the glances, the twitches, the instability in her thoughts at the innocuous question. What possible falling out could have occurred between them? Nick wanted to inquire further yet knew Clare would not appreciate him probing. The broad frizz of her hair, light lining between her eyebrows, and generic jogging pants revealed a depressed soul, but Nick's own foundation would not support him, let alone another fragile being.

"Why did you stop loving me?"

"What?" Nick said, blinking at her, looking around for someone to verify the words.

"What happened? Why did you stop chasing me? You used to be so kind. You had such a crush on me. I miss that, Nick."

"What do you mean you miss that?" He picked up her plate and brought it to the sink. He attempted composure, but fury latched onto the hard notes of the question. "You used and ignored me, Clare. Did you expect me to play puppy dog my entire life? You had no respect for my feelings." He threw a fork into the sink, the clanging reverberating longer than he wanted, yet she waited, no reaction to his outburst. "You treated me horribly when I wanted to make you happy. Why would you want me now, Clare? All this flirtation and games. Do you take pleasure in ruining my general happiness? Julia was a nice girl, and now I have no one." He rushed back to his chair, grasped her hands, and looked into her eyes. "Why would you ask that question?"

"I love you, Nick."

"Why now?" he said, hammering his fist on the table. "Why, when I finally found someone else who meant something to me, who returned my feelings without games?"

"I don't know," she said, eyes tearing. She seemed genuinely frightened by the outburst, which caused Nick immediate sorrow. He felt entitled to his anger but never wanted to cause Clare any visible harm.

"I'm sorry," Nick said, rubbing his hand over her cheek. "Please don't cry. You do understand, right? Quit playing games. I can't take being made a repeated fool."

"I'm not out to make you a fool, Nick. I love you and want to be with you. You were so aloof through high school. I know this is terrible, but you taking care of Isla and having a stable relationship with Julia has changed you. I can see it. You're a better man."

"But how can I feel the same about you? Between your outbursts, drinking, displays of rapid emotion, I never know what step to take that won't cause a meltdown." He stood, knocking back the chair, infuriated by an implication he only just realized. "How dare you accuse me of acting like a child and using my grief to justify some disgusting need to play nurse? You sit there telling me that my refusal to lie down and die has given you some sexual interest. What is wrong with you, Clare? I loved you. Everyone knew. But this is rotten. Could you imagine if I told Isla or your grandma you only want me now after the death of my father?"

Clare kept quiet during his outburst. Nick walked back and forth, picking up the chair, leaning toward her face, then looking out the window. He felt empowered to punish her for the years of rejection she'd made him endure. However, her sudden desire rekindled the boyhood crush he had nurtured for so long. She wanted him. Why was he using this moment to reduce his only chance at the woman who saved him and Isla from leaving?

"I'm sorry," he said. He returned to the chair, pushing his hands into his eyes, unable to acknowledge the distress he'd caused Clare. "Everything you've done all these years, all the wishing you would finally notice me. It makes me angry, Clare. You could have loved me for all those years, a high school time of bliss rather than a feeling of permanent rejection that I endured from you."

"I understand," she said. "Maybe I should leave and give you time to think everything through."

She stood with slow grace, looked at him, her eyes lightly stained from running mascara. Nick did not understand. He could not pinpoint the benefit of punishing her any further. He needed to kiss her, hold her, beg even longer for forgiveness. This was Clare declaring her love for him. Clare! How could he forget the one person he had begged God to reveal the chivalry he would provide in her life? Had not the divine provided in this moment? He pulled her close and kissed her, a soft touch of the lips, a slip of his tongue just inside the sweet opening of her mouth. She pushed him away gently, eyes closed, appearing to breathe in the moment.

"Does this mean you forgive me?"

"I'll try," Nick said, pulling her back into his embrace, savoring the woman of his dreams.

Chapter 22

Clare is nineteen

Nick was exhausted after another late-night rendezvous with Clare, speckled with residual fluids, both too lazy to rise after sex. He looked at Clare sprawled over most of the bed, arms spread, her butt trailing in the air, a light sputtering coming from her mouth. He felt a tinge of endearment at the sight, knowing he would need to wake her soon so she could sneak back into her bed. They pretended the household did not know, but Nick expected they all knew in some form about these midnight escapades. Isla knew outright, as no attempts at sneaking could succeed past the teenager. She expressed no objection, unless she heard loud noises from Nick's bedroom, at which times she would bang on the door, yelling in disgust. She was off at camp now, so this night had faced no interruption.

Nick rolled out of bed, stretched his arms with a grunt, and looked at the clock. Still before midnight, so Clare had some time to make her way back home. He touched the stickiness on his cock and stomach and decided to shower before easing Clare out the door.

The spray of hot water brought relief as he scrubbed briskly. "Dammit," he muttered, remembering he had to wake at six to ride to work with Kelvin. He did not mind the shelf stocking job Kelvin offered him, but the hours were so early, requiring numerous alarms.

He washed his hair, wondering how long he and Clare could continue this affair without confronting the family. He thought Kelvin would be respectful if he admitted to their experiences. He assumed Rhonda despised him, hating the idea of someone of no relation staying in the trailer. Nick could not recall being rude or giving her any reason to suspect him, yet he could feel a certain layer of cool air in her presence. He did not expect Edna to object, given her generosity and assistance already, but he could not be sure. His mind returned to Kelvin, not wanting to disappoint him, but unable to talk Clare into defining their sexual exploits as anything more than pleasure.

He dried off, put on sweatpants, and snuck back into the room. He rubbed Clare's back, trying to ease her up. Small groans but no movement. "Clare, you need to go home."

"Who cares?" she mumbled. "I'm tired."

"Clare, I think your family would mind if they caught you in my bed."

"No," she groaned.

"Clare, you can't stay here until we tell your parents. It's not right."

She groaned, then grunted, pushing herself up in annoyance. "Your morals annoy me."

"I'm glad I balance you out," he said, smiling. "I have to leave with your dad at six in the morning, so you need to head out. If your parents say it's okay, I don't care if you stay over. I'm just not going to ruin a good thing here."

"I know, I know," she said, pulling on her panties. "Gross," she said. "I feel sticky."

"Yeah, we fell asleep right away."

"Great. I need to shower, or I'll reek of sex."

"I think you smell fine," he said, pulling her into his arms, kissing the top of her head.

"I need to talk to you before I say anything to my parents, Nick."

He furrowed his forehead, studying her. She pretended to be sleepy, closing her eyes and yawning at his gaze, but he knew this was a tawdry act. "What?"

"I'll tell you tomorrow. I have something I need to figure out first." She stirred from him, finding the rest of her clothes, scrambling to dress.

"Clare, why the rush? You're worrying me. You can't just be cryptic and leave. What am I supposed to think?"

She patted him on the face and kissed him. "Nothing bad for us. I just need another day. I shouldn't have said anything. Sorry."

"It's fine. Make sure you tell me if you need anything."

"Of course, my knight." She went out the bedroom door, closing it behind her.

He stood in the dark, dumbfounded by her patronizing manner. He simply did not understand what built the foundation for a great relationship. With Julia, he felt that initial excitement, the party, prom, consistent sex that faltered after two months, aligning with his father's death, moving into Clare's backyard, raising his sister, followed by incessant lectures on what he planned to do. How could he plan for anything when the best man he knew had died for no reason? Suddenly, Julia found every decision he made to be a failure, and his delights in relaxing and smoking pot became a foundation of laziness, resulting in sighs of latent satisfaction.

Then Clare rose to his side at Julia's jealous outburst. Nick's feelings of abandonment and rejection emerged, but he grasped onto the thought of a fairytale romance. A boy that holds out for a girl for so long should feel like the knight. He deserved abounding love, a cheerful clutch of the hand, a ruffling of forehead kisses, cooking a dinner for the whole family, a proposal of marriage planned for years. He did not enjoy the sneaking around; the insinuation that they were participating in some forbidden act. He fought off his suspicions, yet he remained with few explanations for her behavior.

Nick sighed, smacking himself on the face, trying to ignore these sordid thoughts. He needed to sleep, dream, drift away from whatever Clare could possibly tell him that would destroy the future he desired. He snuck into the kitchen, taking his weed out of the drawer. He sat in the chair, turned on the television, smoked, and fell asleep to the soft sounds of comedy.

Nick woke to banging on the door. He tried to lift himself out of the chair, falling back, forgetting he left the footrest up. More knocking. "Nick, are you ready? We need to leave in ten minutes."

"I'll be right out," he started to yell, attempting to clear his throat, then croaked.

"Alright, pal. Hurry up. We have a big shipment coming this morning. I'll be in the truck."

Nick looked through his closet and then at the laundry basket for a work shirt, grabbed one—wrinkled, smelled okay. He smoothed the shirt with an iron and sprayed Febreze—still wrinkled but good enough. Khaki pants and proper shoes on, he hurried out the door, hoping he did not smell.

He jumped into the passenger seat of Kelvin's truck. "I'm sorry. I hope we won't be too late."

Kelvin reversed the truck without acknowledging him, turning up the radio to some talk show. Nick curled into the seat, closing his eyes. Kelvin and Nick generally rode with the radio filling the silence, yet Nick felt annoyance in the air today. He loathed being the burden of someone's day—especially a person that he respected. As Kelvin parked the car, turning the radio down, Nick said another earnest apology.

Kelvin regarded Nick for a moment, studying him. Nick simmered in discomfort, reaching for the door latch.

"Just wait, Nick. I want to know something."

He knew Clare should have told him sooner, and now Kelvin would threaten his life for screwing his daughter. He kept hold of the door handle, waiting for any sudden movement of violence.

"You aren't getting high at work, are you?"

"Wait, what?" Nick retorted, less out of the accusation than surprise at the subject.

"People have been smelling weed in the back room, and I know that you partake every so often at home." Kelvin rolled his eyes at Nick's confusion. "Oh, come on, Nick. You've reeked at dinner. No one cares at the house, except maybe Mom if she's in a mood, but you can't be doing illicit drugs at work. I won't have any choice if anyone complains about you. We both know you'll fail that drug test."

"I've never done anything of the sort, sir."

"I thought so," Kelvin said, looking out the windshield, tapping the steering wheel. "You just smell like weed right now, Nick."

"Oh, shit. Really? I'm so sorry. It's a dirty shirt, and I sprayed Febreze to mask the smell. I'll be happy to spray any other cologne. I honestly don't smoke at work, Kelvin. Really."

"I believe you. Let's just make sure we shower and wear clean clothes from now on. Like I said, I won't have much say if someone above me gets a complaint."

"I appreciate you telling me. I'll make sure to be more aware."

"Great," Kelvin said, clapping Nick on the shoulder. "Let's get this day over with."

Nick enjoyed the passive nature of stocking the shelves, every item placed in its rightful spot. Few people bothered him with his hands full, so he worked with his thoughts drifting between Julia, Clare, Clare's unknown problem, and what his future could possibly entail. Saving some money over the year and attending community college seemed admirable enough of an endeavor for the time being if he could keep his relationship with Clare from turning sour. A fervent lover of the dramatics, he usually smoked more before seeing Clare to prevent being swept up in her onslaught of mood swings. Clare had taken to accusing him of still desiring Julia, then apologizing for her jealousy in the same hour. He clung to past emotions, hopeful that the Clare he dreamed to be real would spring forth.

Clare picked Nick up from work as Kelvin needed to stay late to finish paperwork. They drove in silence, the radio playing muffled tunes that Nick could not recognize. He looked amongst the passing houses, fields, a small pond with a dog and boy, the dog jumping into the water while the boy laughed at the splash. A smile drew upon Nick's lips, as he thought of his dad taking him to water parks when his mom was alive. A happier man who'd enjoyed every water slide with the gumption of a young boy learning the joys of speeding faster in cars, tubes, and boats. A gentle handle on the risks of life without ever grasping the danger of death. He began weeping for his losses, eyes focused out the window, hoping Clare would not notice.

They began down the final gravel stretch toward home when she broke the silence. "How was work?"

"Fine."

"You okay?"

"I'm fine," he said. A sniffle caused him to tighten his fingers into his pants.

"You sure?"

"Just allergies."

"Okay. I need to talk to you later. You going to be home tonight?"

"Yeah," he said. "Just relaxing. Maybe play video games. Isla will be home from camp, so I'll catch up with her. What did you want to talk about?" He looked upon Clare's face of pale dread without blinking.

"I didn't know Isla would be home. Maybe we can talk another day."

"Clare, I'm not going to wait around for you to keep telling me you have something important on your mind. Just say it. You know how much anxiety comes from telling someone 'I need to talk.' Good news rarely needs an introduction."

"Sorry. I'll tell you tonight. I just want you to promise to keep an open mind."

"An open mind? What is going on, Clare? Are you in trouble? Are you in debt or something?"

"No," she said, letting the sounds of gravel clinking underneath the car fill the air.

"You better tell me tonight, Clare. I thought we had something good going for us, but you're starting to make me wonder if you plan on leaving me."

She grabbed his leg. "Oh, no. Nothing like that. I'm sorry. I'm making a mess of everything right now. I just need you to give me some time."

"Alright. I'll drop it."

"Thank you."

After a few minutes of muffled music and gravel, Clare parked the car. Nick headed around the house to the trailer. He stepped inside to find Isla holding one of her bras out. She shrieked, then threw it into the hamper.

"Isla, I've seen your bras."

"I know," she said with a breath of exhalation, then nervous laughter. "You surprised more than embarrassed me." She rushed over and hugged him.

"How was camp?" He leapt onto the chair and leaned back while Isla continued her laundry.

"Great! Everyone is so focused on getting better and beating each other, but not gloating about their personal achievements. More like improving as a group. I enjoyed the camaraderie, but the closest girl is two hours away."

"I thought your friend Kayla was going. Doesn't she live nearby?"

"No, well yes, Kayla was supposed to go, but she backed out. I forgot to tell you. She claimed something to do with her family, but I think she was nervous with the top runners all over the country attending."

"Well, I hope everything is okay with her family."

Isla threw her sock down, frustrated at not finding the other one. "She hasn't mentioned anything since her excuse, so I bet she was lying. Not my problem. Plus, I don't want to be insensitive and call her out."

"I know."

Isla began humming while she folded her shirts. Nick looked for the remote within reaching distance but could not locate the small object. Without the energy to get up and look, Nick sighed and closed his eyes.

"Is."

"Yes."

"Can I ask you a personal question?"

"About me or you? I'm not dating anyone, if that's what you want to know."

"No, it's about me."

"Well?" she said after a while. "Are you going to ask me?"

He opened his right eye; she was staring at him, expectant. "Clare says she needs to talk to me tonight. She mentioned handling some task before. Should I be worried?"

"I don't know. If she planned on breaking up with you, why would she need to do something beforehand? Maybe she changed her mind about going to college and needs to talk to her grandma about money?"

"You didn't see her face, Is."

"Well, of course I didn't."

"You know what I mean. She looked upset."

"I don't know, Nick. Clare and I haven't spoken much this summer. Seems like we were growing closer but then drifted apart. She says a few words when she visits you, but otherwise, we don't hang out. I'm away all the time, so maybe that's it."

"She doesn't drink as much anymore, from what I've seen. She sees Ryan less, so maybe he was the influence. But she seems unhappy."

"Have you talked to her about it?"

"Sort of. Can you just ask someone why they are sad all the time? She's hard to pinpoint."

"You could just ask if anything is wrong."

"I tried that, obviously," he mumbled, twitching his head.

"Sorry. I didn't know."

"I know. I'm the one who's sorry for having you listen to my dreariness. I don't know what I want, Isla. I'm so proud of you and your accomplishments. But for me, I only see haze when I think of the future, a listless path where I barely set one foot in front of the next. I'm eighteen and have no concrete goals. Aren't I supposed to know what I want to be now that I'm grown?"

Isla laughed. "Sometimes I forget why you smoke pot. You over-think everything. You haven't talked to me like this in a while. I figured Julia and Clare had taken the brunt of your indecisiveness."

Nick groaned. "This isn't helping. Do you think Clare and I are a good couple?"

Isla placed some of her folded clothes into her basket and walked into her room. Nick heard the opening and shutting of drawers, clanging of hangers, activities of monotonous laundry tasks, yet no response to his question. Nick knew the gist of how Isla felt about their relationship. He did not believe Isla hated or was even bothered by Clare, but Nick needed Isla to tell him what he already suspected, that Clare could not possibly be in a place to date anyone with sincerity, and he would toil for months in a relationship fraying with secrets. His stomach churned, sweat on his palms, a pulse in his balls from the desperation that he had loved Clare only to find that love to be a fantasy. He wanted the best for Clare in every way imaginable, but the extraordinary act of kindness of providing his small family with a home did not equate to a tender relationship.

He never should have started, for what if Clare became cynical, seeking punishment when he no longer desired tumultuous trysts in the dead of night? He wanted romance. Was he merely a patch to Clare's emotional void that he did not want to admit existed?

He heard Isla begin to speak. Lost in thought, he could not comprehend the words. "Isla, did you say something?"

"Have you not been listening?" She sighed and returned to the couch. "Will you please sit up and listen?"

Nick brought the chair upright and gazed upon his sister, her face worried.

"I'm not sure what to say to you that will help. I like Clare in her own way, and I love you more than anything. But I don't think the two of you belong together." She raised her hand, as if anticipating a rebuttal by Nick, though he sat placated, waiting for her reasoning. "I think Clare has taken advantage of you and your teenage crush all these years. I never said anything, because what could I have said that would help you? Dad made his jokes, but he worried, too. You refused to chase anyone but Clare, and she led you along with light flirtations, enough for you to help with her homework, drive her around. I'm not saying Clare is evil or that a woman must either excuse herself or accept every offer. Boys are ignorant, even with the most straightforward rejection. She's worse, Nick. Even now, when she claims to love you, she won't tell her family. Why? I think you deserve someone who will support you like Julia. Clare will always be about Clare. I believe she tries to be a good person . . . I mean, look what she did for us here. Even so, she can still be a poor match for you."

The moment lingered, the clicking of the second hand on the clock keeping rhythm. "Thanks, Isla. You're right."

"I'm glad you took that well," she said. "I was worried you might just let the question go. What are you going to do?"

"I don't know," he said. The room felt distorted and unfocused. One part of him wanted to break up with Clare before she could tell him anything, beat her to whatever bad news, but he knew this would only cause more grief. He would hear her out, then reveal his doubts about their relationship. She needed to understand, truly acknowledge the heartache she'd caused him all those years.

"Why don't you take a nap and hear what she has to say?" Isla suggested. "I'm going for a run in a little bit. Make sure I'm around, maybe in my room, when she comes over. I want to be here for you, Nick. Relationships can suck."

"How would you know?" he laughed. Isla blushed, but he did not pry. "Thanks." Nick grabbed his pipe and weed from the drawer and went into his bedroom. He smoked for a while, not allowing his thoughts to linger on anything for too long. He meditated in his own way, not with any mantra or focus, easing himself into the passage of time, clinging for a clear mind. He fell asleep, upset at the toll that Clare's waiting forced upon him.

Nick gave up on sleep after a couple of hours, exhausted by the bouts of tosses and turns. He did not want to admit the reason he was bothered. Clare had volunteered this trailer, and he had to stay for three years for Isla. Clare had the upper hand, no matter how he felt about her. He suffered under this powerlessness. He looked at his phone—no messages. He texted Clare, asking when she planned to come over and profess. He did not want to wait. She responded with one word: *soon*.

"Isla, you out there?" he yelled.

His door opened. "Yeah, did you need something?"

"No. Clare said she would come over soon. I know you want to support me, but you might want to make yourself scarce. I'm worried Clare will try to tell me another time if she sees you. Do you think you can hide in your room for a bit?"

"Uh, sure," she said. "Just knock if you need anything."

Over an hour later, Clare walked into Nick's bedroom without warning.

"Can we talk?"

"Yes, tell me what's going on. Why do you look so frightened?"

"I don't want to drag this along any further. I'm sorry for how you must have felt today. I needed to talk to Tristen first. I'm pregnant, Nick."

Nick did not grasp an immediate emotion. He thought through all of the day's anticipated scenarios, replaying them, unable to find a declaration of Clare's pregnancy in the mosaic of predictions. The feeling of falling backwards without a safety net lurched through his mind, until he began to take heavy breaths, unable to catch his body with each one.

"Oh my God, Nick. You're hyperventilating." She rubbed his back for a moment. Her comfort ended there as she began crying.

"I'm sorry," he huffed. "I'm happy for us. I'm just surprised. I thought you were on birth control." She did not respond, continuing her soft sobs. "You told me you were on the pill, Clare."

"Sometimes I forget," she whimpered.

Nick groaned, pressing his hands into his eyes to fight his disbelief. "Clare, I would have used condoms if I knew." He then understood her initial words, a sinking of why he needed to wait to hear from her. "Why did you need to talk to Tristen?" Her whimpers stopped, as if his connection frightened her emotions, stalled them to fathom a response. "Have you had sex with Tristen?" Her head tilted reluctantly until she nodded. He flung from the bed and tripped backwards, falling into the wall. Nick's picture of Isla and him at the county fair crashed to the floor. "How could you do this? You must have slept with him recently."

"Sort of," she whispered, a throaty grind coming out. "It wasn't consensual, Nick."

"What the fuck do you mean it wasn't consensual?" He ran toward her on the bed, arm around her waist, face next to hers. "What happened? What did he do? I'll kill him, Clare. I will."

"You remember when he came over that one time to play video games, and you left us alone? That's when it happened."

"He raped you *here*?" Nick boomed. He scrambled toward the door. Clare began to scream. "No, Nick. No. Please. Let me explain."

Nick did not hear her, his mind now focused on Tristen, the creepy bastard. How dare he come into his home and commit such an atrocity? Tristen needed to be dragged, arrested, charged, and brought to justice.

Isla opened her door. "What's going on? Who's screaming?"

"Isla, stop him. He's going to attack Tristen."

Nick did not run, instead adopting a blustering march to punch Tristen's face until he felt relief. Nick was unable to articulate the madness that overcame him at Clare's declaration. On top of a pregnancy, an in-family assault blinded him, requiring him to lash out.

As he opened the trailer door, he felt a hand tugging his arm. He shook the hand off with ease. "Nick, you have to stop. What is going on, Clare?" Isla cried out. "Why is Nick going after Tristen?" Nick stepped outside to see Tristen hurrying toward the back door of the house, feeling adrenaline at the sight of prey.

"You disgusting bastard," Nick said, leaving the trailer, followed by Clare and Isla. "You raping piece of trash. You can't run far."

A chorus of Clare and Isla begged him to stop, but he ignored them. "I'm going to fucking kill him," he said as he reached the door.

Nick stepped into the kitchen. Kelvin looked shocked, papers strewn about the dining room table and floor.

"Nick, what the hell is going on? Tristen just rushed through the kitchen."

"Where did he go?" Nick said through gritted teeth.

"Up to his room, I think."

"Come out and face me," Nick yelled, marching toward the stairs. Clare and Isla were now in the house, both trying to pull on him to stop. Kelvin stalled with the papers in hand. Rhonda stepped out of the spare bedroom, uttering nonsense of confusion.

"Don't go up there, Nick. You don't know what's going on," screamed Isla.

"Shut the fuck up. He's dead."

"Hold on, Nick," yelled Kelvin.

Clare lost her grip as Nick marched up the stairs, though Isla still held onto him, attempting to drag him back. Nick tried to shake her off, beginning to lose his balance but determined to reach his goal. Tristen would not hide from this. He would fess up and face the consequences.

"Isla, get off," he said, wagging his arm behind him as he neared the top of the stairwell. He heard the sudden cry and tried to grab her. He did not mean for her to fall, just to stop the pulling, as his sister flopped down the stairs in three rough tumbles, hitting Clare at the bottom of the stairwell. Clare fell hard on the kitchen floor, her body making a flat thud. Isla began crying, holding her right arm. Nick gawked at the two girls he meant to protect, an already monstrous scenario worsened by his thoughtless impulses. He rushed down the stairs, but Kelvin stopped him, blocking him from going further.

"Explain yourself now, Nick!"

Edna then entered the front door, gasping at Clare and Isla splayed on the floor. "What is going on in here? Why are the girls screaming on the floor?"

Edna reached down to Clare, helping her stand. Clare leaned onto her grandmother, blocking her belly, as if Nick had intended to punch the baby out of her. Nick knew he looked in the wrong, though he did not even commit the act he intended. All these atrocities had happened around him, not caused by him, yet he did not know how to properly explain, so he said the only words he knew would deflect his offenses. "Clare told me she's pregnant, and Tristen raped her."

Isla moaned on the floor, straining to lift herself, cradling her right arm. No one helped her as they swallowed the accusations laid out by Nick. Clare gripped her grandmother so tight, the wiser woman let out a soft cry and loosened Clare's hands.

"She told you Tristen raped her . . . and she's pregnant by him?" Kelvin repeated, catatonic.

Broken from his rage, Nick finally helped Isla to a sitting position. He did not see any bone protrusions but expected her arm to be sprained at best. He would take her to the hospital as soon as these events passed, though his mind still considered the creature in the room above with disgust.

"Clare told you Tristen raped her?" Rhonda said in disbelief. "Did she tell you that they've been sleeping together?"

Nick wanted to throw up, desperate to accuse Rhonda of lying. Nick shook his head vehemently in an effort to show his refusal to hear the words.

"It's true. Clare told me herself, and that it had ended. I wasn't aware of these other concerns," Edna said.

"You've been having sex with your adopted brother?" Kelvin roared. "In my house? And you both knew?"

"What were you going to do?" Edna said without inflection. "Clare told me she had instigated, and I didn't want to see the boy put out, so I didn't mention it."

"She threatened to turn you against me," Rhonda said with disdain. "Remember how you all refused to believe he peeped on her in the bathroom? I caught them one night, and she said she would convince everyone I'm a liar and force me out."

Clare did not raise her head, her hands softly resting on her stomach. Nick began to feel a hatred for Clare that he knew would never leave.

The withholding of this information had caused this present tragedy, as he never would have touched her if he knew.

"Why would you lie to me, Clare?" he said.

"I didn't lie," she screamed. "He did rape me! The last time, like I said. The baby is probably yours," she said in a final whisper.

"You're fucking Nick, too?" laughed Rhonda. "And you don't know who the baby's father is. My God, Clare. Have you any shame left to provide this family?"

"Shut up, Rhonda," snapped Edna. "At least Clare graduated high school before getting pregnant."

"Oh, bully for you, old woman," Rhonda said.

"Let's forego this whole business about Clare's sexual partners," Edna said. "I think we all knew Nick and Clare had been romancing, though I did not know the degree. Why were you heading up there, Nick?"

"To get the truth from Tristen."

"He'll deny it," Clare cried. "He doesn't think he did anything wrong."

"But you were sleeping with him before?" Kelvin said.

"Yes, but Dad, that doesn't matter."

Before Kelvin could respond, Edna said, "We need to take Isla and Clare to the hospital. I'm worried that poor girl broke her arm, and Clare appears to have pain in her abdomen. I'll drive them. We can deal with this when we get back. Nick, I expect you to mind your temper until we hear from Tristen. We will discover the truth without violence." Clare opened her mouth, but Edna interrupted, "Hush, child. We need to go now. Kelvin, will you grab some Vicodin that I have in my medicine cabinet. Isla should have two before we go."

Nick guided Isla to Edna's car, setting her down in the backseat. He apologized, begging for forgiveness, telling her he would never willingly hurt her.

"I know, Nick. I know you didn't mean it."

"Thanks, Is. I can't explain how terrible I feel right now."

"Nick, go home," Clare said softly from the front seat.

Nick wanted to argue with her, but Edna started the car as Kelvin came behind Nick and handed Isla the two Vicodin.

"Please be careful, Mom," Kelvin said.

"Don't do anything until I get back. I think this situation requires all of us to sit at the table and discuss how we want to handle it, including Clare's pregnancy."

"Right," he said.

She drove off. Nick raised a hand to their departure, unable to see if anyone waved back. He turned around and jogged to catch Kelvin heading into the house.

"Kelvin, I'm sorry. Clare told me she was pregnant and that he raped her. I lost my mind. I wanted to wreck Tristen when I heard. It's hard to believe now that I'm saying it, but at the time, she said he took advantage of her in the trailer when I was away. I'm sorry. I am."

"I understand, Nick, but I think we need to hear Tristen's side of the story," Kelvin said, plopping on the couch. "I can't believe Clare has been having sex with that kid. He's only sixteen. Under my roof, and now she's accusing him of this. What am I supposed to think? Why didn't she tell us when it happened? She'll never be able to prove it, even if the baby is Tristen's. Should we destroy that poor kid's life? This is terrible."

"Damn right, it's terrible," yelled Rhonda, swinging her door open. "I warned you about that boy, and now look what happened."

Kelvin rose, moving inches before her. Rhonda squared in place. "You knew our daughter was sleeping with her brother, and you didn't tell anyone? What is wrong with you? I want a divorce. This marriage is dead. You are just as much at fault as both those kids."

"Fuck you, Kelvin. I've been planning to leave for months. And you never would have believed me, and you know it. Clare told me she would lie. Who do you love and respect more?" A silent pause. "That's right, so fuck you. I'm going to bed."

Rhonda slammed the door, causing Nick to jump despite anticipating the noise. Kelvin turned to Nick, lifting his hands up, eyes wide, as if asking Nick to tell him what to do. Nick shrugged his shoulders, exhausted—no, defeated. He needed to process the revelations made to him in the past hour, as he could not decipher any lies from truths in his current state.

"I think we should both go to bed and deal with this in the morning. I'll have a talk with Tristen and then Clare. I'll talk to you afterwards. Nick, please hold tight until we speak. I understand. I would be just as upset if Clare told me that, but with her admitting to consensual sex with him, I don't know who to believe anymore."

"Okay. I'll wait for you at my place. If you need anything, please come get me."

"Thanks, Nick."

Kelvin drooped his shoulders and shuffled to his room. Nick followed pace into the trailer, pulled out his weed, and smoked on the recliner, watching late-night reruns of *Cheers*. He fretted over Isla and Clare, ashamed by his actions, but he could not relinquish the feeling that he had been manipulated by a girl he once loved.

Chapter 23

Clare is nineteen

Nick opened his eyes just before noon, rushing up from the recliner, looking around for Isla. He had kept himself under the perpetual influence of weed ever since Kelvin discovered Tristen's lifeless body in the closet. Tristen had not answered Kelvin's incessant knocking by the afternoon of the day following the debacle. Kelvin eventually broke open the door to find the boy huddled in the corner of the closet. Edna and Kelvin raced him to the hospital, as Kelvin sobbed over the body draped on his lap in the backseat. The hospital advised that Tristen had been dead for some time and ruled it a suicide.

Kelvin, Edna, and Isla all spoke with Nick, assuring him that this tragedy could not be his fault. He did not accept their excuses and blamed himself. Nick judged that he must have scared the kid into his tragic actions.

Nick refused to meet Clare, locking himself in his bedroom whenever she barged into the trailer. She pleaded at his door, but he would not listen to any more lies. He wanted to believe that Tristen's sexual exploits entirely predated his own, but he worried she had lied about the rape, in case the baby turned out to be Tristen's child. An impossible ploy for Nick to forgive. He layered himself with doubts, exploring Clare's possible motives. Had she expected him to act with such frightful fervor in her defense? No one blamed him, yet he'd harmed his sister and caused a child's death, inadvertent or not. How could he believe himself blameless?

He didn't know how to continue living here with these circumstances standing upon his shoulders. Kelvin hadn't required him to go to work for the foreseeable future, knowing the depths of Nick's suffering.

Nick could only manage brief bouts of sleep these last couple nights. The first night he learned of Tristen's untimely death, he could not distract his mind from the image of the boy taking a pill for each moment of fear as Nick stomped up the stairs—the foreboding sounds of punishment without trial.

He constantly returned to that protruding question: Why had Clare not told him about her prior relationship with Tristen? Did she suspect he would be repulsed, or did she have her own regrets that precluded personal admission? This omission by Clare prevented him from reacting with honesty, simply looking to destroy based on the horrid violence he understood to have been committed by the boy.

Yet, with this omission, could he believe her accusation now? In reflection, Nick thought the boy had looked sad and forlorn when he saw him over those last weeks, if not months, as if some dark desperation lingered. Had Clare crushed the boy and then worried that everyone would judge her, so she'd made this accusation in order to prevent said judgment? He did not want to think so poorly of her. But the girl he had grown up with and worshiped and the woman that had caused this recent spiral could no longer be reconciled.

Nick would do right by the baby if he were established as the father. He did not want Clare to believe that he had any intention of creating a family with her, though. Visitation and child support would be forthcoming, but he would never dare a nuclear relationship with this woman.

What had Clare said to Tristen right before seeing him? On the second day, Kelvin had asked, and she said only that she was pregnant, and the baby may be his. She'd then brought up the rape charges, despite the recent discovery of Tristen's body. Edna said that they had to be calm, telling her that there would be no further talk of the kind until after the funeral. No reason to bring up such nasty affairs when the boy was to be buried. Also, his mother would be in attendance, given furlough to come to the funeral. Clare had slept with her adopted six-teen-year-old brother. Nick festered over this ordeal once more. How could Clare possibly justify herself?

A knock on the door forced him to recognize the day.

"Nick, are you up? Are you getting ready? We need to leave in an hour."

"I'm getting ready," he yelled out to Isla.

He did not want to attend this funeral, having to watch the boy he'd wanted to kill only days before being lowered into the ground. Had Nick not succeeded in his claims? A guilt that God had fulfilled his wishes lingered within him. He loathed the thought of meeting the eyes of Tristen's mother and giving his condolences, when he knew this family would not admit the totality of what had occurred. He did not even know if Clare would attend, as he was told she felt victimized by her family.

"She needs to leave the matter alone, just until we bury the boy and set him at peace with his maker," Edna said.

Nick found his suit pushed to the back of his closet, the suit he'd worn to his father's funeral. Tears formed when he realized he would need to place himself into the throes of another's death. He had come to the Chestwick household to escape the cruelty of his situation. Now he wanted desperately to leave but felt burdened.

He left the room, suit on, exhausted. He waited on the lounge chair, fighting the urge to smoke weed prior to the funeral. Isla expected him to drive, and she would be furious if he was under the influence. Isla walked out of her room in a straight black dress and gold necklace with a cross. She must have seen Nick eye the necklace, as she clutched it and said, "Edna let me borrow it."

"What are we going to do, Isla? Should we stay here with these people? After everything that's happened . . . if Clare did not have that fetus, I would ask you to move to Texas today. I can't be here anymore; there's too much." Nick sobbed. Isla pulled him up to his feet and held him as he saturated the top of her head with grief.

"If you want to move, then we'll move. But you have to accept that you may be the father of Clare's baby, Nick."

"You're right," he said, taking an offered tissue and blowing his nose. "You knew Tristen better than I did. Why is this bothering me so much?"

"You think you killed him. You didn't. I know you didn't. But you think you had something to do with his choice. He made that decision, Nick. You didn't force him to swallow all those pills."

"I guess. Let's go," Nick said, putting his arm around his sister's shoulder, leading her to the house. They walked inside to find Kelvin sitting on the couch next to Clare, the television blank, and Edna relaying the funeral address to someone over the phone.

"We're ready," Isla said. Kelvin lifted a hand without looking, while Clare glanced, then turned away. Nick noticed Clare's red eyes of either sorrow or fury, but he did not have the will to ask her which.

"Do you want us to go ahead? Is Rhonda still getting ready?" Nick said.

"She's not going," Clare yelled.

Kelvin gently touched the back of Clare's head, but she pulled away. Kelvin turned to them, looking as if he had a somber task to complete. "Yeah, Rhonda said she's not feeling well, and I don't have the energy to argue. This is a trying time for all of us."

"Mom's not going because she can't look Tristen's mom in the eye given the lies you all want to uphold. That eulogy will talk all about his untimely death and innocence. Lies, and you know it," Clare said facing forward, not speaking to anyone in particular, raging toward the world.

"The boy is dead." An utterance Nick had heard Kelvin say a few times this week with variable inflections, depending on the person. The flattened matter-of-fact tone of this verse led Nick to believe Kelvin had said these words too many times to Clare today.

"Just because he is dead—" Clare began, before Kelvin yelled, "Stop! We talked about this, and you will not say these things today. We will talk about them once the funeral is over and Tristen's mother has buried her son. Not a minute before, Clare. So help me, I'll kick you out of this house if you ruin the service. That boy deserved better." Kelvin erupted with grief, stumbling out to the front yard.

Edna emerged from Kelvin's bedroom, adorned with new pearl earrings. "Clare, please stop. Your father needs your support more than anyone right now. I know your allegations are serious, trust me. But

Kelvin still loved that boy like a son, and he's dead. He would mourn for you no matter who you murdered or assaulted. You must know that. Please tell me you know that," Edna demanded.

"Yes, ma'am."

"Thank you. Nick, will you be alright to go to the funeral with Isla? I would travel with you, but I don't dare leave Kelvin and Clare in the car without me."

"No problem," Nick mumbled.

"Well, let's go," Edna said, grabbing her purse.

Nick watched Edna lead Clare out the front door. He could not understand why Kelvin and Edna wanted Clare to be a witness to these proceedings. What purpose could be served by the presence of someone so righteous against the deceased? Could they be punishing her for sleeping with her adopted brother? He did not want to believe that Edna or Kelvin demanded she go for disciplinary purposes. Maybe Kelvin wanted to show a semblance of family at a funeral that would primarily consist of schoolmates and people who knew Kelvin from work. Kelvin knew that he did not have any power over Rhonda, but he still held sway over his daughter.

Isla and Nick rode in silence while Nick snaked the rolling roads toward Edna's church. He knew little of their beliefs other than Kelvin calling them Baptist-light. Nick did not have enough religious foundation to fathom where that placed them on the spectrum between salvation and judgment and had not attended church enough with his father for independent consideration.

"Why do you think they are making Clare go to the funeral?" Isla said, turning down the murmur of the radio. "This won't go well for the family. She seems ready for a breakdown."

"I don't know. I had the same thoughts. I can't tell if Kelvin is punishing her or wants to present normalcy despite the suicide. He must know he is inviting chaos."

"My only positive thought is that he's hoping she'll wake up and realize that Tristen can't do any more harm. That there's no reason to hold on to anger when he's six feet in the ground."

Nick did not respond, impressed with his sister's mind. In these moments, he remembered why he had stepped up to support Isla's aspirations, as she deserved these opportunities to succeed.

"So, you can tell me if I'm wrong to ask, but do you think Tristen actually raped Clare? I mean, he was so scrawny. Also, they were sleeping together before. Do you think she claimed rape just to cover herself if the baby happened to be Tristen's instead of yours? Didn't she expect their consensual relationship might come out into the open?"

Nick wanted to yell in agreement but could not make Clare out to be so vindictive and cruel. Although Clare could be selfish and aloof, he never saw her to that degree. He peeked at Isla, who studied her cast covered in adorations from friends. He had been the first to sign, at Isla's behest, showing she forgave him.

"I don't know. That question tears at me too. I acted so bullish when Clare told me about the rape. I didn't stop to think of the motive or possibilities of her lying about something so revolting. The past few days, it's been harder to fight off the worst answers to your questions. What am I going to do?"

"I think we should leave," she said, as if whispering dark thoughts that she meant to keep from him.

"Me too," he said, refusing to pretend he did not hear her correctly.

"Then we should go as soon as possible. We move to Texas. Aunt Jeannie and Uncle Jerry may be able to help find us a cheap apartment. You need to get away, Nick. I'm sure if we explained to Kelvin and Edna, they would understand. You could still be in the baby's life if it's yours. But I think we need to leave for a while. I'm fine with it. I can run anywhere. I don't think I'll ever feel comfortable living here again."

"I haven't asked how you're taking all this, have I?"

"No," she said. "But you have a lot going on, and Clare's accusations are at the forefront of everyone's mind. Sometimes I question whether I knew Tristen all that well. I had no idea he was sleeping with Clare. I mean, we didn't hang out or talk about many deep subjects, but I'm surprised you or I never heard at school. To think of Tristen being able to assault someone like that, I just can't piece together. He was so gentle and reserved."

"Well, Clare says she was passed out when it happened, so I suppose he didn't need strength to rape her."

Nick heard Isla's head thud on the window, then lightly tap in even increments. "I never worried about my safety around Tristen. I would have been more fearful of Clare attacking me than Tristen. I have doubts, but now we only have the word of Clare."

"Tristen did kill himself on the same night the accusations came out, though." Nick did not want to point this out with vindication, but rather wanted Isla's thoughts on why Tristen went so far to hide.

"With what we know about Tristen, doesn't that make sense? If Julia accused you of rape, you would deny it too, right?"

"Of course! I've never done anything without consent, Isla. Not that I want to talk about it with you."

"But see how upset you just got? Defensive? Tristen, torn from his home, mom in jail, likely depressed, is accused of raping the daughter of the family he has as his only safety net. Who could he turn to? No one, Nick! No one."

A sob escaped Isla. Nick reached over and placed a hand on her shoulder, maneuvering down the last few streets to the church. He had no retort, for he knew Isla did not want Clare or Tristen to be the villain. Nick needed to talk to Kelvin soon. He would move to Texas, now that Isla agreed.

"We're here, Is. You should freshen up before we head inside." He stepped out, then went to his sister's door to assist her. He never thought of Tristen and Isla as being other than idle friends based on proximity, so he had not bothered to inquire about her own pain. He felt shameful as her caretaker.

They walked through the large walnut doors, greeted by a stranger telling them to sit wherever they liked. Nick's eyes flickered to the carpet floor of blood maroon with strange symbols patterned throughout, edging up to the pulpit and open casket holding Tristen's body. Nick thought Tristen seemed especially small in the black suit surrounded by the oversized mahogany casket. Nick could not recall Tristen wearing a suit before, even at his father's funeral.

Kelvin and Edna stood next to a taut woman, rippled with sorrow. Nick maneuvered to see a face of vague familiarity, struck by the sudden realization that Tristen had been the child of this poor soul. Nick looked for Clare but did not locate her, guessing she'd remained in the car in protest. Isla pushed Nick toward Kelvin as more people gathered behind them. Nick was grateful that Kelvin did not ask them to be a part of these greetings. Edna, poised and pleasant, kept close to Tristen's mom, whispering to her twice, as Nick shook Kelvin's hand, providing Kelvin with repeated condolences. He hugged Edna, then met Tristen's mother with a meek smile. He did not know the decorum in greeting this woman, despite having undergone the inverse only a few months before. Everyone had volunteered a pleasantry that never reached his pain, but he assumed each meant well.

Thankfully, she held out her hand with a smile, though her eyes remained devoid of appreciation. Nick looked below the smile and shook her hand, giving a murmur of his condolences. She nodded in acknowledgement, and he moved on to Tristen's body.

Nick did not intend to stare, but the realization that a sixteen-year-old could take his own life poked at Nick's understanding of mortality; he could step out into the road at any moment to allow the next life to receive him based on choice rather than divine circumstance. This freedom upset him, as he had never considered the alternative to his continued existence.

"He's so small in that casket," Isla whispered next to him. "He does look good, though. Peaceful. They took good care of him."

"Yes," he said.

Nick headed toward one of the back pews so that he could be far from the procession and observe those that entered. Isla sat next to him, spreading out her dress to keep it from wrinkling, then grabbed a Bible to leaf through, flipping and reading various sections without purpose. Neither uttered a word as the congregation continued to grow. Nick did not recognize some of the younger teenagers, assuming they were Tristen's classmates. Nick had told his friends about the funeral but never explicitly asked them to appear. They did not know Tristen, and Nick did not want anyone to be uncomfortable in these circumstances.

Despite the small standing crowd, Nick did not initially see Clare enter the church. Momentarily, he forgot about Clare's lingering hostility, trying to recall more faces, figuring the older figures were Edna's friends from church. A nice gesture in filling the otherwise empty pews. He noticed Clare only when he saw Kelvin jolt. Edna reached out to Kelvin, but Clare stormed toward the casket. Kelvin and Edna stood in place, seeming unsure of what to do next. Nick thought that if they dragged her away from the casket, a bigger scene would ensue.

Tristen's mother did not pay much attention to Clare, ignorant of her intent. She only noticed when she saw Edna and Kelvin's focus. Nick was not sure if he witnessed Clare's action or merely heard that familiar sound that comes from the back of one's throat: a phlegm concoction. Clare spat into the coffin.

Tristen's mother shrieked, yet Clare had not finished her outburst. "Fuck you, you raping bastard," she yelled and began punching the dead body. Tristen's mother cried in wavering sobs with unclear mutterings. Kelvin grabbed Clare's arm and dragged her out of the church without any gentility. Nick expected a hand mark of bruises to form on her arm.

"We should follow them," Isla whispered, nodding her head toward the exit. Tristen's mother covered her face with her hands as Edna and other ladies of the church tried to console her. Another held a hanky, wiping it over the boy in the casket.

"I think you're right."

They tried to sneak out, but many eyes kept to the door after Kelvin and Clare escaped through, likely waiting for further outbursts. Isla pointed out Clare and Kelvin near their vehicle, Kelvin's arm still tight around Clare. She did not squirm or talk back, having spoken her piece.

When Kelvin noticed Nick walking up, he said, "Nick, please take Clare home. She is no longer permitted at the funeral."

"Uh, sure. I'm one of the pallbearers, though."

"I'll find someone else. The best thing you can do for Tristen is to rid him of her." Kelvin bent down until his eyes penetrated into Clare's. "I will not change my mind, Clare. You are no longer welcome in my home. You had no right to be so insolent in front of that poor woman. She lost her son, Clare. Her only son. What did you want to happen? Who did that help? How will that change your accusations? I'm done. I expect you to be moved out within the week." He let her go, walking briskly back to the church.

Isla guided Clare into the backseat. Nick was deadened by the circumstances and appreciated the silence as he drove.

"Clare, Nick and I will be moving to Texas," Isla said. Nick glanced at Isla in surprise. "He'll be there for you and the baby, if it's his, but we need to be closer to our family. I hope you'll understand."

Nick looked in the rear-view mirror; Clare lay across the seat, her back toward them.

"I'm sorry, but it's for the best," he said.

Chapter 24

Today

Clare glared at Nick's hardened face, his mouth puckered. Had she ever loved this man, or simply needed his connection at the worst of times? She had considered him throughout the years with mild interest, yet the manner with which he handled his father's death inspired a maturity from him that she admired, witnessing the man Nick could be if he applied himself. Then the rape, pregnancy, and accusation tore them apart. No, not completely. Nick had chosen to leave when the reality grew too uncomfortable.

Nick spat at the ground, wrestling with his straps, shifting the chair just a few inches. "You are the most selfish person I will ever know, Clare."

"What do you expect from me, then? You show no remorse when I tell you that your actions have left me a husk. If you ask, I will hang from these rafters, never struggling, just accepting your decision."

"Fuck you, Clare. You slept with a child, who killed himself, then you made his travesty into something about you." Nick laughed, his eyes raised to the rafters. "I'm just happy that Isla is in Texas. Would you tie that poor girl up and claim she is at fault too?

"No. She didn't force you to leave. You took advantage of the opportunity, while I was pregnant with your child."

"*My* child! How do you know it was my child? You aren't pregnant anymore, so the child could just as easily have been Tristen's or any other man you failed to mention."

Clare clutched her abdomen in remembrance. The baby had no chance after the stress and chaos caused by her family. Only after did she realize how much hope she had placed on her growing possibility.

"You caused me to lose my baby. Don't you remember pushing me down the stairs?"

"I never pushed you, Clare. You fell from the bottom step after Isla fell. The hospital checked you out and found nothing wrong. People have miscarriages every day, and they aren't my fault."

"This one was."

"You don't know that!" Nick yelled. "You have no idea, Clare. What do you hope to get out of this whole display? Are you expecting we'll beg your forgiveness, and you'll feel validated? No one wants you to kill yourself, but you know that. Quit blaming us for your mistakes. You're going to do what you want to do. That's just your way. I have nothing further to say."

"Fine. I should have expected as much."

Clare went to place the gag back over his mouth—another lost apology and futile attempt at forgiveness. She felt colder at the thought of a tomorrow. Nearing Nick, he began shaking violently, twisting away from her, edging the chair just a few more inches.

Clare backed away, looking at him with distaste. "Nick, you need to stop. You're going to fall off, and you've got a noose on your neck."

"Get the fuck away from me, Clare. I'm not going to let you put that on me."

"I'll get the tranquilizer. Is that what you want?"

"No, just let us go!" More force erupted from him, as he started making the chair hop.

"Nick, you have to stop!" Before she could turn to the tranquilizers, one of the legs broke through a floorboard, causing the chair to lean back, all the force now on Nick's neck. She could hear the muffled screams of her mother and father as she attempted to pull Nick back onto the loft floor, furious that her strength did not seem enough. He flailed in fear, dying before her. She collapsed, turning away, curling into herself until her parents' noises became soft moans.

"No . . . no, no, no. You weren't supposed to die. I wanted you to listen," she whispered. "He . . . he's the one who wouldn't stop. I never thought the loft would break. I didn't give any of you enough rope to tip the chair off the ledge to make sure you wouldn't fall. I'm sorry," she said, numb and lost.

Clare turned to her grandmother, whose face was moistened with tears. Clare took off her grandmother's gag, causing Edna to begin coughing. Clare bent before her grandmother, hands on Edna's left thigh, postured in forgiveness.

"You killed that poor boy," her grandmother said.

"I didn't mean to," Clare whispered. "What do I do? I never meant for anyone to die." Clare began sobbing into her grandmother's leg.

"Oh, child. You have to take responsibility and call the police. Are you sure he's dead?"

"I think so."

"You've taken this too far and will face consequences."

"But . . . but I didn't mean to. I didn't push him."

"You placed us in nooses, Clare. You meant to scare us, and you've succeeded. What do you want? Let me go, and I'll speak to the police. I can help, Clare. Grandma loves you."

Clare looked up at her grandmother, aghast at the words meant to placate her.

Part V: Guardian

"Let the morning bring me word of your unfailing love, for I have put my trust in you. Show me the way I should go, for to you I entrust my life." Psalm 143:8

Chapter 25

Clare has not been born

Edna waved from the front door as Kelvin headed out to take Rhonda home. Rhonda was adamant that her parents would not be accepting, but Edna remained firm that Rhonda tell them. If they insisted Rhonda leave their household, Edna would accept her. Edna already cared for her future grandchild from those two fools, intent that they would not destroy its life. Having kids at this age out of wedlock. She never expected something so irresponsible from her son, but Rhonda would grow that child in her belly as witness.

"Lord, help me," she said, pouring another half glass of wine. "I need your guidance more than ever, as that boy has been easy enough to raise until now. I knew my time for tests would come, but I had hoped for something of quality." Edna did not feel any spiritual response, so she let the silence float onward, resting herself at the dining room table.

She heard a knock at the back door, followed by her father walking into the house.

"Hi, Daddy. What brought you over?"

"I wanted to visit my favorite neighbor," he laughed.

Edna eased up, the two exchanging hugs, then kisses on the cheek. "Sorry, my mind is just in a bad place right now."

"Well, watch your drinking, Edna."

"Would you like a glass?"

"No, no." Teddy sat to Edna's left, both sighing in tandem. "I'm missing your mother tonight," he said. "I'm glad you're so near."

"Me too. You should move into the house already. We have extra bedrooms."

"You know I don't plan on leaving the trailer. I can feel your mom in the space. Keeps me hopeful for when I'm in a better place."

Edna sipped the glass of wine, studying her father. He returned a meek smile, but his eyes showed a gulf of detachment. *He should forget the trailer, but I'll never convince him*, thought Edna.

"So . . . you ready for a great-grandchild?" she said.

Teddy coughed, attempting to speak but only managing, "What?"

"Kelvin got his girlfriend pregnant."

"I hope you're joking, Edna. That's not funny."

"I would never joke about such a thing," she said, tapping her nails on the glass. "They just told me. Rhonda thinks her parents won't accept the pregnancy, so I told her she could live here, but only if they married. I gave Kelvin my engagement ring, and Kelvin proposed right here."

"What did Rhonda say?"

"She said yes, of course. What else could she do? She plans on keeping the child. Won't speak of abortion or adoption, though I abhor both ideas as well."

"He had such a bright future," Teddy said, slumping into his chair. "What's he going to do now? That boy is not ready to care for another."

"I know. That's why I'm having them move here, where we can keep an eye. That girl is so meek, and Kelvin already seems indifferent to her wishes. I think he'll tire of her, but if they get married, maybe the relationship can be saved."

"Oh, Edna. Don't make them get married if you think their union will fail. That borders on blasphemy. Marriage is a sacrament, and it sounds like you're tossing it around as an ultimatum."

"That baby needs both parents, and I'm not having an unwed mother living under this roof. I love Kelvin, and I'll learn to tolerate Rhonda. With your help, I hope."

Teddy patted Edna's hand. She could feel him scrutinizing her drinking, words, general demeanor. "Of course, I'll help," he said. "Have you thought about putting that barn to use? It's been sitting out there since, well, you know. I'm sure you can turn it into a nice place for Rhonda, Kelvin, and the baby."

"No, Dad, and you know I won't."

"It never hurts to ask. It's been seventeen years, Edna. You must let some things go."

"Are you already forgetting how Mother's spirit rests with you in the trailer? Don't tell me how to mourn. Most of Charles is gone from this house. I will not tear down that barn. That was the last thing he did for this family, and it brings me peace as a memorial—better than any gravestone."

Teddy leaned back in his chair, grunting. "I don't mean to fight, Edna. I just worry. Like you said, it's been seventeen years. Have you been seeing anyone? You're still young, beautiful, and a fine Christian woman. There must be plenty of men around here. I just don't want you alone after I'm gone."

"I'm not alone. I've got Kelvin and now Rhonda with a baby." She sighed. "I've dated, not that it's your business, but I never find anyone interesting. I've done well enough without Charles, and thankfully, he blessed us with that money. So overall, I'm thriving, Dad, despite this recent development."

Teddy stood behind Edna, squeezing her shoulders. "You need to let other people help you, darling. You take too much upon yourself. I'm going to head back. I don't want to be around if the kids have to settle in tonight, and they may want to tell me in their own way. I'm sure Rhonda will be quite upset if her family kicks her out. Poor child." He shook his head, walking out the door.

Edna observed him shiver, sparking concern over the state of his health. She opened her mouth to tell him to wear a coat but shut it. He would not listen anyways. She looked upon the remaining glass of wine, shook her head, and poured the rest down the sink. She wanted a clearer mind for the rest of the night. She would set up one of the guest bedrooms for Rhonda, not permitting them to comingle until the marriage became official despite their prior misbehaviors. If they wanted to share a bed, they could hurry their union. Edna's mood quickly soured. She no longer desired a grandchild in the house, unable to view this baby as a blessing. Though she would have missed him dearly, she had been excited at the prospect of Kelvin heading off to college, leaving her with the house to herself. Now, she would endure a new cycle of childhood and adolescence.

"I'm still mad you left me, Charles," she muttered. "I miss you."

Edna went to her bedroom and sifted through her bottom dresser drawer. She found the small photo album with memories of the best man she had ever known. She touched her wedding ring, still enshrined on her ring finger, looking over the memories they made those first few years. Marrying so young, not much older than Kelvin and Rhonda, yet they had married out of want, not out of misbegotten sexual prowess. Two years after their vows, Kelvin came forth. They had just enough money to get by, so Charles built the barn nestled in the backyard in his attempt to farm in his spare time. A silly idea, but one Edna supported, nonetheless. She looked at two photos of Charles and his friends working on the barn. Charles wanted to build it himself, a proof of his skill as a craftsman. Since his passing, she refused to permit anyone to alter that barn while she remained on this earth. She knew Charles would not have let it run into a dilapidated state, small pieces of paint peeling and parts of the wood looking warped, but she did not have the heart to alter his dreams.

She touched a picture of Charles holding a sleeping baby Kelvin in his arms. Charles had his finger over his mouth warning Edna to remain quiet. Maybe she should allow Kelvin and her dad to build the barn back to a better place. It would be a good bonding experience for the two, and she did not want the barn to collapse due to neglect. She closed the book after taking one last look at a wedding photo.

She returned to the kitchen, wishing she had not poured out the wine. *The kids should be back by now*, she thought. *Rhonda must be gathering her stuff. Lord help us.* Edna brought back the bottle of wine and tipped some into her wine glass, then pulled out a flashlight from the hodgepodge drawer of batteries, rubber bands, and other catchalls.

She drifted into the backyard, away from the trailer, past the fire pit, and over to the barn, empty aside from the riding lawn mower.

"I won't turn this into a house, Charles. You can't make me. I know, I know. Kelvin should have his own space, and you gave me the money. But he needs to eventually move out on his own, and if I do this, he'll never leave. No, Charles. I can't change it. Hear me out. I'll let Kelvin and Dad fix it up. I know it isn't the same, but it's all I can handle."

Edna sat on the wooden stairs, flashing the light throughout the roof, not sure what she hoped to find. Maybe a bird's nest to validate that this barn was already a home. Edna had hoped the space would warm her, make her feel connected, yet she only felt a chill and creeping loneliness.

"Maybe a baby would be good for my life. I could use something new," Edna said, still looking around the barn. "I'm just being harsh due to the circumstances. In another time, I would be elated at this news. I'll try to be better, Lord."

"Mom. Mom, are you out here?"

"I'm in the barn, Kelvin."

Edna swung the flashlight toward the barn door. Kelvin's head peered into the doorway, then jolted back at the light. "Mom, right in my eyes."

"Sorry, dear."

"It's fine," he said, sitting next to Edna on the stairs leading up to the hayloft. "Why are you out here?"

"Oh, I don't know. Thought I could use some solitary time in the barn. Haven't been out here in ages. Look at how rundown it's gotten." She took a sip from her glass and placed the flashlight between them, shining at the wall. She no longer cared to explore the crevices for other life. "Would you and Grandpa be interested in patching it up?"

"Grandpa has enough trouble getting around the stairs. Why do you think he'll be able to help with the barn?"

"Kelvin, is this some ploy to get out of my request? Your grandfather is an able-bodied man, and he would be disheartened to hear you talk of him in such terms. Your father built this barn. You should take pride in the handicraft. One of the last remaining pieces we still have of him."

Kelvin kept silent. Edna hated when he refused to engage with her, as if he won by not listening. He would help fix this barn if she had any say. She took a final sip from her glass, placing it on the step behind her.

"So, you going to marry Rhonda?"

"Why are you asking me? You're the one that forced me to propose."

"Well, if you plan on having that baby and living under my roof, then yes, I expect you to marry."

"Well, then I don't have a choice. Rhonda's in the house situating the few things she could grab through her mother's screaming. Her brother was there to help, but I think he really just wanted to fight me."

"Poor family. I wish you two would have been more careful. I thought I taught you better. Where did you put her? Better not be in your room."

"No, Mom," he said with disdain. "She's across the hall in the upstairs guest room. I anticipated your wishes."

"Good boy."

A pause, then Kelvin spoke. "Mom?"

"Yes?"

"You asked me if I still plan on marrying Rhonda. You also said I have to marry Rhonda if we plan on having the baby and live with you. Are you suggesting that Rhonda consider an abortion?"

His question did not elicit any external response from Edna, but she wanted to scream that despite her tried-and-true beliefs against abortion, she desperately wanted that baby to not affect Kelvin's life. Could she truly spout her heart's desire, when she worried the Lord would place judgment on her at the final hour?

"No, but I don't think either of you have properly considered placing the child in adoption."

"Mom, you encouraged me to propose to Rhonda because she refused to get an abortion, but I would have supported that option, I'm sorry to say. But now I'm engaged to her, and she's convinced that we will be able to raise the child in your house. I can't give the child away now. You need to make a choice. Will you help me convince Rhonda of the alternative or help raise the child with me? I don't see a middle way forward."

Edna felt a heaviness loom, as if the grace of judgment became a steel blanket resting upon her body. She wanted to say yes to such a disgraceful proposition—to have her son back in a planned path forward to success. Yet she would never obtain that dream for her child again; the abortion would forever sully her feelings toward him. She pushed against the constriction and breathed out.

"No. I think you've made the right choice, despite the less than up-standing beginning. I'll love that grandchild. I promise. I just hope for Rhonda's and your sake that you discover more in common than what's between your loins." She paused, admiring her glass, then sipping. "I wish you would come to church with me more, Kelvin. I pray every week. Perhaps these circumstances could have been prevented if you had a little more faith. I should have pushed you into church instead of waiting for you to make the right decision. I hope we are not too late."

"No, Mom. I don't think church would have changed anything."

"I'll pray, Kelvin. That's all I can do anymore."

Kelvin stood and leaned against the barn doorway. "You want to head back to the house? I should make sure Rhonda is settling in alright. We can get the marriage license quickly if you want. Neither of us wants to have a ceremony."

"Understandable. I'll wait out here for a bit. Let you two get situated."

He gave a light wave, and Edna fought the urge to run off. She did not want to enter that house and accept these consequences. Eventually, some visualization of the good would be revealed to her, right? She just needed to be patient, wait for the Lord to catch up.

She picked up the flashlight and her drink. Halfway between the barn and house, she turned to study the structure under the moonlight. She nodded her head, affirming she would require Kelvin to begin the restorations. She needed some control, and the re-establishment of one of her favorite places by the source of her discord might help bide her time.

Chapter 26

Clare is two

E dna rubbed her temples, waiting for the lightning of a hangover to strike and terrorize her mind. A soft rumble of pain, but nothing significant. She turned to her darling grandchild on the bed with her, sleeping the wicked night off. A two-year-old's birthday party should be filled with delight and laughter, not the absence of a mother and terrorization by the father.

Edna eased herself up, then collapsed, feeling queasy and light-headed. She had promised to have a good time with the church ladies and had enjoyed herself, until that final despicable display. Those supposed women of God would gossip about her home life, and Edna was unsure about the best steps for damage control. Ignorance, forgiveness, and forgetfulness tended to work in dire circumstances. Edna propelled herself up and rushed to the medicine cabinet, swallowing four aspirin with water from the sink.

"I must have better control," she groaned.

She heard rustling from the bed and prayed her grandbaby would stay asleep. Edna needed time to come up with a plan. Had Kelvin slept with that other woman in her house? Edna's thoughts focused on Sheryl and Kelvin drinking heavily upstairs, though Kelvin had run off after burning that poor doll. Had he left with Sheryl? No surprise. Edna was not fooled about Kelvin's promiscuity.

Clare mumbled in sweet gibberish but stayed asleep. *I will need to speak with Dad first*, Edna thought. *He'll be the only one to mend bridges, and I don't want him to consider leaving.* He had been the most upset by the events, immediately rushing Clare off into his trailer. When Edna checked in on him soon after, he initially refused to allow Clare to leave with her.

"You're drunk, Edna. You have no business taking care of a toddler."

"I'm fine, Dad. Almost everyone left, and I need to put her to sleep." Edna wobbled a little but had enough sense to put a child to bed. However, Clare was not in her bed but lay nestled in Edna's. Edna believed she fell asleep with Clare nearby, intent on keeping a watchful eye on her.

Edna put on her robe and slippers, then shuffled into the kitchen to make tea. Rhonda looked wide-eyed at Edna, a glass of water in hand, and hurried toward the stairs.

"You don't need to leave because of me, dear. Feel free to grab yourself something to eat. I'd rather you get it than Dad bring it to you."

Rhonda blushed, pleasing Edna just a bit. Edna filled the kettle with water, placed it on the stove, then sat down at the dining room table.

"How are you feeling?" Edna said. "Sorry you missed your daughter's birthday party."

"I'm okay," Rhonda said.

"That's nice for you," Edna said, making little attempt to hide her insincerity.

Rhonda looked at her glass of water, then at Edna. "I'm going to head back upstairs."

"Okay. Bye, dear."

Clare's cries reverberated from Edna's bedroom as Rhonda took that first step up the stairs, then paused, giving Edna the moment.

"Why don't you check on your daughter? I think she would love to see you since she missed you last night." Edna smiled, both her hands resting on the table, pleased with the barb. Rhonda's eyes widened, mist forming at such a simple request. Edna hated this constant desperation from Rhonda. She understood being sad. Edna had not felt like much of a person for years after her husband died, yet she strove forward, as she had no one to step up and care for Kelvin. Rhonda was abusing their hospitality, especially her father's. Who heard of post-partum depression taking over someone's life for two years? Rhonda needed professional help, plain and simple.

"I can't today," Rhonda finally said, then slowly marched up the steps to her room.

Good riddance, Edna thought. Edna sauntered to Clare, scooped up her grandchild, and rocked her, the child's head cradled against Edna's neck. Clare mumbled, "Mmmaa mamamama." Edna was used to Clare calling her versions of momma. She hoped she could teach her the proper term for grandma by the time she turned three.

The tea kettle whistled, requiring Edna to hold on to Clare with her hip while the other hand removed the kettle from the stove. She heard sounds from the front door. She turned to see Kelvin walking in with disheveled hair, last night's clothes, and a sheepish grin at his mother.

"You are twenty years old, young man. You need to get your act together. Come take your daughter."

Kelvin rushed to hold Clare and sat at the dining room table. Edna steeped the tea bag in her cup of hot water, taking a seat at her spot next to him. Kelvin kept his eyes focused upon Clare. Edna knew he was avoiding her gaze, not wanting to open himself up to a conversation about his behavior. She waited, sipping at her tea until his eyes adjusted enough to catch her own.

"I understand, Kelvin."

"You understand what?"

"You've already lost interest in her. She's lost all her will and can't seem to get it back. I wouldn't want to be dragged down by such a relationship."

"Mom, I'm not sure you mean what you're saying. Rhonda can't help it. I wish she could, but she can't."

"We both don't believe that. She needs therapy, but she refuses, while Grandpa is forced to speak to her every day as a free ear."

"Grandpa is great with her," he said, nodding.

"Did you sleep with that girl, Kelvin?"

Kelvin looked off, no vehement denial. Edna paced herself with the tea, unsure how to follow. She considered whether she truly did not care whether Kelvin strayed from his marriage, fighting her personal principles with her son's sought-after vices. So long as Clare maintained a home with two parents, then Edna would be hard pressed to judge.

"I wish you could be more thoughtful of your wife. Not a soul at that party would believe you did not sleep with that young lady. Rhonda must be beside herself at everyone knowing. You need to be better, Kelvin. If not for yourself, then for Clare. People will talk."

"What people?" he said, setting Clare on the floor. She crawled into the living room amongst the cascade of toys. "Your church friends? They gossip about everyone—false or not."

"You don't know anything, Kelvin. What about the parents of the classmates that Clare will grow up with? What will they say to her about her drastically depressed mother and whore of a father? You never think of anything beyond the moment."

"Mom, I'm too tired for this. I need sleep."

"Stay seated," Edna ordered. She poured more tea into two cups and set one before Kelvin. "Drink this before you go to bed. You'll feel better." She grabbed two aspirin from the cabinet. "These as well."

"Thanks," he mumbled, sipping the hot tea with the pills, wincing at the scalding water.

"I expect you to start applying to proper jobs now that school is almost over. None of this part-time work that pays for only what you want. You need to start supporting your family. If you do not make an honest effort within the month, I'm going to start charging you rent."

"Mom, that's not fair," he mumbled. "I didn't mean to cause such a scene. I'm sorry."

"Get your life together, Kelvin. You have a daughter. Be a role model, for goodness' sake. I'm not being unreasonable. I'm being a parent."

Kelvin steeped his tea, refusing to engage. Edna greeted this groveling as a triumph. *He has too much freedom*, Edna thought. She was not sure if she could get away with the same ultimatum against Rhonda, though. Her father would protect Rhonda, especially after he mentioned Edna's mother had experienced something similar. Edna recalled her mother being quiet but not distant or absent. Edna supposed Teddy forced this idea of her mother onto Rhonda as an excuse.

Her cell phone rang from her bedroom. She rushed to answer, hoping for some bit of news that would ease her mind away from last night's debacle.

"Oh, Edna. How are you feeling? We all felt so bad for you after your son's display last night," Evelyn said, clearly feigning sympathy.

She took a breath, already disappointed she had answered, "Oh, Evelyn. You know how young couples can be. Just a little marital spat. They've already made up."

"You're telling me that his wife, the one that holed herself up in her room, is talking to him already? Even after he burned that doll? I'll admit that the good Lord forgives, but if I was his wife, it would take me more than a night's sleep to forget. I just feel so awful at the position that puts you in."

"I'm fine, Evelyn. Clare is doing great. Kelvin played with her this morning. No hard feelings between them. I appreciate your call."

"Edna. Sorry, that wasn't the only topic I wanted to bring up. Well, I mean, this has something to do with it but more forward thinking. I spoke with Pastor Wilson this morning. Asked him to pray for your family and such. He thought that some marriage counseling may help Rhonda and Kelvin. He would do it for free with the good grace of Jesus. Isn't he a blessed man? He said he would call you, but I wanted to call you first, so you wouldn't be surprised."

Edna gritted her teeth at Evelyn's revelations to the church. She should have called the pastor and explained. There was no chance that Kelvin and Rhonda would agree to counseling, even with her dear minister. Even if she could convince them, Edna did not dare allow them to air their problems at her church. The walls were too thin, and Pastor Wilson was known to participate in quiet gossip regarding his parishioners. *He's a godly man, but we all have our shortcomings*, Edna thought.

"You there, Edna? You okay?"

"Yes, I'm here. I'll speak with the pastor. I'm sure he appreciates your concern for our wellbeing, but as I told you, they just had a late-night spat. Nothing to worry over."

"What about that woman Kelvin left with? Are you telling me Rhonda is okay with his late-night explorations, too?"

Edna had forgotten her friends likely knew of Kelvin's leaving, hoping she had been the only one to notice. The church would forgive and forget violence against a doll more than sexual promiscuity. Her eyes curved around the room, attempting to formulate an excuse. "Oh, Kelvin just needed to get out of the house. He understood he overstepped and thought he could use some time away. She brought him home later that night, after you left. No wrongdoings between them."

"I wouldn't be so sure," Evelyn said. "Rumors have circulated about your son's affairs. I obviously do not participate in such gossip, but I feel it is my duty to warn you. Last night will surely spread around town. You should warn that poor girl."

"Which one?" Edna said, not caring for the answer, simply curious where Evelyn's sympathies lay.

"Oh, both I suppose, but poor Rhonda. I would not want to be on the receiving end of rumors of my husband's mischief."

"Well, neither of us need to worry about that, do we?" Edna laughed. She knew the stab would hurt Evelyn, given her recent divorce.

"Well, I need to go. I'll be praying for you. Bye." Evelyn hung up the phone before Edna could respond. Edna felt a little troubled by the abrupt end to the call, worried about other potential discussions Evelyn might have with the pastor.

Edna walked into the kitchen to the absence of both Clare and Kelvin. She opened Clare's room to find Kelvin asleep on the floor with his clothes on, a pitiable display. She did not raise a boy to remain a boy. She would talk to Dad. He might be able to put some sense into Kelvin.

Edna snuck around the bed—no Clare. The little girl had been crawling something fierce these last few weeks and loved to hide, delighting in little events that gave her grandmother a fright. Edna thought she acted in this way to get noticed, but the consistency led her to believe Clare might want to stay hidden, rarely troubled in her solitude.

Edna hurried through the house, looking under the kitchen table, around her room, all around the living room, in the two back closets behind the stairway. Clare could not have made her way up the stairs by herself, Edna reasoned. She did not have the strength. Even so, Edna went upstairs, checking the guest bedroom. Edna breathed deep, then knocked on Rhonda's door.

A muffled "come in" came from the other side.

Edna gritted her teeth. "Oh, Rhonda dear. Kelvin's downstairs sleeping, worried he would wake you. I wanted to make sure you knew, so you didn't worry." Edna scanned the room for Clare, then brought her eyes back to Rhonda.

"I don't care, Edna. After yesterday, he can stay down there for a while."

"I'm sure you don't mean that. We all have our issues, don't we? He just got a little frustrated when you felt too ill to come to Clare's birthday party. We missed you. Clare most of all."

Rhonda rolled over, her back now to Edna. "I think I'll take a nap."

Edna wanted to scream at her for being so disrespectful. However, she closed the door, letting the good Lord find the best way for Rhonda to get her due.

Edna walked down the stairs, growing a bit frantic. Edna did not keep a cluttered home, so how could the child have escaped her search? "Clare bear. Don't hide from Grandma. Where's my baby at?" Edna dropped to her hands and knees, crawling around the living room to gain perspective.

"Edna, why are you on the floor?"

Edna tipped to the side, collapsing on her right arm. "Dad, you scared me. I didn't hear you come in."

"I thought you may want to talk after everything that happened. What are you looking for? Did you drop an earring?"

Edna struggled up from the couch. A hangover still hovered, exacerbated by the morning's activities. Maybe she should ask to take one of her dad's pain medications. He always had extras, though he never handed one over without an eye of judgment. That could wait until she found her granddaughter.

"Edna? Are you okay?"

"Just a little dizzy from standing up so quickly."

"You need to watch your drinking. Look at how Kelvin acted last night. Despicable. An embarrassment."

"Calm down, Dad. No harm was done. He's your grandson, after all."

"And I love him. Doesn't mean I can't tell him his attitude needs to change and quickly. Poor Rhonda needs our support, not screaming about the misery she causes while burning an effigy. And Clare. She must have bawled her eyes out for almost an hour, watching that doll melt. Took ice cream to finally calm her down."

"I already yelled at Kelvin this morning. But I think you are giving Rhonda too much of a pass. I know she's depressed, but she can't hole up there forever. Her daughter just turned two, and Clare needs her mom."

"I know, Edna. I know more than you think. But your mother got through her spell with support, not blaming and guilt. I know you don't remember, and we are blessed for that. But Clare is soon going to realize her mother's absence, so we need to help Rhonda along."

"You will do what you think best."

"Where's Clare? I wanted to check on her."

"Oh, gosh. Clare . . . she's hiding. I think. Still trying to find her."

"You lost the baby?" Teddy cried out. "How long has she been missing? When did you last see her? Oh my God, who took care of her last night?"

"She slept in my bed, Dad. Calm down. She was fine. I lost sight of her maybe ten minutes ago. Just help me look. She can't be far."

Teddy sighed. He shuffled around with his cane, doing his best to look down to a two-year-old's crawling height. He pushed the door open to Clare's room.

"Be quiet," Edna whispered. "Kelvin is sleeping in there."

"That boy is sleeping while his daughter is missing!" Teddy opened the door. "Kelvin, get up. We can't find Clare."

"Grandpa. I'm tired."

Edna's phone began ringing. She looked at the name in horror. "Shut up, everyone. Pastor Wilson is calling me. I need to take this. Lord knows what he would think if I ignored him." She answered the call. "Hello, Pastor. I hope everything is well."

"Why is the pastor calling you? What is going on? Where is your granddaughter, Edna?" Teddy fumed.

Edna waved her hand at him, trying to concentrate on the pastor's words. "I'm glad to hear. We had a lovely party last night. I'm sorry you couldn't attend. I know you have your hands full with church duties." She laughed, loathing herself for the ridiculousness. How dare Evelyn tell him her family's business?

"Edna, we need to find Clare. Kelvin," Teddy yelled, "get up and help us find your daughter." Kelvin grunted, then pulled a small blanket over his head. "What is wrong with this family?" Teddy sat on the couch with his arms crossed.

"Are you sure everything is okay, Edna?" Pastor Wilson said. "I heard some mishaps occurred last night with your son and his young wife. Also, did I just hear your granddaughter is missing?"

"No, no. We are playing hide and seek."

"You must be joking," Teddy said, shaking his head.

"Oh, fun," the pastor said. "I thought I should call and offer my services to Kelvin and his wife. I heard they've been fighting a lot lately, and I have a fair amount of experience counseling young couples with immense success."

"Oh, I don't know if Kelvin and Rhonda would be interested."

"Interested in what?" Kelvin yelled. Clare began crying from the far side of Edna's bed away from the door.

"Well, we found the baby," Teddy said, hurrying into the room.

"Just a minute, Pastor," Edna said. "Will everyone please be quiet? Please!"

Forgetting his torment, Kelvin stood and rushed next to his mother. "Mom, what are you talking about? What does the pastor want with me?"

"Is that Kelvin?" Pastor Wilson asked. "Do you think I should talk to him directly?"

"Shut up," Edna said. "Oh, not you, Pastor. Uh, no. Kelvin isn't feeling well. I'll tell them about your offer. If I can convince them to come to church more often, you can certainly ask them in person. Well, I've got my hands full here. You can probably hear the baby woke up."

"Okay, Edna. You take care and don't hesitate to call me if you need to talk."

"Will do," she said, hanging up the phone. "Do you all have any idea how embarrassing that was?"

Teddy rolled his eyes while he patted Clare on the back, struggling to ease her crying.

"Convince me of what? Why the hell would I go to your church?"

"Kelvin Chestwick! That is no way to talk. Pastor Wilson called to ask if you and Rhonda would want counseling from him."

Kelvin squinted his eyes. "Why does Pastor Wilson think Rhonda and I need counseling?"

"Well, you know Evelyn. She told the pastor about Clare's birthday party, and so he called. Now he probably thinks I need counseling, too."

"I'm not going, Mom. We had a bad night, but I'm fine."

"That's what I told him. Go sleep. We can talk about this when you aren't so tired and grumpy."

Kelvin sneered, tottering to the upstairs guest bedroom and shut the door. Edna was thankful he was put away for the time being.

Clare's cries became soft moans in Teddy's arms. "That Evelyn needs to mind her own business. She's always carrying on about other people's lives. Nosey."

"I agree, Dad." She sat on the couch next to Teddy, resting her head on his shoulder. Clare giggled, softly tapping at Edna's face, moving her hands through her hair. "I don't know what to do. Kelvin and Rhonda won't address their problems, and I'm afraid if I push them, everything will collapse."

"I know, honey. We do the best we can. I'll talk to Rhonda later today. You can try to connect with Kelvin when he's feeling better. Hopefully, we can talk some sense into the situation, though I still think Kelvin was out of line. He's better than throwing his daughter's toys in a fire on her birthday. Anyone is better than that, Edna, no matter how mad they are."

"I understand, Dad, but we all have our moments."

"We need to keep one firm thought in mind. Clare needs to be raised properly, without all this anger. Thank goodness she has us."

"We do the best we can," Edna said, echoing Teddy's words as she closed her eyes, leaning her face close to Clare and Teddy's noses. Clare laughed with delight, attempting to wrap her arms around both their heads.

Chapter 27

Clare is twelve

Clare and Edna stood in the middle of the trailer, scanning for anything that could spoil. Teddy's funeral had been a few weeks ago, and no one had ventured into the trailer, even Rhonda, who had taken his death the worst, at least vocally, sobbing at the sound of his name. Edna accepted the sentiment and appreciated the closeness Rhonda and Teddy had shared, but after two weeks, Edna felt drained and dragged further into misery by Rhonda's incessant wailing. Edna would have preferred that Rhonda assist her, but she did not expect any honest help. Thus, she had recruited Clare to remove the awful smell that had begun radiating into the backyard.

"I don't see any left-out food, so I'm guessing all the spoiled smells are coming from the refrigerator," Edna said. "We may want to wear something over our faces in case there's mold."

"Grandma," Clare whined. "This is disgusting. Can't you hire someone to help you with this?"

"No." Edna went into Teddy's room, finding a few bandanas in his closet. "Now put this over your face and hold open the trash bag. I'll throw in all the food. The sooner we finish, the sooner we can escape the smell."

"Why didn't you do this earlier, Grandma? Oh, God. It smells so bad." Clare made retching noises as Edna threw curdled milk, limp and molding vegetables, and other perishables into the bag.

"I've had a lot on my mind, young lady. Your father is working non-stop, and your mother is going through her own grief, so the funeral services and your great-grandfather's estate fell onto my shoulders. Now, hold the bag wider."

"I might throw up. Ugh."

"Then throw up in the bag," Edna said, reaching into the fridge for the last bits of packaged meat.

"That's not funny," Clare whined. "I need to practice my flute."

"You'll have all day. Your whining is not helping this go any faster. Now, open the bag wider, for goodness' sake."

Edna opened the freezer to sweep out all the food in there. She wanted to rid the entire refrigerator of Teddy's food. She certainly would not want to cook any of it, and Rhonda would cry at the thought. Frozen bags of vegetables, ice cream, and pre-prepared meals went into the trash. Edna knew she had waited too long to go through the trailer. She preferred it to be left alone, to remain a shrine to her departed parents. However, the actualities of life forced her to reckon with reality and complete necessary tasks. Edna pinched her face to keep from crying.

"Grandma, I'm taking this out. I can't stand it." Clare then threw up a bit into the bag, before closing and dragging it out of the trailer.

"That child is so dramatic," Edna mumbled. "I suppose she's a teenager now." She pulled out another trash bag from the box, scooping everything else from the freezer. She tied up the bag and brought it outside, noticing the other trash bag next to the door. "Dammit, Clare." Edna grabbed the second bag and pulled both to the front of the house, slamming each into the trash bins.

Edna hurried to her house to wash her hands, disgusted by the whole process. Clare sat on her living room couch with her flute, a portable stand holding her book of music. Clare struggled with a song that sounded like a hazardous rendition of the theme from *Star Wars*.

"Clare. Clare!" Edna said to stop the piercing high notes. "Why are you practicing over here?" Edna went to the kitchen to wash her hands.

"Mom said the music was bothering her. She was on the couch watching some World War II documentary that Grandpa loved. I went upstairs to my room to play, but then the new boy knocked on my door. I told him to leave my room, but he just hung around while I practiced. So I came here. I hope you don't mind. I thought you would be at Grandpa's trailer for a while."

"I suppose it's fine, though I wish you would tell me first. Why is your mom watching that documentary?"

"I guess it helps her think about Grandpa."

"She is determined to make his death about her," Edna sneered under her breath.

"Grandma, you okay?"

"Yes," Edna said, drying her hands. "I'm just tired from lugging both garbage bags to the trash can."

Clare either chose to ignore her or was enmeshed in her song book, flipping to another page. Edna worried for the child, who had shown little emotion at the funeral. Even Kelvin had teared up at the wake, though Edna understood that Teddy was the only real father figure Kelvin knew. She contemplated whether the family would crumble without her father's subtle support. Edna sat on the love seat as Clare began another song from her book. The piercing wails from the flute did not sound correct, but Edna refrained from criticism during the child's practice. Mistakes were meant to be made in private.

"Clare, can we talk for a moment?"

"Grandma, I really need to practice," she whined, slamming the flute down on the couch cushion. "The band director is going to make me third chair if I can't keep up. I refuse to let myself fall below Stacy Tretchler." Clare made a face of disgust, though Edna could not recall her ever complaining about this Stacy before.

"I want to talk about your great-grandfather. I haven't sat down and asked how you feel. I can't imagine your mother or father have asked you either. Are you doing okay? Do you want to talk about him?"

Clare rolled her eyes, thumping her head on the back of the couch. "Ugh, Grandma. I'm fine! I miss Grandpa, but I understand how death works. He was sick for so long and Mom kept saying, 'This will be the day.' When it finally happened, I don't know . . . I guess I had been sad for so long already. I'm fine. Really."

Edna teared up, reflecting on the terrible year the family had experienced with Teddy bedridden. The child was right in that regard. They had anticipated his death for months. *Rhonda deserved better from me,* Edna thought. *She genuinely cared for Dad and was there when I couldn't be.*

"Grandma, don't cry. I'm sorry. You asked."

"Oh, I know," Edna said, grabbing a tissue. "I forget how grown you are getting. Before I turn around, you'll be out of our lives, exploring the world. Sometimes I miss you, even when you're here. I don't know how to explain it. Death brings out a lot of emotions, Clare."

"It's okay." Clare got up and hugged Edna. Edna took a breath, focusing on Clare as she was now: a twelve-year-old girl with her own focused adolescence.

"I didn't know him that well," Clare said, sitting. "He was usually with Mom, whenever he left the trailer."

"He helped raise you, Clare. You must remember that. He watched out for you and made sure you had the best we could provide. I hope you keep him in your prayers because I have no doubt he is keeping an eye on us. He was our protector."

"Okay," Clare said, flipping back through her song book.

Edna stared at Clare, incredulous at her flippant attitude. Would she care so little for her grandmother, as well? Edna could not remember being so isolated and self-involved during those tender years. Edna's mother would never have allowed such attitude in her home. Edna considered a different approach.

"Grandma, are you going to keep staring? You're making me nervous, and I need to get these songs down this weekend."

"Do you want to go back to Grandpa's trailer and look through his stuff? Maybe there's some keepsakes you would like to take to your room, memories that you can cherish?"

"Grandma," Clare whined. "It stinks in that trailer. I'm sure we didn't get the smell out. Do you want me to go back to my room? We can talk about Grandpa later. Please."

"Fine," Edna said, her tone shifting to annoyance. "Doesn't matter anyways. If this is how you feel, you can all forget any inheritance. I'll not have heathens who refuse to appreciate a precious life benefit from it."

Edna stomped up the stairs, slamming her door. She slumped onto the floor and sobbed at her loneliness, never fully appreciating the structure her father provided over the years, believing she had been the one to keep her dad afloat. Clare had accurately pointed out that Edna should have anticipated his death. How could she still be so embittered? She had not been so distraught at her mother's funeral. Guilt panged at this realization. She climbed into bed, upset that her actions mirrored Rhonda's weak emotional state, weeping in bed weeks after the funeral.

"Why do I keep feeling such sympathy for Rhonda?" she raged. She closed her eyes, trying to come to a proper prayer, but only simple conversation spewed. "What is happening to me, Lord? Why do I judge one for having few emotions while another for having too many? Must I control every aspect of this life? Is that why I'm feeling so burdened? As much as I prayed and hoped, I could not prevent my father's death. I know he's with you, but you don't need him. Please bring him back. Please," she begged with hands clasped together like a fallen angel tipped to the side. "I know you won't, but I wish you would. I truly do."

Edna woke later to a soft knock on her door. "Come in," she said.

Kelvin smiled, still in his CVS formal attire. *Management looked good on him*, Edna thought. *So mature.*

"Hi, Mom. I wanted to check in on you. Clare said you went to Grandpa's trailer and threw out his food. She also said you went crazy and started screaming that she didn't care about him."

Edna turned away from him, unwilling to participate in such cold accusations. She felt Kelvin get on the bed with a drawn-out sigh. "Take off your shoes before you get into my bed." The sound of one, then the other shoe falling to the floor. "I didn't mean to yell. I just don't understand why she is so complacent."

"She's a teenager, Mom. They're selfish and have a hard time acknowledging plain emotions. Even so, I don't think you should tell her that she didn't care about Grandpa. You know Clare has a reserved way about her. I blame her mother," he laughed. "Rhonda takes all the emotion available for herself."

Edna turned to look at her grown son strewn on her bed. He looked tired, but still smiled, attempting to support her. "What about you? I know how much you must be hurting, yet you've barely mentioned him. Don't you miss him? Remember all the times he took you to Cub Scouts or helped you with school projects? Don't you want to reminisce? Your sentiments at the funeral were endearing, but I'm worried our family is already forgetting. We've all moved on so quickly, which hurts me."

"Mom, I miss him so much that bringing him up hurts more. I just don't talk to you about it." He paused with his hand on her shoulder. "I'm sorry." He stood, slipping on his shoes. "Clare said you wanted to look through his stuff. Why don't we head over? We can look through everything and try to figure out what you want to do. We'll go at your pace; there's no rush. You get ready. I'll grab the air fresheners from your bathroom to help with any lingering smells." On task, he slowly shut the bedroom door behind him.

Edna slumped to her vanity mirror, exhausted despite the nap. She looked upon the creature who was just beyond fifty, worried about her growing outbursts. She feared death more than ever. Had she lived a full life? She helped at church, supported her family, and prayed for the Lord to make her better every day. But when she thought about the remnants of her father in that trailer, his body lost in the ground, she worried that after only a few days of absence, the world simply saw the burdens you left behind. The soul, with its profound circulation of memories, would fade, and she would soon forget the face of her father. She cried at the creature she saw in her vanity. She missed her parents. She missed her husband. She missed the woman she had been thirty years ago. All this regret culminated into a tantrum toward her granddaughter—a girl not yet embittered by the growing shadow of death, a whistling bud at the cusp of discovering the sun.

A soft knock on the door caused her to blink, realizing she had been lost in thought. "Mom, are you okay?" She took delight in Kelvin's interest in her wellbeing.

"I'll be right out," Edna said. She took one last look in the mirror. She did not need others to see her running makeup. She took a few slow breaths, fixing the smudges, and headed downstairs. Kelvin sat on the couch, waiting in silence.

"We can go. Thank you for offering," she said. Kelvin placed his elbow out, escorting her around to the trailer. Despite his bouts of selfishness, she believed her son had grown to be a good person.

"How's Oliver handling everything?" she asked. "Poor kid had to go to a funeral less than a month into being here."

"I asked if he wanted to be put with another family. Explained that we would love for him to stay but did not want to make him uncomfortable with the situation. He said we were nice people. I don't know if you noticed, but he was a gentleman at the funeral, quiet and reserved but respectful."

"I suppose I wasn't paying attention with everything happening. I'm happy he decided to stay."

Kelvin stepped first into the trailer, spraying Febreze before him. Edna walked into the smell, not bothering her now that she had rid the place of the moldy food. Kelvin continued to barrage the trailer, beginning in Teddy's bedroom, then the spare bedroom, and finally the bathroom.

"I think we're okay," Edna said.

Kelvin opened the fridge, spraying inside for thirty seconds. "There," he said. "I think that will do."

"I feel awful letting this place come to ruin so soon after he died," she said, sitting on the couch. "But I couldn't bear the thought of being here until I had no alternative. What am I supposed to do, Kelvin? Do I sell his television, his couch, his lounge chair that he adored? Who would want them? I don't want to throw them away. I would feel terrible removing him."

Kelvin lingered near the refrigerator. She waited for him to respond, her mind drained of thought. Sought-after guidance and prayer did not fulfill her in this moment.

"Leave everything here," he finally said. "Why not? We don't have any reason to remove the trailer, so why get rid of Grandpa's stuff? We can use it as a guest house. You don't need to do anything you don't want."

Edna brushed her hand along the deteriorated brown fabric of the couch, wondering if this trailer would become another dilapidated memorial like the barn, always aging, never improved despite passing desires. Was she capable of ever letting herself lose someone? She clasped her hands together. "The Lord guides me. We'll keep everything the way he left it."

Chapter 28

Clare is nineteen

"I'm terribly sorry, Pastor Wilson. I don't know what came over Clare. I've never seen her make such an outburst, especially at a funeral. I think she's just upset over the poor boy's death. I promise I'll speak with her."

"See that you do, Edna," Pastor Wilson said, pinching his nose, his glasses tilted. He sat behind his desk, rocking himself in the raised wooden chair. "I spoke to that young man's mother for almost twenty minutes, apologizing for Clare's display. Her only child, Edna, and Clare screams and spits at the boy. What is this about rape? I told the mother that I knew nothing of these allegations. Why would Clare spout something so dreadful at a funeral?"

Edna leaned forward, easing her hand onto the pastor's desk. She made a quick decision to let these rape allegations rest, as no one could possibly win in the situation. No proof would be forthcoming, even if the baby happened to be Tristen's, God forbid, and no punishment could be issued either way. Best to pretend the matter had not happened, though she worried about lying to a pastor. She reasoned that she did not technically know the truth, so vague allusions to a misunderstanding would not be a sin.

"I think she felt lost, needing attention. You know she's a good Christian, though she has drifted from the church in her teenage years. Like

I said, I'll have a talk with her and place her back on a righteous path. I hope we did not cause you too many disturbances. This whole experience has been awful," Edna said, wiping her eyes with a lace handkerchief.

"That poor child taking his life at such a young age. I haven't discussed that part with you, have I? Were there any signs, Edna? What led this boy to take such a dark turn?"

"I truly don't know," Edna whispered. "I've spoken with Kelvin and Rhonda and neither saw the boy moping or seemingly depressed. Some underlying issues at school, I would guess."

"Do you think his suicide could have any relation to Clare's allegations at the funeral?"

Edna sat up, considering the pastor's question with precision. "I would expect that if Clare's claims had been brought up before, Tristen would have spoken with Kelvin. They had a close relationship. I expect some other dark recess of thoughts led him to take all those pills." Edna grabbed a tissue from the pastor's desk and blew her nose. "I'm sorry, Pastor. I don't think I can talk about this any longer. Kelvin is waiting for me. Please call me later if you want to talk more." She stood to leave the pastor's office, waiting for him to open his door, as he was known to prefer.

"I'm always available to speak with any of my congregation, including Clare. Make sure she knows, Edna." Pastor Wilson hugged Edna, then led her out of his office.

"Of course," she said with an unintended half curtsy.

Edna hurried through the area of classrooms for children's Bible study, up the stairs, and out the door toward the parking lot, worried Pastor Wilson would try to stop her with more inquiries. She felt utterly humiliated by the whole ordeal. Between the suicide and rape allegations, her family would be the source of church gossip for the next month, if not the entire year. She saw Kelvin's head vibrating against the window, as loud bass rocked his truck. She knocked and then opened the door, as he turned down the music.

"How did everything go with Pastor Wilson?"

"As well as can be expected from a man who oversaw the burial of a suicidal teenager followed by the caring of his mother because of rape allegations at the funeral."

"I'm sorry, Mom."

"Can we please drive?" Edna rushed into the passenger seat, trying to mentally prepare for the rest of the day.

He sped out of the parking lot in tumbling force. "I'm not letting Clare live with me anymore."

"Oh, Kelvin. How is that going to help anything? We need to approach this cautiously. I told Pastor Wilson that Clare had been acting out in general. I doubt he believed me, but he seemed to accept the possibility."

"What possible good could have come from Clare screaming those accusations at his dead body? That poor mother. I can't forgive her, Mom. She's out."

"She'll live with me, then," Edna said with a sigh. "I can't let her sleep on the streets. This ordeal keeps piling on, and I'm afraid for our name in the community."

"It's your house. She just won't be in mine."

"I understand your frustration, but I'm worried that you're only making the problem worse."

"I loved that kid! He deserved better. I don't know what happened between Clare and him, but I do not believe that Tristen is the only one that did wrong. He was her younger brother, for God's sake. Did she have no sense of decency?"

"This happened under your roof, Kelvin. You let your home run astray."

"Do you think he raped her?" Kelvin said softly. "Do you believe her?"

"I believe she believes it. I don't know what good could come from talking about it any further. I'll speak with her. I'll try to explain without belittling her claims."

"You didn't answer, Mom."

Edna gazed out the window, the summer fields of corn swaying in the wind, the trees ripe with bloom. She ached at the thought of accusing Clare of lying. She loved her grandchild. But why would this boy kill himself if he had been innocent? Something occurred between the two that would never be known to anyone else.

"I don't believe he physically assaulted and pinned her down, no. I believe that some alcoholic scuffle may have occurred that could be misinterpreted. Perhaps Clare has regrets and was using this to win support if the baby happens to be Tristen's. No, I don't believe Tristen raped Clare in any feral manner. Clare was also not innocent in the sexual escapades that seemed to have been a normal occurrence between the two."

"Her younger brother, Mom. I just don't understand."

"Enough mayhem has happened today. Can she please move out tomorrow? I'm hoping everyone will be settled and separated when we get home."

"Fine, but she's out tomorrow."

Edna closed her eyes, attempting sleep. She could not pinpoint which wrong turn the family had made and when. She missed her father in these moments. He had been a stable man who could have prevented these terrible events. He would have noticed Clare's sexual trysts with Tristen and rightfully spoken with both regarding their consequences, well before these circumstances. He could have conferred with Clare regarding her accusations, found a solution that would not end in such travesty, a lingering bitterness that stained all three homes. Edna would attempt to emulate her father's spirit, caring for her granddaughter while discovering the root causes of her instability.

She felt a shake on her shoulder. "Mom, we're home. You can sleep in the truck, but I didn't want to leave you sweltering in the sun without the option."

"I'm coming. I didn't realize I fell asleep," she murmured. She exited the car, walking with Kelvin to their joint front porch. "Will you be able to enter your house without screaming at your daughter? It won't help, Kelvin. I know you're hurting, but so is she. Please try to be kind."

"She screamed abhorrent things at a funeral. I'll try to be rational, but I cannot forgive her."

Edna sighed, pinching the back of Kelvin's elbow.

"I hate when you do that!"

"Then keep a level head. She'll live with me soon enough."

Kelvin walked into his house without further word. Edna went toward her door, then thought of Isla and Nick. She should ensure their wellbeing before retiring for the day—another step toward resolving the disturbances encroaching upon her home. Edna strolled over and knocked on the trailer door, waited a minute, then knocked again, believing both may have taken afternoon naps until Isla opened the door.

"Oh. Hi, Edna. Please come in."

Edna smelled the marijuana in the air and tried to fight a face of discomfort. She did not detest private use, but she hated the idea of young people wasting valuable time in a haze. She especially detested her father's home absorbing the distinct smell. Nick jolted up from her father's chair at the sight of Edna, almost tripping on the footrest.

"Sorry," he said. Edna realized she'd failed to mask her disgust. "I needed to relax after today. I hope you don't mind."

"It's understandable, I suppose."

"Would you like a drink?" Isla said, heading to the kitchen.

"No, dear. I wanted to make sure you're both doing okay after today's events. I'm grateful you brought Clare home. I was worried that she would continue her ravings, causing you both distress."

"She was upset, but we coaxed her to bed," Nick said.

"That's good. How's your arm, Isla?"

"Fine," Isla said, resting on the couch near Edna. "Though I feel my running is still off just a little. I hope to find a good stride within the week."

"We plan on moving," Nick stammered out.

"Oh?" Edna said. "To your aunt's place?"

"Maybe," Isla said, elongating the word. "We haven't fully decided, but we think it may be best. I hope you understand, though I wish Nick would have given us more time to figure out the details before telling you." Isla glared at her brother, then returned a smile to Edna. Edna enjoyed Isla's attempts at subtle behavior, knowing she would move on to greater endeavors than her brother.

"What do you expect to do about Clare's pregnancy, Nick? I don't suppose you plan on leaving her alone if the baby is yours."

Nick looked from Edna to Isla, as if expecting his younger sister to speak for him on all matters of importance. Edna initially thought that Nick's gesture in caring for his sister was an act of courage. She still did to some degree but began to see that Isla may have been the guiding force in saving them, unfortunately being three years too young to decide for herself.

"I guess we can get a paternity test. I'm just not sure how I'll be able to facilitate a relationship with Clare given these circumstances. *If* the baby is mine, of course." Edna noted the emphasis on "if," observing the unfathomable hope that he would not be tied to Clare any further. "If so, then I would do my best to be in the baby's life, including providing any financial support that Clare required. I would not want to be an absent father. I just … and I don't mean any disrespect to you, Edna, but I would not be able to continue a relationship with Clare given these newfound circumstances."

Edna tutted, rubbing her thumb over the fingers of her right hand. She agreed that Clare had been erratic and lost, but she did not care for the words coming from this man, who may have impregnated her granddaughter only to move a thousand miles away.

"I think you are being quick to judge a woman who is pregnant and has possibly been raped in the last few months. Have you considered her feelings? Discussed any of these accusations with her? I seem to remember you coming to her rescue only a few nights ago, resulting in your sister's arm here."

"He didn't mean to," Isla interrupted.

"That may be so," Edna continued. "But your instinct then was to protect Clare, yet some volatility has scared you now. Perhaps she did sleep with her adopted brother, but she claims this was before your relationship, so I don't see how that should bother you. A pregnancy by Tristen would have been possible only from this alleged rape, correct?"

"We don't know that, do we?" Nick said, his eyes squinting. "We know that she admittedly slept with this kid multiple times and was possibly raped in this trailer with no witnesses or proof. She only brings up the accusation once she discovers her pregnancy. Have you considered that she could be lying to excuse herself from being pregnant by her own brother?"

"Adopted brother," Edna said. "Let's not defile the situation more than necessary."

"I can't see how you could approve of that situation."

"Whether I approve of it or not does not matter any longer, does it, Nick? Tristen is dead, so I don't need to explain to you the impossibility that leads to any ongoing issues in that regard. As to you moving, I've changed my mind. I think that may be best. I don't see how Clare or this baby could benefit from someone who has decided to abandon them at a whim."

"I'm not sure that's fair, Edna," Isla said softly.

"I don't believe that matters, dear. The fact remains that your brother likely impregnated my granddaughter but sees fit to abandon her in clear distress. I cannot see how having someone like Nick around will ever be to Clare's benefit." Edna rose, patting Isla on the knee. "I came here to ensure that you two did not need my help, and it seems obvious that you have made your own plans. Please make sure to tell me when you leave. I do like to be informed of such matters."

"Edna, I'm . . ." Nick stuttered.

"That's enough," Edna said. "If you have anything further to say, I will ask that you do so without being under the influence of drugs."

Edna walked out the door, exhausted by her haughty defense of Clare. She despised the immaturity of not accepting responsibility for one's actions. Nick was using this ordeal to escape his obligations. Edna began to wonder if caring for Isla had materialized as a gift for Nick, keeping him from moving forward as an adult. Edna pushed this final thought off, not wanting to believe that someone could be so engrained in a selfish plot.

She entered through the back door of her old house, hoping to find a sleeping household. Instead, she heard screaming before the door fully opened.

"Fuck you, Dad. You believe that dead, suicidal maniac over your own daughter. Accept it. You never wanted me!"

Clare was screaming at the bottom of the stairs as Kelvin walked down them with handfuls of her clothes in his arms. He marched down the stairs without acknowledging Clare, though he paused briefly upon seeing Edna, clearly surprised. Edna remained in the doorway, unsure as to who was likely at fault. Kelvin brushed past Clare toward the open front door, throwing more of her stuff onto the front porch. Edna then noticed the ongoing pile, insinuating this fight likely had begun soon after Kelvin arrived home.

"What's going on?" Edna said, unwilling to raise her voice.

"Dad's a lunatic. He says he never wants to see me again. His own daughter." Clare threw herself onto a kitchen chair, banging her fist on the table.

"Clare," Edna said, brushing the fitful girl's hair with her hand. "This behavior cannot be good for the baby. Please stop so I can speak to your father." Clare pounded her hands a few more times before crossing her arms.

Kelvin marched up the stairs. Edna followed him, hoping to trap him in Clare's room and obtain a direct explanation for this fiasco. She found Kelvin sweeping more clothes out of Clare's drawers, piling them onto the bed.

"Why are you doing this, Kelvin? You need to calm down," Edna said in necessary soothing tones. He rarely acted with such ferocity.

"Look at Tristen's room! Look at it, Mom. Look at what that monster did." Kelvin slumped on the floor, beginning to cry, covering his face.

"Please stay here. I'll look."

Edna rushed to the room across the hall. She saw a running crack at the bottom of the door, as if someone had repeatedly kicked at it. She opened the door, pushing hard against some heavy object. The door relinquished, and she gasped at the mess in the room. Anything breakable had been flung against a wall and shattered onto the floor, clothes were spread all over, and sheets were ripped off the bed and cut up. The worst was the word "rapist" spray painted all over the walls, bed, and floor. Edna did not understand this abhorrent destruction. What did Clare possibly expect to gain by such garish actions? How far did she need to push? She needed Clare to move into her place, now. Waiting would only cause further strife and heartache.

She softly closed the door and went into Clare's room. Kelvin held a picture frame. Edna walked to his side, brushing her poor boy's hair with her hands. The cracked picture was of Clare at band camp a few years ago. She looked so happy amongst her friends.

"What happened to her?" Kelvin said. "What did I do wrong? Is it all Rhonda's fault?"

"No, Kelvin. It's not. I think you need time to heal from this whole ordeal, and being around Clare is not helping. I'll help her move into my spare bedroom immediately. Do you think you can bring her stuff down without throwing everything onto the front porch?"

"Yes," he said, focused on the photograph.

"Where is Rhonda? I'm surprised she didn't hear all the commotion."

"She did, but she locked her door. She wants nothing further to do with this family."

"I can't wait for that woman to leave. I will never understand her."

"Me neither," Kelvin sighed.

Edna patted Kelvin's shoulder, then went downstairs to find Clare slumped on the floor.

"Clare. Sweetheart. You'll be moving in with Grandma. I think you and your dad need some space apart. Is that okay?" A slight nod. "Good. Now, please help me with the clothes on the porch and bring them into my house."

Edna pulled on Clare until she stood. Edna guided her to the porch, each taking a handful of clothes, then dropping them onto the couch in Edna's living room.

"Sit, Clare."

Clare looked exhausted, having lost the battle she'd fought with her father moments ago. Perhaps she only needed this soft guidance. Edna considered the best means to bring peace to the family and knew that quashing Clare's animosity would be most effective.

"I need you to stop all this."

"But Grandma . . ."

"No! Clare, you are done speaking. You have disrupted this family long enough. Whether that dead boy raped you or not no longer matters. You cannot get justice against the dead. You can only cause yourself and those around you ongoing misery. Enough. You want that baby to live, you must start taking care of your health and begin acting with more peace in your heart. Pastor Wilson wants to speak with you about your behavior, but I convinced him to let us handle our family's matters alone. Please look at me."

Edna saw the defeat of Clare's spirit and felt relief. She could not consider the burden of the baby and would leave that to the Lord and her personal prayers.

"Let's get you into bed." Edna eased Clare up the stairs and to the bed in the guest room. "Now, please think of anything other than these last few days, love. You need rest of mind and body. No more thoughts of rape and violence. We will move forward, prayers on our lips and in our hearts, seeking guidance from the Lord."

Chapter 29

Clare is nineteen

Edna relaxed at her dining room table, steeping two bags of black tea. Her body yearned for the extra caffeine this morning after Clare's late-night scare. Edna had woken to Clare's cries from the guest bathroom. Clare begged for Edna to leave her alone, but Edna opened the door anyways. Clare sat in the bathtub, her knees to her chest, arms crossed over her abdomen, pain riddled on her face, begging for it to stop. She offered to call an ambulance, but Clare cried out, "No, I'll be fine. Please leave me alone."

Against every instinct, Edna had closed the door and gone back to bed. She did not care to be screamed at anymore. She felt guilty at the selfish impulse, worried Clare might be miscarrying, yet what could she do when Clare had refused every offer of help over the last couple of weeks? Neither Rhonda nor Kelvin had come to offer any support or inquire about their daughter's wellbeing after Clare's relocation to Edna's guest bedroom. Now Edna felt tied to this moping creature, as Clare rarely left her room for anything but food and the bathroom.

Edna fought with disgust the developing prospect as she steeped the tea. This elongated fit in Clare's body led Edna to believe that Clare might lose the baby, which would alleviate numerous complications down the road. She had come to the resolution that she could not discuss an abortion with Clare; her principles would not allow her to utter that possibility. A miscarriage, though disheartening, would propel the family toward healing. Otherwise, that baby may be a perpetual reminder of that poor suicidal child.

She looked at the small wooden clock hanging just above the stove, the seconds ticking toward 9 a.m. She would attend church soon. Pastor Wilson had called a few times, supporting Edna's decision to stay with her family during these difficult times, but warned her of straying too far from the church. He assured her that the congregation missed her, and no one would speak of the events at the funeral. She did not believe him, though she hated to think of her pastor as a liar. She had assured him the day prior that she would make an honest effort to attend.

She sipped at her tea, wincing at the singeing of her tongue. She grabbed two ice cubes from the freezer and dropped them into the cup. She did not have the time to wait for matters to cool if she planned to attend that day's services. As the ice melted, she walked up the stairs and knocked on Clare's door. "Honey. I'm planning on going to church. Would you like to come?" No reply, so she knocked louder. "Clare. You okay?" She opened the door to see Clare sprawled out on the bed, tangled in the sheets. Clare rotated into the fetal position at the creak of the door. "Clare, didn't you hear me? I'm going to church. Would you like to attend with me? I'm sure the Lord would serve you well during this time."

"No thank you," Clare moaned. "I'm still not feeling well."

"Don't you think it's time for us to take you to the doctor, then?"

Clare turned her head, though she seemed to be looking past rather than at her grandmother. Edna saw the disheveled hair, the tired eyes, the despairing smell of clothes worn for multiple days.

"I'm fine. I just need to rest."

"If you say so, dear." Edna sat on the bed, brushing the hair out of Clare's face. Edna had hoped Clare would heal with time away from all the stress, but Clare seemed lonelier than ever, despite Edna's consoling. Edna fretted that Clare had been broken beyond repair and this baby stood little chance. Edna's conscience panged her once more at the prospect that Clare's pains would alleviate her troubles. She kissed Clare on the cheek. "Please call me if anything happens, okay?"

Edna closed the door, unable to understand why Clare refused to go to the doctor. Did she honestly feel better, or, more likely, was she worried that these cramps were something worse that she could not control? Edna would not force Clare to the hospital against her will. She would pray for the health of her granddaughter. Edna sipped at her tea while dressing in one of her favorite floral dresses—navy with a red, white, and pink flower pattern. She placed her favorite pearls upon her neck with matching earrings. Edna expected gossip, but she certainly would not allow anyone to belittle her style and looks.

She finished her tea, gazing out the window above her sink. She observed the dilapidated state of the barn in its rustic condition. She was saddened by the structure, yet felt content with its sturdiness, never bowing despite its years. She still desired to have the building restored, but akin to the trailer, she never felt the time was right, despite her half-hearted requests to Kelvin all through the years. *Let these matters remain as they are*, she thought.

She hurried out of her house, unsure how half past nine had arrived so fast. She knocked on the neighboring door. Kelvin opened, surprised at his mom's early morning visit.

"You okay, Mom? Come in," he said, moving to the side for her.

"I'm doing well. Heading to church. I wanted to stop by, see if you would come with me. I'm not sure I can stand it if I have to hear any belittlement of our family. I could use the support, Kelvin."

"Well, I guess. It's short notice, though." He scratched at the back of his head, leaving the door open. Edna heard rustling from the kitchen, observing Rhonda scurrying into her separate bedroom and shutting the door.

"She's still a pleasure, it seems," Edna said.

"Yeah, well, I think she's planning on moving in with her brother, so there may be peace soon."

"So, you are going forward with the divorce?"

Kelvin rolled his eyes and sighed, walking toward his bedroom. "Has this ever really been a marriage, Mom?"

"I believe you made a vow, Kelvin."

"Oh, please. I'll get dressed and go with you, as long as I don't have to be lectured."

"Fine," Edna said, smoothing out her dress.

As Kelvin entered his bedroom, Edna knocked on Rhonda's door. Despite no audible reply, Edna entered the room. Rhonda lay curled in the fetal position, a mirror of her daughter.

"I thought you should know that Clare has been feeling unwell. I'm going to church with Kelvin. If you feel capable, you may want to check in on her. I left the front door unlocked."

Rhonda did not acknowledge her. Edna saw a small rip on the corner of Rhonda's shirt, the disheveled hair, the underlying smell of sweat and sadness. Edna did not believe that this woman wanted a divorce from her husband. Maybe just a different life with him, one that started with a natural romance rather than a child at graduation. Edna pitied her and closed the bedroom door.

"What did you need from Rhonda?" Edna clutched her chest, not expecting Kelvin to be standing nearby. "Sorry, Mom. I didn't mean to scare you."

"No. I'm fine. Clare hasn't been feeling well but refuses to be taken to the hospital. I told Rhonda so she can check in on her, if she pleases, though I have my doubts."

"She rarely comes out of her room. Are you sure we should go if Clare is sick?"

"Yes. I need to at least make an appearance at church, and I'll be late, unless we leave right now."

Kelvin handed her his keys, then paused as Edna walked to his truck. She sat herself in the passenger seat, draping her dress so as not to wrinkle, waiting for Kelvin to hurry along. After a two-minute delay, Edna felt on edge as Kelvin stomped to the porch, slammed the door, and stormed into the car. Edna sat in silence as Kelvin spun out of the driveway onto the road.

"Well, what was that all about?" she said, annoyed.

"I asked Rhonda to check in on our daughter. She would not look at me, refused to turn around, even acknowledge my presence. I can't stand her anymore."

"I know," she said. "And it's for the best. I'm sorry if I made you feel guilty before. I'm sure the Lord will understand."

"Thank you," he said, easing his grip on the steering wheel.

They sat in silence, neither reaching for the radio to drown out the sounds of pitching gravel, passing birds, or the grazing wind. She enjoyed the general emptiness along the roadway, houses set far back within the land, trees close enough to caress vehicles, shadowing their journey. She adored the sanctity of the church, but something about the wilderness made her know that the Lord stood with her. She could handle any situation, even Clare's present condition and the ongoing family troubles. She loved the child and hoped to cultivate a lovely woman in time. She looked at her handsome son, appreciative that he had stayed so close over the years. She knew that he could have moved at any point, but his resilience and support showed patterns akin to his stalwart grandfather.

"I see you found a shirt to match my dress," she said, delighted with his nice attire for the occasion. "I think a mother and son matching will help ease the gossip."

"I thought it wouldn't hurt," he laughed. "The shirt was there when I opened the closet, and I knew I had to wear it." A moment passed between them until Kelvin said, "Do you think I should take Clare to the hospital?"

"She's an adult. We can't drag her against her will. She's fine. I hope you two reconcile, but I'm not sure that can happen during her pregnancy."

"Maybe you're right. Her complete lack of sympathy for Tristen and his mom still bothers me. I never knew I raised someone who could be so vile at a funeral. Sometimes I reflect over that day and feel ill. I hope the baby will help Clare grow up a little."

"One can only hope," Edna said. Minutes passed as she tapped on her bag to break the silence. "You must know that just because I told her to let the matter go does not belittle her personal feelings. I agree that her manner at the funeral is hard to forgive, but if that boy did take advantage of Clare, she has a right to her bitterness and anger, Kelvin."

"We don't know what happened," Kelvin yelled, slamming his fist on the steering wheel. "We will never know because that poor boy is dead! She took advantage of an underage boy and is now trying to protect herself." He slammed his foot on the brakes. Edna lurched forward, then backwards, hitting the side of her head on the window. "Get out, Mom."

"Kelvin. Please."

"No. Get out!"

"Everyone is expecting me at church."

Kelvin shifted the gear into park, got out of the car, and opened Edna's door. "Get out, now."

Edna grabbed her purse and shuffled out of the car. She did not feel scared, just disappointed in his behavior. In the past few weeks, she knew to let this subject alone, yet he had instigated the discussion. How could she have known he would still overreact with such fury? Kelvin sped off in the car, spraying dust into Edna's face.

Edna stood in the ditch, overgrown with weeds and garbage, including a pile of rusted beer cans. Kelvin's reaction had been unwarranted and childish. Despite being his mother, she wanted to kick him out of the house this instant. Lord knows he had never paid rent or even offered. Her heels sunk into a patch of loose dirt. She wanted to take them off but worried about unseen metal in the grass. She stepped onto the road, immediately unable to fathom walking the more than ten miles back to the house that included the gravel stretch. She thought through people that would be willing to pick her up: friends, the pastor, possible work colleagues, yet she fretted over telling them the reason for her predicament. How could she explain her fragmented relationship with her own son? She had only meant to have a discussion, but he had become so defensive without rational judgment.

She sat in a dip of grass without debris and looked through her phone. She knew of only two people she could call who would not have reason to gossip. She did not want to deal with Nick after her biting last words. She wanted the boy to leave without more fanfare. Calling him might escalate the situation, despite his sister relocating last week. No, she had only one person remaining. She hesitated, abhorred touching the call button. The phone rang—voicemail. She called again. Then a third time until Rhonda picked up the phone.

"Can you pick me up? Kelvin left me stranded at the side of the road."

"Have your friends pick you up. Why do you need me?"

"Because I don't want them to know, okay? Please pick me up, Rhonda. I'll be in your debt."

An audible sigh and sounds of a struggle to get up, presumably from bed. "I don't owe you anything, Edna, but I'll accept a future favor."

Edna grimaced at the forwardness. That woman had lived for free all these years with little effort to help the family beyond listless caretaker yet had the audacity to claim Edna would owe her a favor. Edna prayed and held her tongue, again regretting her part in Kelvin and Rhonda's marriage.

"Where are you?"

"I'm close to the intersection of Sullivan and West County Road. Just drive south toward Sullivan and you'll see me on the right."

"Fine."

Rhonda hung up without a farewell. Edna crouched further into the ditch. She fretted that someone would recognize her and offer help. She had no explanation except for abandonment. Waiting, she reflected on the escalation of the renewed fight, curious as to why her son took such a vicious stance in support of Tristen without even listening to his daughter, or in this case his mother. Sure, she understood that Clare had committed a heinous act at the funeral, along with her sexual relationship with the boy prior to his suicide. Edna also knew that her decision to stifle Clare from further discussions on this point had probably not helped the situation between father and daughter. Perhaps they needed to scream and yell at each other, rip at the wounds until they festered. Then they could heal. Or, Edna feared as the notion took root, her family was broken and no amount of praying would fix it. Edna began crying, mopping the tears furiously so her makeup did not smudge. She did not want Rhonda to believe she had cried over this silly incident.

Fortunately, she soon spotted Rhonda driving slowly down the road. Edna waved at her, greeted by a beep in acknowledgement. Edna breathed in deep, hoping she did not look as miserable as she felt.

"I'm glad I found you so quickly. I passed Kelvin on the road, but he didn't seem to notice."

"Thank you, Rhonda. I genuinely appreciate you picking me up."

"It's fine," Rhonda said, making a U-turn toward home. Edna peered over to find Rhonda in her same drab clothing, then pushed the judgments aside. Rhonda had picked her up, and Edna wanted to be more considerate for the effort.

"I want you to know that you can stay at the house however long you need. There's no rush."

"So, Kelvin told you, then? My brother says he has the room. I'm not sure what I want to do anymore."

"You could work on your marriage, Rhonda. I know Kelvin loves you, and you've been together for more than nineteen years. That's a long time to throw away."

"Your son no longer loves me, Edna, but you know that. This is the same man who just left his mom on the side of the road, so please don't defend him to me. I'm grateful for your hospitality, I suppose, but please don't pretend that I have a marriage anymore."

Edna looked at her unsteady, clasped hands. She did not have a warm response, wanting to remind Rhonda that two people had to fail a marriage, yet the words would not settle.

"Well, I wish you the best."

"Thanks, Edna. You too."

"Did you visit Clare?"

"No," Rhonda said, reaching for the radio, turning up the volume. Edna did not attempt to speak over the country music. No further lecturing or admonition would help. Edna closed her eyes, praying, deep and wholeheartedly, for tranquility.

Edna bumped into the car door as Rhonda swerved sharply. She opened her eyes to the warm sight of her home. Rhonda drove furiously and jerked Edna's car into place. Before Edna could provide any more thanks, Rhonda rushed out of the car and into the house. Had she been so terrible to this woman for her to act with such disdain? Or was the looming divorce raising the tension between Rhonda and all of the Chestwicks? Edna braced herself up and out of the car, exhausted. She did not have the strength to support all these emotions. She would read some of her favorite passages from the Bible, pray, and rest. That was what the Lord needed from her today.

Edna entered her house, feeling a blanket of sorrow as she heard soft cries coming from upstairs. Edna dropped her bag and walked up the stairs without vigor. She moved to Clare's door, then realized the cries came from her private bathroom. She knocked on the door, then knocked again, waiting for Clare to respond. The cries continued.

"Clare, I'm coming in."

"Don't come in!"

Edna ignored the scream and opened the door. She gasped, her stomach twisting, as she observed Clare on the ground, her pants around her ankles, blood stains between her thighs and on the floor, the toilet seat streaked with blood. Edna grew nauseated by the thought of the contents of the toilet. When she saw her grandmother, Clare's wailing increased, as if the recognition on Edna's face brought the reality closer. Edna, frozen at the door, tried to will herself to help her granddaughter. More than a minute passed before Edna came out of shock, grabbing towels from the linen closet, throwing them on the toilet and floor and gently providing two to Clare.

"I don't know what I did, Grandma. I thought the pain would go away. I didn't realize how bad it had gotten until I went to the bathroom. I'm sorry, Grandma. I'm so sorry."

Edna dropped to her knees, gritting her teeth at the graceless pain. Edna crawled to Clare, unable to keep the blood from staining her dress. She wrapped her arms around the child, shushing her, softly humming the lullaby "Hush Little Baby." Clare continued to whimper, clutching at her grandma, grasping at the pearls around her neck, now blemished with blood.

"It's okay, baby. You'll have other chances. The Lord works in mysterious ways. Maybe this is his way of helping you." Clare's grip tightened.

"You're telling me God wanted my baby to die?" Clare pushed her head back, glaring at her grandmother. "Please tell me that you don't think God wanted this." Edna hesitated and looked away, not sure if she meant to be evasive or felt otherwise guilty. "You wanted this, didn't you?"

"No, Clare. Not exactly. I never wanted you to go through a miscarriage, but there was so much misery surrounding this child," Edna said, feeling a strain in her back.

"But you think God didn't want me to have this baby. Why?"

"I don't know, Clare. I can't speak for the Lord."

"I . . . I can't believe you." Clare's sniffles of misery had stopped. She looked furiously upon Edna. "Get out, Grandma! Get out. I can't stand any of you. I don't need your help. Not anymore."

Clare flopped her head to the floor, face in one of the towels, the wails reverberating, tearing at Edna's soul. Had Edna wanted this? She did not want to lie. She knew the loss of the child would help the family heal, but she never thought she would be faced with the repercussions of such a desire. She pushed herself up and shut the door, leaving Clare to her pain. Edna removed her dress, used makeup wipes to remove Clare's fluids from the fabric and her skin, put on a nightgown while she waited to shower, opened her Bible, and began reading and praying for the broken.

Chapter 30

Today

Clare could no longer meet her grandmother's gaze, so distant and patient. Instead, she looked upon the dangling body of Nick, the crick in his neck, the vacant look in his eyes. Purpose was now lost by his lifelessness.

"Everything you did, Grandma. Do you honestly believe you helped me by belittling Mom, hammering on Dad, forcing Nick to leave, and telling me to keep quiet about the rape? And then . . ." Clare began crying, then smacked herself, desperate to finish. "I know you wanted that miscarriage. I know you were delighted—that a burden had been lifted." She spun in the loft, delirious and tired. "You are the crux of all of this, Grandma. You have always wanted me stifled. Were your prayers worth it?"

Clare finally returned her grandmother's stare, still brimming with tears. Clare began to pity this woman, waiting for her parting words. Clare needed this one showing of responsibility. Why were none remorseful for their clear failings in their own lives that had caused others such misery? She glanced at the empty rope.

"Look what you've done to your family. If you wanted an apology, an honest discussion, why did you need this whole display? How much misery could we possibly have caused you to place us in these confinements and murder your friend? Nick did not deserve his fate."

"I did not murder Nick! He fell on his own."

"Again, child. You placed us in this position. You knew the repercussions and could not have believed that our deaths were unimaginable. You are disturbed, honey. You need to stop this, let us down, and we'll handle this as a family. Please understand that we never meant to hurt you."

Clare slapped her grandmother. The impulse, still shaking in her hand, surprised her, yet Clare's face jutted and dared her grandmother to continue. "Your hollow words don't fix anything. I'm a shell because of you."

Her grandmother closed her eyes and began reciting the Lord's prayer. Clare, defeated by her grandmother's refusal, looked at her mother and father—eyes agape, as if worried that Nick's fate would be their own. She walked to them and took off the gags.

"You killed Nick. How could you?" cried her father.

"I warned all of you," she screamed. "I told him to keep still, yet he kept shaking the chair, even after I begged him to stop. Don't you understand? Tell me you understand," she pleaded, pulling on his shirt.

"Are you going to leave us here?" her mom murmured.

"No. I never intended . . . I just wanted you to understand."

She considered them, flinching at the position of Nick's body, no longer clear of her intentions in this senseless predicament. The plan seemed so clear when she was curled in bed following all that loss—forcing them to confront and recognize how much grief and pain their inane deeds had caused her and each other in a semblance of threats on their lives. Maybe she was no better. Had she only been seeking to punish with no intention of receiving genuine confessions of regret resulting in her forgiveness?

Once the tranquilizers had been bought, propelling these events, this point of loss and shame was so apparent in its inevitability. She had sought to cause them fear in hopes of reflection, considering the totality of their actions in causing these extremes. However, they only saw the monster that had been wrought outside of their perceived control, fearing for the *what* she may do rather than the *why* she had done any of it. Unfortunate considerations far too late amongst more death.

She stepped away, finding her cell phone near the stairs. She dialed 911, and a lady's voice asked her about the emergency.

"I'm at 147 Granite Peak Road. I found my family tied up. I don't know how they got there. Please send someone, as soon as possible. I can't tell if they are still alive." Clare heard the woman ask follow-up questions, but she hung up.

"Thank you," she heard her mother whisper.

Clare reached out to Nick, determined to place him properly before help arrived, terrified as to how she would explain. She pulled on a lifeless hand, urging the chair up, yet the one leg remained wedged underneath the loft. She tried to reposition Nick, unwilling to be blamed, when she tripped over a broken piece of the loft, flinging onto Nick. She wrapped her hands around the body as the chair tipped further off the landing. As she tried to edge her feet back onto the loft, she heard mild cracks until the roof beam broke. She found herself falling with Nick, striking her head and then body in turn, as she grew distant from the affair, disappearing into silence.

Epilogue

Edna clutched her purse and phone, waiting in the parking lot of the church. She fretted over Pastor Wilson's tardiness, worried he might back out of this visit. She could not handle going alone. Her nerves had forced her to swallow one of Rhonda's reserved Xanax, a precaution she had taken as soon as she parked her car. Thankfully, Pastor Wilson had volunteered to drive, welcoming Edna's request for him to attend with her, despite Edna's failure to appear at church in three months.

The wind rustled at her dress, but Edna let it flow. She enjoyed the breeze, the smell of late fall, the trees swaying with gentle waves. A car passed by, waking her from the peace. She dared not look, afraid some nosey congregation member would offer insincere condolences along with inquiries about her life to find out some semblance of truth. She had blocked two of her past friends' phone numbers for this exact reason, once she discovered that her reliance on them had only resulted in information spreading to others.

A small maroon Toyota pulled up next to Edna. Pastor Wilson waved, then unlocked the door. She gripped the handle, her hand slipping, then pulled harder, causing the door to creak as it swung open.

"I'm sorry. I'm sure you remember that this car has lived quite the life."

"Oh, it's fine," she said, firmly closing the door. "I would expect thriftiness from a pastor. I think that shows character. Do you have the directions?"

"Of course," he said, smiling, showing the papers tucked in his lap. "Call me old-fashioned, but I prefer hard copies of directions. I'm always worried about getting lost with no phone signal. I'm sure you can understand, living in the country."

"Yes," she said as he drove out of the small town. She closed her eyes, hoping Pastor Wilson would allow this trip to maintain silence.

"I was awfully glad to hear from you, Edna. I know you have been handling so much. I think it's wonderful that you are making these efforts. Healing takes time."

He placed his hand on her leg, likely a small bit of kindness without ulterior motive, yet she did not want to be touched, so she moved her legs closer to the door. His wavering hand went back to the steering wheel. She squirmed, wanting to be more amiable, knowing the pastor meant well.

"How's the congregation?"

"Oh, everyone's doing fine," he said. "You and your family have been in our prayers. I hope the Lord has seen to your wellbeing."

"As well as can be hoped," she murmured.

"That's good. How's Kelvin been doing?"

"Working. He works so much that I rarely see him anymore. But I understand; keeping busy is good for him."

"As long as he takes the time to properly grieve," Pastor Wilson said. "He can't expect to run from those feelings. They'll eat him up. You let him know I'm always here to talk."

"I'm sure he knows, Pastor. He's always tended to himself during difficult times. I try to take solace that this too shall pass, then I begin to wonder how much more I can take, but I wake the next morning, going through the motions."

"That's all you can do, Edna. Time heals. Grief dissipates to sorrow, so you must be vigilant. Taking this trip is a big step. Know that I and the Lord are proud of you."

Edna sickened at the pastor's sentimentality, finding him vague and superficial. Had Pastor Wilson always uttered such clichéd advice? She did not feel acknowledged for her pain, time be damned. The further they drove, the more dread crept into her.

"How's Rhonda?"

She figured he wanted gossip. He knew about the divorce and needed more. Childish. She had nothing to hide.

"I haven't spoken with her since the event. She moved in with her brother after the hospital. With her arm broken and back issues from falling off the ledge, her brother felt it best he care for her. The divorce is close to finalizing," she said, observant of the pastor's hunger for more information. "Rhonda is making claims for alimony, even trying to get money for the house. Too bad for her, the house always remained mine. We may need you to testify at the trial, Pastor, regarding Kelvin's character. We hope to resolve amicably, but trials do happen. Can we count on you to help?"

"I'll help in ways that bring your son and daughter-in-law peace."

"My son is at peace now. I'm thankful he had the strength to finally move forward. I hope you and the congregation don't seek to judge him."

"Goodness, no!" Pastor Wilson said, shaking his head. "The Lord is the only one who stands to judge. I'm here to merely assist in the divine plan."

Edna laughed at these religious ad-libs—no teeth to these quips. She was bemused at the idea, knowing she must have espoused some personal wisdom of her own over the years.

"What's so funny?"

"Nothing. I feel a little delirious. To be honest, Pastor, I took a Xanax in the parking lot. I . . . I don't know what to think anymore."

"That's fine, Edna. I think going to visit her is brave. I'm glad you asked me to drive."

"You know I did not cause this, right? I did the best I could for that girl." She choked for a second, then began coughing. Once she caught her breath, she continued, "I never thought so much death could happen around me."

"We know, Edna. We know. Have you thought about seeing a therapist? I may be able to counsel you with the Lord's words, but another professional may be of some assistance. Few people could have endured the trials you have this past year."

"Lord knows," she murmured. Confession welled within her. "That girl had demons, Pastor. Some of them fair, but she never understood how her actions affected others. To force us through her rambling grievances, claiming that we forced her into that predicament. She wanted us to suffer, terrorizing us and then claiming all she needed was an apology. We did our best. Just like any family." Silence lingered until Edna asked, "Are we close?"

"Maybe fifteen minutes. We don't have to talk if you don't want. I'm not here to pry, Edna—only support."

"We burned down the barn after the investigation finished," Edna whispered. "I couldn't stand the sight of it. I felt nauseous every time I saw it. I asked Kelvin, and he obliged without pause. I'm thinking of ridding myself of the trailer, too. Bad memories everywhere."

"Have you considered moving?"

"No. But maybe I should. A fresh start would do us good, but then we would be away from Clare."

"Well, she's being cared for, isn't she? You could still visit her periodically. You need to live for yourself, too. You must not forget."

Edna turned up the radio. The gospel singing irked her, but she had no more words for the pastor. He may have been a good person, but she was tired of the passive support. She wanted to be alone. Pastor Wilson did not question her further as they swerved off the highway, suddenly turning into a parking lot surrounded by a fence and barbed wire coming to a sprawling, three-storied brick building. The officer at the gate waved them inside. Edna appreciated the pastor's formal attire, figuring the guards would respect a man of the cloth.

Pastor Wilson parked the car and turned to Edna. "Well, we made it. Do you want me to wait out here?"

"Oh, no," Edna said, recognizing she had offended him. "I'm sorry for being so abrupt. Please come inside."

They exited the car, following the signs for the visitors' entrance. Edna's queasiness grew as she walked through the front door. She paused, leaning against the wall. Two guards eyed her but did not offer assistance.

"Are you okay?" Pastor Wilson said, tendering his hand for support.

She took it for his sake, nodding her head. "I haven't seen her in weeks. She was in the hospital for so long. They honestly don't know how altered her mind is, since she won't speak. They think she's getting better, though she still doesn't have use of her legs. I'm scared, Pastor. I shouldn't be, but I am."

He nodded, guiding her off the wall and toward the check-in desk. He said their names.

"You're not on the visitor list," the officer said, looking through the computer. "She is, but not you."

"Oh no," Edna said. "I'm so sorry. I never even thought of that part of the process." She turned to the guard. "Are you sure he can't visit with me?"

"I'm sorry, ma'am," she said, shaking her head.

"I'll wait, Edna. You need to see her for at least a moment. Don't worry. I'll be here."

Edna looked from the officer to the pastor. She slowly nodded her head, taking the visitor pass and walking through security. A social worker met her on the other side and guided Edna down the broad hallways, past doctors, nurses, and patients.

"So, you're the grandmother? I'm Robert. Terrible events. I'm sorry. Clare is doing better. Says a few words but mostly mumbles. I'm not sure if she'll ever get all her faculties back. She tends to keep to herself. Sits and looks out the window. Right now, she's in our day room with a handful of our less violent patients. Please make sure to stay calm and don't antagonize other patients. I know you won't, but I'm required to say it," he said, smiling with obvious exhaustion. "I can stand to the side if you want some semi-private time. If anything happens and you need help, please do not hesitate to motion to us."

The social worker guided her to a large room with nine people inside with scattered tables and chairs, a few of the patrons playing cards. She saw Clare off to the side, her head tilted to the right and leaning against a window. Edna tried not to cry, not wanting to upset Clare, but she could not stop. Soft sobs shuddered as Robert handed her a few tissues. When she felt a little more in control, she nodded her head and walked toward Clare.

"Hi, Clare," Robert said, squatting down. "I have a special surprise for you today. Look who it is." Edna bent over, trying to get Clare to look at her. Clare kept her eyes to the window—no acknowledgment. "Don't take offense, but do you want me to stay?"

"No, we'll be fine," Edna said, pushing herself up, wanting to hug Clare but afraid.

"I'll be around. Again, if anything happens, please get me or one of the nurses."

Edna nodded. Robert walked to the nurses' station. Edna turned back to Clare, who remained keen on the outdoors. Edna peered out the window, noticing the beautiful flowers, colors of amber, lavender, and peaches. Small birds twittered in the trees. Edna felt such sorrow at Clare's gaze. She got to her knees, grabbing one of Clare's hands. No reaction as the skies darkened with passing clouds.

"I'm so sorry, Clare," Edna said, tears drifting once more. "I'm sorry you felt such loss, so lonely, so defeated. I never meant for this. If . . . when you get out, you'll live with me, and I'll care for you." She paused, swallowing hard. "I hope you'll forgive me some day."

Edna felt a light squeeze of her hand, and she looked upon her granddaughter's face. As the sunshine returned to blanket them, Clare slowly turned her head with a gentle smile at her grandmother.

About the Author

Tony Heck works in the legal profession, devoting more time towards his passion for creative writing. Originally from Indiana, he presently resides in New York City with his fluffy pup. *Tribulations* is his first novel.

If you want to learn about any upcoming works, please follow him on Instagram @heckintony.

www.ingramcontent.com/pod-product-compliance
Lightning Source LLC
Chambersburg PA
CBHW020123310726

48970CB00006B/1701